COUP D'ETAT

Coup d'Etat is a masterly analysis of the human motives that lead to tyranny, feed it – and ultimately destroy it. But it is also a powerful love story. The story of Vangelis, Chryssa and Michael, their commitment to each other, their passion and their guilt.

The time is 1967. The Colonels are in control of Greece. Vangelis, a young lawyer fights in the law courts against the tyrannical military control. He is arrested and disappears, and so Chryssa his wife begins her long and solitary search to trace him. The authorities block her every move and in despair she turns to Michael, an English journalist and friend from carefree student days.

Coup d'Etat is also the story of Leonidas, Chryssa's brother-in-law, as he manoeuvres himself into Government, and it is the tragedy of his disaffected son Alexis and of the sacrifice of the young of the nation.

John Harvey's *The Plate Shop* won the David Higham Literary Award for the best first novel in 1979. In his second novel John Harvey's canvas is wider, his aims more ambitious and he succeeds triumphantly. *Coup d'Etat* is a literary *tour de force*.

Coup d'Etat

—◇—

JOHN HARVEY

COLLINS
8 Grafton Street, London W1
1985

William Collins Sons & Co. Ltd
London · Glasgow · Sydney · Auckland
Toronto · Johannesburg

BRITISH LIBRARY CATALOGUING IN PUBLICATION DATA

Harvey, John
Coup d'etat.
I. Title
823'.914[F]   PR6058.A6989

ISBN 0 00 222795 9

First published in Great Britain in 1985
Reprinted 1985
© John Harvey 1985

Photoset in Linotron Plantin by
Rowland Phototypesetting Ltd,
Bury St Edmunds, Suffolk
Printed and Bound in Great Britain by
T.J. Press (Padstow) Ltd, Padstow, Cornwall

For Julietta

CONTENTS

PART ONE

<><>

The Cruellest Month

1

The gravel crackled as the General's boot scuffed it. 'Where the hell have they got to?' he muttered. They were the first and last words that he said to Kostas.

'It's nearly seven,' Kostas offered.

The General ignored him. Still the military bus did not come, that should take them to the Pentagon; and no vehicle came, no staff-car, no jeep. They turned where they stood, scanning for trouble: but all they saw was the still bright morning, with the huts and chalets of the summer camp spaced between olive groves as far as the sea. Just sleeping silence, not a child had woken; and the sea was as calm as a bowl of water.

The General fretted fiercely: an officer of the old school, broad, barrel-chested, tautly erect; with thick tight-curled moustaches, and eyes that frowned whatever they saw. Beside him, tall, lean, sleek in his uniform, his papers neat in his slim portfolio, Kostas stood like a dagger. They had nothing to say to each other.

Still no one came, and the bus did not come.

Kostas took a slight stoop of respect. 'Shall we take a taxi?'

The General turned and seemed just to make out, like some dot on the horizon, Kostas. He gave a guttural snort: they set out for the main road and presently caught a taxi.

The taxi drove quickly through the suburbs of Athens. The roads were empty, it was like a Sunday morning.

'Eh, where is everyone?' the driver cried; he was just driving in himself, from the village where he lived. He turned on the car radio, but got only atmospherics or military music: he twiddled the knob, but it was as empty of voices as if the world had died.

He looked round at his passengers, shrugging enormously; and they looked about them, puzzled, at the still sunlit city. A tank was parked in a side street, its gun-barrel levelled. It was so much what they were used to seeing every day in the barracks that they had passed it before they blinked: what was it doing here? Then they passed two tanks, driving at full speed – grinding fast like careering lorries – the way they had come. The General's face sharpened, his breath came hard; but he made no remark.

All they saw, as they drove into town, were blind houses and dead avenues, shining in the morning, where nothing stirred except isolated tanks, crossing the white face of the city like giant ironclad beetle creatures.

When they reached the Pentagon they found the entire dual carriageway blocked with soldiers, and the Pentagon itself ringed by tanks: its bleak yellow cliff walls just showed over the lined gun turrets.

They got out of the taxi, and a soldier they had never seen before, a sergeant, bawled out to them to say who they were. He carried a machine gun casually; he spoke as rudely to the General as he did to Kostas. Other soldiers came forward, and frisked them in a series of hard knocks: the General's hat came off. Kostas prepared to protest; for any breach of respect was distasteful to him, and he was not afraid. But when he saw that the General bore these things with no trace of reaction, with a face like concrete, he decided that wisdom was to do the same.

From what regiment were these soldiers? He had never seen them.

'You can go to your offices. Stay in them!' the sergeant shouted, and turned away. They were dismissed.

More soldiers, armed, stood at the gates, and more again at the doors of the Pentagon. Kostas kept glancing at the General, thinking he must explode with fury; but the General did not explode, he only glanced witheringly at the strange soldiers and marched between them, going where he wanted to go.

Only in his own office did Kostas find someone he knew; and all he heard then was that the unknown soldiers had taken over in the night. They were from some provincial garrison, it was not clear who was in charge of them.

There was a clattering racket outside, the room went dark, a helicopter was descending into the courtyard. Kostas looked out and saw, between long blades turning slowly, soldiers hustling men out of the machine – men in odd clothes, in pyjamas and dressing gowns, in loose slippers. Another helicopter landed, and more half-dressed men were bundled out and stood around in the courtyard at a loss. Among them he made out, looking like real people – unshaven, grey-faced, blear-eyed – politicians he had seen only on television before.

The first helicopter rose again, another one landed, and thereafter there was no pause as the huge machines slowly rose and sank between the courtyard and the sky in a continuous drumming thunder, while the men in dressing gowns were herded and sorted and shipped away again in other helicopters or lorries.

Eventually these movements slackened; later, when Kostas again dawdled at the window, he saw a slightly ruffled and crumpled young officer, with no hat, walk hurriedly into the courtyard. Other officers scurried deferential beside him. Kostas stared at the hurrying man with the sallow, plump face: and of course he knew him.

'Hey Couli, come here!' he called, 'It's the King!'

As the King approached the main entrance, a small troop of soldiers stationed there came to attention but did not present arms. The King walked past them and out of sight.

Presently Kostas invented a reason for visiting an office at the other end of the Pentagon, and ventured into the corridors. He walked briskly, as if under orders; at every corner the unknown soldiers, in full battledress, stood with their guns. The guns especially disconcerted Kostas, for though the Pentagon directed wars he had not seen soldiers with weapons inside it.

He passed a large hall, the Theatre of Assembly, where they had concerts, theatricals, receptions. And this was the strangest thing of all, for it seemed that, in the midst of the invasion, there was a performance going on. Through the entrance he could see that the hall was crowded, and the guards at the door were leaning in; yet it was quiet, everyone there was attending to something going forward on the dais at the far end.

With a face of urgency Kostas pushed in, and got as far as he could before the crowd grew too thick. He looked about him bewildered, for the hall was crowded with soldiers and officers of all ranks, none of whom he had seen before. On the stage there was a long table: at one end sat the King, at the other sat several officers, one of whom had a moist bald head. Kostas thrilled: he was witnessing history.

The King looked assured, he seemed to speak firmly: but though everyone strained to hear him, still the low noise of the stirring crowd obscured his speech, so his words were passed back by relay to where Kostas stood. The man in front turned and quoted, 'Gentlemen, this is ridiculous. I give you till 2.30 to return to your barracks.'

The hall grew quieter still, for one of the officers was now replying; but his voice was too fine, they could hear the silk of courtesy in it, but his words had to follow like an echo, 'We thank you, Your Majesty. You say you give us till 2.30. We give you till 1.30 to sign.'

The King fingered a sheet of paper: it looked like any piece of office paper, with some typing on it. All eyes studied him, the room hardly breathed. He rested his cheek on his hand, and sat at the table like any young officer, looking thoughtful and depressed.

The crowd shifted and jostled, there were comings and goings at the rear of the hall, but the room stayed whisper quiet: it was – the contest.

The King sat straight, took up a pen, and signed the paper. He and the officers stood: there was a general sigh: and everywhere men began quietly talking, leaving the hall.

The atmosphere in the corridors had relaxed, and Kostas walked back to his office unwatched. He was moved by what he had seen: it was a solemn moment. The soldiers in battle-dress stood easy with their guns, some chatting, as though it were the most natural thing for them to be there. They were legitimate.

In the afternoon, by stealthy telephone calls, Kostas and his friend Coulis began to learn who the new men were: they were hardly wiser, for the names meant nothing to them, with the exception of a colonel who had once inspected the setting of the guns at a time when Kostas was adjutant to the Sergeant Major of Ordnance. Kostas and the Sergeant Major had disagreed about the angle of the guns, but the Colonel saw at a glance that the setting was correct, and congratulated Kostas. Kostas remembered him well, he was a short man with wide energetic eyes and a high bulging forehead.

'He was decisive, up-to-date – impressive, I thought. Who knows, perhaps he's the man Greece needs.'

Coulis nodded but shrugged, it was early yet to commit oneself.

The day ended quietly, there was only one mishap. Kostas had gone down to the transport yard, which was packed with the extra traffic of the day, lorries, tanks, jeeps, armoured cars, military buses, staff cars, motor-cycles, all milling and quivering in a sour haze of dust and exhaust. At a distance, in their own gritty tornados of dust, helicopter gunships, used now as transports, descended and rose. Spaced through the traffic and smother, officers of all ranks stood about, waiting to go; while the occupying soldiers, still with guns in their hands, tired and harassed, tried to direct the vehicles clear of these unfamiliar barracks.

Absently, Kostas heard one of these soldiers ordering the driver of a truck to a particular depot.

The driver leaned out of his cab, shrugging with all his shoulders and arms, 'What the hell should I take it there for?'

'How do I know? Just take it!' the soldier shouted hoarsely, waving his gun.

'Ach, the idiots! What the hell good is it there?' The driver clambered down, and walked towards the soldier, who was peering fretfully at his papers. He looked up and saw the driver.

'Get back,' he shouted. 'Get back there!'

'Who the fuck do you lot think you are? Don't tell me to get back! What have you got on that paper?' The driver strode quickly towards the soldier: he was a hefty broad-built man with an inflamed angry face, he rolled his eyes with rhetoric and waved his arms.

'Stop! Get back!' the soldier shouted, but the driver didn't get back, there was a sudden rattle and crackle of shots, he jigged in the air, jerked, in a collapsing dance he tumbled heavy on the concrete. Everyone moved, but the soldier who had shot him crouched where he stood, holding his gun wedged tight into his body, and swinging it from side to side covering all of them. At the top of his voice he shouted 'Get back! Get back everyone!' They all froze, but the soldier still jerked his gun round at them.

15

Eventually he relaxed, and they could proceed. He shouted to others, who came and lifted the inert body onto a stretcher. The soldier continued dispatching the transports, his face wide-eyed, and as tight and stretched as if a hand behind him were straining to pull the skin off his head.

It was the only bloodshed. In due course, Kostas took his seat in the military bus to the summer camp, and in the rear window the long yellow bulk of the Pentagon shrank away behind telegraph poles and apartment blocks. The officers chatted about the takeover: it had been well planned and well carried out, it was a clean operation. Kostas nodded, with excited eyes; he was impressed.

So the National Government was installed: parliament was suspended, and the powerful hand of the army took all of the country in its control. Of course there was fury and outcry from the demagogues and political adventurers, and whining from foreign capitals. But for Kostas the new government was the saviour that Greece had needed for so long. For the country was breaking up: there had been so many 'democratic governments' that all collapsed, there had been marches, riots, strikes, fighting in the streets, anarchy already here, and nothing ahead but the fast slide to communism. If ever the army was needed, it was now. Kostas burned with enthusiasm, for work for this government must be his real life's work: even at home he was like a new convert, pale and tense and radiant with mission.

In the Pentagon he made this clear: and it was a time of opportunities too, for there would be great changes in the army. Virtually all officers senior to those who had taken power were removed at a stroke; and the new loyalty tests cut great swaths through the officer corps. Almost everyone who survived jumped several ranks at once; and Kostas observed drily that this low consideration played its part in making the National Government popular in the army. His own loyalty was pure: he lived for the day when promotions would be posted.

And he went up only to captain: it almost broke his heart. What important work could he do as a captain? And others he knew took greater leaps, who were not sincere as he was. So he learned, the new government was not perfect. It was still what Greece needed; yet even so he was surprised at some of the men who survived. Even that stiff general with whom he had waited at the bus stop – whom he deeply suspected of being not at all a National Government man – he evidently had said what he was expected to say, for Kostas still saw him stalking haughtily through the corridors of the Pentagon, proud beyond contempt before junior officers.

He lay awake at night, smarting with injury.

'Don't let them get ahead,' said his wife Kiki, 'you should look after yourself, you should press.' He lay still, but his nervous tightness kept him awake.

'Kosta, tomorrow you'll go and see Uncle Theodoros.'

'Tomorrow, tomorrow,' he said, like a brisk salute.

The next day he crossed to a far limb of the Pentagon, and tapped at his uncle's door. His uncle was a stout lethargic man, who had however risen to be a major general. There he was comfortable and there he stayed, serving his country mostly by sitting down, as now he sat, reclined pot-bellied on the large cushion of his swivel chair, like a cushion on a cushion. He ordered coffee for Kostas, exchanged some family small talk, and then, incalculable behind dark glasses behind an incense of cigarettes, he volunteered his views on who counted in the army now, and on whose staff Kostas ought to get. His voice was a slow guttural reverberation, as though he let his words go only after he had swirled them round with peppers and raki in the great churn of his belly.

'You must be careful, Kosta. How many coups have there been in Greece this century? You must think ahead. If you got to the top with these people . . . in a few years time there might be another coup . . . who knows, you might be shot. Cigarette?'

So he advised: Kostas should choose between going high now, and going not so high now, so as to go higher later. Best of all would be to get to the top five years or so before he retired: that way he'd have a full career, and at worst be pensioned off, and on full pay too. He couldn't plan for that, of course; the moral was, to be very careful. He himself had been careful; and he wouldn't ever be a full General; but on the other hand he had arranged things so that different coups and governments would come and go, but he would stay.

17

Kostas gazed at him tautly, acknowledging his shrewdness, despising his caution.

'Uncle Theodore, you have wisdom,' he said, leaving; he had made a clear note of the tips his uncle gave, as to the officers and relatives he ought to approach.

He had never intended to use such aids. The new government took a stand against corruption: there would be no more jobs for friends of friends and relatives of relatives. Kostas believed this with passion: too long the old families had hung on and run things, now they were out and with a kick in the arse. But the right people must replace them if things were to get better, and Kostas must use what means he could. And his uncle had urged him to see his cousin Leonidas – Leonidas Argiriou. He was only a civilian, but he had at one time been a deputy for the Conservative Party and he had now come out for the National Government: even before the coup he had written articles in the newspapers on the dangers of anarchy and the need for strong leadership. If the cabinet of the National Government were to admit civilians, he was a man that they might choose: he was a man it would be wise to know.

So, one Sunday, Kostas put Kiki in her loveliest clothes, and put her, his child, and a pile of presents, inside their small Citroen, and they drove to the suburb where their cousin lived. It was true that Cousin Leonidas had given no sign that he wanted to see them; never mind, he couldn't turn his relatives away. Hospitality would get them in, and the presents would make them welcome.

At the door of their apartment they listened close, and heard not many voices: it seemed their relatives were in, but without other guests.

The door was opened by a small lean smart woman; her handsome face had a fatigued, not pleased expression. It was Leonidas' wife Patra. She was a dry stick, they would have to make the best of her.

'Patra!' Kiki cried, while Patra still blinked, catching for names, 'how well you look! Marvellous! Lovely to see you!' Kiki was a good wife; she ran on as though she were the hostess and Patra the guest, and the thrust of her voice, and of the gift-wrapped presents, and the tilt forward of the whole family, drove Patra back, so they came in.

Patra had their names now. 'Kiki,' she remarked, and gave her a peck; she was a closed hand.

But Leonidas' hand was open. There had been a hush in the living room, as he eavesdropped on the introductions; but now he strode forward, as knowing them of old, 'Kiki, Kosta, lovely to see you, marvellous that you came!' He shook hands vigorously and shouted out welcomes to them and their child in his resonant voice that he liked to hear. He made them sit in the best armchairs, while he sat back at ease taking all of the sofa: the host. He had evidently been to some lunchtime reception, for he had on a shimmering suit that looked new from the tailor's. With his round, Roman-nosed head set back, and his heavy eyelids drooped, he held court like a pasha.

'We brought you these – uh! – presents,' Kiki said, belittling them but handing them over. A rare brandy for Leonidas, his blood warmed as he counted the stars; and a fine gossamer material for Patra. With Kiki's help she held it against her, imagining the dress she would make of it, ravished. And now, truly, the hosts felt hospitable.

The children sized each other up; the women chatted like silver bells, getting together drinks and snacks; and Kostas fell into conversation with Leonidas. And he had the right touch, Kostas, nothing servile, but clipped, bluff, man-to-man; they told each other what they should do like equals – Kostas being careful to tell Leonidas only to do what he wanted to do.

Patra handed round thimbles of liqueur.

'The Greek Army!' Leonidas proposed.

'The National Government!' Kostas returned, as though it were the body Leonidas belonged to. He bowed his head, pleased.

'I was in the army,' Leonidas recalled, 'I drove a tank.' He reminisced about his military service. He had developed an interest in army gossip, and presently, lightly, asked about generals. Kostas made much of working in the Pentagon, and was good at seeming inward with the higher secrets. From Uncle Theodoros he had two or three pieces of real news, which he released at strategic intervals. Leonidas nodded and took them in, betraying his interest only by his silence. He in return gave Kostas only opinions, but Kostas responded seriously, grateful for the tip. And after all, what he was grateful for, chiefly, was the opportunity to make it clear that he was grateful for anything.

The women withdrew, the men poured themselves whiskies and became more companionable. Leonidas confirmed that he had been to a Government reception that day, and presently he seemed indirectly to imply, in strictest confidence though no clear words were said, that he had some expectation of entering government. Kostas tensed with excitement, he had been wise indeed to come today. Obliquely he gave his cousin felicitations.

'Quietly,' Leonidas murmured, and significantly eyed the kitchen. As the whisky mellowed, he betrayed that even he, with all his good status, had some domestic problem. For his wife's political loyalties were less clear cut than his own; and her family were something of an embarrassment to him. For she had a sister, who had a husband, who was known to be a critic of the National Government. Fortunately, since the coup, the two families did not meet.

Kostas commiserated, all large families had their problems. In consolation he said, 'Cousin, you must come and see us at work.'

An entry to the Pentagon: Leonidas' brown eyes burned. He inhaled deeply, and then said, not lightly, 'I should like to see the War Room.'

Kostas glanced at him sharply, and wondered whether he dare mention the final information that Uncle Theodoros had given him. He settled for a question.

'Are you expecting war, cousin?'

'I am a patriot, cousin,' Leonidas said seriously. Their eyes met: they knew they would help each other.

In every level of the carrier, which rested on the flat plain of dark blue sea like an iron peninsula, bells and sirens sounded. Absorbed men shoved missiles on trolleys like patients rushed to surgery, and snugged slender pencils of rockets home in their cradles. Pilots squeezed into cockpits and flexed gloved fingers over massed controls. In the carrier's deck plated doors opened inwards, and out of the dark bustle below folded up airplanes smoothly rose and spread their wings: the writhed web of cables and hoses was pulled away from them, their engine roar rose to a knifing shriek, they began to crawl forward while all the carrier wavered and shimmered in the molten scorch of their jets. Then the release, one after the other the planes shot from the deck like bullets, accelerated in tearing screaming, and disappeared.

The iron sea raced below them, they felt only inches above it. Their earphones crackled with messages from the carrier; and now a new voice intercepted, 'Hey, you idiots, where are you going?'

They heard the lead plane answer, 'Where do you think? We're going to Constantinople.'

'Constantinople? This isn't the way to Constantinople,' the man said; then they heard him shouting, 'Hey, Niko, who are these arseholes? They say they're going to Constantinople.'

They didn't bother with him further, for now at the end of the sea a tiny white pucker appeared, it grew to a line of mountains. Together the planes tilted and changed direction. Now a coastline swung at them, inlets, bays, and then dead ahead the huge sprawling city stretching miles in brown haze. Docks and docklands then apartment blocks zipped below, the bony spike of Lykavittos appeared, and the yellow bars of the Parthenon, and now their target was in sight, standing clear over houses and flats, yellow, dingy, like a great hospital or prison, its thousand windows all unprotected. It grew towards them; hands tightened nervously on rocket and bomb controls. Their earphones crackled again.

Inside the Pentagon officers dived for the floor as in a sudden shatter the jets passed overhead and away into distance. News of the uprising had come some minutes before, but no one supposed the Pentagon would be attacked. Kostas had found time to ring Kiki.

'It's a mutiny – a coup d'état,' he shouted. 'Get stocked up and stay indoors.'

In the distance they heard the jets turning. 'The bunkers!' someone shouted, they all scrambled for the door.

The corridors were full of running men: adjutants, generals, colonels, majors – men in shirt sleeves, undone jackets, with odd handfuls of paper. One of them was calling, as he passed Kostas, 'The King's behind this.'

The bunkers were deep underground, it would take time to get there; and again the planes screamed overhead, some men plunged for the floor, others tripped over them, there was shouting and confusion. But still, no hits, no rockets.

'Is it a warning? Are they trying to scare us?' Kostas wondered, but didn't stay to see. And now some ingenious officer had tuned in the intercom system of this part of the Pentagon to the frequency of the attacking jets, so that even as they ran they heard overhead the buzzing amplified voice of the lead pilot. He was pleading with someone. '*Let* me bomb them,' they heard him say. 'We got through, we're here, we can bomb them out of existence. Give me permission!' His voice rose again, then was drowned as his own aircraft passed overhead. The officers wasted no more time, they sprinted. Only, at certain places, there were officers who didn't run, as when Kostas turned a corner and saw ahead of him, standing rigid as a pillar while the others pelted by, the general who had waited with him at the bus stop. He stood to attention in the scrambling corridor, and looking upwards with exhilaration shouted above the radio and the jets 'Bomb us! Destroy us! Long live the King!' Kostas dashed past him, but as he joined the greater crowd, crushed to the elevators, still there were other officers who impeded the flight, shouting where they stood as they waited to be bombed 'Down with the Junta! Long live the king!'

The King did not give permission; the jets were helpless and flew away. The officers emerged from the bunkers, and within hours the King's coup was crushed and the King himself a prisoner. Order returned, many prompt arrests were made in the Pentagon, and Kostas was not to see again that senior General, of whom his suspicions had proved correct.

The loyal officers could sigh with relief, and the only surprise remaining to Kostas was when he returned home that evening, a weary man, to find he could hardly get into the flat for boxes of tinned dolmas, cans of olive-oil, plastic sacks of olives and cheeses, salt legs of animal, loaves of bread, bottles of ouzo and tins of coffee. Their flat was like a warehouse; for his good wife Kiki had remembered his instructions on what to do in a coup, and had emptied the supermarket below, preparing for the siege. He gave her a dazed kiss and found a space to sit down, a bemused man who saw his needs provided for months ahead, and a rich home atmosphere of cheese, and vegetable, and spiced sausage in abundance.

In the Pentagon, the days that followed were good days. From time to time Kostas and Coulis would look at each other, and shake their heads and sigh with thanksgiving: for the National Government had had a narrow escape. It was now confirmed that the Prime Minister, and all the senior officials of the Government, were in the Pentagon at the time of the attack. They were assembled in a conference room when the first jets arrived.

'Everyone went down like this!' Coulis cried, suddenly keeling over at his desk, 'except the Prime Minister. He just sat – like this.' Coulis sat up in perfect composure. 'They dived again, and again they didn't fire, and he said, "Uh! They cannot attack." And he went on with the agenda.'

Kostas gazed rapt into distance and said, 'He is a great man! He is a leader!'

His disappointment was subdued by the Premier's courage, and he put all his energy into duty and work. He had been assigned to Domestic Security, now a limb of Military Intelligence. This was not his true vocation – foreign policy was that – but Domestic Security had an urgent mission in these days of danger. As the mutiny showed, the National Government had powerful and treacherous enemies; this was a national emergency, and there could be no complaint now about arrest without trial, or prolonged interrogation, or the need to vet everyone. All loyalties must be checked.

The work went well: for many people had joined the mutiny, or shown sympathy for it, and all these enemies were caught at once. They, under interrogation, betrayed more traitors. In another six months, the anniversary of the Revolution came. There were receptions in Athens, and in the Pentagon great parties: the new generals danced while the new colonels clapped and shouted '*Opa!*' Kostas sang, in his fine voice, a royalist song from the Civil War; he was moved with satisfaction and pride. The National Government had passed the period of its test; it pursued its policies with vigour, and all Greece acknowledged its authority. Wherever you drove you saw tributes: placards at every roadside showed a Greek soldier in silhouette against the powerful body of a phoenix that surged triumphant from the fires of destruction; at the entrance to every village a white bridge of loyal slogans spanned the road; the walls of old Turkish forts, that crumbled with age on promontories and crags, cried 'Long Live the Revolution' in dazzling white; and into the living rock of the mountains the great message was cut, so that from a pass many miles away you could gaze across space and read, small in distance but strong and clear, the bold white letters proclaiming the April date that brought salvation to subverted Greece. Kostas drove his family through the country, and the drive felt like a triumphant procession.

In the following year he was promoted to major. His cup now was full. Not everyone's plans had gone so well, he reflected with sympathy: for his cousin Leonidas also had ambitions, and still wrote articles supporting the Government. Yet his name had not appeared in any list of new appointments. Reviewing his acquaintances, now he had risen, Kostas wondered whether there still was point in cultivating his cousin. He decided there was. 'You never know,' he told Kiki, 'it's always good to have friends.'

Leonidas, when they met, would still occasionally complain about his wife's sister's husband, Vangelis Tzavellas. He had not been arrested, and he had not given up. He was a lawyer, a legal pedant, he was even trying now to take the Government to court.

'Let him try!' Kostas laughed at the thought.

2

The plane jerked, plunged, then banged, bounced as though they were belly-landing on rock: yet when Michael looked outside, all he saw was sunlit emptiness. The sky was violet, they could be in space, far underneath them the thick lower atmosphere stretched to the horizon like a purple sea: scattered clouds, glistening fleeces, rested on its surface like grazing creatures. But again, in the stillness, the plane shook as if it would break: he knew with each bang he was crossing a boundary, into the danger world.

Were they safe, his friends? It had been such a shock, invisible, on a still day, shaking his heart, when he heard of the coup: he knew the change must mean danger to them. But when he spoke to them on the phone, they sounded undaunted. It was only recently that he heard a trouble in their voices that told him he should come.

He shifted his cooped limbs and craned to the window. The plane was slanting down towards that thick ocean of lower air. Dimly he made out a brown country under it. Now he had crossed the frontier he saw his friends more clearly, they seemed to hover at the window: a dark earth-coloured figure like a stone, and a figure swirling, turning as she laughed.

A dazzling bloom of cloud grew steadily till they drowned in it. Lights flashed, hands fumbled for belts; as the air-pressure spiked everyone's head, the several babes in arms on the charter flight started to howl. The cloud disappeared, and a brown-white city turned slowly below them as if on a wheel. The plane wing separated in a ladder of slats, and they bumped, roared, braked and taxied to the airport buildings.

As they crowded to the door, the burning Athens air devoured them as though they had stepped into a furnace. It took away the power to breathe. Half blinded by sun dazzle, Michael looked round at the soldiers, who stood about on the runway holding small machine guns, idly attending to the new arrivals. Beyond the airport, palm trees and city blocks shimmered like a mirage.

In the terminal, fortunately, there was shade and coolness, as they queued to be inspected by officials who had before them tray after tray of small dog-eared cards. Each card had a photo stapled to its corner: these evidently were the regime's enemies. The official nodded to Michael; at his leisure, sardonic, he inspected the spare, thin-faced, long-legged Englishman, and shrugged him through.

He took a taxi to the centre. He looked out hungrily for the ancient city, but what he saw were marinas of bobbing yachts; roofless nightclubs with their neon lettering switched off and pallid; a long space-age fairground; and a beach so gorgeous in the city swelter that everyone had gone there, the sand couldn't be seen, the blue sea showed through chinks in the brown bodies. Then the taxi turned inland, and the streets were lined with new apartment blocks, which seemed to be no buildings at all but just layers of balconies stacked into the sky. It seemed no one lived in houses any more; occasionally, between the blocks, he glimpsed a dusty mansion of fracturing stucco swallowed by creepers. Traffic converged, car tyres screeched; there was a brief surprise of woodland, with slender columns standing higher than trees; then they came to a stop in the drumming traffic strangle of Constitution Square.

From here Michael walked through side streets, dodged and retraced, took another taxi, and headed for the suburb where his friends lived. He announced himself to the buzzing grill.

'Michael?' said Chryssa's distant voice; he recognized her timbre, low, musical, lively. The glass door of the building hummed hospitably and he pressed it open. He summoned the lift, but then, in the dimness, leaned back on the cool wall: he felt moved, nervous, in some way weakened. The years disappeared. Through the wire sides of the shaft he watched the lift descend like a vehicle of fate.

He was delivered into a pitch-black corridor, at the end of which a door opened, releasing light and a woman, small, taut, a figure of energy, brown and bright.

'Michael? Welcome!'

She had a strong voice, the corridor vibrated. She came quickly forward, and seized him and kissed him, and he kissed her. 'Come in.'

They entered a long living room, that brightened steadily to a sunlit balcony. Here they took each other in, she in a firm, up-drawn stance that had a bright defiance of his English height. Her dark brown eyes were alight with yellow sparks, brimful of pleasure-to-see-him and in some way amused also.

'So – after a decade – you come to see us!'

'At least I wrote.'

'Uh, letters. I'm sorry, Michael, I'm bad with letters. I need to see someone when I talk to them.'

He gave his presents: records, whisky, books they might not so easily get now. Some of them she had read, some she was glad to get. She offered coffee, and they went into the small kitchen. As she measured out water, sugar, and the snuff-fine dust of Turkish coffee, he secretly studied her. He guessed there was slav blood in her family, her sweet face was broad, with high clear cheekbones, and a short but not receding clear-shaped jaw. Fine face! he thought. As she turned and stooped to the stove he recognized poignantly the tender curve of her unclassical profile.

She asked what he did, and he described his work on the foreign news service of a London paper.

'You see the world, then.'

'I see a lot of airport lounges.'

'Are you on a "story"?'

'What I'd like to do is to write about you and Vangelis, if there's a way of doing that that's safe for you.'

'Safe?' She looked up quizzically. 'If we only did what was safe, we wouldn't open the window. But we'll talk about that when Vangelis is back.'

'How is Vangelis?'

'He's well,' she said seriously.

The thick glossy liquid slowly mounted in the small metal coffee pot. Chryssa poured it into little cups like egg cups, which they carried back into the living room. She indicated mischievously a giant chair, and for the first time Michael registered, and wondered at, the furniture they had. There were some modern easy chairs, but these hardly noticed beside the main suite of massive broad-shouldered, stout-armed, plump-seated, bulbous-legged chairs – with table and stately sideboard to match – richly, elaborately carved in black wood. The whole suite looked at first glance like some marvellously ripe fruit and flower market magically frozen into timber.

'Vangelis married these chairs when he married me. He calls them Balkan baronial. My father had them made.' She plumped down in one of them, for a moment like an impudent child in its carved embrace. Her father was a businessman, Michael knew; these chairs must date from the time of his prosperity. Michael suddenly had a picture of the way, as a child, Chryssa had bounded on the new-made chairs when they were things of awe and hardly to be sat on.

Michael sat in a throne.

'How do you feel?' She was amused to see him, a man with the physique of a too alert and famished hound, attempting to sit in state.

'Grand! They're palatial. Did Vangelis marry the rugs as well?'

'Yes, he married a hundred rugs.'

It looked so, the floor was spread and overlaid with rugs, of oriental design, in a warmth of brown and grey. 'And we'd nowhere to put them but on the floor.' Chryssa stretched her foot, toeing the soft pile.

'They're very beautiful.' He looked round wistfully at the married home of Chryssa and Vangelis, with its lovely balance of abundance and space.

She spoke about their life together. They had delayed having children, for the usual reason, to establish their careers.

'We should start a family – though it's difficult to think of children now.' The rich wooden abundance had suddenly an emptiness: there were real fruit not there that should be there. The child Chryssa in the chair was no child now but a woman from whom, like a release of carefully contained radiation, a wave of sadness poured through the flat and out over the sunlit day outside.

He asked, 'Is your work safe?'

'You mean, have they sacked me yet? No they haven't – universities aren't high on their list of priorities. But they'll get to me. They're putting the civil service through a sieve, and chucking out everyone who isn't theirs.'

He was startled by her hard tone, she had been in such a different mood.

'And they can catch people pretty easily here. They know if you read *Vima* fifteen years ago.'

28

'*Can* they last long, though? They seem just a gang.'

'They're strong, Michael. Have you seen them in interviews on the telly? They've got a tone – "We're here, and you can think what you like about it." What's the word?'

'Truculent.'

She paused and nodded. 'Yes. Truculent.' She smiled, with a bitter relish of the word.

Her fluency in English had felled his Greek. He asked, 'What can you do against them?'

'Well. Vangelis is a lawyer, and we do what's possible with the law. They make a big noise about strict laws. We gather evidence, depositions, we send them abroad when we can. We have some material for you to take back, if you'll be our "postman" – you should think about it carefully before you say yes. And Vangelis takes cases – against the Government. He has one now, about a schoolboy. This boy joined a resistance movement, I don't even know if he knew what he was doing, but the police took him in, and when he came home he had brain damage. All the same, he *can* say what happened, slowly. It is – terrible, listening to him.' She paused, nodding to herself, rocking slightly. 'Vangelis has worked very hard on this case, he has been very strong, very clever. And because they did not think the boy would be able to testify, and because he *is* a schoolboy, and some people who are for them are shocked, he has been able to get people to the stand – doctors, policemen, even an interrogator – he never thought he would get. They underrated him, and let it all go forward, and he has built up *such* a case. It's hard for them to drop it. This is why we hoped you'd come. Because this case must be known. We can do more here, if it's known about outside Greece. And Vangelis is near the end, and if he can just get there – if they let him finish – they *must* let him finish –'

She stopped, her face strung between hope and misgiving: she murmured, 'I hope . . .' but her tone said, 'I fear . . .'

Michael nodded. 'Whatever I can do, I will. I used to think reports, exposés, counted for more than they do. But I can make Vangelis' work known.' They paused, wishing; she had spoken of Vangelis with anxiety and trust and great love, her voice had a softness he had not heard before.

In that silence they presently heard the muffled whirr of

the lift rising through the building. Michael could see from Chryssa's face that she knew this was Vangelis: she looked as if she had stopped breathing.

A latchkey turned: a large man entered, and stopped and stared at the stranger; and in the quick sharp way those black eyes darted and fixed him hard, Michael knew at once the old Vangelis. But he'd changed! Michael remembered him as thickset, serious, a stone man down from difficult mountains. The new Vangelis was mature-bodied, stout even, and professional, important, in a taut light suit; and he had, a new thing, a thick, jet-black Balkan moustache. But his eyes were constant – sharp, even rude, till, as now, he recognized the stranger.

'Ah Michael! Hello!' He quickly crossed the room, his dark-skinned hand gripped Michael's hand hard, and they bumped cheeks, his black stubble grazing Michael.

He said no more: no formal Greek welcomes, he did not waste words, but stood, his solid rotundity upright, buoyant, while his black eyes, sparkling, inspected Michael with zest of old friendship.

'You're doing well, Vangeli.'

'And you're pretty spare.' Vangelis nodded ruefully. He put his case down, kissed Chryssa, and stood with his large arm resting round her, while she stood, pleased, within his embrace. 'These are bad times, Michael, we *need* to see friends!' Yet he did not look as though, today, he found the times so bad: his eyes shone excited, both Michael and Chryssa could see there was something else that pleased him, apart from Michael's visit.

'How's the case, Vangeli? You're making headway?'

'Tell us, Vangeli!' Chryssa said. 'You've pulled off something, I can tell.' She and Vangelis spoke English to each other, in hospitality to Michael.

In modesty Vangelis slightly ducked his head, like a buffalo menacing. 'Today, perhaps, I gained a point. I'll get drinks.' The others must wait while, in light exact movements, he was all about the flat, till he put into their hands glasses of ouzo, clinking with ice blocks, and rested on the table a dish with olives and pieces of cheese. He sat.

'I've a new witness taking the stand on Monday.'

Chryssa looked at him.

'The Security Commissioner – we've actually sent for him. The other side didn't like it, but they weren't quick enough, and the order was made. So! If he turns up – then I have them.' He swirled the ice and ouzo in his glass; Michael watched with pleasure the satisfaction of his friend, who was now a full-fledged lawyer but whose face in profile still showed its vehemence.

'Very good, Vangeli!' Chryssa's strong voice vibrated; but her face was tense, Michael noticed, she was biting back on some misgiving. Vangelis glanced up quickly and caught that look; he frowned, then he turned and sat upright.

'Well, young Michael, what have you been up to?'

Michael gave his account: his period as a foreign correspondent, his work now as part journalist part manager for the foreign news service of his paper.

'And you, Vangeli! You haven't let the grass grow?'

Vangelis ran over recent years. From criminal law he had moved steadily into labour law, he had several times represented a large trade union; he was at work on a book on boundaries and property; he and Chryssa were campaigning together for the elections when the Junta came. He shrugged as he finished, 'That's all stopped now.'

'Interrupted,' said Michael. 'They'll collapse soon, surely?'

In reply, Vangelis jerked his head upwards, and made a tongue-and-teeth 'tst' sound. Michael had forgotten this emphatic Greek way of saying 'No', which could seem if one weren't used to it, like a scoff.

'They'll be with us for a while,' Vangelis said; then turned to Chryssa, 'You don't think they'll let me win on Monday, do you?'

She said earnestly, 'You've built a strong case, an unanswerable case, Vangeli.'

'But I've got carried away, right? You don't think they'll let me get away with it, do you?' He sat forward, and said to her gently, with a hot vibration of urgent appeal, 'But the case is so strong in law, Chryssa. And it is *their* law, they are committed. They cannot get out of it.'

With an emphasis almost of tears she said, 'My love, you've done so much with this case, you've achieved so much – I want

31

more than anything for you to win. But what can I say? Can I say "Of *course* you'll win, of *course* the Junta will put themselves in the dock"?'

Vangelis looked at her, but she would not say more: evidently he saw she was worrying for his safety. He sighed, shook his head, and with an edge to his voice began explaining to Michael, 'You see, Michael, we are trying to use the law. There are other forms of resistance – bombs, guns. But do bombs and guns work against a military government? I don't think so; they have too many soldiers and too many policemen. And the more you bomb them, the more they clamp down. But, still, they do keep up a *sort* of legality, they have laws, "rules of procedure". They make a great brag of them – "Come and see our justice!" They are concerned for their "image". So we try to use these rules here, and also to get evidence abroad. Of course, what we do isn't going to get them out. But in the long run, with everything else, it can tell. And in the short term things can be . . . less bad. That is our plan. But if – if, even *with* their law, we cannot get anywhere at all, if when a case is clear, and the law is clear, if even then they will not allow . . . *some* justice . . . They must, they have to, they cannot get out of it now.'

Michael agreed, but Michael's agreement was not what Vangelis needed. He sat gazing blank ahead, his new moustache jutting: and just in the way he sat, gazing fiercely into obstacle, Michael recognized the young Vangelis. So he used to sit. He didn't see his way clear but he had obstinacy plus courage, no difficulty would deflect him.

But also he was not a man to be simply stuck. He sighed; there was a sharp report as he slapped his thigh. He got up. 'Well, enough! We have the weekend, it makes – a rest. I shall collect myself, and on Monday I shall tread' – he looked pointedly at Chryssa – 'very carefully. I shall be subtle, I shall catch them quietly. Well! These are bad days, let's think of old times.' He talked on energetically, reminiscing, by willpower talking his way clear of foreboding. He had avoided looking in Chryssa's direction, while she gazed downwards, troubled; but now, almost shyly, he glanced at her, his eyes bright with tender humour. He recalled an episode that she also remembered, and she picked it up. All three worked at the conversation, which presently gathered momentum.

Vangelis poured more ouzo, Chryssa brought snacks, with zest they recalled an earlier life.

They had all met in England, the two men first. Michael and Vangelis found themselves sole graduate students in a crenellated soot-crusted fortress of a Victorian lodging house. Vangelis, slightly older, had taken time off from his main legal training to study international law; Michael was a linguist, with only books to speak to. They knew no one else in the cold dim north London suburb, and drew together for company, chatting in a mutual aid mix of English and Greek. They each had the forlornness of the lone young researcher tipped far from his nest. Vangelis was oppressed by the damp and cold and early dark, and by the absence of anywhere to go but pubs; and behind Michael's chat, when his cheerfulness guttered, was some undeveloped, obscurely desolate English mood. He consoled himself in the daytime by riding hard a thunderous heavyweight second-hand motorbike. In the evenings they sat in armchairs drawn to the gas fire, nursing small cups of Turkish coffee, half listening to Rebetika or Chris Barber, and talking.

They told each other their life-stories to date. Michael's upbringing, in a small market town, had been quiet in comparison with Vangelis's; all their work in the daytime was English, in the evenings Michael liked to listen while Vangelis talked, with the obsession of distance, about Greece. His father had been the schoolmaster, his mother the doctor, in a village in the northern mountains. For most of his childhood the village had seemed nothing but a track for straggling armies, first the Italians, then the Germans, and then alternately, in the Civil War, the Communist guerillas and the royalist troops. He had glimpses of wounded, their bandages bleeding, and dead bodies under greatcoats. Cavalry pranced down the summer street in a whirlwind of burning dust; in the winter they returned, slithering in the mire. His father was an isolated man, a bookish socialist: he was hated by the royalists and mistrusted by the communists. Vangelis described with great affection the obstinate idealist, with his village physique and learned glasses, who used to take him for walks of explanation. For all the struggles, he had happy memories of his father, stooped very close to him, describing a plant or demonstrating, still in his city suit, how a car engine worked. Of his mother he had less

33

clear but more luminous memories: looking up exhausted from her surgery desk, or stooping to him with a young bright face in a swirl of pretty dress. She died while he was young, in an epidemic that accompanied the war. After her death his father had changed: he was desperate, cynical, also violent – but of these years Vangelis hardly spoke. Life brightened only when he left the mountains, and began to study law in Salonica. He was in a way like his father, argumentative, idealistic, a man on his own, guarded. Justice must come to Greece – but he could not see how it would come. In England, during the long talks with Michael, he had moods of determination, and moods when, in this cold foreign place, he sank almost out of sight in a darkness he carried everywhere with him.

Michael had no such riven childhood: he was a child of the war, but all he remembered of it was occasional throbbing flights of bombers. Otherwise his childhood was sheltered, happy, on the small fruit farm his parents had. The only warfare was playing fortresses among the stacked bales of the farmer next door: when the walls of bales and children fell, they landed soft in yellow straw and throat-drying strawdust. Then he boarded at a school he disliked, where he grew tall and stretched and angular from endless cross-country running round the edges of plough under the heavy broken English sky: it was how his adolescence had felt to him, a solemn effort of running into the blind cloud of his fate. His eyes were shy but lively, eyes of the runner still, reconnoitring glances, eager for true experience, such as Vangelis had a surfeit of, but which had not yet touched him.

Into this inertial, dark-futured, something-missing world of the bachelors Chryssa suddenly descended. Michael and Vangelis sagged in their chairs one evening deep in desultory philosophy when there came a tap on the door, and a girl's worried but buoyant voice asked, 'Do you understand fires?' They sat up, for with her there crept into the room a sharp smell of burning. They followed her into the deepening smoke of her own room, where they just made out the red glow at the base of a paraffin stove, badly adjusted and now one cake of soot, with thin red flames emerging from its grill like long fingers that turned at their ends to strings and spirals of black smoke.

34

Knowledgeable in technology, the men dowsed the burner and dismantled the apparatus, and urgently invited her into their room, hers being full of smoke. She thanked them with brown bright yellow-glinting eyes. She had just come, she was pleased to meet them: she too was Greek and exchanged histories with Vangelis, also she was interested to meet the Englishman.

She toured London with them: this was her first voyage abroad, she was determined to enjoy it. She could be exhilarated even by the dark, cold suburb, by the sheer excess of Victorian gloom in the towering shut houses with their Greek temple porticos: her low voice laughed loudly with amazement as she held herself together in the sudden gusts. She was enterprising and inexhaustible, she got them to films and to marches they'd only talked of going to. She discovered street markets and Oxfam shops: she flaunted her purchases, and would return to the lodging house promenading towards the men with a suave far-flung swivel of hip, while one jaunty hand cocked the brim of her wide pink hat, and in the rose shadows under it her raised square face fluttered eyelashes, taunting. Her English developed quickly. They became a threesome going everywhere together; they even went to see *Jules et Jim* together.

Abruptly, she had to go. Her father's business had failed, she was sucked back into family trouble.

'You'll come back?' Michael murmured; he found his throat was clogged and hoarse.

She didn't look up. She sat frozen, perhaps sullen, a deep dejection: he realized he was seeing the other side of her flamboyance. But then she looked up with brilliant eyes, 'Come and see me in Greece.' She kissed him quickly.

So Chryssa left: part of her seemed used to surprises of trouble. She didn't come back. Michael wrote, but she was preoccupied; and in any case, with new interests, new plans, their correspondence stretched to a point. His planned trip to Greece was postponed.

Some years later Michael was invited to the wedding of Chryssa and Vangelis: he found he was surprised they had married, they had seemed so different and from different worlds. He sent a present, and wistful good wishes. The correspondence was renewed interruptedly, they invited him

35

several times to visit; now they had invited him with more pressing reason, and now he had come.

On Sunday they went sightseeing. Chryssa guided them first to the National Museum, 'You must see the smile of *kouroi*, Michael.'

She led the way through the cool halls. Michael loved walking behind her, as she wove through the exhibits and the visitors with a graceful swing and swerve. She moved like a young actress, amused to find she was acting herself.

They arrived among the marble youths.

'What does that smile say?' Michael mused. 'It must be important, they all have it.'

'It's the eyes that make the difference' – Chryssa imitated them – 'they're so open. Otherwise they'd be like any cheerful person, wrapped up in their own happy ball.'

Vangelis was impatient. 'Perhaps it's the only expression they could carve then. So these are the "athletes" our ancestors loved. Oh, they had it coming to them.'

'What a rationalist you are, Vangeli!'

'Yes, that's true, I always have been.' A man of hard material himself, Vangelis looked stolidly round at the statues; and the tall white *kouroi* stood over him, smiling still, their eyes wide and their smile calm and permanent, heralds of some great benignity, inscrutable now.

They went to the Acropolis, and laboured up the crag in the scorching heat. They picked their way between the pillars of the Parthenon, wondering at the gigantic elegance of it: the summit of Athens, the archetype of temples. There was a brutality in the colossal stone blocks that made it.

Then the cool walk down wooded hillside, through olive-groves and evergreens, to the Temple of the Winds, and the *agora*. Vangelis and Chryssa debated, interpreting the ancient street plan; Michael, no archaeologist, wandered the scorching stones trying and failing – except for a gaudy recollection of Hollywood Rome – to imagine the buildings that had once stood here, full of business and emotion.

From the *agora* they crossed a street, and were in the flea market. They wandered slowly down the long narrow alley, where every shop had so many wares it couldn't contain them,

36

and overflowed the pavement – copper vessels, ironwork, earthenware, souvenirs, stands holding trees of shoes. T-shirts and jeans dangled overhead like a limp foliage. When Michael found a chased and studded copper coffee grinder he wanted, Chryssa said 'Leave it to me', and all her father's passion for bargaining descended on her like a radiant mantle. Her head jutted forward, her voice rose and hardened, she picked up a copper lamp which she didn't want, looked at it with indulgent contempt, and asked offhand what the shopkeeper charged for it. She dropped it like a hot brick when he named his price. She circled, sauntered, and idly picked up the coffee grinder and turned it over unimpressed. 'What do you want for this?' she asked. He said. 'You're crazy,' she said, and dropped it. He came and looked at it, 'What would you give for it, madam?' Casually she muttered a price; he turned away in disdain. With his back to her, making business with his higher shelves, he said, 'You can have it for four hundred drachs.' Now Chryssa was all disdain; she fingered other items in the trays and dismissed them, and slowly made her way out of the shop: she was leaving: yet she did pause on the threshold and call back wearily, 'Two hundred drachs.' 'Two hundred drachmas!' the shopkeeper exploded; in wrath and indignation he came swarming through the shop, enraged, enlarged, a tornado. He swept up the coffee grinder and thrust it into her hands, 'Here madam, take it, have it for nothing!' He waved it at her. She frowned, she wouldn't take it for nothing; but presently she offered something a little above nothing. The shopkeeper shrugged, but his price came down; and so at last in the countdown they stepped towards each other grudgingly from price to price, and met, and the purchase was made. And now Chryssa frankly admired the coffee grinder, and consulted the shopkeeper on where it came from and how to look after it, and he genially told her all about it. Weary but pleased they left the shop, and walked on down the street inspecting the coffee grinder with a pleasure truly earned. Vangelis, who had looked on during the bargaining, admiring Chryssa's capacity, came in now with connoisseuring observations on the quality of the copper.

Michael was awed at her generosity of passion: giving so much emotion to make a purchase. And, the purchase made, the bargaining fury would drop from Chryssa as completely as if a possessing demon had given her up. The only cost Michael could see, after a couple of busy bargaining hours, was a trace of tightness, tension in Chryssa. Then Vangelis, alert, took over the guiding while Chryssa recouped: more and more Michael noticed the unobtrusive tender cooperation there was between these two different people.

They were all tired now; on their advice Michael took them to a restaurant beside the sea, where at leisure they recovered.

It was after midnight, Chryssa had gone to bed. The two men had had a long session, in which Vangelis gave Michael all the details of the present case, and an account of other cases also: now they sat smoking on the balcony. The city itself was still awake. On balconies for as far away as they could see other families and friends sat chatting, smoking, quietly enjoying the night. They were facing Piraeus, and the sea beyond the buildings was dotted back into the distance with ships all brilliant with lights.

Michael savoured with the smoke the warm night air: unbelievable, after England, the gentle midnight air of Athens. During these days it had seemed to him that all their old rapport of a threesome had sprung back at once into life, as if it had been laid aside only for an hour; now he and Vangelis sat talking and not talking like two people who saw each other daily. But though his body relaxed, Vangelis did not relax; his old intentness burned all the time, like a blowtorch focused to a point. They discussed now reports Michael had heard in England, that another coup had been planned before the present one, but the Colonels had got in first.

'Yes, that's true,' Vangelis said. 'There was another coup planned by the Generals. These people jumped the gun.'

'They say in England that there was a split in America: that the State Department wanted an Establishment coup, but the CIA thought the Colonels would be more – efficient.'

'Maybe it was like that. Of course, there are people here who say that the British were behind the first coup plan, but then the Americans got ahead. I don't know. For us these questions are academic now. The Colonels are here; and they'll stay as long as the CIA and NATO believe they're good soldiers. "Protecting the eastern flank", you know. I don't think there's any other consideration.'

'Are they good soldiers, though? Does an army stay a good army, if it turns into a police force, and keeps having purges?'

'Well, but they may have military aims too. They aren't only fingers of the CIA.'

'What else are they?'

'They're something from our past, they're the skeleton in our cupboard. Sometimes they frighten me seriously. I don't mean for now, now they are simply NATO's policemen. But if they stay a long time – you don't know the things they believe in, in the Greek army. The Great Idea, even.'

'Which idea is that?'

'The Great Idea means the Greater Greece – Greece as she was before the Turks came. We went to war for that in 1919. Of course, there are different things to fight for now. We are looking for oil in the Aegean; if we find it, there will be a lot of pressure here to make Greece *the* power in the eastern Mediterranean. The army would like that. So I don't think that in the long run these people will do *only* what NATO wants. And a new war. . . .'

With his mind's eye, Michael scanned uncertainly the geography of the area: Bulgaria, Istanbul, the Dardanelles, 'The Balkans'. His thoughts chilled: such wars were past, surely? They sat in the dark: the saltpetre crackled in their cigarettes, the warm breeze from the sea brushed their foreheads.

'Well,' Vangelis sat back, stretching his arms, 'these are tomorrow's problems. Today we have more urgent ones.'

'But still I wonder, Vangeli, if that is what these people are like, how far *can* you get, working against them just with the law. Can anything that isn't military bring down a military government?'

'Not now, of course; and in the longer run . . . I don't know. I know about law, and I do what I can with that; other people do what they can. Perhaps we will achieve less than nothing at all. But we cannot sit by. It is a trust.'

Michael looked at Vangelis with admiration, but also with doubt: so that presently Vangelis said with energy, 'No Michael, things are not so dark. You used to call me a rationalist, and I will tell you, this is a rational trust. It is true we have a tradition of tough government here, whether its right-wing, monarchical, military or whatever. It goes back to the time of the Turks. And it touches everything. The ruler is a pasha, every bigshot is a pasha, every husband is a pasha, every first-born son is a pasha-to-be. But Greece has two traditions, and the other tradition is "freedom fighting" – against the Turks, against the Italians, against the Germans, against whoever comes on top of us. And it is a democratic tradition: we have had dictators, but we have had parliament after parliament. Perhaps other countries are either democracies *or* dictatorships, but here the two things fight all the time. That is our history. That is why my trust is a rational trust. I know that the reason I am resisting is not just that I was born loving freedom, but because I am a child of that history. My father was. That history means I can't do nothing. Other people are the same. So I work; and I have to hope that not everything I do is waste, because I have put my life into this work.'

He looked at Michael steadily, with the wall of face Michael knew from the old days: obstinate, pugnacious, his lower lip jutting. The shadows fell now so his eyes looked cavernous, but with a slow-burning mineral in them like phosphorus.

'Tomorrow you'll strike fire,' Michael said, moved; the warmth of their friendship flowed from the past into the present.

Vangelis sat back; he smiled keenly, 'Tomorrow . . . we shall see. I shall go carefully, as Chryssa says – but there will be some "courtroom drama" tomorrow.'

He looked out over the still night-time city. His face in profile was jagged, determined, aware of the chances.

In good time the next morning Vangelis went to the metro station near their home, and climbed into one of the ancient carriages of varnished wood. There he sat, the impeccable lawyer travelling to court, in a light smart suit and a fragrance of aftershave, still in self-possession while the train swayed and jarred, and the crowd shoved past, and the massive peasant woman next to him leaned bulgingly his way. Within he was a stealthy animal, all taut, on the alert, creeping close to his giant enemy.

He was swept with the escalator crush into Omonia Square, and briskly walked the short distance to the massive grimy street-long block of the law courts.

He glanced at his watch: the train had been delayed, he was none too early. As he pushed through the chipped swing doors someone shouted to him, but he couldn't stop: he hurried up narrow stairs and along dingy corridors where the strip-lights were off or failing. In a dim brown light that filtered through from side-offices with yellow-stained windows, dark groups of people in trouble sat on old benches as though they had been dumped there, or looked anxiously round hanging their sight on each new person, or killed time by pacing slowly. Somewhere a client remonstrated with his lawyer. 'Hideous place!' Vangelis thought again, with zest. He felt nervous but ready, his thought was focused.

He arrived at his courtroom, pushed hurriedly in, and came to a dead stop. He had expected a general milling, officials and policemen chatting, waiting to start. But the court was in session.

'Wrong room,' he murmured; but it was not the wrong room, it was the same room as before, with its yellow walls and an icon off-centre behind the judge's chair. The judge sat there preoccupied, listening to some address: and in Vangelis's place, another lawyer stood. This lawyer faltered when Vangelis came in, his wide eye glanced round; but then he resumed and spoke on loudly, and the judge turned all his attention to hear.

Vangelis's eye searched out the parents of the schoolboy. They were staring back at him with a look of such bewilderment and hurt and appeal and weak anger that he wondered what hideous mistake he had made. Slowly the schoolboy, sitting crouched, raised his head; slowly his heavy eyes swung to Vangelis.

'Mr Tzavella, you look confused,' an official was saying to him, courteous and kindly. 'Come and sit outside a moment, take some air.'

A policeman also had come, and by pressing close the policeman and the official forced Vangelis into the corridor. There the official told him, 'Your request has been granted.'

'What request?'

'Your request to be excused from the conduct of this case.'

The official gazed at Vangelis with stony eyes, his earlier blandness gone.

'That's rubbish. I made no request. I am going into court.'

'But you can't, Mr Tzavella. The judge has announced to the court that he has received your request, and that regretfully he has granted it. Another lawyer has been appointed.' He spoke brusquely, with annoyance, as if Vangelis had been lying; and with that he left, and walked back into the courtroom.

'Excuse me, I am late for court,' Vangelis said, in his sharpest courtroom voice, that resounded in the corridor. But he could not move an inch: the policeman held his arm quite locked. He could not free himself without a public struggle.

Another policeman appeared at the door of the court, and shouted down the corridor 'Order in the courts! Silence!' He stationed himself at the door.

The policeman holding Vangelis let go, and Vangelis walked away some paces. The policeman watched him off, and presently went and sat down on a bench. There he lounged, an arm on the bench-back, his belly slack, his bright eyes watching. He had a tiny moustache, he looked like the fat one of Laurel and Hardy.

Abruptly Vangelis walked fast down the corridor to pass him; but the policeman heaved himself up and fatly slouched into Vangelis' path. Vangelis paused, and retreated again, while the policeman's brown eyes sparkled.

Vangelis didn't want to leave, but didn't want to stay where the policeman could see him. He wandered into the first room to hand, the tiny *cafeneio* that served this floor of the law courts. There were a handful of rickety chairs and tables; a patched white cloth hung from the four corners of the room in a drooping canopy, to give some shade from the heat of the roof lights, but even so the room was stifling, airless. At least it was empty: Vangelis could pace and turn there, in his own hot box of outrage and frustration. Surely, surely they wouldn't simply *forge* a letter from him, asking to withdraw – not such a crude lie?

But he must act: he made himself be still, he reviewed the possibilities, and he made his plan. It involved waiting hours in this corner of the building, and never such hot hours passed: then he emerged, hurried downstairs, along another corridor, and up other stairs. He knew the building: he dodged the policemen, and at the right time came to the Judge's private office. He went straight in.

The Judge was there; Vangelis had him. He was a youngish man with an old manner, with big sallow cheeks: he blinked up like a frightened baby owl.

'What is this nonsense about a request to be relieved?'

'Nonsense!' the Judge queried, with an effort at indignation. He was younger than Vangelis, a career judge who had never been a lawyer, trapped in his den: he felt at several disadvantages. He snatched a paper off his desk. 'I have the letter here. It came this morning.'

'What letter?'

'Your letter; your request to be excused.'

'Let me see it.' Safe behind his desk, the Judge held the letter up like a proclamation, so Vangelis could read it. He saw, the sheet had his own letter heading, there was a straggly signature that looked a bit like his. It was a request to be relieved, but in messy typing and with spelling mistakes: Vangelis almost wept.

'Your friends could have done a better job. Do you think I can't spell?'

The judge kept touching his fingers to his brow: in a high voice he said, 'This isn't your letter?'

Vangelis gave an impatient head toss.

The Judge was an owl in panic now. The letter twanged in his fingers as he held it up and said in a shrill voice, 'Well – it looks to me very like your typewriter.'

'My typewriter? How do you know if it's my typewriter or not? Do we correspond? The letter's a forgery. You can see that. Can't you?'

Vangelis insisted: but it was too much for the judge, who opted for frantic anger, 'How dare you suggest I would be party to a forgery? I shall have you ejected from my office. I shall cite you for contempt. Officer!' Not giving Vangelis time to go, he kept on shouting, 'Officer! Officer!'

Vangelis didn't wait; he had a desperate new misgiving. He dashed from the building, jumped into a taxi, and even as the taxi raced through the streets he sat sharply forward urging it on. He ran upstairs, and through the outer rooms of his firm to his own private office. It was still locked: he fumbled with the key, and got in. The blinds were down and the dark furnished room looked much as it should. His typewriter sat on his desk uncovered – but how would he know if it had been used? He went to an old wooden chest where he kept special papers: and his heart missed a beat, for there were scuff marks and splinters round the lock. He opened it: and his files were there, compressed, bulging – but yet not all of them. For all his papers for the case in hand had been kept here: and he searched thoroughly: and those papers had gone.

He sat down at his desk; he had come to a dead stop now. *Such* methods, *such* cheating, and all he could say was, How was I such a fool? Why didn't I expect it?

Vangelis didn't immediately go home: Chryssa would be at work, and also he must walk off his passion before he could discuss what had happened with anyone. He left his office and walked fast through the hot crowded streets. But today's passion could not be walked off: for he had come to the end of a road he had travelled for the past two years. He had put all his energy into that work, he had thought he made progress, with his testimonies and depositions, and it was all wasted labour: at any time they wanted, if they were ever in danger, they could step in quite easily and bring it to nothing. That poor boy had been made to suffer again, for hours on end describing what had been done to him, to a hundred greedy eyes: that too was for nothing. And he himself would be watched, he wouldn't get so far with any other case. His thoughts could only go round in circles, now haranguing the Junta, and now protesting to a higher tribunal in his mind at the unfairness, the cruelty, the perversion of justice.

He heard the sound of his own voice in his ears: he realized he had been talking to himself in the street. He paused, shocked, and then in a curious detached moment thought: now I understand why it is that people talk to themselves; it isn't themselves they are talking to, they are arguing with someone else, in vain, and that's why they can't stop. Then his own inner arguing caught him again and swept him on round the maze of tight backstreets.

When he got home to Chryssa he was exhausted, flushed, confused. He found it hard to go back to the beginning and

44

tell her just what had happened that day. His thoughts wouldn't stay still, and the effort to speak caused him physical pain; he kept breaking off in mid sentence.

'Vangeli, please – you owe it to me to tell me what happened.'

'Chryssa, I'm sorry, I'll tell you properly.' But still it was difficult. Something had happened to him while he walked in the streets, as if the emotion he had been alone with had grown inside him till it passed beyond any words he could say to other people; and now it was sealing itself in. He could be lost to other people in sheer helpless indignation and rage: there was a knot inside him coiling tighter.

He made himself talk, he told her clearly all that had happened. She was outraged also, she wept with indignation: but her indignation only fed again his own, till he was crying to her, 'What was the point of all we did? It was all for nothing, you realize that?' Even speaking to her, he couldn't keep aggression out of his voice. 'The people who use bombs, they fight the right way. Fighting means fighting. There's no other method.'

'So what are you going to do, Vangeli? Get a gun and shoot a policeman? A lot of good that would do.'

'A lot of good! Is that how you describe . . . the fight?' He looked away; doubt from her was not what he wanted. For a moment he felt weak.

Presently she rested a hand on his arm and said, 'Vangeli . . . my love . . . of course you must be angry. But not with me. We only have each other. We mustn't fall out.'

He still looked away.

'My love,' she said again, her voice firm, her hand on his shoulder, firmly loving. Looking round with exhausted but tender eyes, he reached up and took that hand gently in his; but presently again his hold turned to a hard grip, without love.

So they were when Michael came, and Chryssa in anger and sadness, and Vangelis in a harsh, ironic, scathing voice, told him what had happened.

Vangelis ended, 'So. There's nothing to report after all. We needn't have dragged you here.'

'I shall report what happened – all that happened. That's important, isn't it?'

45

Vangelis gazed back with small eyes, ironic, bitter, his thoughts elsewhere.

'You'll keep on with your work, won't you, Vangeli?'

'Oh yes,' Vangelis said, quietly and privately, 'there's no stopping us. We shall keep fighting.' But he sat at that moment as if alone in the room, gazing ahead intently: and Michael watching him had a momentary vision of Vangelis driving on now in a closed, armed vehicle, and Chryssa outside it beating on the windows; and himself the mere witness, the outsider, looking on helpless while they drove into danger.

3

Some days later there was a brief announcement in certain newspapers about Vangelis' case: there had been irregularities in the proceedings, and the judge had accepted an application for the case to be dropped. With Vangelis' help, Michael prepared a report.

He stayed some days further with them. Vangelis was busy with other cases, so Chryssa showed Michael the places in Athens he needed to see. Discreetly, in her shadow, he took photos of shuttered offices, old warehouses, where interrogations went on. She translated for him when they visited acquaintances, or housebound politicians, or clients of Vangelis whom he wanted to interview.

In these difficult times, Chryssa was glad of his company, she was pleased to walk round Athens with this alert, diffident nomad, who always pressed forwards to walk her off her feet. What he was hurrying from or towards she could not tell: his blue, kind but restless eyes seemed always hungry for more than they saw, and more than his newspaper ferretings found.

'I envy you and Vangelis,' he said.

'You're a free man in a free world, Michael.'

'Free? I'm too free. I travel too light, I feel sometimes I'm everywhere and nowhere. You have a home, marriage – *and* a fight you're in the thick of. Things are bad here, I know, but I'd rather be here than where I am. I'll help all I can.'

He was always moving, and very soon he left. 'I'm sorry he's gone,' Vangelis mused, not, after all, having said very much to him. They were both more touched by his departure than they had expected. Being an old friend, he had brought back not just himself but all their good past together, so that in meeting him they met their younger selves: youth and freedom came back, young irresponsibility. Now he left, he took these things away.

In the following days Vangelis was taciturn, absorbed in thoughts he didn't confide. Chryssa pondered privately what course they should take: then she was called away. Her sister Patra rang. They had hardly spoken in the last six months, having separated after a run of family arguments about the Junta.

'It's an emergency, Chryssa, we have to talk.'

'What is it, Patra? Dad again?'

'Of course it's dad.'

'What's he done?'

'Chryssa, I don't know. Mother says he's bought a warehouse.'

'Bought a warehouse?'

'That's what she says, I don't know what she means. Can you come round, so we can talk? We haven't seen each other for so long.'

'I will,' Chryssa said; the separation weighed on both of them.

Patra came to pick her up in the capacious Rover that was her husband's pride. The sisters kissed; then Patra fought with the handbrake, and in a purring throb they moved into the traffic.

'So tell me, Patra – what has he done?'

'He's emptied a warehouse. He's bought everything that was in it. They told him he'd get a bargain price if he took the lot. So he collected all the money he and mother have, and he borrowed a whole lot more – and he bought everything! Can you imagine? All that money gone to waste! Where's he going to keep these things?'

'What are they, anyway?'

'I don't know. I don't think mother knows. She's in a state. We'll ring her later, see what we do.'

Impatient cars closed in on all sides, as they drove into the centre of Athens. Patra grew sharp-faced, nervous and competitive, harassed by the drivers behind, afraid they were trying to overtake. She darted and veered – when they crowded her and hooted, she passed on the curses to the cars in front – but she fought her way through the city, and Chryssa even found that their itinerary was taking in several stores in passing, where Patra stopped to collect goods. Evidently Chryssa's company was a godsend to Patra, giving her a second pair of

48

hands to carry to the car miscellaneous antiques, old curtains, little tables, brass lamps from old ships.

'Are you buying Athens?' Chryssa asked.

'They're for the villa!' Patra panted. Chryssa nodded. Patra and her husband lived for the villa they hoped to build.

Patra drove into the green hilly suburb of Kifissia, and parked by a large block of modern apartments. Laden with furniture they staggered in, let their burdens topple in the living room, and sank into deep chairs.

'Euphrosyne, bring us coffee!' Patra shouted hoarsely.

'All right, Mrs Patra,' a distant voice grumbled.

The room was hot but dim, for Patra kept the blinds down to keep some coolness in the scorch of midday. It was crowded from wall to wall with more pieces of furniture – tiny chairs from Skiros, bow-legged cabinets, different styles of table lamp – which evidently were waiting for a villa to go round them. It was a dark clutter: yet, unexpectedly, something in the room gave Chryssa deep comfort. Then she realized why – the packed shadowy room reminded her of the real warehouses their father had, in the days of his prosperity; she remembered their crawling as children through a twilight magic forest of furniture. She lay back in the hot velvety armchair, while her life seemed to slow and fill from the memory.

Euphrosyne, a stout powerful middle-aged woman, brought in the coffee, and bent with a weary sigh, like one laying down briefly a burden of toil, to rest the small cups on the table.

With a tired sharpness Patra issued her instructions for lunch; she suffered greatly from her maids. Euphrosyne sighed, and padded slowly away.

Then the sisters rang their mother, but this time they could get no clear account of the crisis from her: her voice shrilled on the line, agitated, lamenting, explaining nothing. Puzzled, frustrated, her daughters tried to calm her, and eventually rang off.

'We'll have to go there,' Patra said.

Chryssa nodded: she rang the airport, and booked tickets for Salonica the following morning.

'So. Tomorrow we'll know.'

The sisters sighed, drank their coffee. Chryssa told Patra about Vangelis' case and the way it had been stopped. Patra nodded, sighed, was sympathetic, but made no comment. She complained about Leonidas, not about his politics but about his appetite, his ambition, his ego, his feasting, his gambling, his nightclubs, his mistresses: she couldn't cope. Her complainings overrode Chryssa's; she was still the big sister.

The phone rang; it was Leonidas himself to say he was on his way and wanted lunch. Patra answered tersely, and hurried to the kitchen to harass Euphrosyne who was ponderous and stolid and not to be harassed, and went her way regardless. She picked up carelessly the aubergine which she had simply rested naked on the electric ring to cook, so it burst green all over her and the cooker. Patra wailed and badgered and banged on the kitchen units so all their doors flapped open; and through it all Euphrosyne steadily continued, and out of chaos produced a lunch, and if there was anything that should have been there but wasn't, she made shifts without. She had the strength of the villages and nothing could stop her: when she couldn't find the tin-opener, she simply took the breadknife and cut the tin through, to release the dolmas that Leonidas loved.

Keys rattled at the door, then a loud voice called, 'My wife, where are you? Wonderful news! I have an invitation from Manoli.'

'An invitation to what, Leonida?'

'To hunt on his mountain. And do you know who will be there?'

Patra didn't ask who would be there; while Leonidas spoke, there had been clumpings in the hallway, and he now came into the kitchen.

'What a sight,' Chryssa said. He had taken his clothes off as soon as he got indoors, and stood before them in his underwear, a large figure with stout round limbs and a soft potbelly. His big body was ruddy to start with, and tanned deep brown all over, and on top of that was overgrown on chest and forearms and shoulders, and on the parts of his legs where his trousers didn't rub, with a curling scrub of black hair. He stood in the doorway, fat and fit, in underpants and black socks, like Worldly Success in person, stripped naked but unashamed.

'Oh. Chryssa,' he observed; they kissed quickly, coolly.

'A good day, darling?' Patra asked.

'A good day,' Leonidas nodded with satisfaction. Neither he nor Patra said a word more about the invitation: Chryssa supposed there must be some political advantage in it, that was not for her ears. But Leonidas was hospitable.

'Chryssa, sit down,' he said, and without more ado he sat himself at the table and made a start. He piled his plate with dolmas and yoghurt and aubergine and taramasalata; and with fish he had caught himself, fried to his own recipe; and with a mountain of pilaf. Chryssa watched the mountain disappear. Leonidas' family had been poor, he went hungry for years: now he was rich he ate with fury, he devoured, he ate like a man who would never be full. But not selfishly: constantly he interrupted himself to cry 'Ah, wonderful food, marvellous food!' He would pick choice morsels from his plate – a khaki twist of entrail, a piece of fatty skin, a kidney – and cry to Chryssa or Patra, 'Ach, this is the best piece, *you* must have it!' He fed them in turns as though they were pet dolphins, while he told them how much they enjoyed their food.

And food notwithstanding he talked as well; and if Chryssa or Patra had any idea of conserving temper by steering clear of politics, or of touching such matters glancingly, or of tactfully not going in too far, Leonidas blew up any such caution at once. He began immediately to tell Chryssa how wrong Vangelis was.

'Can't he see, doesn't he know, what this country of ours wants? We *need* a strong government, it's all that can save us. We were sliding into communism. Has Vangelis seen Bulgaria? Has he seen Rumania? Albania? Is that what he wants? Because it's that, or the National Government. There's no middle way.'

'That's nonsense, Leonida. We were sliding towards elections and that's all. The communists wouldn't have won, they wouldn't have come near it.'

'Ach, Chryssa, have you no memory? Don't you remember the riots, the anarchy?'

'Of course I remember. It wasn't anarchy – except when the police came to beat up the students. There were protests, yes – and the only reason for those was that the King didn't want elections, and kept appointing new governments so he didn't have to have them. That's what brought Greece to the boiling point. And why did the King do that? Because the men with the money were afraid they'd lose some. And that's why you like this government – because it likes the money men, and all it wants to see is them getting more.'

'Excuse me! Sorry!' he shouted across the table, scattering food. 'Do you think I support them for money? Do you think they can buy me? I do it to save us from communism. Don't talk to me about elections, I know about elections. Socialism today, communism tomorrow. You, Chryssa, you don't understand. You are young, you didn't see the Civil War, you don't know what it means. What! Excuse me!' He interrupted himself, and stared at a fish head Chryssa had casually put on the side of her plate, 'Oh, Chryssa, no, that is the best piece, you haven't eaten the best piece!'

'The fish heads?' Chryssa said. 'I won't have them. You eat them.' She delicately picked up the fish heads one by one, and laid them on Leonidas' plate.

Leonidas stared, his face swelled: more hurt than furious he cried out loud, 'She isn't eating the best piece!' He took it himself, crunching and sucking the tiny, brittle head, then smacking his lips and rubbing his stomach, 'Mmm! Here, Patra, you have one!' and he held out the next head to his wife.

Patra eyed it with disgust. '*Take* it away, Leonida.'

'What? What did you say?' The plates rattled, the table shook: he surged up in the cramped kitchen and stood over them, thrusting the fish head at his wife, 'Patra, you will eat! It is a delicacy. Eat it, I say!' He boomed at her, in authority of the husband. Patra scoffed, took the fish head, and put it down on the table top, among the crumbs. Leonidas looked on as though his eyes would burst; and Chryssa stared, for Leonidas was beside himself. All day in his office he had to be cool, at home he let rip: and, when he did so, his wife froze in dislike, and he was baulked. But he found an answer.

'Euphrosyne, come here! I have something for you.'

Euphrosyne approached, sweet deference, her voice dipping like a curtsey, 'And what is that, Mr Leonida?'

'Eat them, Euphrosyne, they are the best.' He piled fish heads in her hand. She crunched and sucked, while he took one back and savoured it, 'Ach, Euphrosyne, aren't they sweet? They are delicious!'

Euphrosyne nodded, sucking the small skulls dry. Leonidas, justified, looked at his salt wife with yellow eyes of hatred; then sat down, ignoring her, and picked up his argument where he had left it.

'No, Chryssa, Vangelis should *support* the National Govern-

ment; he should not take cases against it. All this court business
of his – he shouldn't do it. But I know why he does it.'

'Why is that?'

'For his career, of course!'

'You're insane.'

'What! Excuse me, Chryssa, I know how he thinks. He looks
forward to the government *after* the National Government, he
thinks he will have a good name then. He isn't stupid. But he
shouldn't do that, he should be with us. Of course! He says
he is left, but he is middle class. We are all middle class, and
we have one enemy – the communist!'

'This isn't the Civil War, Leonida.'

'Chryssa, you are very superficial. Things do not change,
the communist is there. And me, I have made my way from
nothing, I have slaved, I have earned my money. And I will
not give it to the communist!'

'All right, Leonida, all right. Calm down. You won't give
your money to the communist. We understand. Where is
the communist anyway? Is he under the table? He's half
your invention, you know – your money invents him, it's
thinking of your money that invents him in your mind. He's
what you've got instead of a conscience. Really, there are
more communists in your head than there are in the
party. And that's the crazy reason that we have this crazy
government. That's why children get beaten until they've
got brain damage.'

Leonidas interrupted, 'Excuse me, Chryssa. No one has
proved that the National Government uses torture. Vangelis
did not win his case.'

Her voice sank a tone. 'Do you know what happened in
"Vangelis' case", Leonida? Shall I tell you how justice works
with the National Government?' And she told him, quietly, in
order, the progress of the case. Leonidas listened glowering,
bridling, seeking loopholes, irritated with these details. When
she finished, he pushed all she had said on one side, 'Chryssa,
these are personal details. They are not the point. The point
is – the plight of Greece.'

'The plight of Greece, Leonida? The plight of Greece is that
it's run by thugs and spies and arselickers for people who
grab.'

Leonidas stood up again. 'What did you say? Thugs? Spies?

Chryssa, no one – *no one* – calls the National Government thugs in my house!'

'Keep your house, Leonida, keep all your houses.' She got up to leave.

'Chryssa, please,' Patra cried, following her down the passage. 'Stay.'

'I can't, Patra.'

In the hallway Patra got in front of her. 'Chryssa, he was stupid, please stay. We haven't seen each other for months because of rows like these. Let's not go back to all that.'

Leonidas had followed them down the passage; he hovered at a safe distance, his face inflamed. Chryssa saw him, and looked away.

'I can't talk to him.'

'Don't talk to him. He won't say anything. Do you hear me, Leonida? You will keep your mouth shut, shut, shut.'

'Stay, Chryssa,' Leonidas said quietly.

Pale now, subdued, the sisters returned to the table; Leonidas went out onto the balcony and lit a cigarette. The plates were cleared away, and Euphrosyne got out the watermelon. At Patra's bidding Leonidas returned and sat down, on his dignity. Euphrosyne now distributed the pieces of watermelon, sighing *'Ach manamou!'* loudly and grievously as if all the suffering had been hers.

Fortunately the watermelon was red and sweet: on tasting it, Leonidas exclaimed with delight. He decided he had the best piece, and this was possible since Euphrosyne had given him the biggest. He forebore in tact to press it on Chryssa, but, with a slight trip of hesitation, risked offering it to Patra. 'The best piece, darling?' She made a face, but, in tact, accepted it; then she and Chryssa smiled to each other, and shared the best piece, and the meal finished quietly.

After lunch Patra and Chryssa went to the bedroom to lie down; Leonidas, displaced, lay on the sofa in the living room. The sisters were too agitated to sleep, but presently they heard, rising and growing regular, the long snoring of Leonidas.

Stretched on the bed, they reviewed their travel arrangements for next day, and discussed what to do about their father. He was long past the retirement age, and he had almost no money, but still he would not stop trading. His activity kept him fit, he would go on for ever to new ventures and new disasters.

'He *must* stop. He must take his pension.'

'He won't, Chryssa. And if we sort things out this time, there will be more warehouses.'

'Uh, the warehouse! What are we going to do about the warehouse?'

They turned the problems over, and couldn't find good answers. Then they made coffee, and drank it slowly, dressing; Patra would run Chryssa home. In the living room they passed Leonidas, who lay on the sofa on his back with his legs apart, his arms wide, his mouth agape for his tremendous snores: a naked, enormous, exposed creature, sleeping freely and unprotectedly, like a child. The sisters studied him – he was a sight – and left.

The following morning Chryssa and Patra took an early flight to Salonica. The plane climbed rapidly till, looking east, they saw arches and caverns of cloud lit a hundred colours by the low sun. But almost as soon as they reached this height the plane dipped down again, and within the half hour they were descending over dried brown river courses to Salonica airport.

At the airport they rang their mother, to tell her they were coming; they had not rung sooner, in case they scared their father off. Then they took a taxi: it drove them down a wide coastal avenue, which slowly thickened with heavy traffic to become the main street of the hectic overcrowded northern city.

They got out by their parents' home. Their father loved business so much that he had to live in the busiest place, and his flat overlooked this main road through the city, where all the lorries drove. It was at the top of the building, and every day he liked to sit out on the balcony, sipping his coffee, and looking down on the long dazzle of shops, and the streaming crowds, and the endless traffic, drawing life in his age from the bustle and racket and familiar sour smell of dust and exhaust that rose to him through the roadside trees.

The building was dusty, dingy, not well looked after. When they got in the lift, its light switched out: they cranked slowly

and jerkily to the top floor in darkness, and tripped as they
got out, since the lift always stopped two inches below the
floor level.

They knocked on their parents' door, and eventually heard
sliding steps shuffle towards them: their mother.

She opened the door, then stepped back, and expressed
her pleasure to see them by frowning hard. 'Ah! You!' she
exclaimed. She pulled them to her and hugged them passion-
ately, one in each arm. Then she stepped back onto the two
pieces of blanket on the floor behind her, and shuffled ahead
of them into the living room: she always, while walking,
polished the floor.

They sat, recovering from travel, looking round the familiar
room. Their father was restless, he must change apartments
often, but the same home reformed in whichever building they
moved to. The room was large, but dimly lit, for only half the
egg-shaped bulbs would come on in the enormous cumbersome
carved wooden candelabrum, which stuck out of the ceiling
like a dragon's leg, or like the bottom half of a tree which had
its trunk and branches in the attic above. The room was
crowded with more of that suite of black wooden furniture of
which Chryssa, on her marriage, had inherited a fraction: big
upright wooden armchairs in which, even now, both sisters
could if they wanted sit together as they had as children; a
table like a catafalque; a cabinet of glasses and decanters and
Bavarian china; and on all the furniture their mother's fine,
bright coloured embroideries. All these things were there; but
their father was not there.

'Where's dad?' they asked.

'He's out just now,' their mother said; she sat uneasily in
the large chair, blinking sharply at her daughters.

'How are you, mum?'

'Terrible. I don't sleep well, I don't digest, and I have pains,
I'll show you, I have pains here, and here. . . .' She was,
visibly, strained and tired, but still she got up nimbly to show
them where she hurt. 'And your father, oh, the life he leads
me! Aman! My God! I don't know how I can cope!'

'Yes, but where is he? When's he coming back?'

'Ach, that man! He's normally home at this time. Who
knows where he is?'

The sisters looked at each other, and began to ask her about the warehouse. But she was troubled and confused about this now; she was not sure what he had done; she was sorry she had dragged them here all the way from Athens. And all that happened, as they continued talking, was that her face grew slowly sadder, till it showed only grief. Her face was like Chryssa's, squarish, clear-boned, slightly slav, with small features: an old but pretty face, which, as it lost sternness and grew sad, grew younger too.

Patra's face was like their father's, handsome, sharp, nervous. 'The point is, mother, he has to retire. The pension's there and waiting, he has to take it. If he goes on with business, warehouses, trading in this and that, he'll lose everything.'

Their mother didn't argue, but also didn't seem fully to grasp what they said. Her head sank lower; and then, by the tiniest change in the way she sat, they knew she was crying.

'He will kill me, that man,' she sobbed. 'He will be the death of me.'

The sisters paused and looked at each other helplessly.

'Mother, when is he coming?' Chryssa asked.

'He'll be here soon, my child,' she said through sobs.

They waited; their mother sobbed inaudibly, almost invisibly; the daughters sat at a loss, while tears collected slowly in the corners of their eyes.

Time was passing; then, abruptly, Patra sat forward and said sharply, 'Where is he, mother?'

Their mother jumped, and stared at them, blinking.

'Come on, mother, where has he gone?'

Their mother stared about her mistily, bewildered; at last she said numbly, 'The island . . . I said, didn't I? . . . He's gone to the island, he'll be back as soon as he can. . . .'

The sisters gazed aghast: their father had a favourite island, where he was especially well known to the shopkeepers. He always traded there, though more and more they cheated him.

Patra stood over her mother with her hands on her hips, shaking her head. 'You see, Chryssa, you see? She's covered up for him. She's kept us here while he got away – running from his daughters. Ach, parents!'

At this their mother flared, she was on her feet at once. 'What did you say about parents? I'll tell you something about parents, Patra!' She spoke sharply, but her voice was not strong; she was shaken, flustered.

57

Chryssa stood also. 'Mother, you should have told us. This isn't helping him. Patra, we must hurry, we've got to catch him.'

'Catch him? He'll have got all that stuff on the island by now. He'll be trying to sell it! Ach, can you imagine? The "bargains"! The loss!'

'How did he go, mother? When did he leave?'

·'The bus . . .' their mother murmured, weak-voiced.

The sisters sped from the flat.

Their mother, when they'd gone, stepped back onto the pieces of blanket and, lamenting quietly, shuffled round the flat while the floor shone ever brighter.

Hurrying from office to office, the sisters hired a car, and set out overland for Kavala, the port of embarkation for their father's island. Patra drove. Bends hurtled at them, mountains tipped the road up, tiny villages swerved at them, swallowed them and vanished: sunburnt aged men in white shirts and grey caps at café tables; old women shawled in black; chickens, sheep, goats, all flashed like snapshots and fell away. The sea swung beside them then left them; oncoming buses missed them by centimetres; and everywhere, endlessly, the white signs and slogans of the National Government clacked at them, vanished, and jerked up round the next bend to pester them again.

Driving fast made Patra talk fast, in monologue, and Chryssa's worries put her in mind of her own. They had troubles with their son Alexis, he and Leonidas could not get on. Alexis was quiet, mild and happy-go-lucky, and Leonidas was at his wits' end wondering how to make his son a man. He was full of crazy remedies, he made Alexis take boxing lessons, he wanted him to get into the army early, he gave him money to go to a brothel – and Alexis gave it back saying, 'Never mind, daddy, I can't be bothered.' Leonidas was mortified, he put the blame on Patra, and his anger fell on her when she tried to shield Alexis.

'Ach, Chryssa,' she said, 'the sufferings of the family! Tragedy is alive today!'

They climbed a curving mountain road and passed through a gap in the rocky hills; and all at once the stony landscape fell away, and below them they saw, tumbling down the hillside to a crowded harbour, the old town of Kavala, all warm yellows and long shadows in the lowering sun. Beyond Kavala stretched the calm sea; and far out, huge, ghostly in mists, humping like Leviathan, was the mountainous island where their father traded.

They wound through old streets till they came to the water-front. There was little chance they would catch their father before he caught the ferry, but still they kept watch while their car purred along the front to the ferryboat landings, slowly, stealthily, like a car on tiptoe.

Chryssa cried, 'It's him.'

They parked, and approached their father: he was standing by himself on the quay, a small restless figure in silhouette against the water, which caught the low sun like a dented piece of bronze. He moved his arms nervously and walked to and fro, beside a mountain of ferryboat luggage. He hadn't seen them, he was gazing out to sea: evidently he had missed the ferry he wanted and was waiting anxiously for the next one.

He turned when they were very close: for a moment he stared at them, then he cried out loud like a man in a surprise of pleasure, 'Aman! Is it you? Are *you* here?' He came towards them with his arms held out, he raised his head for them both to kiss, then he stepped back to look at them holding each by the hand. 'Chryssa, Patra, well fancy seeing you here! My daughters! Who'd have thought it?'

'Dad, we came after you,' Chryssa said seriously, but he seemed not to hear her. He bore them forward in his sweeping arms, 'Fancy seeing you! What a coincidence, what a surprise! Let's celebrate! Come, I know a good café, the man there is a good man.'

They crossed the road to the nearest café: he gave them seats with their backs to the sea, and sat himself so that he could see past them all the time to the mound of luggage and the open sea. He rapped loudly on the table with a fork, and hollered across the café, 'Hey, Alecko, two coffees, and ouzo for me! Immediately! At once!' He looked at them, 'You'll have coffee? He's a good man, Aleckos.'

The café owner appeared in the doorway, hulking, un-shaven, dour: he did not look like a good man. He said nothing, and returned to the kitchen.

Chryssa and Patra poised to begin; but their father didn't wait, he shouted across to the next table, 'Yianni, how goes it? Isn't business terrible!'

'Abysmal, Mr Niko. Are these your daughters?'

'They're my daughters!'

Then Yiannis, an aged bent man in the uniform of old men, grey cap and trousers, collarless shirt and maroon pullover, with a thick silver dust on his brown chin, slowly came over and sat at their table. 'Congratulations!' he said.

'Alecko!' their father called again. 'An ouzo for Yianni! Quickly, right away!' Again Aleckos came to the doorway, looked at him, said nothing, and went back in.

Now the sisters had Yiannis to deal with, in addition to their father, whose pleasure at seeing them seemed more than he could contain. But Yiannis was not a problem, for once he had sat at their table, their father ignored him; and Yiannis himself was evidently content just to sit back looking at the two women with a shrewd inspecting smile that seemed to tell them without end that he approved.

And they were not to be put off. 'Dad, were you waiting for the ferry?'

'The ferry, Chryssa? Oh yes, that's right, I've got to go to the island. Business, business, I promised I'd go. But never mind that.'

'But is that your stuff over there, dad – all those cases and boxes?'

'Cases and boxes, my child? What cases and boxes?'

'Over there, on the quay.'

'Oh, those things – I think they must be luggage for the ferry.'

'But where's your luggage?'

'My luggage? My case is there, don't worry, I'll keep an eye on it.' And he did, his eye wouldn't leave the pile of cases for an instant.

At last Aleckos came, manoeuvring his heavy bulk carefully between the close tables. He rested the order on the table, while he and their father gazed past each other into the middle distance.

Chryssa, about to resume, was forestalled by Yiannis, who picked up his glass, smiled broadly at her and Patra, and said aloud, 'Your daughters, eh, Mr Niko? Congratulations!' He dashed his glass against their father's as though these daughters were that moment born. Then their father gazed on them with public pride: but they, the ingrates, stayed stony.

'What business is it, dad?'

'Business, my daughter?'

'On the island.'

'Ah, my child, yes. Business, business, I always have business, I get no rest. And I'm an old man now, how can I keep up with it all?'

He had given them their chance. 'Well, dad, why not stop? You've worked so hard all these years. Why don't you rest, and take your pension? That pension is just sitting there waiting for you. Take a holiday, dad, do.'

He had looked strained as they spoke, but now, suddenly, he banged his glass on the table and said, 'My children, you're right! Let's call it a day. I've earned my pension, haven't I? I've a right to take it easy!' He protested hotly.

'Ach, dad, our little dad, that's such good news! Look, come back with us now. This business on the island – let it go. The car's here, let's put your things in, and go home.'

He sighed, 'My children, thank you, you're true daughters. But I can't come now, I must finish my business. I gave my word. You go home. You're such darlings. I'll take my pension – tomorrow: I promise you.'

They worked on; their father dodged; Yiannis sat and listened and smiled. The red sun hovered on the rim of the Aegean, and people came out in smarter clothes to promenade along the front. Their father toyed with his glass: he had the patience of the merchant, but the pressure of their urging told on him. A little knot of muscles at the corner of each jaw started to throb and beat.

Someone shouted greetings to Yiannis, who answered loudly but waved them away: he was busy listening.

The knot of muscles beat, the lines in their father's face deepened, they saw they had come to the impasse: he had to take his pension, but he could not give up business. It was his life, he could not stop. And he had other worries too. Evening deepened and all Kavala promenaded on the quay, and he kept losing sight of the luggage: and beyond that, as the ferry still didn't come, they saw the fear grow – his desperate fear – that he had missed the last ferry.

Yiannis at last came into his own. Chryssa asked him, 'Mr Yianni, tell us, when does the last ferry go?'

'The last ferry? Uh! Poh! It's gone. It went hours ago.'

Their father's face fell, he looked round wild, he could no longer make any pretence. Their hearts melted. He got up and hurried in agitation to the quay, to the mountain of luggage. He started checking the items, counting them frantically: he seemed to keep counting them, as though between one count and the next something might have been stolen.

'Put them in the car, dad. Let's go home.'

'Let's go home, dad. Put the things in the car.'

Patra brought the car close, its large boot yawned for the luggage.

'We'll return the stuff where you got it, dad. We'll insist that you get your money back.'

But he stood, and stared, and could not budge. He was in great agitation, his mouth munched. It was his golden bargain, his coup. They saw that if they took everything away now, it would make him mad.

They stood at an impasse, till Chryssa said, 'What things are you selling, dad? Let's see. Do they have to go to the island? Can't you sell them in Salonica?'

Their father looked at them with dazed eyes, and then stared hard at the boxes, almost as if he had become so desperate in guarding them he had forgotten what they contained.

'The island, the island,' he murmured.

'Show us the things, dad. Let us see.'

To their surprise he complied at once. He pulled off the stack an old blue tartan suitcase, big, battered, which was hardly secure since the corners were dented and the hinges broken and the locks not working; and which was yet hard to open because their father had so tied it round and over with string. They fumbled the string together, eventually the knots slipped – and the case exploded, for it was crammed, and what burst from it was – a world of plastic: plastic hats, plastic spades, plastic buckets, plastic water wings.

Without a word the daughters took another case. Under the tall white lamp-standard on the quay, between the black sea and the promenading locals – who paused and stared and didn't speak – they opened more cases and more till they stood surrounded by a devastation of open trunks and breaking boxes. Out of them rose a swollen crowd, a flood, of plastic things: ghastly, ghostly, half their lurid colour bleached out of them by the dim electric light: plastic boats and plastic shoes, plastic dolphin, plastic liners, plastic hats with plastic feathers, plastic rakes and plastic shovels, plastic masks, plastic beasts and oh armfuls of hard plastic flowers.

'Dad, is *all* the stuff like this?'

He nodded, looking on bewildered, and half in tears Chryssa asked, 'Dad, dad, how can you sell these things, on the island? It's September.'

He murmured, 'September . . . that's still summer, Chryssa . . . Next year. . . . Buy early for next year. . . .'

'It's September, dad. Who wants these things now. You'll never sell them. Dad, how could you?'

He gazed perplexed at all his wares laid open on the pavement. 'How could I . . . I don't know . . . my mind now . . . but Chryssa, Patra, it was a bargain price, *such* a price. . . .'

They hugged him hard, while the tears ran down their cheeks: he only looked about him, his brows high, hopelessly confused.

The repacking began. They knelt on the quay and gathered the plastic shoes and hats and boats and toys, and packed them back in the cases and boxes, which they crammed into the boot of the car, and into the back seat, and piled up high, precarious on the roof rack. All that mound of luggage proved to be their father's things: they didn't dare imagine the fret and trouble he must have had, coming, shepherding all these things from bus to bus. They squeezed into the car as best they could, and Patra put the lights on and gingerly set off.

The sisters were exhausted, they had nothing left to say. They were cramped together in the front seat with their father beside them. He was perplexed, desolate, he looked very old. Chryssa observed him tenderly. He was the merchant: once he made a fortune, spreading cheap furnishings through the villages; now he was old, his day was gone, he must retire. Chryssa dozed, but her father did not, and later in the journey, when the lights of an oncoming car suddenly lit up all the inside of their car, she would see his face for several moments: aged, scored with lines, but again hard awake, hook-nosed like a bird of prey. His eyes had a hard gleam like glass eyes; at the corner of his jaw the knot of muscle throbbed, throbbed, like a creature in his skin. He had not given up, he would not: his turn would come, it must. Through her sleepiness she saw him; her heart died; but she was worn out, and lapsed again to sleep.

4

A quick fire of excitement that needed no fuel kept Leonidas
taut and fresh through the hard drive to the hunting party. He
and Patra argued about what to wear: what was appropriate
for meeting a minister? Alexis, indifferent, lolled in the back
of the car, reading.

They crossed a flat, interminable plain dotted with long
white barns with wilting cardboard walls, where tobacco was
dried. There were mountains in the distance. The land rose,
and they began to climb and wind through foothills. Eventually
they ran into the scorched, dusty, deserted square of a hilltop
town; a dozing dog opened an eye then closed it.

They paused and enquired, but the party they were going to
was further on, up in the hills. So they drove up a narrower,
steeper, more winding road, breathing the sweet keen scent of
pine trees, and stopping, where they saw many cars stopped,
in a high saddle of the hills where the trees thinned, and where
a fire was burning, and the sound of voices carried on the
air.

Here was the party. A sheep was roasting, an old man beside
it turned the spit slowly. People stood round talking, laughing,
drinking. A musician was playing a pipe, individuals would
dance. They saw their host, a vigorous middle-aged man with
close-cut hair, a tough style, wearing a sports shirt among the
suits.

'Hello Manoli!' they called.

'Leonida! Patra! Wonderful that you came!' He hurried
over, embraced them brusquely, and began to show them his
domain.

'We used to own this mountain,' he said, then pursed his
lips, 'but we let it go.' Now all they owned was a textile factory.

He poured them drinks and ushered them in, making introductions. Leonidas' sharp eye scanned, seeking the man he
wanted most of all to meet, the Minister of Coordination,

Sotiriadis. Years before, he and Leonidas had actually, briefly, been law students together.

Now Leonidas saw him – he was almost hidden behind other men who stood round him in a horseshoe, chatting, admiring. He was a short lean man, wizened but ardent: his eyes shone feverishly, with excitement of success. And the eyes of those talking to him shone, they were all excited. Leonidas could see what was happening: the flatterers all beside themselves, buttering the Minister. He would not approach now: it was too important to do it right, he must wait till he had the Minister to himself. Then he would pay his own more manly, more upright respects.

And he was meeting important people: people in textiles, in shipping, the best wealth of Athens, he was not wasting his time. He voiced well-chosen opinions firmly, and let his expertise as a consultant show. He started to enjoy himself: the air was sweet, the wine was good. He studied the barbecue eagerly, for it had been a hard drive and he was ravenous. The shining flesh turned slowly, the fat dripped and sizzled in the charcoal chips.

Conversation paused. A large, well-fleshed man – a successful Athens doctor – was going to dance. With his head down, his arms held out, he jumped, turned, made small runs, stooped suddenly to slap the ground. He danced well. The people round cheered and shouted 'Opa!', the pipe music skirled and whirled, hands pressed bank notes into the musician's pockets or stuck them onto the sweat of his forehead.

Leonidas clapped, and saw Patra across the clearing, clapping cheerfully. The only fly in his ointment was the brief sight he got, between people, of his son Alexis sitting against a tree looking sulky. He had made himself ill, reading in the car all the way there. Now he lay like an invalid, with the book responsible beside him.

'We'll put some blood in his veins tomorrow,' Leonidas murmured, thinking of the hunt. His eyes lingered grimly on his son.

'The meat is ready!' Manolis cried.

They all hurried over, except Alexis, who lay watching his father pull apart a large piece of hot mutton. He had a spasm of dislike, watching his father chew so the fat ran down his chops; now he was laughing, over the greasy meat, and his

66

loud false laugh banged like a clapper in Alexis' head. He watched his father's large brown eye look steadily at a big-breasted, big-buttocked ash blonde girl, a white plumpness, who laughed to all the men. His father and his father's friends! Alexis seethed, the dislike was under his skin, he'd have to scratch off his flesh to be rid of it.

He waited under the tree as if he'd fallen from it, full of poison. And now they came over to him, Leonidas, Manolis, and two other men – big, wide-bellied, laughing and chewing as they sauntered.

'So here's the young hunter, resting for the morning!' one of them said.

'Ah, his father's son!' Manolis chimed. Leonidas smiled, uneasy.

The other stout man said, 'And so, young Alexi, what will be your line? Will you advise foreign countries, like your father?'

Abruptly Alexis spoke, 'I wouldn't do that. I'm an honest man.'

He had heard someone say this to his father once, as a joke; and he thought before he said it that he also meant it for a joke. But he heard something in his voice so thin, so acid, so sharp – he knew it was not a joke, and that no one could take it for a joke. And the others were drunk, drowsy, none of them found a quick remark to save them; they only withdrew, their conversation stopped, in awkwardness. Presently Alexis saw his father detach himself from the group and walk away down the hill by himself. Alexis could see from his walk that he was not happy now, he had been humiliated in front of his friends. Now the dislike in Alexis' skin turned to a prickle of disgrace, embarrassment, self-dislike, frustration. His mother came to comfort him, bringing meat; but he was irritable with her. She presently left him, and went off to talk to Manolis' wife about husbands and sons.

Evening deepened but the party didn't stop. An enormous amber moon hung over the plain to the east; and with its rise, Leonidas returned, and in good spirits. Manolis had found him, and told him: they would be up before dawn for an early hunt. And in their party there would be Leonidas, and his son, and Manolis, and – the Minister.

'Opa! Bravo!' Leonidas cried, as the doctor danced again.

67

The moon was a high silver coin in the blue-black sky, before the couples and groups sporadically drifted down the mountain to their cars. The charcoal glowed; the car lights wound away between the hills.

Leonidas' deep voice breathed in the darkness, 'Alexi, are you awake? It's time.' He sounded doubtful, afraid Alexis would be ill, or sullen.

Alexis awoke to these words. He felt confused and sour from yesterday; but at his father's near voice in the dark, something jagged and hard inside him melted, he wanted to make a new start on the new day.

'I'm awake, dad. I'll be with you.'

Leonidas was pleased. 'I'll wait outside.'

Alexis put on the thick trousers, large boots and tough jacket his father had left out for him, and went outside. It was night time: the cold nipped, the stars stood out white, with the black hump of the mountain sharp-edged against them. As they tramped to the rendezvous their ears were filled with a constant streaming, rushing noise: it was the push of wind in the trees, combined with the rushing splash of water. The town was split by gorges, where the torrents ran that once powered the textile mills. Wherever you walked in the town, you heard the sound of water.

There was a light on in a small shed; they went inside. Manolis and the Minister were there, drinking coffee.

Manolis introduced, 'Mr Minister – I believe you know Mr Argiriou,' and as the Minister gazed hard, working to recall, he went on loudly, 'Leonida, good morning!'

The names clicked, the Minister held out his hand, 'Leonida! Good to see you after all these years. You're doing well, I hear?'

Leonidas returned courtesies, they stood talking. Alexis looked round the hut, with its dead animals, trophies, guns; and at the people – Manolis was lightly dressed for the mountain cold, tough in shirtsleeves, while the Minister, spare and bony, was enclosed in a large shaggy tartan coat which looked as though he had bought it yesterday in Canada. He was excited, nervous, no veteran of the hunt. Manolis passed round peaches: they chewed while the juice ran down their fingers, and sipped the strong sweet coffee which seemed to thread their bodies and wake up every cell.

They came outside. Manolis suddenly roared into the night, 'Jack! Hey, Jack!' and a rough-haired dog came loping out of the darkness towards them. Manolis scratched him hard, then opened the boot of his car, 'Jack, get in!'

But Jack didn't want to, he slunk away behind a flank of the large car. Manolis grabbed his collar and lugged him quickly in half-throttled, slamming the lid down before he could get out.

Leonidas laughed doubtfully, 'Jack doesn't like that too well.'

'Oh, that's nothing,' Manolis vigorously explained as he opened the car doors for them. 'He was in there four hours yesterday, that's why he doesn't want to go in now.' Alexis thought he heard a whimper from inside the boot; but he couldn't stop, for Manolis was in the driver's seat now, revving the engine in sudden peremptory roars that hustled the others in quick. The Minister got in the front, Leonidas and Alexis sat in the back.

'Let's go, Manoli!' Leonidas slapped the strong shoulders of Manolis, who was a good example to Alexis of what a man should be.

Manolis was tough and *macho*, and had a Minister to impress with his driving. The engine revved; a glare of headlight lit up in front; abruptly the car wheels ripped round, and gravel rattled on windowpanes behind them. A white blinded housefront leapt at them, and passed; now they saw the road winding ahead, now in harsh headlight a cliff wall of rock, now the pale beams of the headlamps reached endlessly through space, out over the precipice. They took corners on roaring handbrake turns, accelerated on the straight, decelerated as violently; and through it all Manolis sat relaxed but taut, in control, knowing the road, smoking evenly while his arms spun the wheel, his hand danced on the gear lever, his feet pumped the pedals. He was *macho*; but Alexis would never be *macho*, and if he was car sick before, he had car vertigo now. And Leonidas and the Minister, they too were hardly the *macho* type, they were more the pasha, more for limousines and chauffeurs than for racing driving. They smiled a wan sickly smile, and weakly cried 'Bravo!' while Manolis, regardless, drove on as though he hated his passengers, shaking them up like old watermelons in a truck.

As they climbed, a grey light grew. The trees thinned. They were emerging into a dim grey upper world that consisted only of a yawning grey-white misty gulf stretching away into dimness, while out of it vague blunt humps of mountains pushed, far apart, stirring uneasily as the car swerved.

The road gave out but Manolis continued up the stony side of the mountain, slithering on stones, pebbles clanging and ricocheting on the car's underseal like bullets.

Abruptly, without coming to any particular terminus they could see, they stopped, on a bare shoulder of mountain. Manolis was out at once, drinking joyous breaths into his large chest, striding on the rocks, muttering for weapons; while three shaken hunters, and a sick, dazed, debilitated dog, staggered from the car. But the high air was keen as a knife. They soon revived; and now the sun appeared. It was a dull red wheel on the grey horizon, but it brought light, so that they saw they stood on a high promontory over a dazzling sea of mist, white, radiant, out of which, across distances, wooded uplands and sharp peaks stood clear, like separate islands scattered away in a long archipelago.

'Ah, *this* is the life!' the Minister said, blessing the hunt. 'Why work in Athens, when there's all this?'

They armed, pulling heavy belts of cartridges out of the car boot, and comparing rifles. Leonidas gave Alexis his second-best rifle, and studied the Minister's, agreeing with Manolis that *that* was a rifle. The Minister pulled out of his pocket something like a large floppy leather bag, and balanced it on his head, letting down two loose furry lugs that flapped against his ears. Manolis looked on askance, tough, bare-armed, his tanned skin rasped with goose-flesh. 'We're after hares, not elephants,' he remarked, taking a liberty, showing no politician could buy his praises. The Minister laughed.

They crossed the small plateau, and started climbing again, into thickening woodland. The trees over them made a cold shadow, and their boots slithered on the loose stones and the dewy, slippery grass. Jack disappeared into the undergrowth.

'He'll send the hares our way,' Manolis explained. Knowing the mountain, he led the way, while Alexis lagged, enjoying the morning, and Leonidas walked beside the Minister, passing

70

him cigarettes, seeing they exchanged brief snaps of remark, improving the rapport.

They seemed to have the woodland to themselves; then they heard a barking, and three dogs came loping down the hillside towards them, and a hunter in grey stood out from the trees ahead and waved and shouted to them, 'Go back! Stay there!'

Suddenly two hares shot across the ground in front, and after came the dogs: now there were shots, the dogs barked, and the hunter and the dogs hurried on down the hillside.

'Ah, the quarry!' the Minister said vigorously. 'We'll shoot here, eh, Manoli?'

'Uh!' Manolis tossed his head and continued. 'This is not the place.' Against the evidence, he insisted there were no hares here.

So they walked on, till they came to a stretch of woodland that looked no different from the country they had passed through, but here nonetheless Manolis stopped, unslung his gun and loaded and cocked it, and told them, 'Here we are, *this* is the place!' They looked round, not clear why especially this was the place.

'Jack!' Manolis called, and a moment later Jack stepped out of a pocket of bracken and stood beside them looking bored, with no sign of embarrassment at having failed to send any hares their way.

'Let's go!' said Manolis. Now there was a peaceful time as the four hunters thinned out and waded through bracken and fern. The sun was higher, and came through the trees in thin shafts; the air was fresh, sweet; the only sounds were the occasional cries of 'hup!' and 'hey!' as they tried to start hares from thickets; and the distant barking of Jack, who, if he had found hares, seemed bent on chasing them in the other direction.

Eventually they met again; evidently this was not the place, after all, and Manolis, forgetting it ever had been, said, 'We must go deeper. We'd better split up, or we'll shoot each other.'

'Be lucky to shoot anything,' Leonidas muttered to the Minister, who smiled: the joke joined them. 'Alexi,' he called, 'you go with Manoli. *He'll* teach you to be a hunter.'

So they separated, Leonidas cheerfully wading through the

71

fronds with the Minister, and seeming to lead him, as if he now knew where the good places were.

'Come with me,' Manolis said confidentially, 'we may find partridges.' Jack stalked ahead; Manolis walked carefully, concentrating, making low clucking and purring sounds to start the game. Alexis studied him: he disliked Manolis, with all his toughness and harshness, with his beetling brows, with his black tufts of hair underneath his eyes, where his strong beard grew too high up his cheeks to be shaved. But, after yesterday . . . his father . . . and he didn't want this other man to think he wasn't a man. He would hunt. He trod warily, his eyes scanned ahead, swinging to each small tremble of a leaf; his hearing sharpened, he caught tiny sounds, breaking twigs, easing boughs, somewhere water dripped. He was all alert, he held his gun lightly, making small passes with it, in readiness to aim and shoot.

Abruptly something started, there was a whirring and flapping, a bird stood in the air just in front of them, big, plump, like a winged ball: he aimed and fired. There were two reports; his shoulder jolted; the bird dropped, dead.

They had both fired, it wasn't clear who hit it. 'Bravo!' Manolis cried, and slapped Alexis on the back; it was a fine partridge. They congratulated each other; then Manolis put the partridge in his satchel and they walked on. Alexis hoped, hoped, it was his bullet that hit the bird, that he brought it down: he walked on, the hunter, listening, seeking, confident now, on the alert.

Leonidas also, as he parted fronds and ducked under bushes, scouting for the Minister, was the keen hunter: last of the Mohicans. But it was the man, not the animals, he was stalking. Now was his chance, he must tread carefully, quietly, the quarry was in his sights.

First they must be friends: tracking game together, they must realize how well they worked in partnership. So for now Leonidas only was the good, businesslike comrade-in-arms; and it was not hypocrisy, this comradeship, for all his instincts were in it, it came to him naturally from the heart of his wish.

'Go round those firs, round to the right,' he said; from time to time he directed the Minister, letting his great respect show through his curt remarks. He made it clear he expected the Minister – great man though he was – to show a proper respect for him also.

So they hunted together; and they found game; and fortunately the Minister shot a bird, and though it was a thrush Leonidas found himself convinced it was some rarely seen, most special, mountain top species of game. It gave him something to congratulate the Minister heartily upon.

'What a morning!' Leonidas said. 'Let's take a breather, we've earned it.'

'A good idea,' the Minister said, sweltering in his coat: he blessed Leonidas for suggesting a rest. They squatted down on a grassy platform of rock, below which the woodland plunged steeply down into the valley. The sun was well up, and hot on their skins; the ferns and grasses round them were sharp and bright in the sunlight, the misty air of the valley gleamed. From below, the voice of someone singing in the church just rose to their ears, a faint rising and falling of chant. Across the valley, above the haze, the mountain peaks shone blue and clear, with scattered glittering facets of white.

'Such air!' Leonidas said, passing a cigarette to the Minister.

'Wonderful!' the Minister agreed, and they sat enjoying the scene, and their catch, and the fragrant smoke of their cigarettes mixed with the pine scent of the mountains. The Minister lounged relaxed, and Leonidas seemed so. *This* was his window, his chance; but he mustn't push. He squinted at the peaks, and let the Minister speak first.

'So Leonida,' the Minister said, stretching his arms, 'we've come a long way since we were students.'

'Well, well, we've made our way. But one of us has gone a bit further than the other.'

'Uh, well. . . .' The Minister was modest, smoking contentedly. 'So, tell me, then' – he paused – 'fellow student' – he was pleased with Leonidas' attentions, he would give him this sugarplum – 'how do you find our policies?'

It was all the start Leonidas needed. He had done his homework, he knew the facts: he admired one policy, he did have a question about another, in a third case the tactics were – a master stroke, they took his breath away, and yet, as a long-term strategy, he wondered. . . . And of course the control of wages was a tricky issue, when after all Greeks could earn so much money working in Germany. The solution of course was to bring more foreign businesses here, and as to this he himself could play a part. He had only praise for the procedures used in appointing the secretaries of trade unions. He ventured, suggested, paused, and let the Minister draw him on: but in each word he showed what a colleague he would be. Let the Minister take note, here was loyalty and long-standing fellowship, here was insight, judgement and executive skill. Greek politics needed new blood. Let the Minister see, here beside him was the man of men for the post which Leonidas knew he still had to fill, that post so vital to any minister, the post of second-in-command, of Secretary to the Ministry. Government. Government. Leonidas' heart pounded, he was talking for his life.

'And foreign policy, now, Leonida, what are your thoughts there?'

'Ah well, sir, which foreign policy?'

The Minister sat forward, 'You're right, Leonida, there's policy – and policy. Is it your view that we should be – enterprising?'

Leonidas was silent: his brow knit, he turned his cigarette over and watched the smoke-trail coil and spread. Then he said tensely, in a close voice, from the heart, 'In two days we could be in Ankara!'

The Minister started: his eyes suddenly glowed, brilliantly, with fever, as if with the glare of a bomb exploded far behind them. He nodded shortly, regaining composure; then he changed the subject.

They talked on; till Leonidas knew they had talked enough, he had done all he could. Now, for his career, he could only wait, and pray. He let a pause in their talk extend.

'Well,' said the Minister, 'this isn't filling the pantry.' He got up, stretched, and they resumed the hunt.

Eventually they found Manolis and Alexis.

'What have you got?' they shouted to each other. They had between them a handful of birds. They shared praises, but the catch wasn't good, they still had not caught a single hare.

'Poh! Don't worry,' Manolis said firmly, 'I know a field where the ground is a *carpet* of hares.'

They set off for this field. The sun was high now, and hot: they took off their coats, and still sweated heavily as they climbed. Swarms of tiny flies had woken, and buzzed round them in clouds.

They came at last to the field Manolis meant; which was not precisely a field, but a stony upland scattered with clumps of scrub.

'Eh, Manoli, where are these hares?' Leonidas cried.

'Wait,' said Manolis, and he picked up a boulder, crept forward, and suddenly hurled it down so it spread-eagled a bush. At once he raised his gun, swung round. And yet, there was no hare. However, he explained to them that inside all the bushes, except this one, a hare would be hiding, they had only to throw stones to start them.

So they commenced in this new way of hunting; and other hunters arrived to join them, for it seemed that this high stretch of mountain was where all the hunters came at last, here the hares were run to earth. Alexis only watched: he was new to hunting, and his earlier excitement had been exhausted by the sight of too many tiny blind bulge-eyed heads hanging crooked from plump throbbing bodies. And he saw his father grinning like a crocodile, full of sly pleasure; he had obviously caught whatever he had been hunting for. All Alexis' dislike of him boiled and swelled. He watched now while this slope of stones became peopled with farmers, businessmen, his father and his father's friend, the local field policeman, a government minister also – separate men, they stalked plants, shouted 'hup!' or 'hey!' at a bush, and if the bush didn't answer they threw a stone at it, and moved on to the next, like men with mad hopes.

5

Chryssa and Patra had returned the plastics, and by vehement joint insistence retrieved a portion of their father's outlay. He thanked them with tears of gratitude, but from day to day put off the question of retiring from business. For all his prevarication, Chryssa made some attempt to sort his affairs; but it became clear that this would take weeks of work, and she needed to be with Vangelis.

She flew back to Athens, but not to the old life. As the plane, in midflight, passed the barren crags of Olympus, she felt she was crossing a cold barrier. She still shivered as they descended into the bowl of Athens heat.

Vangelis had come to meet her. He looked at that moment keen, excited to see her, and also, unusually, vulnerable: she hurried to him and they hugged each other hard as if they had been apart for weeks.

'Has anything happened, Vangeli?'

'Uh! Nothing good,' he smiled quickly to her. His black eyes glistened wistfully as if there were something he wanted to tell her but wouldn't. In the taxi she looked at him solidly sat, his large head tilted down: her husband, but also an impenetrable presence, like a hot statue beside her in the car. Perhaps from anxiety and anger, he had lost weight in the last few weeks, and the result was that his still plump face was younger looking, more handsome. Abruptly he looked at her, his eyes now very dark, anxious, bright: she was uneasy, puzzled.

It was only when they embraced calmly in their flat that she felt the full relief of being home, and a release from the tension of her trip north. Her father's unresting activity wound tight the nerves of everyone round him. Vangelis also was restless; all his movements were exact, guarded, tight.

He stayed taciturn; it was hours later that he said directly, deeply unhappy, 'I'm not sure where to go now, love.'

'Vangeli, we continue. You've achieved a lot.'

He raised his brows quickly in a muted 'no'. 'I failed with that boy.'

'My love, we'll have failures. Of course. But you shouldn't call that case a failure. What more could you have done? People still come to you, don't they?'

'No, I failed, Chryssa. It's true people still come. They bring evidence, witnesses – I've even got a tape of an interrogation. But I can't represent them now. I'm too much a known quantity. And can I keep their evidence safe? The police have been in my office once, what's to stop them going there whenever they want to? And I don't believe now that I can make progress – not by the law. That's the big difference.'

'Vangeli, we *knew* they would use – bad methods to stop you. We didn't expect to beat them this year.'

'I know. It's my fault. As I got further with that case, I let myself hope more – I shouldn't have, but I did, and that's why it was a great blow –'

'My love –'

'The question is, would I have begun with that case, if I'd known at the start it would end as it did? I don't think so. There would have been no point, and it would have been too cruel to drag that poor boy through it all – he was out there *hours*, trying to remember things he should never be asked to remember – if it was all for nothing. So: do I start on other cases, when I know they will end like that? I don't know. I can't just do nothing.'

'If we can still send evidence abroad, stories to Michael –'

'But I don't think we can; they know about us now. Any package we send will be picked up, and it won't just be bad for us, it will be bad for the people who gave us the evidence. We were lucky to do what we did. But Chryssa, I *can't* just sit taking notes all day and keeping it secret – there's a place up here in my head, that when I hear these injuries, I feel it get hotter and hotter, till I think my head will explode. And every road's blocked. I know now what's the worst thing with a "National Government", it's that everyone shuts themselves up, in their own cage, for safety. If you come out, you're caught, and then you can do nothing at all. Either way, you fester in a cage. Well, a lot of people don't mind that, they're cautious anyway. Or they say, "We'll work within the system,

77

we can do more that way." That's a nice lie to tuck yourself in bed with –' He stopped. Chryssa held him.

'Vangeli, I don't know what we should do. We just have to think, and work out what is possible. You always said that what we did would tell in the long run. So we know now *what* a long run it will be. Still we keep going.'

'*If* there is a long run, we keep going.' He glanced at her with a stricken face.

'What do you mean?'

He turned, his eyes focused on her so hard she felt as if his hand held her, hurting. He unclenched and clenched his hands; brought his fists hard down towards the table top but at the last moment froze them, so they tapped it precisely. Then he turned, and gave a great shudder, as if to shake himself clear of all his locked thoughts.

'How is the merchant, then?' He meant her father.

She saw he hadn't been listening when she told him before; but she spoke on with emphasis, with humour, to draw his thought clear for a time of the hot place where it was caught.

Bitter weeks extended, in which they made no advance. Previously all their effort had a strong forward momentum, they moved from task to task, an active couple keen with purpose, like two mariners in a storm steering their vessel, regardless of risk, into the face of wrath. Vangelis, in his intentness, had seemed to Chryssa at times like the spirit of resolved opposition to dictatorship there in person beside her.

And now, so soon, they had come to the limits of what they could do. They were briefly cheered when Chryssa found, in the English papers in the university, some of the stories that must originate with Michael. Sometimes Vangelis was mentioned by name as an active opponent of the government, both in the courtrooms in Greece and in representations to international bodies. For some days then they knew they had made progress, and believed the fact that they were known abroad would give them some immunity in their work. But their progress was not visible in Greece, and Vangelis was not able to send more news to Michael: even communication with him was not safe. He considered warily the different

78

possibilities. Chryssa watched him grow more doggedly, more desperately taciturn as time passed.

The knot of his frustration tightened. He found he could not listen to things people said on other subjects, even to what Chryssa said. She might talk very tenderly about matters touching both of them, and he would gaze longingly at her loving or hurt face, but he could not take in her words; he was shut inside a trap of his own.

Even her emotion made him guarded, uneasy. A lawyer they both knew died in custody: and Chryssa wept, crying freely in anger and grief. Vangelis' eyes smarted, his voice broke; but he could not cry, at her tears his own eyes dried. What good were tears, they didn't help, they discharged passion the wrong way. He watched her with hot eyes, frustrated, while a bitter creature inside him was exasperated beyond measure. He felt wretched, and resentful, he was jealous of her clear emotion.

'My love, my beautiful love,' he might say at night, moving nearer her in bed. Then his thoughts were abstracted, his hand caressed her like a mechanism, back and forth, with a controlled violence. It froze her feeling; he, baulked, retreated, angry.

She woke to the knowledge that his anger with the Junta could steal his soul; it was already a third person in their lives, it bled into his life's blood that bled into it. She remembered his father, the elderly man with sharp, almost wolfish eyes behind round gold spectacles, who sat in his corner between bookshelves furred with dust, and smiled at her when he was aware of her: but it was hard for him to be aware of her, he kept sinking back into black preoccupation. The thought of Vangelis being like his father froze her.

It seemed, now that they had stopped moving forward, that the only movement available was movement apart. Vangelis was often out, busy with his court work which did not slacken; and when he was at home, he sat beside her like a locked-up room. His work on his book had completely stopped. More and more she wondered, as she had at the airport when she returned from Salonica, whether he had a secret from her.

'What has happened, Vangeli?' she asked, on a sure instinct.

Her voice was hard, demanding an answer: he looked up, startled, and in his flickering eyes she saw his secret darting to hide. He escaped her look by taking her in his arms, but she

79

stayed set hard within his embrace, and he didn't tell her his thoughts.

The woman in the building opposite sometimes looked across, and saw Chryssa, whom she knew as an energy, standing now periods at the black window in some way blind and sometimes bitter.

Early in the new year, Vangelis visited the Ministry of Justice: he often had to go there, making representations on behalf of his clients. Rotund and businesslike he strode down the corridors, pleased by the brisk light rap of his steps. His route today was a new one, however: he tapped tersely on a tall, panelled door, and, barely waiting for the answer, went in.

'Mr Secretary, I am Evangelos Tzavellas, I should be grateful if you could spare me some moments.'

The man at the desk raised sceptical eyes: he was hawk-faced, cavern-voiced.

'Mr Tzavella, come in. I gather you are often here.'

'I'd as soon not have to come.'

Standing, Vangelis outlined his request. The official stretched back, listening without sympathy to his claims, and at the end he dismissed them shortly. Nonetheless, he did leaf through the folder Vangelis passed him, and in the course of returning it he handed Vangelis a packet of papers that had been on his desk.

'Good morning,' Vangelis said brusquely.

'Uh,' said the official, turned already to other matters.

Vangelis took the papers to his office; and that afternoon he was visited by a psychiatrist friend who had worked with him on the case of the boy with brain damage. While they discussed cases drily, Vangelis opened his file. Behind their thick glasses, the enlarged eyes of the psychiatrist swung to the brown-paper packet which Vangelis handed to him. As he clasped it, he sighed, as if all his worries for a moment flowed easy.

'Not a word, eh, Vangeli?' he said quietly. 'Not even to Chryssa, not to anyone.'

'Tst,' Vangelis nodded: he didn't need reminding to be discreet. The psychiatrist shook him vigorously by the hand and quickly left, with the packet among his papers. What it contained – a list of names, details of future policy, military matters – Vangelis did not know. Over the winter months he had begun quietly to work for the resistance group the psychiatrist belonged to, yet still he knew very little. He realized more than before what a dispersed ghostly creature the resistance group was, so protected by secrecy that even its members could scarcely see it, and gave no more trust to each other than they were absolutely forced to. In the present case he knew only that the official in the Ministry of Justice was working with them: and this he must tell no one, it was their most important secret, it was a secret even to other members of the group. Vangelis knew only because he had easy access to the Ministry of Justice.

He hid his work now, even from Chryssa: for he had moved so stealthily to join the group that somehow he had never found the right time to tell her. He knew she would question what he was doing. In the past they had both been doubtful about the groups: how could a few men, with either pamphlets or weapons, take on the army in direct combat? They would fail, and the only result for others would be new repression. But Vangelis could not talk for hours to people who worked so bravely, so dangerously, who endured such tortures without a growing heat of shame at his own safe inaction. And as time passed and his own work showed no gains at all, it only seemed to him steadily more inevitable that he would join them. Sometimes he thought, 'It's too late now, we should all have worked together at the start' . . . but the more desperate the prospects, the more it seemed to him that he had no choice. Still he had few contacts with them, he saw only the psychiatrist, except for one occasion when he attended a meeting in an Athens flat. There were present, beside himself and the psychiatrist, two students and a young doctor, none of whom he knew, and a Professor of Medicine from the university, an elderly man, whose hair, as he spoke, stood out in white tongues round his passionate face. The group was larger than this, but who its other members were Vangelis did not know.

And he had not told Chryssa: for he found it in practice a difficult question, how does a man tell his wife that he has joined an organisation that can put them both in danger? He should not tell her names; he could not tell her plans; it was safer for her to know as little as possible. But it was a betrayal to tell her nothing; and also he needed to confide in her. His eye would slip from hers when she looked at him; he thought, 'She can see I'm keeping something from her.' This made him nervous, and she must see his nervousness. Later, it seemed easier not to tell her: keeping his secret had become a habit. But it made a new tension and estrangement between them.

Then, in the paper, he read that two students had been arrested: their photos were shown, they were the two students who had been at the meeting he attended. The paper said they had been identified by security forces as members of a 'terrorist group', and that grenades had been found in their lodgings. Vangelis found a way to contact the psychiatrist, but all he said was 'Steer clear, Vangeli. Know nothing about it.' There his resistance activity paused. Just what the students were planning, whether it was part of the group's plan, whether or not they really had grenades, or even whether he himself was endangered, he did not know.

Chryssa must not know, he told himself. If she's ever questioned, she must know nothing. But, more than ever, he needed to tell her.

As he left their flat one morning, Vangelis glanced back: there was a man close behind him whom he thought he recognized, but could not place. The man had a worn, weathered face, he might have been a fisherman or a villager; he looked hard-up, in his frayed overcoat. Vangelis met his eyes, and the man did not look away; but he made no acknowledgement. Vangelis shook his head, puzzled, and proceeded.

That evening, as most evenings, he came home on the metro. It was one of the new trains, all plastic, metal and glass. He sat on the curved seat, staring absently at a glass panel in front of him. It was crowded with the pale reflected faces of the people sitting behind him: in the murky glass, all the faces looked like ghost faces, his own included in the centre. Then, above and beyond them, his eye caught another faint face: haggard, hollow-eyed, searching. He realized this face was looking into his carriage from the connecting doors of the carriage beyond. Faint with distance, it hung in the doorframe like a picture: and slowly he realized it was looking at him. It was the man he had seen in the morning; he had failed to know him because his face looked different in the pale train lights.

Now the train was on a bend, the coaches went out of line, and the face in the doorway slid out of sight. Then, as the train came straight, the drawn transparent face swam slowly back across the glass.

At the next station, Vangelis ducked out of his carriage abruptly. Glancing behind him as he hurried down the platform, he saw the man strolling after him, among the other passengers, as the train with its bright lights slid away.

In the streets above he dodged and turned, and after a time he failed to find his follower; perhaps he had shaken him off. He hurried home.

So he was followed: each day, as he went to work, he picked up a pursuer. Sometimes it was the worn man in his late forties, sometimes it was a sallow hard-eyed twenty year old. They kept their distances, and now he knew them, they didn't try to hide. If he shook them off sometimes, they were back again the next day; some mornings they weren't there – evidently, occasionally, they took the day off.

Through these long months of frustration, he had still thought of himself as a creature on the prowl, secretly stalking the Junta: now the position was reversed, they were hunting him. Sooner or later they would take him, and he knew too much about them not to fear. In the cold dead of night, when he lay frozen still beside sleeping Chryssa, he knew what lay in wait for him, the wolf underworld, the human pack following hard, on the scent. How crazily rash his past actions looked: for what had he done, in the last year, but shout to the world that he was their enemy? He could have let them be, as others did; instead he had attacked them, with all his passion and with fascination also drawing him on. When he joined the resistance group, they needed nothing more. They would watch him for a time, to see what he would do. But there was no question any more of his acting against them: their watching immobilized him. The interrogators were waiting. He realized they saw his worry and fear, they sniffed it, he saw their glint.

There must no longer be secrets from Chryssa; she must know the danger. Closely in their home he watched her. By the light of the art nouveau lamp she sat reading: her brow was knit, it was a difficult treatise. But the page did not turn: he saw she was not reading, but pondering a difficulty. As if he were deep in a cave, he observed her: he liked the dark knitted dress she wore, with, across the breasts, a spread of rainbow beams from left to right. He watched the delicate tremors in her brow, as her thought unfolded. He thought: intelligent, lively, firm-featured face! Then she looked up: her brown-yellow eyes met his. She quivered a moment, as if she missed a breath or a heart-beat. In a level tender voice she firmly said, 'Tell me, Vangeli – everything you should tell me.'

He told her, without names, without details, but all that she needed to know. She came beside him.

'My love, I knew it was this. You should have told me. We have been very far apart, and we shouldn't be in these days.'

He wanted to weep; they held each other close for the first time in many weeks.

As the days passed, they grew used to surveillance; and then, for a time, their life had a crazy normality. They went to work in the mornings, were together in the evenings, just as in old times, and the only difference was that Vangelis took everywhere with him, at a certain distance, a shadow. After a long interval, he and the psychiatrist met, on a legal pretext; and, in spite of the danger to their own group, the psychiatrist had still a guarded optimism. A reorganisation of the resistance groups was occurring. The communist underground had split in two, but other groups had made new alliances: there were ties between the socialists and the monarchists, and also between the civilian resistance and a group of disaffected naval officers. There was said to be discontent among the officers in the large northern army on the border with Turkey: that army was too far from Athens, and too sure of its tanks, to be thoroughly purged. To Vangelis it seemed now that though individuals might be caught, resistance to the Junta could not be stopped from growing steadily like land rising from beneath the sea, while slowly the small islands expanded and joined. This conversation revived in Vangelis, what he thought he had lost for good, trust and hope – even though this growth of the resistance, if it were true, only made his own arrest more certain. He must use the time he had. He even, accompanied by his shadow, made a further collection from the official in the Justice Ministry.

'Vangeli, you didn't.' Chryssa pressed her face in her hand. 'Oh my dear love, you won't stop, will you?'

'Don't worry, Chryssa. They didn't see, I know. While they watch me, I can watch them.'

'My God, you're obstinate, Vangeli! Be careful, my love. Where will you take us?'

He paused; then suddenly, on an impulse, said, 'I'll take us out. Why should we be cooped up here all the time? I've been morose. I'll go and ring Simo.'

She stared a moment, then seemed all one smile. 'Do. Let's go out.'

From nowhere, in their dejection, the appetite to see people, to see friends, to get out of the house they had been imprisoned in, rose and swept all fear before it. They hurried to change, feeling suddenly as if lead harnesses fell from them, as if they could fly.

'What shall I wear?' she mused, rummaging. 'My grey? My blue?'

Whitebearded in lather, he frowned in the mirror as he worked to remember these different dresses. At the best of times, his memory for her clothes was bad, and his forgetfulness hurt her. He worked cautiously, afraid the effort of remembering, like a clumsy hand knocking over the thing it reaches for, would scare his timid recollections away. But tonight all veils parted, her dresses rose through his mind like a fountain, like a sudden remembering of many blanked out things: the red dress, the turquoise, the silvery grey, the black with its island embroidery, and bits of broken mirror sewn on here and there.

'Wear the turquoise,' he said, 'I love you in that.' She always called it blue.

'Hm. Do you think so? Tst. I'll wear the grey.'

'Uh huh.' His advices always met this fate: in their home, as in a dress shop, it seemed it was always his job to pick out the second-best item and hold it to the light, so she could see what was wrong with it and then choose right.

He came to the bedroom and reviewed his shirts. 'Which one do you think?' he enquired, nonchalant, hiding his reliance on her advice.

'The blue, I think.' He looked at it, and it was the best: his taste worked the other way from hers, it was only when she

85

told him which shirt to wear that he saw clearly what a good shirt it was.

Looking over her head in the dressing-table mirror, he combed his jet hair, and trimmed his thick moustache, thinking, 'So I'm overweight – it's a strong head nonetheless.' Her hair dryer whirred. Eventually they were ready; in the hallway he admired her. Even after winter her skin was warm brick-brown against the silvery blouse, her brown eyes shone, her new-blown hair was feathery and fine.

On the pavement, they looked round for Vangelis' pursuers. Sometimes they waited in the entrance of the building opposite; but tonight they weren't to be seen. Evidently they were so unused to Vangelis going out at night that they had gone home.

They took a taxi to the rendezvous, the indoor room of a taverna where, in the summer, they liked to sit out on the roof. Though the room was crowded, and the air a shining veil of smoke, they had no trouble finding their friend Simos, a large-limbed man who dwarfed his chair and table, and sat back, in his good humour, like a spreading large-branched tree. He had a broad high-domed head, a nose that was big but broad and snub, a wide big-lipped mouth; and small grey eyes, and fair curly hair. He didn't look Greek, he didn't look anything; he was like the aboriginal human giant from which the lesser, particular races sprang. His wife, beside him, was small, svelte, smart: she had a beautiful face with a high brow, clear bones, a small perfect nose, a full-lipped mouth. She was made-up, neat and brisk where he sprawled huge, she was like a robust bird poised on his branches.

Simos saw them: at his leisure he rose, and his large arms reached to them like the father of the prodigal, 'Come, you miseries, where the hell have you been these months? Is your home a monastery? Are you proud because you've got your name in foreign papers?'

First Chryssa then Vangelis disappeared in his embrace, then his wife Clio was absorbed in their embrace. Then they all sat, and after the long separation simply were pleased to be together. Effortlessly, without his moving forward, the large arm of Simos swung round and filled their glasses. Clio had just visited her family in Crete: her conservative uncles were excited, telling her that one member of the Junta came from a village near their home. In a tribute to his birthplace, he had ordered a motorway to be built from the coast to that village: its daily traffic consisted of two donkeys and a three-wheeled truck.

Clio spoke briskly, vivaciously. Simos, once seated, was a quiet presence, listening massively, his face screwed up in puckers and trenches; peacefully he slipped his worry beads from one hand to the other, and expressed disagreement by rearranging his limbs at leisure. Vangelis had not discussed his resistance work with Simos, but several times this evening he noticed Simos looking at him, his sharp grey eyes thoughtful and worried. When Simos saw him looking back, he glanced away quickly, stirred momentously, and steered Clio away from politics. They recollected different trips to Crete, to the plateau of Lasithi with its windmills, to the mountain village of Anoyia where all the men were beautiful, to the caves in the south where the hippies camped.

Their talk changed topics, speakers, mood, with a pleasant rhythm like lively music. They were joined by other people they knew: by Cosmas Matziris, a trim-moustached, horn-rimmed, bow-tied solicitor, who sat down beside Simos and argued vehemently with him. Simos absorbed his emphases with crumplings of brow and gave occasional quiet answers. Cosmas argued loudly about opposing the regime, in the way one safely could if it were known one did nothing. Vangelis half listened to him, undisturbed by his own better knowledge; he was deeply relaxed, smoking calmly, admiring Chryssa and smiling to her when she caught his admiration. He was thinking how much he enjoyed her voice: he loved its deep tones when she sang; its ripple when she laughed; it could whisper so his hairs rose; and it could rise to comic squawks when, as now, she imitated the old peasant woman Kyria Styriani scaring the birds. He was tickled, he loved it, to see exhilarated, laughing-eyed Chryssa momentarily absorbed in preposterously globing her cheeks round the birds'-blood-curdling cry.

A small space in the centre of the restaurant grew larger, as people scraped back their tables and chairs to make way for dancing. Already one of the diners stood up: with his arms outstretched he danced precisely, watching his own staccato footwork. Chryssa had not thought she would dance: it was late, they were tired. But still she found, as she watched and listened, that she steadily sat more upright, her weariness dissolved like thickening mist, each fibre of her body seemed to come alert and have spring in it. Though she didn't move, her mind danced with the dancers, the rhythm's vibration travelled her limbs. The black past, the black months, were no reason for not dancing; they were a reason to dance, to defy darkness by dancing.

The group had enlarged, and she joined it. She knew at once she was dancing well, with confident crisp movements, the right balance of expertness and joy, with a rhythm inside her that had sunk deep in previous dances beating clear in time to the music. All eyes were on her, she had called them to her. She was either no good and sat down, or she was excellent, the best. She rose to the challenge unworried, inspired, happy to be the centre: she knew her quick hops, her swoops of arm, her sway of body, were clear not timid, the dance was dancing her. Through her jumping eyes she saw the solemnity of the dancing men: not to be like them, she let happiness, comedy, into her dance, let her quick feet and flying fingers shimmer like laughter. She saw Vangelis sitting at their table, happily watching, no giant like Simos but consolidated, solid, frowning even in admiration: she smiled at the sight of the set brown figure, always slower to dance than she was. Well, let him be a pasha, a potentate on cushions, she would be the dancing girl, and catch and spurn his lazy admiration. So to his eyes, elated, she danced her independence, till, catching his eye directly, she smiled, laughed. Love flowed between them, and all of that game became an old joke behind her while, looking elsewhere but knowing he watched her, and seeing him watching in her mind's eye, she danced again for others, for all the restaurant, so absorbed now in her own movements, in new warm waves of energy the dance released in her, she no longer felt like anyone's self, but the dance there in person that everyone was dancing, too absorbed in moving even to say that moving like this was perfect happiness.

Vangelis, his small eyes hooded by frown, sat still in delight, seeing all her exhilaration turned to the dance. He noticed then how the woman next to Chryssa had her head slightly down, so as to see from the corner of her eye what Chryssa was doing: her movements followed Chryssa's a split-second late, and were vague and timid where Chryssa's were sure. He felt for this woman, for he was liable, dancing, to a similar self-consciousness, a failure to be possessed by the dance. He returned to Chryssa, she was the star: and it was something he loved in her, that she could so easily enjoy being centre stage, with humour, exhilaration, innocent self-delight, enjoying herself without heavy ego. As a child she had wanted to be an actress, and it seemed to him like a divine gift she had – he didn't have it – this ability to do things perfectly, even with everyone watching, and to know this and enjoy it with no sort of pomposity or personal preening. It was a quality children had, and the greatest performers: he was different, even in the courtroom, when he was good, he was still often tense. And the dancing men that he watched didn't have it, with every solemn gesture they made they seemed to demand special plaudits.

She danced on, not dancing to him, the light rippled on her, her feet flickered, she seemed very tall and slender. Her jaw lifted showed its clear line; catching the light, her raised face seemed to glow; her yellow-brown eyes, reflecting many lights, sparkled. Now as he watched she danced steadily towards him; and abruptly, crazily, a phrase from the bible came into his mind, 'Lift up your heads O ye gates.' It had always moved him though he'd never made sense of it – till now her arms opened towards him like the doors of a city previously closed, and at the same time she raised her head in exaltation though her eyes still gazed to him, both movements wonderfully generous and welcoming, as if she were a city that danced, and after long separation welcomed him in. He was moved, his eyes moistened. Why had he let them be estranged? He felt a warming in his spine, that had felt made of rock, a loosening in his still solidity, his own will to dance steadily gathered and with good momentum he rose to join in, at a certain pausing and widening of the circle. At first very upright, puckered-browed, frowning, he danced with gravity like a patriarch dancing: but his energy flowed, his movements grew free, he danced before Chryssa like a dancing tower.

He was stout for dancing, but exact, crisp, his feet stepping lightly. Gradually, with dignity, he stooped as he danced, his arms swung lower in wide clear curves, almost he was dancing on his knees: then with precision, finesse, he slapped the floor sharply, the boards resounded as though a shot went off, and he quickly rose like a man released.

Later Clio and Cosmas danced; Simos sat; time flowed peacefully. Before going home, the whole group together walked along the waterfront. The air was keen but still, beautifully fresh after the warmth of indoors. Beside them, the rush of traffic along the coast road was so continuous that it resembled a river. Out over the sea, lights moved through the sky as planes approached and left the airport. A plane turned with its landing lights blazing ahead of it, looking like a car in midair. High overhead, another plane crossed the moon: the red and green lights went out, and, tiny against the white disc, they saw momentarily its distinct black cross. They chatted desultorily, in an easy space of fellowship.

Chryssa and Vangelis arrived home in the early hours, pleasantly relaxed but scarcely tired. They undressed at leisure and lay for a moment enjoying the bed; but almost at once Vangelis scooped Chryssa in his arms, and caressed her. She warmed and melted to him, and he embraced with a tremble of love in his voice that seemed to say sorry, sorry, sorry, for the cold wall between them there had been.

That evening, afterwards, seemed an oasis.

In the dream the man was hammering, hammering. 'What are you making?' she asked, but he only hammered on.

Blearily they stirred, confused. Who was it knocking on their bedroom door? 'Come in,' Vangelis growled in his sleep, and turned over. Then his eyes snapped open, he was wide awake in the dark.

'Quickly, Chryssa, they've come.'

'Who?' she murmured, then 'no!' and jumped out of bed. Her 'no' had pure horror in it, it chilled him more than his own fear.

'Quickly, the papers.' Already he had run to his desk, and stood at it, naked, leafing through a sheaf of papers. He had everything arranged already, but still he made sure. After a moment, he handed several sheets to Chryssa. 'Just these.' As she left she glanced back, and in a spark of vision snapped a picture that stayed with her afterwards of Vangelis standing as if planted, naked, swarthy, all his body rounded and firm, with his tanned head – his frowning eyes, jutting nose, dense moustache – directed hard at the papers he checked, while the loud knocking at the door continued, knock knock knock, like a machine hammering nails in their heads.

In the bathroom, Chryssa hurriedly set light to the papers over the sink, then flushed their crumpled ashes down the lavatory. When she came back, Vangelis, in his dressing gown, was going to the door. 'All right, all right!' he shouted to the men outside.

She caught hold of him and pushed him back. 'No, Vangeli, don't open it. You're not going to.'

'They won't go away,' he said.

'We don't have to let them in. You're not opening it.' She stared at him wide-eyed as she stood solid before him blocking his way; then she bawled at the door with all the force of her lungs, 'Go away!'

'Open the door,' a voice outside shouted. Then the knocking stopped, evidently the men out in the corridor were trying to catch what they said. Chryssa and Vangelis held their breath; there was complete silence.

'Open the door,' they shouted again. 'It's the police.'

'At this time of night!' Chryssa shouted.

'You have to let us in, we have an order.'

'Who is the order from?'

'From National Security. Open up.'

Vangelis unlocked the door. The moment it was open, Chryssa sprang in front of him. She faced five men: they didn't look like policemen, they wore T-shirts or old jackets. They looked strong and used to it; their hair was cut short; they might have been soldiers in civvies. 'You're not the police. Who are you?' she shouted. But they ignored the indignant woman who stood before them in her nightie, and shouted past her.

'Are you Evangelos Tzavellas?'

Vangelis didn't answer.

'Get your clothes on,' one of them said, with contempt, like a sergeant bossing a raw recruit. They trooped into the flat, making for Vangelis.

'What are you doing?' Chryssa snatched hold of one of them as he tried to push past her, she was jolted, shaken, she started punching him on the chest, arms – and he punched her back, hard, in the face. 'Aaaah!' she shrieked, more in outrage than in hurt. His hot swollen face filled her sight then he moaned, very low, and folded down, she had brought her knee up. The others all came for her, faces spun round her like Saturn's

91

moons; she was confused by vague knocks and heard Vangelis shout behind her, 'Leave her alone!' She turned to see him, just as two of them grabbed for him: he seemed as he fought them to have several arms. Then they were all tangled in one big scrimmage, in the middle of which Chryssa, twisting, kicking, hitting, suddenly found her head yanked hard back behind her, someone pulled her hair, he was jerking to uproot it: she shrieked now furious to wake the building, but still was dragged back, back, and forced into the bedroom. Before the door closed she had a glimpse of two men holding Vangelis, his arms bent behind him, while already a third man stooped at his desk, shovelling papers into a polythene sack.

The man who had dragged her here stood against the door, rasping, getting breath. He looked alarmed, but also enraged. Panting, she realized her nightie was ripped in tatters, she saw bruises on her arms which hadn't started hurting yet, her scalp felt as though it had been pulled so hard it was loosened from her head. While the man stared but stayed by the door she put on her dressing gown.

Presently, outside the door, a voice called, 'Okay, Vasili.' The man shoved her hard across the room so she stumbled on the bed, while he slipped out, pulling the door to.

Chryssa ran through the empty rooms of the flat and out onto the landing. For a moment she saw blurred figures standing cramped behind the frosted glass door of the brightly lit lift: then the lift slipped down below the floor.

She ran downstairs, stumbling and tripping in the dark, gasping as she went, not able to catch the lift. When she reached the ground floor, the men had gone. She ran out into the street, and saw Vangelis stooping to get into a car, and looking back at her troubled as she called to him. He was pulled into the car sharply, like a puppet snatched; the other men got in, and even as she pelted down the pavement shouting, the car started. She ran after it down the middle of the road calling at the top of her voice, 'Stop! Come back! Vangeli! Vangeli!' In the rear window of the car, one of the men's faces turned and looked at her. She continued running and shouting after the car had turned the corner and disappeared, while lights came on in all the flats nearby. Blinds and shutters were cranked up, other voices called. She reached the corner, and the road beyond was empty as far as she could see: then, as though a string in her snapped, she just sat down in the road where she was, and cried, loudly, heartbroken, like a child boo-hooing in the street, while people in pyjamas and night-gowns one by one like stars at night came out on the balconies stacked above her; then the first of them appeared in a doorway, and came to pick her up and help her back to her flat.

6

They helped her upstairs, but got no sense out of her; eventually she was left, sobbing steadily, in a flat that was all a shambles. The separate drawers from Vangelis' desk were scattered on the floor like boxes at a market, with the odd leaf of paper here and there among them. She realized only now that they had taken also her own research notes – papers that would baffle them. Not only was the desk ransacked, but cupboards, wardrobes, kitchen cabinets: all the flat was inside out, Vangelis' clothes lay everywhere. She made a move to collect them, but stopped when she picked up his jacket, and collapsed back again gasping as she hugged the empty garment.

She smoked, paced, stroked hairs from her head, while the hours passed like ages. At first light she sat by the phone to ring friends, to get advice, noticing only now that their phone diary had gone – but of course they would have taken that. She knew the numbers she needed. She rang Simos and Clio: they wanted to come round, but she postponed seeing them, she must be out searching. She took their advice, and the addresses of police and security offices she could go to.

She went to a police station in the city centre. The main office was large, pompous, all marble slabs and bright lights like a fishmonger's stall: young policemen stood at leisure, tall, thin, with handsome sharp unfeeling faces. Their dry eyes flicked to her face and flicked away again. They knew nothing about Vangelis' arrest, they sent her from desk to desk and asked each other across the room if anyone knew anything about it. She persisted, and eventually a middle-aged police officer was produced from the inner chambers, corpulent, important, with knots and braids of white cord winding over his green uniform like a string sling. He wouldn't speak to her directly, but, after glancing at her once, stood at a distance, talking to the young policeman who had called him.

'We've no record,' he said shortly, wanting to make an end.

'No record!' Chryssa called. 'You must have a record!'

He spoke again to the young officer. 'If there is a record, it hasn't come here yet.'

'There must be a record,' she shouted. 'You know that. Who booked him in? Where was he taken? I've a right to know that.' Her clear voice echoed off the marble.

Finally the officer turned to her. 'He isn't here. What can I do, madam? We haven't got him. There's nothing on our books about him. How do I know where he is?' He heated indignantly, the pestered hard pressed public servant. She saw there was no point in going on, he would only become furious and tell her nothing.

'Will they know at Bubulina Street?'

'They may. You should go there.'

'Will you ring?'

'Ach, madam, who shall I ring? I've work to do. How can I ring?'

But he rang; she listened to him being brusque on the phone, and at the end of the short call he had nothing to tell her.

She went from police station to police station and from office to office. Some were large halls, some were dim hot rooms, blinds down against the sun. As she grew tired, she was more often shouted at: Vangelis' name meant nothing to them, they knew nothing about it, they didn't know who would know. How could they keep track of all the criminals? Athens was huge and the offices far apart; travelling between them she stood cramped in stifling buses, weak from sleeplessness, her head drumming. Her body hurt all over from the fight. She visited government offices, accosted officials, but no one knew anything. Her headache clenched like a steel cap screwed tight. She had expected to be appalled, sickened, at the travesty of a charge they would bring against Vangelis: she hadn't expected that he would be just – gone, vanished, no traces left, and a grey opaque sea shut over him like iron.

In the following days she tried to find Vangelis, in the nights she dreamed again of his arrest: many men, with blurred faces, forced their way in through doors and windows. She woke crying 'Vangeli!' and reached to warn him, but her hand fell through the place where he should be.

She sought help, rang friends. She tried to ring Patra, but she and Leonidas were out of the city.

After a week she heard that Vangelis was being held in a police barracks in the suburbs of Athens. With Simos and Clio she went there. Her famished eye fed on the old brown building, which looked simply like a block of cramped flats, with flaking plaster and wooden shutters hanging askew; bars criss-crossed the lower windows. She scanned them for faces. The small office inside was a stale oven; the bleak-faced man at the desk was brief, businesslike. Yes, they were holding Evangelos Tzavellas; she couldn't see him, but he would record her visit. He couldn't say when it would be possible to visit him, the investigation was serious. At every pause Chryssa listened with fear for shouts, distant cries. But there were no cries, only boots in a corridor, a typewriter somewhere, someone loud and exasperated on a telephone; it was just cramped and ordinary and dirty.

The man at the desk would say no more. He sat down, waiting indifferently for the visitors to go; but presently remarked, 'You can bring him a change of clothes, if you like.'

The next day she returned and handed over the counter a suitcase full of clothes for Vangelis; sometime later it was brought back to her. She didn't open it there or in the bus, but crouched over it all the way home as if it contained a treasure. Her mouth, her face, were locked shut; it was also a bomb that she carried. As soon as she was home she opened the case and pulled out his clothes, and as she unfolded shirt and underclothes she found in this place and that small blots of rust, then, opening another shirt, she found a large patch, a flower of dried brown blood; the shirt was stiff and brittle with blood.

The world was unsteady, she was terrified of ordinary things. A dazzling shark of aeroplane dived shrieking over her, and left her in trembling bits. At the roadworks near their flat a lorry tipped slowly up, releasing molten asphalt, black, slithering, like the substance of nightmare pouring through a break in the world onto the street. Her sight was jangled: at a glance a person's face would look deformed, half-gone, horribly birthmarked, aflow, yet when she looked again it was only a face, cut by deep shadow.

In a calm moment, reaching for the touch of a voice, she rang her mother, told her Vangelis had been arrested.

'My God! My God!' her mother cried.

'I hope they'll let me see him soon,' Chryssa said; she found herself trying to make the arrest sound less serious, as though it could hurt her parents more than it hurt her.

'But what's it for, my child? What has he done?'

'He hasn't done anything, mother. It's political.'

'Is it political, my daughter? Ach!' Her mother gave a long deep groan, as if Chryssa had named an epidemic devouring the land, which Vangelis could have avoided if he'd had his vaccination.

'Ach, my daughter, what a thing to happen! What will become of us? Ach! My God, my little God!' Her mother's great sympathy grieved at the other end of the line, and Chryssa was moved by it, and then checked, for it was the same sympathy that her mother brought readily to any catastrophe in the family – illness, lost money, arrest, a missed train. But it was the sympathy born of a suffering life: to any misfortune her mother gave all her heart.

Her father came on the line. 'Has Vangelis been arrested, my child? You must be careful. You must look after yourself.' He encouraged, strengthened; in the background Chryssa heard her mother's sobs.

'And what is it he's done?' her father asked again; but again she heard his bewildered silence after she tried to explain. He was so deep in his own troubles, he was long out of practice at worrying for other people's; she pictured his forehead wrinkling in the effort of attention, trying to work out what was wanted of him. Then he hit on something.

'My child, has he got a good lawyer?'

'A lawyer, dad? But. . . .'

'No, my child, excuse me, it is the most important thing. Tell him he must say nothing till he sees his lawyer.'

'As to that, dad –' But her father had a head of steam now, 'And not a lawyer from Athens, Chryssa; see he steers clear of them. They're all crooks in Athens. He wants a good lawyer from Salonica; that will save him. Now let me see, who's the man we want? There's Neologos – ach, no, he's a coward, he's no good. There's Arvanatis – mmm, but he'll fleece you and do nothing for you. Wait, I know, there's Kotsos! Well, still, but really, he's a crook too. I don't know, Chryssa, when you think about it, they're all crooks. . . .' He paused, enmeshed in his memories of litigation.

'Yes, father, yes, Vangelis knows this. Vangelis is a lawyer.'

Her father came to, the mobile merchant as ever. 'And so he is, my child! And that's my point. He's a lawyer. Remember, Chryssa, a lawyer will be all right!' He repeated to her encouragingly what he used to say to her about Vangelis in past times, winking, the two of them being sly about a third sly one in the family. 'Eh, Chryssa? A lawyer will be all right!'

The misunderstandings went on, but when Chryssa put the phone down after half an hour, she felt, in spite of all, raised up. A tangled rope of old connections, family memories, was let down to her: when she caught hold of it, she felt, for some time, stronger.

Chryssa sat with Simos and Clio, discussing what to do. Simos' great face was a puckered map of sympathy: from his experience as a lawyer, he advised her on the offices she could visit.

'But I must be honest, Chryssa, you must know that nothing you do will have an effect now. All that will happen is that the police will watch you more, and if they can get you, they will. You must be very careful. There must be *no* resistance contacts, no fireworks, no phone calls to foreign journalists, nothing. You must be – spotless. But you should keep going to see the authorities: you should go again, again, again. You must make them know that you are someone who won't go away, and who knows the law, and will try every means, every device, and will not stop. It may make them a *little* more careful now. And in the long run, it may help. It is a terrible thing to say, but later on, time will be on your side. Right now Vangelis is useful to them, or if he isn't, they aren't sure that he isn't. Because any information he has is up to date. But after they've kept him some . . . months – I'm very sorry, Chryssa, but I should say this – after they've kept him that time, his information won't be up to date, and anyway they will know more than he does. And he won't be a threat. Then they will be less interested in him, and that is when your work will bear fruit, and you will just persist and persist and persist, so they get fed up in a way that makes them want to be shot of him and you together.'

Chryssa nodded: things she could not have faced without collapsing, if they had come as her own fears, she accepted grimly, resolutely, when they arrived with Simos' grave matter-of-factness.

'Ah, but Simo, I must know about the law. I'm married to Vangeli, but I'm no sort of lawyer; you know that.'

He rested on her a giant hand of encouragement; it was like the hand of God, she could have sat on it.

'We shall have a seminar.'

All afternoon his slow voice rumbled; motionless, frowning, Chryssa rehearsed.

Chryssa embarked, and proceeded again from official to official. She was better armed now. It was a different insisting from any she was used to, having to harp on the letter of the law. The officials she encountered were at home in such pedantries, they'd try to catch her out, they'd talk through her to other men because she was a woman, they'd postpone the appointment each time she came. It was her hardest role ever, acting confidence in the offices: she would catch herself ready to fold to the floor, or wanting to gape her mouth and shriek, and quickly she grabbed herself and by force of will she sat erect, her square firm head must again be the battle turret. Yet just with very persistence of effort she grew used to striding these long closed corridors; before long she heard legal arguments snap from her lips, impatient, familiar. She was becoming what she acted, the legal insister.

It seemed, sometimes, she was gaining ground. She addressed a taut-skinned, sharp-nosed, tight-mouthed face, with dark glasses like facets of jet: it was a face totally closed to her, and she received, at the outset, a rude refusal. But she argued on till, about the black blank coins of the glasses, the round face grew strained and flushed, it seemed close to tears. I'm getting there, she thought, but in the end he only said, high-voiced, 'I cannot do it, madam. I can't.' She saw it was true: in theory he had authority, but in practice he had none.

Security went its own way. He could refuse her petitions with confidence because he had no power to give. As she left, he took off his glasses, and wiped his inflamed unhappy face.

At last she was shown into the plain office of a high-ranking civil servant, an elderly man in a light-brown summer jacket: a stooping and drooping man, with big ears like sails, long puckered jowels that hung down, a large rubbery nose that drooped heavily, and eyes almost hidden by folds and puckers of hooded lid. He leaned forward, his head lowered, and all his drooping folds composed in attention: and yet she had barely started, when he raised his hand and stopped her.

'Madam, you will have many good points to make, I can see that. Let me say now, nothing can be done.'

'Nothing? But there must be . . . something . . . in justice . . . .' She was tired from many efforts, and for the first time her words failed.

He leaned foward and all his droopings folded towards her, like wings closing gently. 'Madam . . . you speak of justice?'

A man in a T-shirt came in, carrying a small swinging tray with two cups of coffee. The official took one cup for himself and rested the other near Chryssa. He waited in courtesy, then sipped his own, and presently said, 'Would you really prefer it if, instead of me sitting here, there were a brigadier?'

She didn't answer; he pushed the coffee cup a little nearer her, and this time she picked it up and sipped from it. He observed her with the same weary abstraction with which he observed everything. Her eyes were reddened and glistening, but she kept her face firm; she wore dark, smart clothes; she was attractive and serious. She had prepared wisely for this difficult visit. He volunteered, 'Madam, you're right to send in petitions. Carry on sending them. I suggest you address them to Mr Vouthouris and to Mr Banakas – and to me, of course.'

She glanced sharply at him, wondering what this tip meant; but her eyes, meeting his, seemed only to gaze into old wells she couldn't get to the bottom of. She saw, he had seen much; how he judged she would never know; he was kind, but he would do little; he acted within the limits set. He was telling her, as Simos had, that perhaps, in the very long term, her applications would tell. . . .

He saw her out with patient courtesy; and just his touch of

tired consideration, in turning her away, brought home to her, as blustering refusals never would, the hopelessness of her attempts. The wall she beat against was high, thick, it would be months, years, before she breached it, and by then what would have become of Vangelis?

'Courage!' said Simos. 'What did you expect?'

She nodded quietly, seeing by the light of his kindness that, even at this low ebb, she had the strength for a long campaign.

7

Vangelis knew it was morning not from any first, warming glimpse of sun, but from a slight change in the quality of the cold. Had he slept? He felt he had been awake all night, cold in the dark, while the pain in his legs throbbed as if separate hearts beat inside them. His legs hurt so, he had to move them, but each time they stirred pain wrenched, pierced, took a nerve and tore it, so he collapsed back, waiting immobile, while the after-shocks of hurt travelled at their own will up and down his legs.

The relief of morning: boots clanged in a corridor, he heard voices and cleared throats, a toilet flushed in the distance. His eyes had grown so sharp, having nothing to gaze on but boiling darkness, that he noticed at once when a faint grey crack appeared at the bottom of the door of his cell: it meant that somewhere in the building – not in this corridor or the next one, but further off – a yellow electric bulb came on, and the light from it fell down a stairwell and died down one passage after another, till a glimmer that was almost no light at all crept under his door. It was all the dawn he got: for days but it might be weeks they had kept him in the dark.

There was a slight mitigation of the cold, and now morning had arrived a drowsiness came over him, and for perhaps an hour he lay in the comfort of an uneasy cloudy stupor.

A nearer light came on, feet passed outside his door. He wondered, could he get up? With enormous care he swung his legs slowly round and, like a large cautious crane, lowered them gradually towards the floor. The soles of his feet were so sensitive that, however slowly he lowered them, always when they grazed the floor razor pains cut them. He didn't know any more whether that shock was the anticipation of pain, or the pain itself: but he had become businesslike, he now just sat and waited for the pain to retreat, and when his boredom with waiting grew greater than the pain he slowly flexed his muscles and tried to stand. His legs weren't ready, one ankle exploded, he staggered back for the bench but caught it badly and fell.

Patience: with time the pain diminished, and he began to crawl forward. He thought, 'Why do I do this? I'm not going anywhere,' but even here he couldn't be still. Though the floor was filthy with dirt and shit he no longer smelt it, his main fear was that in dragging his wounds across the ground he could pick up infection. But it was better to move, to keep up circulation in his bloated legs; and he had given himself a job, in the dark he was counting the rough flagstones that made the floor.

He crawled, counted, in a manner time passed: he didn't think of other things, his life had shrunk to what he did here. Far off but shrill, a telephone rang; he started, as if it could be a call for him. For a few moment echoes of voices that could be on that line fell round him like blossoms . . . Chryssa . . . Simos . . . Cosmas . . . Chryssa . . . The bell stopped, he heard a faint barking.

Had they forgotten him? After the first round of interrogations, they had left him alone so long that he caught himself at moments almost wanting to see them again, simply for company, to relieve the boredom. But everything stopped, he froze, when presently he heard them come: boot studs clanged on the stones outside, stiffly his lock was cranked open. Two policemen came in.

'On your feet, tub,' they said, but they knew that was more than he could manage, and bent to lift him. Hoisted between them, he was dragged down the passage: he paddled weakly with his legs, not to walk, but to reduce the pain as his feet dragged.

As they climbed a staircase, he recognized his light, his sun, the bare bulb hanging from a twist of flex that gave him light in the morning. His fear peaked as he saw ahead, at the end of the passage, a plain wooden door: behind it they would be waiting, pig face and dark glasses, with the doctor in attendance, and the chair and the bed frame that at different times they strapped him to, when they beat his feet or worked on his hands. He would have struggled but his strength had melted. He was falling again back into the underworld; under all countries this world waited, thousands disappeared here and no one knew. There was no way out, and they knew that, the men who waited for you here, and their excitement kindled but they would take their time.

The door swayed towards him: then they turned and walked past it; they weren't going in. What could this be? Release? That was not possible, but still hope stirred.

They took him up more stairs, and along corridors cleaner, more airy, than those he had been used to. At a large panelled door they stopped, knocked, someone inside called brusquely. They entered a room with a big window: it was so full of light it hurt his eyes. Blinking, looking down, he saw there was a patterned carpet on the floor. Slowly his eyes focused on the large desk in front of the window, and on the person who sat at the desk, an officer of the security police in full uniform.

'Mr Tzavella – come in.' The officer motioned to an armchair in front of the desk: the policemen sat Vangelis down in it, then withdrew.

'Mr Tzavella, I've been wanting to meet you.'

Vangelis found the self-possession to murmur, 'Oh?' He couldn't say more, he was seeing for the first time in the clear light of day, through the tatters of his trousers, his own legs. They weren't his: at the ankle especially, and higher up also, they were irregularly swollen, many-coloured, soft with fluid, rough with scab, filthy.

Noticing that the officer observed him, he said curtly, in a surprised, indignant voice, 'Don't you worry about your carpet?'

'Uh!' The officer made light of the hazard. He had a wide mouth pulled down at the corners, showing his teeth: it looked to Vangelis like an animal mouth. But the officer said, still with his tinge of courtesy, 'Is there anything you'd like, Mr Tzavella?'

Vangelis kept his face opaque: what crazy game was this? He thought carefully – he must ask for something they would be likely to give him.

'Yes, there's something. I'd like a bath. I haven't washed in weeks.'

'Haven't they let you have a shower, Mr Tzavella?' the officer said, with a slight exertion of indignation. He called the policemen back, 'Take Mr Tzavellas to the shower.'

They dragged Vangelis down another corridor, and pushed him into a small room.

'Where's the shower, then?' The room was simply a crouch-down lavatory, the hole was choked with stools and crumpled pages from a photo-strip magazine.

'There it is.' One of the policemen pointed to the antiquated cistern above the lavatory. It was rusted through in places, drops of water gathered at one corner of it, and fell in an irregular trickle.

They left Vangelis there, and he took his shower. Slowly and carefully, to reduce the pain, he stripped off his torn clothes, and stepped under the tank. He huddled shuddering as the first drops splashed chilling on him, and winced wherever the water trickled: only on his burning legs the cold drops fell with sweet shock, cutting pain, easing where they ran. For minutes he let the cold rain soothe his legs, then he gathered the water in cupped hands and began to wash himself. He had no soap, he thought it would take him an hour to be clean; but he continued rubbing himself in the trickle, till finally he was clean and still stood under it, used to the cold, fresh, revived. He inspected his body, and tautened his stomach and slapped its hardness, pleased to find he was still a firm man. Truly it was the sweetest shower he had had, he didn't want it to stop.

Eventually they came, and asked with mock courtesy, clumsier than the officer's, if there was anything else he would like. He asked for a razor, and this also they gave him. It was blunt and it hurt – it was obviously much used – but it served. He shaved only his lower jaw; for they had cut off his moustache when they brought him here, and he took a satisfaction in shaving now so as to restore its outline to his face. With pleasure he rubbed the bristles on his upper lip against the grain: he had good growth, they felt like cut ends of wire.

Then they brought him clean clothes, which Chryssa had left for him. Realizing that she had brought them, he felt, in putting them on, that faintly she touched him. 'My love,' he murmured.

He felt now renewed and fresh in a way that earlier he wouldn't have believed possible. It was a crazy feeling, they would catch him for it later, but he should make the most of it while it could last: it gave him a chance to recharge his reserves.

Helped by the policemen, he limped back to the officer's room, and sat down again in front of the desk.

'Mr Tzavella, you look better. Cigarette?' He passed Vangelis a cigarette, and lit it for him. Vangelis allowed himself – even to the officer's slight annoyance – to sit back plumply in a moment of comfort, and inhale deep the long sweet draught of smoke.

'You know, Mr Tzavella, you don't belong here. Wouldn't you like to go, to be shot of us all?' He himself now lounged back leisurely, letting Vangelis savour the thought of freedom as he gazed through the window at the clear sky.

'Well. So.' The officer inhaled again. 'There's not a lot we want, just . . . you know, the odd piece in the jigsaw.'

Vangelis didn't move, but all his senses sharpened: they were back to the interrogation.

'This meeting, for instance. We know who was there. It's only confirmation that we want from you.'

Vangelis' eyes darted to him, drilling: his courtroom stare.

The officer was disconcerted. 'Mr Tzavella, please. We *know* you were there. Come, let's not waste time on these . . . these stupid preliminaries.' He appealed to Vangelis, man to man.

Vangelis shrugged. The officer sighed. Gazing sadly past him, Vangelis saw the free light beyond the big window receding from him again.

The officer was patient, he raised his brows, scratched his head. 'Mr Tzavella, this is just – stupid obstinacy. *You were there*. You worked for Democratic Action. Everyone knows that.'

Vangelis didn't answer. He had decided to say no word further, but he was still anxious to provoke the officer as little as possible. It was good, sitting in this bright office smoking: he wanted to stretch the session as long as he could. And the officer let the session extend, for he was exerting himself not to lose patience: he talked at leisure about freedom, seeing one's wife, one's friends, one's colleagues at work. . . . But Vangelis had dug in. He had had time enough in his cell to work out his strategy, and he knew, he must hold them at their very first question. If he gave them one answer, they would move to the next question, and so to the next: then he would be driven back. Even these first, obvious questions he couldn't afford to answer.

Eventually the officer said, urging and threatening at once, 'Tzavella, show sense. Cooperate now, it'll be worse otherwise. Will you answer my question?'

Vangelis jerked his head back, surveyed him a moment, then gave a single deliberate 'tst'.

The officer lost patience: he shouted abruptly, and, as though they had waited at the keyhole all the time, the two policemen sprang into the room again. The officer waved them to cart Vangelis off, while he stood with his back to them, smoking tautly at the window. With a terrible tearing and wrenching inside him, Vangelis turned away from that window. How could he face returning to torture? But the choice was taken, already they were shoving him down a flight of stairs, and, as he expected, they stopped this time at that plain wooden door which previously they had passed. There they waited, his familiar demons, pig face, dark glasses, the doctor in the rear. He hadn't seen them for a week, but it was just as if he had seen them yesterday. They strapped him to the chair, and kicked it back, so he dashed his head on the floor as it fell. For a time they didn't bother with questions but simply worked on his feet. They didn't strike many blows with the metal rod, for not many blows were needed: a touch made Vangelis nearly faint. He vomited once, just with pain: they let him choke himself clear, and began, then, their questions. Who was at the meeting? Who was in the group? They knew the names already, but he must say them. Who ran the group? What were its plans? Who else had he seen? He gasped, choked, tried not to listen: he would not answer them, he would not budge, however it maddened them, he would hold his line.

But today was a short session, irregular. Within an hour he was dragged back to his cell and dumped in pieces of pain on the floor. Later an orderly came and shouted through the door 'What do you want?' He meant, to eat – he was going to the canteen.

Vangelis moaned, then answered, 'Steak': his request was always, in some form, for meat.

The man went away, and was gone a long time. But later the door was banged open briefly, and something was chucked in. Vangelis crawled to it: it was, as every day, a congealed chunk of macaroni, which, as every day, had been thrown in so that it spilt out of the scrap of paper that held it, and was scattered in the dirt. Vangelis gathered it as best he could, and lingered on each mouthful: it was his dinner, he must try to enjoy it. And he had, for relish, the knowledge that, still, he had held his line. They had got no answers, they had got nowhere. There were some answers, of course, he was unable to give: what *were* the group's plans, who *really* ran it? These things he could not tell them. But one secret he did have, which they would work with all their strength to get from him, if they once guessed he knew it: and this was the identity of the official in the Justice Ministry who had given him messages. This secret he had kept, they did not even know of it. They were an army, but he was a soldier too. If ever they broke his first line, they would have to fight him back through many defences before they came near it.

He clambered with difficulty back onto his bench, remembering only as he lay down the shower they had allowed him: for that cool trickle of running water he still was grateful.

8

Chryssa caught the bus in the centre of Athens, and set out to visit Patra and Leonidas. She had heard now where they were: they were camping out on some land they had bought, overseeing the preparations for the building of their villa. On the phone Patra had wept with sympathy, and begged Chryssa to come and see them: it was bright spring weather, she should give herself time away from the city, and also Leonidas might be able to help, he was a well acquainted man.

At the end of its long journey, the bus was nearly empty: at every stop, people got out. Chryssa sat by a window, glad of the breeze, gazing at the low bumpy hills that rippled past: through breaks in the land she glimpsed the sea.

In a wide space of empty fields the bus deposited her, and for some time, gazing dazzled into the sun, she watched after it as, shining, diminishing, it ran steadily downhill to the last village on this road. In an odd, tired stillness she hadn't known for weeks, her heart went out to that village which she had not got to, with its low white houses set between trees and the bright sea beyond: it seemed in another world, that she could not enter.

She branched off down the earth track that led to the land of Patra and Leonidas. The landscape slightly undulated, she walked between wide fields scattered with young melons, crouched among their dusty tentacles. The spring sun was hot, the track might lead anywhere, she walked on till she felt lost in the wilderness. But slowly the undulations sank into valleys, which then plunged into broken rifts; she saw a strip of hard blue sea beyond the dipping fields, and heard activity – an engine, voices.

Cresting a low hump in the track, she looked down and saw the 'land'. On the edge of the cliff, the scrub had been cleared from a large patch of brown earth: there were a tractor, a lorry, a parked car and several motorbikes, and workmen moving to and fro with timbers and shovels. The villa was under way.

She came slowly down the slope, and arrived unnoticed at a busy site where she had to hop across ditches and pick her way between large pipes and rolls of wire and stacks of wooden planks. Men stripped to the waist, with ragged straw hats obscuring their faces, carted bricks and tiles and wooden boards. In the centre of them was a man who wore only a swimsuit, who was hirsute and stout and big-bellied, and covered in sweat and dust and sand and earth, who strode the site waving his arms and shouting at the labourers and arguing with them: this was Leonidas, directing the works.

He seemed not to see her; Chryssa hunted for Patra, and found her busy at a corner of the site, squatting down and buttering a mound of rolls, among columns of salami and jars of pickle. Her head was tied up in a scarf, her face had the sour expression it took whenever she did work which by rights should be done by someone else. Chryssa saw at a glance that Patra had quarrelled with Euphrosyne and lost her. Seeing that face, Chryssa feared for her trip, but when Patra saw her she gave a cry and jumped up, and her face opened in sympathy.

'Chryssa, dear sister, how terrible, we're so sorry!' She embraced Chryssa, weeping; Chryssa, tired, was numb and slightly resistant in her clasp.

They walked over to a small shelter the workmen had built, made of dried reeds rested on a thin wooden frame. There Chryssa told her, with more detail than before, all that had happened.

'Leonidas will help, Chryssa, I will see to it.'

They looked out at Leonidas, hectic amid the building. Evidently something had gone wrong: he looked out of temper, strained, he was bawling at the men. Chryssa could sense, from the way he would not look at her, that it was her arrival that had put him in this tension: why, she could not guess.

Now he was quarrelling with the driver of the bulldozer, shouting, and waving at a pile of earth. The driver argued back: but something had happened to Leonidas' patience. The next moment he clambered up on the footplate, and seemed set on driving the machine himself.

'Now what's he doing?' Patra muttered, and the women went over.

Leonidas and the driver were swaying at the controls, still arguing. They heard Leonidas shout, 'I'll do it. Of course I can drive a tractor! I can drive a tank! It's just the same.'

The driver looked at him; laconic, he remarked, 'A bulldozer is not a tank.'

But Leonidas insisted: the driver shrugged, and Leonidas plumped down on the seat. He revved the heavy engine so black smoke poured from the exhaust, with a bang he let the shovel descend into the soil, with a crash he let in the gears, and with a great convulsion the engine stopped.

The driver made no comment; eventually he said, 'I will show you.' Smarting with chagrin, Leonidas got up, the driver sat, and while the sisters and the workmen gathered closer, the driver said to him, 'The machine is delicate.'

'Delicate, eh?' Leonidas muttered, blackly ironic.

The driver started the motor, which pulsed and throbbed and quaked in thunder. Over the noise he called to Leonidas, 'How much shall I take? Ten centimetres?' Down came the shovel, forward drove the cumbersome machine, and left behind it a track ten centimetres deeper than the surrounding soil. He turned the machine. All were watching. He held up a finger, and remarked offhand to his audience, 'One centimetre.' He adjusted the shovel, clanged the control, and the quaking, racketing, smoking machine ground forward, lifting one thin skin from the soil, and delivering it in front of Patra and Chryssa.

'Bravo! Opa!' the workmen shouted. Leonidas grunted, 'I've got it now.' The driver rose and he sat; he jerked in the gears and the machine moved forward, but not now smoothly, it bucked and wallowed. Leonidas' tense face worked in anger: he brought the shovel down and shoved, but the earth he took was not a centimetre skin, it was more like the entire topsoil. Patra gasped as the earth of their garden disappeared. Now losing all control, Leonidas banged on the knobs and levers, the tracks starting turning in opposite directions, and before their eyes the bulldozer began to rotate. In a rising choking smother of exhaust and dirt, in a brown cloud, it revolved on the spot and started to dig itself into the ground.

Patra's voice rose in a thin knife of shriek, 'Leonida, come off that machine.'

He did, he had to, he could do no more. Unable to look at the driver, who refused to look at him, he climbed down and strode off the site up the hill. For a little Patra watched him go, then, saying 'tst tst tst' to herself, shrugging to Chryssa, she ran after him. Catching him, she caressed his arm and soothingly said, 'Come, my darling, my darling boy, you can't do everything, come now, come.' He was like a boy in a sulk, but she cajoled and comforted him, and slowly talked him down from his dudgeon and wrath, and led him back to the others.

They all stopped work now, and sat around the site, eating the rolls Patra had prepared. She plied Leonidas with best cuts of salami, nursing his mood. Chryssa was still not clear why, at the outset, he had been in such ill humour. Somehow it was her fault: even now, as he came to say hello, his eyes glared involuntarily.

'So, Chryssa. I'm very sorry about Vangeli.'

Now he spoke, he was serious enough. He questioned Chryssa, and listened attentively to what she told him, taking bites at intervals from a large slice of watermelon. When she finished, he pondered, frowning, then spat out his pips and said, 'You know, Chryssa, Vangelis was very stupid.'

Chryssa hardly moved. Leonidas' voice rose, 'Don't look at me like that, Chryssa. Vangelis is honest, he is brave. But what he did was very stupid.'

'All right, Leonida!' Patra snapped, low-voiced.

Leonidas turned on her, all his pent annoyance bursting, 'Don't say "all right" to me, woman! Vangelis was stupid to expose himself. Now he's in a cell. What can he do there?'

He paused and glared at them: it seemed of paramount importance to him to establish the point that Vangelis had been stupid. He could not succeed in making Chryssa agree with him: she sat white-faced, biting her lips till they bled, gazing at him with eyes he could not meet.

He turned from this topic, said, 'Anyway. Well. So.' He rolled himself a cigarette. 'The point is, what can we do about it? Who have you been to see, Chryssa?'

Chryssa nerved herself: she must swallow his harangue, and beg his help as well. She felt irritated, weak: it was the age old, bitter, inescapable situation, the poor suppliant suing to the rich relative, the lord, the pasha, who, if she begged sufficiently, might extend his powerful hand to save her. True, she didn't nowadays have to kiss the ground or the corner of his robe; and actually this lord had no robe but only bathing-trunks, and though he lounged soft bellied he lay on cement bags not on cushions; but still he was the lord, and though she spoke briefly, in firm short sentences of asking, clear-voiced, still she had to watch him slowly stretch, enjoying the fact of her supplication, as if her words had stroked his stomach.

This lord's wife, however, was no houri from the seraglio. 'Get on with it, Leonida. Tell us what you can do.'

He eyed her with hostility, but he acceded: there were people he could see, a certain civil servant . . . a businessman close to the Government . . . a cousin he had, who worked in the Pentagon. . . . He guaranteed nothing, but he hoped his word counted for something.

Chryssa sighed. 'Leonida, if you can get Vangeli out, I shall be – we shall be – so grateful.'

Her thanks didn't cheer him: on the contrary, he seemed deeply dejected. His brows were raised in an arch of nobility; he got up presently and walked off by himself.

'He will do what he can,' Patra said.

'Ach, Patra, if he can do anything . . . But tell me, why have I made him *so* depressed?'

'Uh, you're not to know. I'll tell you, but you must keep your patience. The point is that Leonidas has had – ambitions. He met this minister when we went on that hunting trip, and they got on well, and the Ministry needed a Secretary. He thought his chance had come, and he's been waiting. . . . And now Vangelis has been arrested, and Vangelis is a relative, and you know how politics are here, and, well, I don't know what you'll think, Chryssa, but Leonidas feels that what has happened to Vangelis will cost him his chance of joining the Government.'

'Joining the Government!'

'All right, Chryssa, all right. We have different views about that. Anyway, it hasn't happened.'

'Different views? We're out of sight. My God, how can he?' With no adequate words for her mixed feelings, Chryssa glanced at Leonidas, who stood on the grassy edge of the cliff gazing out to sea, smoking gloomily. He would intercede for the man who had cost him his career: he was consumed with tragical nobility. Poor Leonidas, then; but poor Vangelis, and poor – so many people.

'Is Alexis here?' Chryssa asked.

'Alexis is all right.' Patra led the way to a small promontory of the cliff, and the sisters squatted there, looking down. The rough earth cliffs tumbled lumpily down to the shore, which was corrugated with small coves. In the bay just below them Alexis was swimming, while a girl friend lay stretched on a plastic raft: in sea water so calm and clear that from up here it looked finer than glass, just the sight of it seemed to wash the eye. Except for the white splashes round them, the two tiny brown figures could be flying. Gazing down, Chryssa realized how much, after these weeks, her whole body, all of her, ached for the sea. She wanted to run there, plunge, hurl herself in, and then swim, swim, limbs moving freely like dancing in midair.

'Patra, it's beautiful.'

'Hm. You know Leonidas' plan? He wanted to build a lift from here to the sea. Can you imagine?'

They looked across at Leonidas; and then they realized that, though he might have given up the lift, he had not given up all his plans. He looked as though he had a new idea; he was striding along the cliff top in long paces, measuring areas, counting under his breath. Then he walked back to the site, shouting to the workmen and calling also for the bulldozer. At his instructions, it came reverberating over the rough ground towards the cliff edge. Leonidas was again on the footplate and arguing with the driver, who eventually shrugged.

'Let's go,' Leonidas shouted, and the bulldozer began driving nearer to the brink.

'Leonida, what are you doing?' both sisters shrieked.

From the shuddering footplate Leonidas shouted back hoarsely, 'Patra, I've had such a wonderful idea. We can make a road right down to the beach.'

'A *road* to the beach?'

'Yes, woman, a road. We'll be able to go to the beach in our car.'

They stared, began to protest – but Leonidas had had too

many disappointments, he would allow no more. He gazed round him with yellow eyes, lowered his head, and through his clamped teeth gravelled, 'Elia, go ahead.' The driver looked at him, at the cliff, at the women, at the sea; he shook his head bemused, and with affection patted the bulldozer's flank. Leonidas stood over him, 'Will you get started?' The driver sighed, and gave a great slow shrug as if to say, 'Well, I may be killed, but at least it's no fault of mine.' He engaged the gears, lowered the shovel, and the machine moved forward, running now beside the cliff edge. The cliff top land sloped downwards at this point, descending in rough hillside towards the shore; and out of this slope the machine began gouging a steep ramp, shoving forward in front of it a large mound of earth that continuously fell away down the cliff-face. Alexis and his girl friend looked suddenly upwards as the small avalanche began to splash round them. Above them they saw the bulldozer lurching and shuddering slantwise down the torn edge of cliff. The driver black with dust bent desperate at the controls, and over him the silhouette of Leonidas stood like a man possessed, like a demon charioteer, forcing this vast smoking ten-ton bulk of machinery onwards downwards in a cloud of whirling smoke and dust, in an explosion of stones and a hail of earth and sand. On the clifftop women shouted, workmen stared aghast.

The difficulties increased as they forced their way on; and then the cliff curved inland too sharply for the machine to manage the turn, and on a hanging crumbling edge machine and men came at last to a stop. Leonidas stood on the brink consumed: all the world conspired against him, it had beaten him now, he wanted to weep.

They had other problems also, for the bulldozer, having worked its way so far down the slope, found it not easy to get up again; in places its tracks slipped, polishing the hard ground smooth, and then it could get no purchase and only slithered on the steepness, slipping sideways towards space. The sad end to Leonidas' endeavour was that all the labourers, Leonidas himself, and Patra and Chryssa too, and Alexis and the girl friend from below, had all to make their way there, and put shoulders to the bulldozer, and all together heave and pant and sweat and shout, and gradually help the tired machine to climb; and now it seemed they would all go over the cliff, and now it seemed the cliff itself would break and collapse and sweep them below. The engine raced, they were all covered deep in dust and soil: but the machine got traction, at last they raised it, and returned to the cliff top, where Leonidas' problems were far from done for Patra confronted him, and told him all her thoughts and ended in tears, that he had not only failed in his mad idea, but in the process had demolished half of the beautiful cliff they had paid for.

Leaving the arguing group, Chryssa dawdled to the cliff edge. It was late afternoon and a warm light fell on the sea, deepening its blue almost to violet. A breeze had got up, making tracks and lines on the surface of the sea, all racing together offshore with an effect like perspective that made the sea seem endless. Fishermen had started to gather and their small dinghies and speedboats bobbed bright-coloured, red and white, some distance out to sea: in the clear light she could make out the tiny still figures like flames, hunched to their lines. She and Vangelis would never have such a place. Her heart flew on wings out and away, over this sea, to a faint shore where a white haze of city glimmered like a mirage.

The following day she returned to Athens. In the evening she sat again on her balcony, watching the dusty blocks, with their strips of balcony round them, recede from her to an inflamed sunset. The country, and help, seemed far away; yet this place, also, was not her home – cruel, chalky, jerrybuilt city in a hot smoke of dust, city of spies and indifferent people. Over the sharp bone of Lykavittos dark blurs moved in the cloud. All of it was her enemy.

Before Vangelis was taken, she had a clear sense of things. The Junta was a nightmare, but she recognized that nightmare and understood it and knew how and why they must fight. But now, though the arrest of Vangelis ought only to have made everything more terribly clear, actually it had the other effect: the world became strange, obscurely menacing. It was not the Colonels any longer, it was the world that was treacherous: cruel world, she didn't know from where it would strike next. There was a glimmer of horror at the edges of everything.

The sky moved. Two rips in the dark cloud over Lykavittos

became hideous torn eyes looking down, blind and seeing at once, with a message she dare not read. If they looked at Vangelis, she shuddered and shrivelled to think what they saw.

9

A screw shut, his fingers writhed, yet he saw the hand lying alone on the floor, waving spider limbs. Whose hand. He was separating. Somewhere apart from him there was a swollen bolster of leg, the pain that jagged in its nerves got through to him. But he was just a head on the floor, and otherwise nothing but a stretched and pinned out web of hurt. The enemy was broken too. Now an army came towards him, there was a boot heel, a fist, a cigarette end, an eye by itself rolling and swivelling, yellow teeth. A fat hand took hold of his hand, he had a brief clear sight of, alone in space, two hands gripped, for a disembodied plump yellow hairy hand held in its fingers a damaged hand, dark skinned, plump fingered, but its finger ends clotted with black scab. He saw only these two things in space, while somewhere else a hard object hit him, his spine shot straight.

For a time the split bits of him descended in smoke. Faces cleared: the fat faced one with the huge arse, who always wore dark glasses even in the cells. The glasses shone: sometimes he knew it was the glasses that saw, there were no eyes behind them. And the round white face with little nose and little eyes, pig face Vangelis called him. Dark glasses was only brutal: it made him furious to see someone vulnerable in front of him, his lips parted, he ached to put the boot in. But pig face relished the intervals between pain, he fed on the man's fear as he hung on the wires, and no matter how brave the man's spirit was, his body still feared, it winced, flinched, squirmed, when pig face came near, his small round nostrils like two drilled holes sniffing for fear.

But worst was the third face that hung in the background: old face, a long head, narrow as if pressed between clamps, the slack cheeks sucked to the bone. It only watched, never approached, occasionally murmured, 'Slowly.' This face he hated most, it pretended to guard him while actually it told dark glasses and pig face what they could do. This was the doctor; he had to see Vangelis wasn't killed, or damaged in ways too permanently obvious. Sunken withered face, the mouth when it opened showed yellow teeth in a twisted jaw that was shaped in a grin, while the lips themselves sagged down at the corners.

They had left him some time, there was a hold-up, they were talking to each other. In the interval he murmured to himself the words he clung to: Nothing, still they've got nothing from me. There's no communication. While there's no communication, they can get nothing from me.

He heard their voices, across the room, crinkle with some new interest. Then boots disturbed the concrete dust. Something waved white, a proclamation slowly descending. His muzzy eyes focused on a piece of typed notepaper. He knew it by heart, they had shown it to him often; it was a page from something longer, it attacked the National Government. Always when they showed it to him, they told him they had found it in his flat.

They held it before him, but they didn't, this time, ask any questions: instead, to his bewilderment, they lowered towards him another piece of paper. He could see it was the same sort of paper as the first, but it had handwriting on it that looked like his. Surely it was his own writing? It looked odd because many of the words were the same as on the typed sheet, though there were many crossings-out. Slowly the two papers slid into one, as the knowledge distilled that they had found a page of his own rough notes, it was the draft of a pamphlet attacking the Junta, which was to be distributed by Democratic Action. He thought he had destroyed it all: but they had found a page, they had their evidence. Now truly, they would start.

You wrote this, didn't you, tub? He didn't answer.

We know you wrote it. We found it in your flat. It's your handwriting, isn't it? It isn't anyone else's.

He looked at it, he recognized the handwriting. He thought: they know I wrote it, I know I wrote it, but I mustn't say I wrote it.

You wrote it, man, look at it, you can't deny it.

The pain burst up his leg: the whole swollen sack would break.

Admit that you wrote it. The evidence is here.

He turned away. They grabbed his head hard, yanked it round. And now while one of them held his head, the other lowered in front of him a third piece of paper. With difficulty he focused on it.

Look at this, it's a letter you wrote, right? It's got your signature. It's in your writing. It's the same writing as this, isn't it?

Still he didn't answer. They jarred his head on the concrete.

You wrote this. Admit it.

It felt as though a meteor, red-hot, ploughed his leg.

Admit it, man, we know, you can't deny it any more.

You wrote this, admit it.

You wrote this, you wrote this, you wrote this.

Yes. Yes, he nodded. Yes, I wrote it.

They stood back, and sighed. They had his first concession, he could tell their relief. Walls fell, cities tumbled in his mind. They watched him now, they saw his spirit flag; and he knew, and they knew, that now was the time for them to press home.

You wrote this pamphlet for Democratic Action – don't deny it, we found the copies. Slowly now dark glasses trod on his foot.

Yes.

You worked with Democratic Action. The boot poised again on his foot: and he thought, why deny this? They knew it anyway.

Yes.

You went to a meeting.

He didn't answer.

You went, with your – *psychiatrist* friend, to a meeting, in a flat in Athens. No? We know you did. We know who was there.

He wouldn't speak: it was clear to him now, here he must stop, he must give no more ground. If he once started giving names . . .

You were at that meeting, we know you were. Again the studs of the boot began to press his swollen foot. All of him was a coiled wincing, back, away, from his own foot. And he wanted to talk, he wanted to answer, now he had begun speaking it was harder than it had been before to stop and tell them nothing. But he must, he would resist them here, he must go no further.

You were at the meeting. The slow pressure of the boot caused stabs of pain like arrows shot in his foot, his closed eyes were streaming.

You were there, at the meeting. They stamped on his foot. Still he said nothing.

You're not stopping now, pig face said, you will tell us. He held up an instrument that caught the light: through swimming eyes Vangelis saw it, and knew it. It was a small slender metal stem the doctor had provided, it was used in treating venereal disease. It was inserted up the penis: when it was in, a catch was turned and small flanges rose from its surface, so that as it was pulled out it would scrape clear the infectious matter inside the penis. Pig face passed the instrument to dark glasses.

Vangelis writhed, twisted, he wanted to vomit, he blacked out a moment then hatred swamped him, if only ever he could get back at them, if only some day he had them before him, what he would do to them, his fingers in their eye sockets, his hands on their balls. But these feelings changed, usurped by fear, as the instrument sank below his sight.

You were at the meeting. They shouted the date. Don't tell us you weren't. You're going to tell us who else was there. We know, but you're going to tell us. Will you tell us now?

He slightly shuddered, he made no other movement.

Pig face opened his trousers and took his penis and stroked it steadily, while dark glasses waited. Vangelis' eyes were shut. When the metal touched his flesh each nerve shrieked. While they held his penis carefully, he felt the slender rod slowly slide into him, he wanted to wince, shiver, but didn't dare move, transfixed on the cold metal.

You will tell us.

He opened his eyes a crack, and saw just before him two big brown eyes with huge pupils that swam in veined, inflamed whites like rolling planets: they were strange eyes, and he realized, dark glasses had his glasses off. He didn't speak. Then, twist, the flanges opened, and now out, scraping his fibres, nerves, shredding him, shrieking, he fainting and the pain so sharp he couldn't faint, unending rising wave of pain.

It was out, he sank collapsing, but they banged him upright, shouted the date. You were at the meeting, we know, we saw, you will tell us who was there.

He couldn't speak, he shook his head. You were there,

weren't you? Tell us, we know. Again they held his penis, touched the metal on it. Tell us now, you were there.

Yes.

What did you say?

Yes, I said yes.

What do you mean yes?

I mean I was there, I was at the meeting of Democratic Action.

Bravo the loyal comrade! dark glasses said with contempt. They allowed him a brief rest now, and he realized this rest was his reward for talking. When he spoke, he would have a reward.

So you were at the meeting – they held him again – who else was there?

He didn't answer. Again they applied the mechanism. He fainted momentarily, woke to their slaps.

Was Simopoulos there? He set rigid. He couldn't keep out of his mind the picture of Simopoulos sitting foward at the meeting, his hair shaking, as he spoke, like tongues of white flame.

Was he there? We know he was there.

Presently they were shouting, You agree he was there? And he realized he had lost now the power or the will or the resolve, or whatever it took, to deny what they said: he could only stay silent.

You agree he was there? Right? He didn't deny it, he said nothing. They said, Good, and proceeded to two more names. When he didn't answer, they said, Why do you hold out on these two? You agreed easily enough that Simopoulos was there. He thought, Did I tell them that? No, I said nothing. He tried to shake his head clear. He thought, But why did I say nothing? That told them he was there. Have I betrayed my friends? He was confused now, uncertain. He saw their skill: now that he might have betrayed his friends, his strength was failing. His uncertainty weakened him. Everything was moving, shifting, sliding.

He thought, I must stop, I must hold them, this is the last chance. But he wasn't any more a soldier at a wall, he was a battered man slipping over an edge, hanging by his fingers, about to lose hold. How could he raise himself? – he had no strength left. At even the thought of resisting further, all his nerves shrieked. He mustn't look at them, if he met their eyes he would show his weakness. But how could he deny them? – he was pushed below language. They came again with questions. With shut eyes, curling, turning from them, he murmured almost inaudibly 'tst'.

They paused; evidently they looked at each other.

What did you say? They bent closer over him.

Slowly he turned over, till he lay on his back facing them: but he shut his eyes, he shut them out. With no sound he jerked his brows up, jerked his head back.

What's that? What do you mean?

I mean No, he said clearer. Do you understand? No. Simopoulos wasn't there.

The noise and smell of them was close round him, their breathing was against his skin. In his ear a soft very close voice mouthed, But you said he was there. You told us he was there.

He clung to denial. I didn't. He wasn't there. I wasn't there. There was no meeting. Repeating the denial, he felt his fingers take a firmer hold of the ledge where he hung.

Now they came for him, they were angry, furious. At the first touch, every fibre, every cell of him wanted to hunch and shrink and curl up small, he wanted to curl into a tiny ball, smaller, smaller, so small they couldn't find him. But he was flesh, he couldn't melt from their hold, their fingers bored in like talons. Oh he had exasperated them, their faces were close now, spitting, blood-eyed, was he going to cheat them?

Simopoulos was there. We know it. You know it. You told us he was there. They were attacking his foot, were they jumping on it, ripping it? His whole leg was splitting. And he saw the meeting clearer than ever, Simopoulos speaking shining eyed, his hair white wings. And, No, he said, louder than before. No, he was not there, there was no meeting, there is no group called Democratic Action. He heard his words clearly.

They returned to the instrument. He kept thinking the pain was such that he must faint, that he must break to atoms. But he didn't faint. And in the centre of pain he said, There was no meeting, I wrote no pamphlet, there is no group that you can catch. Through all their blows he clung to the idea that he was now dragging himself back up the sheer wall he hung on. However they attacked and broke him he was beyond the point now where he could do anything other than repeat denials. He was splitting, fragmenting, dissolving in pain: but he knew he had made his way back to the parapet. They could mash him, they had lost the power to get anything from him.

They continued however, till, at a certain point, either they were tired, or doubtful of their tactics, or the doctor advised caution, but at least for now they stopped. Sourly they called in two policemen from outside to drag Vangelis fainting away.

Dimly he came to, swimming in pain, being roughly lugged by two policemen so his swollen legs stumble-dragged along the ground. Turning a corner in the corridor he saw three figures coming the other way towards them, and they also consisted of a man in the middle being dragged by two police-men. The corridor was long and dim, both groups moved slowly, the noise of someone in a side room gasping and sobbing was half muffled by the racket of a diesel-driven generator: the motor was normally switched on during in-terrogation sessions. The two groups moved steadily towards each other, till Vangelis wondered, was he looking in a mirror? He had the odd expectation that when the two groups met, they would merge in one. There was something curious about the others, about the head of the man they carried. It was too big. Was something wound round it? Now he saw clearly, the head was hugely swollen, the flesh was crimson with wound and inflammation, one eye was invisible in blackened swelling, the other was a squinting slit, the mouth was hitched up to one side, torn at the corner, it made sudden hoarse sucks of breath that sounded like choked laughs, horrible noise. As he looked at the swollen head, he kept thinking, Is my head like that? But also he thought, that isn't a man, he's stopped being a man; it was a damaged animal he saw. As the figure came closer in the deceiving light, a tremor of shock passed through Vangelis. What was it in this face he knew? The enlarged head twisted slightly, there was an odd tremble in it like a nod, and in the hoarse sound that came from the torn mouth he caught his own name. A sudden wash of horror shock melted his legs to running water. He knew this man. It was the young doctor who had been at the meeting he attended. And he was so shaken by this discovery that he hadn't the presence of mind to give any reply, any greeting, and now it was too late, the

man had gone, and anyway, just with the thought that *this* was
he, all Vangelis' substance folded up, he breathed no No NO.
Now truly the policemen supported him. Afterwards he did
not know, and knew he would never know, whether this
meeting came by chance or was arranged.

They left him in his cell. Shut up in the dark, his hurting
eyes were all activity, stars flashed, patterns jangled luminous,
he thought he was seeing his shattered fibres. Later he sank
and rose in a slow delirium, and the pain he was in was inside
his thoughts so he could not stop asking himself questions. He
wondered, what volume of pain did he contain? and he thought,
pain is a quantity without volume, it is the fourth dimension,
it can be small as a pinpoint and intense as the sun. He himself
was inside a pain that was bigger than his body, but still he
wondered, whereabouts inside the pain was he?

Later he thought, I knew about all this, how did I let myself
come here? He had taken them on, he had got involved in the
fight in such a way that in the end, consumed, he was driving
himself into their hands. He looked back now with pity and
wonder: that young Vangelis, so easily inflamed, what inno-
cence, what ignorance, he had known nothing. For without it
happening to you, you could not know how it was, when you
had disappeared inside the torture machine, chewed by hooked
wheels in the dark. Then as his head cleared he thought, Today
was a big battle, did I win it or lose it?

The pain returned in calming waves; eventually, from exhaustion, he sank towards sleep. In sudden banging shock he woke.
Had a bomb gone off? – and bang on the door came the iron
noise, and again, who was pounding on his door? – would he
be arrested?

What is it? he called, they paused in the banging to hear
him.

Wake up bastard!

Presently they stopped banging, it seemed there was silence
though his ears still rang with the din; but slowly he lay again
to rest.

He jerked awake, bang bang bang went the racket on his
door, his nerves trembled panicked to the shock, the bangs hit
him like blows on his wounds.

Stop it, stop it, he cried.

They stopped, in time, and he lay down.

They did not let him sleep, every half-hour they knocked again, till he felt like a sack of broken glass, and each blow shook the sack so the bits clashed and splintered and broke on each other. But late in the night he dreamed he was with Chryssa, in the mountains near his village, where they had once stayed together; between the bright peaks her clear face turned to him. This dream was interrupted, but it didn't disappear. By morning he was weak and sick with sleeplessness, yet he felt at the same time as if Chryssa had visited him during the night, leaving with him a secret present of strength.

They dragged him to the room, and prepared for a new day's work: but as he sank in faintness, a low voice inside him said, You must tell yourself: yesterday was a victory, they might have broken you and they didn't, though you retreated, you fought back, it was a victory. He pictured the young doctor: he had resisted, he had fought. He thought, I'm not alone, we're not alone, the resistance will win. Their hands took him, with a tremor.

10

On returning to Athens, Leonidas did apply himself to helping Vangelis. He did not anticipate great difficulty, for he was a man of substance and good acquaintance. Yet the task was not so easy. He consulted the Athens police, and cousin Kostas in the Pentagon, and was advised who in the Justice Ministry he should quietly talk to. But this person, after enjoying the quiet word and Leonidas' hospitality at a bouzouki, proved after all to have little information and less control. Leonidas found himself referred on from official to official without really getting further, till he had moved into a zone of authority within the National Government that was altogether foreign to him.

For the result of his enquiries was that he found himself one afternoon knocking at the plain door of a closed down office block in a dusty suburb. There was no plaque or board on the building to say what it was. He was let in, and led down a corridor to another door, which again had nothing on it to say who was there. From somewhere distant he heard the clatter of a typewriter, and then a noise of footsteps, which stopped dead as a door slammed shut. His assurance wilted, he tapped on the door like any secretary.

'Come in,' a clipped voice rapped. He entered a small bare office with empty walls, one closed filing cabinet, and a plain table with few papers on it; behind the table sat an officer of the military police, vertical, tight uniformed, a closed face and lizard eyes.

'Afternoon! Leonidas Argiriou, industrial consultant.' Leonidas advanced vigorously, holding out his hand.

The officer glanced drily at this presumptuous hand and then looked away, as if he were being offered something he did not wish to eat. He nodded slightly at a chair, and Leonidas, his aplomb now under strain, lapsed into it. His loyalty to the National Government deserved more courtesy.

He tried again, 'Cigarette?' The officer blinked upwards.

Leonidas looked pensively at the packet, and put it away.

So Leonidas began, and, paying tribute first to the way the National Government was saving the nation and the deep debt all owed to the vigilance of the security forces, he let it be known that he had this distant connection, this person attached to him by distant relays of marriage, no kin by blood of course. The man had been arrested, and this was fair enough, most likely he had shot his mouth off in a taverna – ach, but he didn't imagine the man had done anything, he was an ass but he was harmless, Leonidas could vouch for him, and when there were so many true enemies of the state, so many people rightly arrested, pursued, interrogated in depth, people who deserved what they got . . . surely this harmless lawyer, this dolt with a head full of clichés, wasn't worth the state's trouble?

All these recommendations, with their detours and stops by the way, the officer ignored as though they had not been said, and only enquired, 'How many years did you say you've known him?'

'Known him? – oh, it's a good ten years he's been about.'

The officer carefully reordered the few papers on his desk. 'You've known him ten years. And you meet from time to time?'

A slight thread of uneasiness stirred in Leonidas. 'Well, not really. Hardly at all. We're on opposite sides, you know. But we meet, now and again.'

'You meet where? At your homes? In tavernas?'

'Oh, in the name of God, man, what's the point of all this? I can vouch for the man, he's a relative by marriage.'

At this the officer permitted himself a small laugh that did not move his mouth, it was a quick dry hiss. He looked Leonidas coldly in the eye and said, 'If I were you, Mr Argiriou, I should be very careful.'

'Well!' Leonidas flustered, 'I hope my loyalty to the National Government – to the Revolution – my dedication – my devotion to Hellenism –'

Then and only then the officer's face slightly cracked in the copy of a smile, 'Ah, Mr Argiriou, *your* record is not so bad. All the more reason for you to be – very careful.'

Leonidas was thrown: was he under surveillance? *He?* A part of him stirred in indignant wrath; but through the wrath ran a chill of fear and, all disturbed, he stole away.

He had it in mind, in the following days, to address some complaint to those he knew in high office; and then he found he was afraid to do so. He knew that in his meeting with the officer he had unexpectedly touched a tough steel framework within the National Government. It was nothing to do with the public politicians, like the minister he had met: there was an authority behind them, and probably it watched them also, as it watched everyone. With that authority, his word counted for nothing. As to Vangelis, he saw he could not help: Patra would tell Chryssa that he had tried.

He was shaken, on his own account, by his failure. He had taken it for granted that the National Government was *his* government; it was a government that believed in men like him. He began now to put certain questions to himself: for things still happened under the National Government, which the National Government had been brought in to stop. There was corruption, the relatives of army officers easily got good contracts and jobs. And all that business of iron discipline – that could go too far. He had not thought previously about this side of the Government's work: even with communists, he talked of discipline and pictured nothing. But Vangelis, whom he was powerless to help – he did not like to think what had happened to Vangelis.

He said to Patra, 'They're all soldiers in this government, the ones who count. Well, soldiers have their place, they're brave men, the heroes of the nation! But, when you think about it, what are soldiers? They're men who like being told what to do, yes sir, no sir, they like marching everywhere together in time. And they're puritans, schoolmasters. They're afraid of the man of spirit, the independent man, the man who makes his own career, the real individual. That's why they've kept me out, I know. It isn't just Vangelis, it's because I've got a mind of my own, it's because I say what I think when they only want to hear "Yes sir!" Well, they won't save Greece that way. Ach, Patra, it makes you want to weep. And I had such hopes for this government!'

He continued to proclaim his loyalty, he still wrote praises and exhortations in the press, in a traffic jam a businessman in the next car would wave a copy of the newspaper, turned to his own article, and shout 'Bravo!' But these were sour fruit now, and his own praises were hollow: he felt excluded

129

unjustly, and his private thoughts were increasingly negative. He spent little of his time, these days, in Athens: whenever possible they were on their land, supervising their villa and being rural. He began to tell Patra about his plans for a farm. 'We'll have sheep and goats, and watermelons and nut trees and a vineyard and stables. . . .' The farm, like all his plans, expanded steadily till Patra said, 'Sheep and goats, Leonida? What do you know about sheep and goats?'

He turned on her a martyred eye; but on days when the workmen weren't there, he would sit on a breeze block, amid the silent uncompleted workings, while the onshore wind blew steadily past him and away over the grasses; and in his mind the farm extended, and added now an olive grove, a plantation of evergreens, a work force of hundreds. He surveyed his hectares: he would plant these slopes. He turned his back on the city, and on the vanities of career and money and political intrigue.

'The country life is best,' he told the wind sadly.

Patra sunbathed naked, now the workmen were away. Leonidas surveyed her with weak desire; he was a disappointed man, he was not the man he had been.

He looked round; their son Alexis still sat in the car, reading a book.

'Alexi, come out of there, and get on with some digging!'

'Yes dad,' said Alexis, and continued reading. Later he eased himself out, and sauntered feckless over.

'Dad, *why* has Uncle Vangelis been arrested? Really why?'

'Because he's a donkey!' Leonidas snapped.

'But what was he doing? I know he was against the Government. But did he have bombs? Did he have weapons?'

'Weapons? Hey, Patra, did you hear that? Can you see Uncle Vangelis with a *cannon*? In the name of God!' He gazed at his son's wide, soft, innocent, feminine, deeply troubled eyes, and cold rage exploded in him, an ice bomb.

'Pick up that spade!'

He took a pick himself; and while his son desultorily stirred the soil, he himself began to make inroads, chasms, in the baked dry rock-hard earth.

Later they swam; Leonidas prowled the coast, spearing creatures.

They returned to Athens tired and low, to find the phone

ringing. They heard the bell, distant, incessant, as they stood in the lift; while they fumbled at the door, still it summoned them. Shivering with premonition, Leonidas sprinted to the phone and snatched it. The family's heart stopped beating, Patra stood frozen in the doorway, still holding the day's luggage, her wide eyes fixed on Leonidas, who, welded one with the earpiece, listened more than spoke, while his face took a gravity, a serious importance, and all of him as he listened seemed a little to expand and fill out and swell.

He spoke in breathless snaps, 'Yes . . . an honour . . . I must consider my commitments . . . important affairs . . . I shall let you know.' Gravely he put the phone down, and as he turned fully to them his face expanded beaming like a boy of joys.

'Patra . . . darling . . .' He took her hands, he sighed. 'They have asked me . . . if I will be . . . Secretary to the Ministry of Coordination.'

'Leonida!' Patra cried; they embraced. Alexis looked on, perplexed, excited.

11

Days now passed without new interrogations, and the days became weeks. Vangelis scratched their number on the wall, to keep count. Was it possible they had finished? They had learnt little from him. But perhaps they were tired of him, or believed they had got from him all they could; or they were busy working on people arrested more recently, who knew more; or they were lulling him into a false security, and would spring on him suddenly with a new shock of torment.

Two policemen helped him stumble to the room of the commanding officer, with its carpet and large window. Beside the officer sat a short stout man in a brown suit whom Vangelis had never seen before: he kept wrinkling his nose as if a smell there offended him.

'Come in, Tzavella.' There was no play of courtesy this time. The officer cleared his throat, 'Evangele Tzavella, you will be tried in three days time by a military court for the crime of sedition.'

A trial? In three days? He couldn't take it in. He collected himself sufficiently to mutter brusquely, 'I must see my lawyer.'

'Of course, of course. In the meantime, if you have any difficulty in making contact with your lawyer, Mr Tsanakas here will give you what advice he can.'

Mr Tsanakas sniffed and wrinkled, looking bleakly at Vangelis.

They led Vangelis back to his cell: he was still dazed. His trial? He realized he had stopped believing that he ever would stand trial: he expected only questions and torture, without end. Now he should be anxious about his trial: the short notice meant he couldn't prepare his case properly, the trial would be a travesty. But, immediately, he couldn't worry about that: for the unbelievable had happened, the torture had stopped. After the trial he would go to an ordinary prison, he would have a plain, clean cell, he would see other prisoners, he would see the sun, be fed, sleep – it would be paradise. He could hardly believe that in three days he would move to such a place.

He lay on his bench in one sigh of relief. They had given up their siege: he had kept his secrets, he had defeated them. Now they departed. He shook his head where he lay, and murmured over 'Thank God': he was not a praying man, but he needed to give thanks.

In view of the trial, they permitted some relaxation in his conditions. The doctor arrived, and treated the sores on his legs. In the period in which he had been left alone, the swelling had begun to go down, and he was able, with pain, to hobble. He was allowed to take another shower, standing under the dripping cistern in the stinking lavatory. He was given a further set of clean clothes that Chryssa had left for him some time before. He was even allowed pen and paper, and wrote urgent letters to Chryssa and to Simos, whom he wanted to be his lawyer. But there was apparently a delay in communications, for in the three days before his trial he received no reply to any of the letters he sent.

Never mind, he would prepare. They had thought that by giving him only three days, they would catch him crippled and dazed, unable to defend himself: but he would surprise them. In another trial they had silenced him, but in this trial they must listen to Evangelos Tzavellas. He dispensed with Mr Tsanakas, and spent the remaining days in his dark cell, sitting in the positions that hurt least, considering and planning.

They made it hard for him. He was given no information, even the charges were vague, he could get no particulars. And he was much reduced. He was afraid at first his brain might be damaged, for often he couldn't find the words he needed, he couldn't complete sentences, even half an hour's concentration was such a strain that he would lose his argument, and find himself starting to cry. He needed *some* support, *some* help.

But the following day he was in better heart: his defence was planned, snatches of cross-examination began to occur to him. He imagined his voice, quiet, controlled, with deliberate pauses, cutting the courtroom fog. The damaged engine of his mind was creaking and sliding into motion. By the end of the last day he was clear and resolved. The trial would be a travesty, but it would be an opportunity. Observers, journalists, foreign correspondents would be there: he knew how to defend himself, and he would expose the Junta. His only reservation was, did he have the stamina? But he must make sure he did: all his resistance work came to a head here. This was his chance; he would not waste it.

Afterwards he wondered whether it was because he was weakened by prison and questioning that he had so lost his sense of reality as to think that anything of this kind could happen.

He was taken in a police van to a military barracks, and was stationed at the door of a crowded room. When his guards leaned in to study the scene, he also could see inside. There were so many people there, shuffling in the dim electric light, that at first he was confused; later he made out the long raised table down one wall, with six high leather-backed chairs behind it. At least, with such a crowd, his case would have attention. With every chance he got, he looked round. She must be there; he realized how completely he had counted on her presence. But he could not see her, or any of his friends. Michael, who might have reported the case abroad, had not come. No journalist whom he recognized had come.

He looked again at the people in the crowd: they were listless, bored, not wanting to be there. It was odd. Why should his courtroom be crowded with men who seemed only to have been shepherded there, while they waited to go somewhere else? But then he saw, from the grey and green shirts, that many of them were policemen, and the others, with their heavy faces and cropped hair – they were either plain-clothes policemen, or soldiers out of uniform. He saw now what had been done. At this moment Chryssa and other friends might be outside, at some other entrance, hectically trying to make their way in, insisting they had a right to be there, while the officer agreed, of course they had a right, they had a perfect right, but the court was full, there was no room.

The guards muttered to each other, ignoring Vangelis. When he looked into the room again, he now saw people whom he did know, though he had hoped not ever to see them again. Pig face and dark glasses sat, serious and patient, on the front bench. They were clean shaven and clean, their uniforms new and smart. Pig face sat like a virtuous boy at Sunday School, his feet tucked under the bench, his back upright, his brows slightly knit, his round face patient but hurt: he looked like an officer who deserved more promotion that he had had. Dark glasses, his uniform sleek and his hair slicked back, sat with fat arms folded and his bulging face slumped in seriousness, so the glasses seemed just dark front windows to the sombre patriotism within. They seemed two such dutiful officers as had seldom been seen in an army before. Behind them Vangelis saw, still in his old coat, the weatherbeaten man who had followed him round Athens.

There was a disturbance in the room, and the people crowded there showed their militariness in the way they all got to their feet at once. Four army officers and two civilians filed behind the long raised table, and sat. In the centre, in a grander chair, sat the President of the Court, an elderly officer of irritable dignity, who evidently found these proceedings tiresome. He nodded brusquely, and Vangelis was brought forward.

Vangelis tried to stand with presence. He repeated to himself 'a hostile courtroom is nothing new to me', but still he was in difficulties. It was partly that he found it unexpectedly disconcerting to stand there as the accused, and not, as he used to be, the aggressive lawyer; also he was aware he'd lost weight, his clothes were loose, it was difficult to take his old court stance, stout and foursquare. He mobilized his eyes, his glances, stares. He felt weak, disabled, as if he were exposed to them with part of his body removed. He realized that, of all things, they had damaged his aggression. He breathed deep; he must, he must regain strength.

The hearing began. The first witness got up from the bench opposite: and now Vangelis recognized him, he was one of the men who had come to arrest him. He wore an old T-shirt then, he wore a police uniform now.

'On the evidence we had at that time, I had no alternative, sir, but to order an immediate arrest, which we proceeded to put into effect.'

That was his testimony: almost before he knew it, Vangelis had his forum, the court was his. But he was ready. His own voice sounding sharp in his ears, he said across the room, 'Will you please indicate to the court the nature of that evidence?'

'No.'

Vangelis glared. 'I'm sorry, but you have to answer my questions.'

Rapidly, mechanically, evidently much rehearsed, the police-officer said, 'I cannot cite the evidence for reasons of national security.'

Vangelis' heart missed a beat; but he collected himself quickly. Of course, of course, it was obvious they would say this. He continued, 'Nonetheless, though the details of the evidence may not be given –' But here he was interrupted by the President of the Court.

'Mr Tzavella, I cannot allow you to pursue this line of questioning, since it cannot proceed without trespassing on national security.'

'But the evidence, sir – the evidence against me –' Vangelis began, in the stress of the moment losing momentum.

'Proceed!' the President said, loudly, with annoyance. By now Vangelis had his character: he was a solemn, fixed-minded, patriotic officer – for the people brought before the court he could have no feeling but dislike and contempt, which he worked to restrain. His mind would be harder for Vangelis to penetrate than a concrete fortification.

The next testimony was equally brief, for again the evidence was withheld for reasons of national security. While Vangelis strained to organize a new attack, two more witnesses were called, heard and dismissed. The case was being rushed: already pig face had taken the stand. Quietly, coolly, with well disciplined indignation, he recorded that the accused had confessed during questioning to being a member of a terrorist group which aimed at the overthrow of the Government. It was Vangelis' turn: and this time he had better hopes, for he would not ask for evidence, he would offer it. While speaking, he avoided looking at pig face, to preserve his concentration.

'Mr President,' he said, not loudly but clearly: he would make them sit forward. 'I submit that the testimony given by this officer is invalid because it was obtained by the use of torture, by the use of brutal and atrocious methods which I shall now detail to the court. Not only the phalanga was used –' Vangelis proceeded to describe the torture, but almost at once the prosecuting officer interrupted, his voice vibrating with indignant anger.

'Mr President, I must protest at this vile smear and slur on a Greek officer. By your leave, sir, I shall ask a question. Captain Moraitis, did you employ any of these methods which have just been described to us?'

Visibly hurt, aggrieved but with dignity, pig face called clearly, 'No, Mr Prosecutor, I did not.'

'Mr President,' the prosecuting officer shouted, 'I demand the court take action to stem this foul vilification, by a traitor, of a loyal officer.'

'Mr Tzavella,' the President said, 'you must withdraw the remarks you have just made, or I shall sentence you for slander.' He spoke gravely, in presidential anger; but still a twinkle crept into his eye, he could not help relishing the clever trick being played by the prosecution.

'For slander? Mr President, slander is not within the jurisdiction of this court. You cannot sentence me for slander here.'

'Do you withdraw the remarks you have made?'

'Withdraw? When I have been tortured – when my legs –'

'Silence. Tzavella, I sentence you to two years detention for slandering the security forces of the nation. Proceed.' The twinkle had gone. He was purely determined, bleak: he would discipline the traitor.

Proceed they did, and the prosecution was soon complete.

'Mr Tzavella, what have you to say in your defence?'

Vangelis looked round at the courtroom of soldiers, at the rows on rows of hostile faces which were mostly bored, though lit occasionally with the glare of some private fanatical hatred. He felt suddenly the absurdity of even arguing here. He was a lawyer, he used strategies and tricks in court, but always he had a sense of true process: there were laws, rules that were agreed, kinds of fairness. Whatever the case or the courtroom, always they were in the court of justice. What stunned him now was the scale and completeness of the cheating and lying. It was too wrong, some god of law of justice should descend on them in anger, but none did. On the contrary, their justice worked like a perfect machine, because they all cooperated to see that it did. For a moment he was overcome by his own isolation: but he stood up, and for the first time that day he recognized fully his old courtroom voice, echoing loudly in the room.

'Mr President, I am not brought here by just process of law. I have committed no crime. All my work has been only to preserve justice, and to help others find it. The people with whom I have been associated, and who are abused in this court, are people whose one crime has been courage – whose "fault" is honesty – whose "treason" is that they will work and fight to restore to the nation visible justice. Sir, I challenge the jurisdiction of this court. Even so, I am willing for the court to try me: but let the evidence against me be heard. Let my wounds be examined. Let my claims of torture be proved or disproved. Let my "activities" be described to the court. Let the court be told in what way they are treasonous. For it is not for what I have done that I am accused, it is not with any evidence that I may be convicted. . . .'

The President, who had sat in rising irritation, broke in at last. 'Mr Tzavella, this is no defence. You abuse the patience and the time of the court, you insult the officers of the court and the government of the nation. I sentence you to a further two years detention for slander, and to an additional two years for contempt of court. Be silent now, or you will be removed forthwith.'

He turned to the other officers, they spoke briefly, in curt whispers. The court waited. Vangelis stood firmly. He had no expectations.

The President cleared his throat, resumed his gravity. 'Evangele Tzavella, for the charges of treason and sedition which have been found proved against you, the military court sentences you to sixteen years imprisonment.'

Almost before the words were spoken, the policeman took Vangelis' arm and hustled him from the court. His trial was over. It had not lasted half an hour. As he was hurried out, another defendant was hurried in: if justice was brisk, it was because justice was busy. The officers of the military court had a long day ahead of them.

'Let me pass!' Chryssa cried, outside the courtroom, as she pressed and strained at the broad resisting backs that blocked her way.

She had had difficulties getting here. She had been informed of the trial only that morning; she had been directed to the wrong barracks, and then to the wrong courtroom. Still she had arrived in time, she saw in the distance the courtroom

138

door: but she could not get through, it seemed she was in a crush of deaf people who, at her shouts, only glanced at her blankly and then looked away again. She elbowed and shoved, now she was pushing with all the strength of her body: and the wall of backs only flexed harder, and shoved back against her. Her eyes were smarting, she drew herself tall and shouted 'Let me through, I must get in there,' in a hoarse but clear voice. She shouted as Justice might, straining to enter this courtroom and failing.

She wrestled and pushed, and finally made progress: she had reached the door, there was movement in the chamber beyond.

'Which case are you here for?' the man at the door asked her.

'Vangelis Tzavellas,' she gasped.

'He has been sentenced, the case is over. Next case!' he shouted; he would say nothing more.

Chryssa made an easier but no quicker progress back through the crush. She was dazed. Her eyes burned but she would not weep here. Some of the soldiers looked at her quizzically; they were possibly sorry for her, but she had let herself in for this.

She emerged from the barracks into a throbbing street in the stark sun. She looked at the strange world, the city traffic ploughed past hectic as if it were any normal day; the sunlight out here was naked, blinding; she walked shakily, holding upright.

PART TWO

The Woman
at the Prison Gate

1

At last, all changes over, doors slammed, shouting voices muffled now, no more being knocked and kicked from vehicle to vehicle, with blinding sun not seen in months cutting his sight like a razor so he stumbles darkened into the next container,

but just stillness and the slow coming to for the men shut up in the tight dark panelled room: until the room itself starts slowly to rise, pauses, hangs on the edge, then sinks, drops, subsides into soft cushions and slowly, irresistibly, starts to rise upwards again; the men shifting to keep balance and shaking heads to clear them, but head is no problem, problem rather is that as body is lifted, stomach rises at a different speed, and when room and body sink down and rise again part of them continues down to pull stomach inside out

till after hours or days, there's no knowing in the sick-heaving room where no meals are given (but no food is needed), the swell changes, voices call, there's bump scrape and crash of landfall, and doors thrown open at last and a staggering emergence. The long voyage is over, they are on new shores: but in a derelict country with few lights, an empty café, a faint radio crackle of bouzouki. Wavering, light-headed, the weak men are trudged up steep alleys, past houses falling down, to a large sheet of rusted iron that opens to swallow them. They stagger in, are punched upright, and indoors now in harsh electric light blear eyes inspect them. To Vangelis it seems like changing trains in some bleak railway station up in the mountains: in delirium of hunger and tiredness he thinks, that's where they are, the train has brought them winding up a sickening pass, now they're dumped at the old backwoods mountain station that's half a castle. In the yellow electric glare the tired officials, who have stayed up late to receive them, study papers and check their faces: but how will they make the connection here, when will the new train come, the new express with a fast smooth ride for all?

But it seems they'll stay the night; they are helped down corridors, a door opens, here are his quarters: and actually there's a bed here with mattress and blanket. Surprised, touched, he keels over and rolls himself up in the coarse thick luxury of blanket. But still, tired beyond exhaustion, for a long time he can't sleep for the slow motion of the wooden room has not stopped, and now the whole of the stone building he is in slowly rises, hangs, and drops back into cushioning seabed: the whole country is breaking adrift and rocking in the water. But the swaying movement that sickens him lulls him too, slowly down into sleep deeper than he has known in months.

Gingerly, as if they hurt, Vangelis opened his eyes: there was a brightness of daylight in his cell, and between the bars he saw blue sky, very pale, very bright. The air was sweet; and he realized slowly something strange, there was no noise here, no traffic, no sound at all. He wondered, what place had he come to?

Later the building stirred, he heard a muffled noise of feet, barks of shout. A curt guard brought him a tin plate with a piece of bread, a piece of cheese and a cup of coffee: he ate slowly, extracting every atom of taste from the hard cheese, savouring the bitterness of the coffee and the sweetness of the half-dissolved sugar. A change of clothes was thrown through the door; later still a guard let him out into the corridor, where the other men from the boat trip stood looking about them, dazed as he was. They were marched down corridors and out into an open space, and there they were left. He could hardly believe what he saw: they had the freedom of a wide plain of sandy ground that stretched away to enormous battlemented walls. And crowds of men, too many to count, wandered at liberty there, or squatted or lounged in the shade. Vangelis couldn't immediately step out into space: he moved along the wall till he stood in the sun, and there, feeling weak, he sat down, with his back on the firm stones and his stretched body drinking the hot light that burned his skin.

A well fleshed balding man with curled, grizzled hair came past and squatted on his haunches near Vangelis. Presently he offered a cigarette, which Vangelis took, but he said no more. Vangelis would glance sidelong at him – at his Armenian nose, at his chin of stubble – but the man was inscrutable, squatted there motionless with his eyes wrinkled into the sun, drily exhaling smoke. But eventually he turned and asked, 'Where were you?'

Vangelis said the name of the police barracks.

The other frowned and nodded, blew smoke, 'I was there.' Presently he asked, 'Who did you have?'

'Who? I had . . .' Vangelis searched his mind, it was a name he thought he would never forget, but it would not come. 'He had a round face, piggish, no nose.'

'Uh! Moraitis, I had him. He was a sweet one, eh?'

Vangelis was still wondering what had happened to his head, that he had managed to forget the name of pig face. He looked up, the other had swung round and with energy held out his hand, 'Stamatis Vassios.'

'Evangelos Tzavellas,' Vangelis said, with some of his old briskness. He held out his hand: and the hand flinched, it had its own fears of contact after these months. But the two men shook hands, with some formality and with the vigour of veterans: a long handshake that left Vangelis moved, for he realized it was the first friendly touch he had felt since he was arrested.

'What did you do before?'

'A lawyer. And you?'

'A surgeon.' Stamatis recalled his work: he had secretly tended a number of people, after police beatings. Two of his patients were implicated in a bomb plot: he was arrested as an accessory and given a hard interrogation.

Vangelis listened, and at moments attended, and gazed hard with a knit brow: but talking like this was still unfamiliar and difficult. He had been a long time alone with only himself to worry for, and he realized he found it hard to attend to someone else, even when that person had suffered as he had. Stamatis' sufferings reminded him of his own, and in dwelling again on these he ceased to listen.

Stamatis was patient: they returned to stray reminiscences of the police barracks. Vangelis spoke slowly, for his mouth, his tongue, his thoughts, his words, everything seemed to creak and ache as he brought it stiffly, with trouble, back into use; but there was a kind of help in gaining, retrospectively, a companion in torture.

145

Stamatis broke off to shout, 'Yasou Andoni!' then murmured to Vangelis, 'He was there too.'

The man he had called gave a jerky smile, and limped over to join them on legs that moved like artificial legs, though Vangelis could see from the ankles that they were made of flesh and bone. The man's face was haggard, starved, oddly lit up, with something too wide open in his eyes: a scorched face. He hardly spoke, but listened to what they said, and nodded constantly.

Then a young man came over to them quickly, 'Mr Tzavella, is it you?'

Vangelis got to his feet, staring at the young man with the level dark brow, while the memory of him partially returned. He was a student, he had been one of Vangelis' first clients after the coup: yet that case was far off, he could remember little of it.

'You remember me, Mr Tzavella?'

'Remember you, how should I not remember?' Vangelis said indignantly, but avoided saying his name: he wondered again, had they damaged his head?

The small group talked; later they were joined by a short, stooping man, with a face cut deep with lines of irony, a mobile, knowing, subtle face. He was called Christoforos, he proved to be a civil servant, an agriculturalist; but how he had come here Vangelis could not gather. He was so out of the habit of company that he couldn't take in names and faces, all he could do was to register, dazed, the presence round him of a friendliness with many faces that came on many feet to meet him. Their words he kept missing; he listened simply, as to a new noise, to this friendly timbre the human voice could have. Already tired, he looked round at the sunlit yard; at the deep blue sky that was almost too pure, with no wisp of vapour anywhere; and at the ancient walls that loomed over them on every side. He wondered again how it was that nothing showed above those walls, and that no sound of any sort came over them. He and these other people, with their different past lives, were all assembled in this blessed place like dead heroes arrived in Hades. He asked himself again, What is this place?

Then they were ordered inside, and he alerted with alarm. The guards approached, guns at their belts, their peaked hats pulled low so they had animal faces, eyeless, just snout and teeth under the helmet. As the prisoners trooped in, his eyes wandered over the crumbling block of the main fortress, its sheer wall lined with broken rows of black slit windows, and he was seized with helpless shivering in the sun, for he knew that behind one of those windows was another Vangelis, as much himself as he was, being tortured: in the dim light his body arched.

That night his old acquaintance joined him: he knew they could not be far away, they were his familiars, and he waited paralysed as the round noseless face, and the face in dark glasses, the fat blind man's face that saw, bent towards him.

2

Secretary to the Ministry of Coordination – it was the post Leonidas had stalked up in the mountains. He feared he had lost it, he heard that a famous lawyer was to be appointed, and again that the Acting Secretary was to be made permanent; and in spite of all the post came to him. In the first days he knew no way to contain his happiness. He sat around the flat, with a drink but not drinking it, with a cigarette but not smoking it, just heaving from one easy chair to the next not able to stop smiling; so also at his office, he lolled in his wide black leather chair, and gazed on his partners, on the secretaries, on the hard-driving German and Scandinavian businessmen who were his clients, with a wide moist look of happy affection. He knew he did not look then like a man of fierce acumen – but what could he do? The dream of his life had come true.

Of course, some of his acquaintances disapproved; and he himself had recently had doubts about the National Government. The President was a genius, but some of the others were – second-class men, amateurs in Athens, they gave jobs to their peasant relatives. The police now thought they were cock of the walk, and he had never been a special devotee of the police. There was torture in the police stations, he didn't for a moment doubt. And again, some of these soldiers were such puritans, such moralists, that pleased him not at all.

But these reservations, that had buzzed in his ear only days before, dissolved like blown mist now. For the honour was so great, and it would give him – such opportunities. He could only think of what the National Government *would* be. Torture, police bullying, jobs for relatives – these things belonged to the past, even if for a little they still persisted in the present. His heart swelled and his ambition soared till he felt himself one with the Government: and it was hard for him then to see that the Government had faults that mattered.

His better friends were pleased; and Patra was exhilarated, through fashionable tavernas they moved demure and radiant, aglow like twin suns. Notwithstanding this, Patra could not soar quite so high as Leonidas, and after a little it did come home to her that he was the Secretary and she was only the Secretary's wife, for he had speedily developed a more corpulent manner of demanding her favours. And then she was less awed by the non-stop way he purred at home, and beamed on all the world as if he were a buddha, in this odd limbo interval before he took up office.

So Leonidas found that, even at the outset, not everything was perfect. He found Patra on her dignity, and (Patra aside) he found the nightclub singer Varvara, whom he had long admired and whom he now sought out, late at night in her dressing room after the bouzouki – not so beautiful, turbanned in towels, her pale face glistening with the cream that wiped her make-up off – he found her not ready to yield to him and melt, in the way he had expected, when he drew close to her and told her he was a Secretary.

And his son Alexis did not appear to be boasting at school of his father's appointment, as in filial duty he ought to have done. He knit his brows, and seemed unable to find anything to say, when Leonidas told him of his plans for Greece. And then Leonidas understood.

'It's the school, Patra. Well, we'll find a new school for him.'

In the first flush of promotion, he bought a library of books on political economy, he had some hasty homework to do: but he was too excited, his concentration was not good, he must put off reading them till he began at the ministry. For he had, he soon found, so many things to do. He must separate himself formally from his consultancy business, his sleeping partners must be woken and put in charge; for he, officially, would be somewhere else. In some ways his work might not greatly change, but it must be made to seem to change. His work as a consultant consisted in advising foreign companies on the siting of new factories, or on the buying of new promontories for leisure development, and on personnel, pay and labour conditions in a particular area, and on grants and loans and legal exemptions that might with skill be obtained from the government, and on the arrangements it would be necessary for executives to make to secure proxy ownership of property in Greece. It was the policy of the National Government that such trade should thrive, bringing investment to Greece; at the same time, Leonidas' fees and commissions were related to the profit that left the country, as he secured advantages for the company that retained him. And his job now would be in part to trim those profits, playing foreign company against foreign company – not but what he would respect old friends – securing more advantage to the national interest. Personally, he would be making great sacrifices, for his pay at the Ministry would be less than he was used to, and all in drachmas; but he would be contributing to the salvation of the nation, and of her crippled economy.

He left his office; and now they hurried, for the following morning he was to start at the Ministry, and this evening they were invited to a government reception. The President himself would be there. After their last hectic shoppings and rearrangements, Patra lay down, to let the breezes of Kifissia, wafting with pine-scent through the window, soothe her headache, so she could recoup and shine at the reception. Leonidas still had too much energy to do other than shuffle his papers, rearrange the furniture, flick through the volumes of political economy, prepare his clothes, shower, and sit down, relaxedly gowned, intelligent-faced, slightly frowning, cigarette in hand, scanning a confidential government report, and savouring arrival.

His peace was not long, for presently his cousin Kostas called, to pay his respects, slim, taut, in a short-sleeved but sharp-cut summer version of his uniform. He shook Leonidas fervently by the hand, and looked him in the eye in a vehement glare of congratulation, then stood back, erect, businesslike, sheathed in self-respect. With a large grandeur, his belly slack, his robe flowing like a pasha's on the wind, Leonidas walked before Kostas onto the balcony, seated himself in the most comfortable chair, and weakly waved at another where Kostas should sit. They had installed a new phone line in the apartment, and, calling their new servant on the balcony phone, he asked for coffee to be sent.

They had a curt conference, Leonidas finding a way, without the indignity of asking, to intimate that he was now, more than before, a person who might be offered, as appropriate tribute, any information about the highest military personalities that Kostas, working in the Pentagon, might have. And Kostas, who had come today with no other wish but to be allowed to give presents to his great relative, laid before Leonidas like sweetmeats his tastier informations. But several times he paused, and hung as on the edge of secrets, looking Leonidas hard in the eye, seeking from him the password to proceed.

'Ach, Leonida, this is just army gossip,' he said after one such pause, 'and an army should have – more interesting work.'

With a vibration in his voice Leonidas asked, 'Do you mean, in the east?'

'In the east, Leonida, beyond the Hellespont.' Kostas sat forward, they both sat towards each other, and their glances darted round them as if they feared that behind the blinds in distant windows, or in the dark bubble of helicopter thudding overhead, or in the cars parked beyond the garden, there were ears and eyes on the alert, surveillance devices leaning their way.

'I believe you know already, cousin,' said Kostas, 'that there is a band of us in the army who believe –' But he paused, and wouldn't say what they believed; again, Leonidas had to volunteer, 'Who believe in the Idea.'

Kostas retreated behind a veil of cigarette smoke. 'We are patriots,' he said.

'And I am a patriot!' Leonidas said throbbingly.

The coffee came; their heads receded; they eyed each other. When they were alone, Kostas raised his cup and said quietly, 'To the Idea.'

'The Idea!' said Leonidas, and sipped solemnly, in thought. He believed deeply, in his bones, in the cause Kostas spoke of; but there was danger in these thoughts. He was new to the Government, he must tread carefully, he must not be committed yet. But still he knew he was approaching, through secrecies, what could be the great cause of his life. It was a cause one could die for, the Idea: and he was in the government that could bring these things about.

He worked now to make clear to Kostas, while saying little, his interest, his sympathy, his dedication. He knew that Kostas, sounding him, had expected more than this; but he must put off till later any clear declaration.

Patra woke; Kostas paid his respects to her and left. The important couple must prepare for the reception.

Leonidas carefully did his toilet, in a calm deep excitement; at the end he sat rigid, like a sacrifice, while Patra dabbed and trained and arranged his hair. Keeping his head still, he told her of a plan he had recently formed. He would lure to Athens a cartel of international developers, who would clear away the older, disreputable parts of the city. In their place, in parks kept green with water from the new desalination plant he would install, towers of apartments would arise, skyscrapers. They would be painted different bright colours; and he would take the poor families out of their derelict tenements and put them here, and to prevent snobbery he would put different types of people above each other in the same building, here a priest, above him a factory worker, and an accountant. There would be no rich towers and poor towers, they would all live together. A new Athens would arise, towering over the little Acropolis: the Manhattan of the Eastern Mediterranean.

As Patra listened, her brown eyes grew slowly smaller, her tugs at his hair grew slightly harder, till she said to him quietly, but like a quiet scythe, 'Are you telling this to the President, Leonida?' He was caught off guard, hurt, and all the pastel happy towers, Manhattan shimmering on the shores of the Aegean, hung insecure in midair, and dissolved as they fell. He gave her melancholy thanks for making his hair beautiful.

Now they were gorgeous. A government car collected them, and bore them through bright-lit streets to an area where traffic queued, and a policeman in full uniform, suddenly lit up silver-green in the beam of their headlight, shouted and blew a whistle and ordered the crowd to part for them; and so to the foot of a broad staircase, where policemen and army officers milled. In a dazzle of cameras they were conducted upwards to a high threshold where, beyond pillars, in the shining bowl of the hall, evening-dressed men in decorations and orders, and ladies in light scintillations of gown, moved at their ease, heads high. Leonidas' chest swelled, he breathed a new air: in state (though a new boy), grand as a minister, he and his lady advanced.

Generals and ministers glanced at them, curious, not knowing who they were. Then Leonidas realized that the power that was gathered tonight had for him its sting: among engineers and managers he was a prince, but he was no one here. Still he was content to gaze, for around him there were not just generals and ambassadors and archimandrites, but, above them, the great men of the nation. He heard a vigorous clapping laugh, and saw not far off a man completely bald, with a sharp face, narrow eyes, a powerful neck; and another with a long face, a supple mouth, and slow, considering, heavy-lidded eyes: founders of the National Government, faces he had seen only in films before, but real men, breathing, talking, only an arm's length away.

They located Leonidas' minister, and went to join his party.

'Ah, Mr Secretary!' the Minister exclaimed, in generous recognition, 'and Mrs Patra.' He introduced them to his wife and to his other companions. His wife was a large woman with strong features, heavily made up, nervously voluble, who took Patra firmly by the arm and in sudden sharp shouts told her about the government wives. The Minister in the meantime expanded on the measures to be taken concerning Greeks who wanted to work abroad. He moved and turned constantly as he spoke, energetic and nervous, fixing the eyes of all of them; and especially his excited, feverish eyes would shoot again and again to Leonidas, making sure he agreed, and was impressed, instructing him to nod, and assent, and pausing for him to come in with more support. Impatient, demanding, he was making sure of Leonidas' obedience at once, and Leonidas complied.

'The Minister is right,' he said. 'When half the Greek work force goes to Germany, of course that pushes up wages here. How can you control wages, when the workers are in Germany?'

'Well, but they send money back,' one of the others said.

'Ah! But how much?' the Minister snapped, his eyes glittering fierce. But then he paused, evidently he was not sure how much. He glanced sharply at Leonidas – and Leonidas had done this piece of homework, and came in prompt with the figure.

'Bravo, Leonida! Mr Argiriou is my new secretary,' he explained again, and his hungry eyes glowed tight approval. Leonidas saw, he had secured his position.

So Leonidas was launched. He attended and supported while the Minister in his anxious jaggedness held forth; and at the right time he came in, deferring but firm, knowledge at his fingertips. The others, he saw, began to take note of him; his interventions grew longer. He found his feet: he realized he was beginning to take hold of the company, just as in a crowded boardroom he would gather in the attention of everyone, till all waited for his next, well-spaced, sharp-toothed word. The Minister found himself more often listening to Leonidas than watching him listen, and his tight-skinned eyes fixed on him watchfully, keen but not altogether easy.

But Patra was watching, while she nodded to Mrs Minister, and 'Easy, Leonida,' she mouthed in his ear. Reluctantly Leonidas doused his light, and returned to being audience. But while he listened, his attention ranged, and took in everything: the chandeliers, the huge bouquets in buckets round the walls, the suave waiters, the jackets glowing with military decorations, the glittering jewellery – everything shone, it was a mirage of glory to a music of confident voices. And everyone he noticed had their own deep glow, a something inside them that crinkled the corners of men's mouths and eyes, and sparkled in their wives' eyes and smiles, and made blood run warm, and air hurry into full lungs. Beneath each face of assertion and denial and expostulation and astute contained humour there was one expression, it was the slow deep smile of importance, success, of enjoyment of power. If the people went the smile would stay, in the looped chandeliers, in the festoons on the walls: all the air of the room was a gentle smiling. Leonidas knew the smile was on his face, and on Patra's, just as in the Minister, for all his agitation, the smile shone in his glittering eyes. And now, as in a vision, the people ahead of Leonidas moved slightly, and across the room, through a valley of shoulders, he saw a head: round, with a high-domed forehead, with strong brows, with eyes of energy, with a small but set mouth, the President himself. Leonidas gripped Patra's hand and squeezed it. He remembered with disdain the cheap phrases people had used of the Government – 'the Colonels', 'the Junta', 'the dictatorship' – and all those little words, which in the past had made him smart, shrank now and died: vain words, from people who knew nothing, out in the wilderness. For this was a Government, it was nothing else. Now he was here, all doubts dissolved: here was authority, importance, power, here were the people who governed the state. And he was one of them: he stood in vision, his eyes dazzled. He had come into a new world.

'The President is a great man!' he told Patra as they left, deeply moved, as though – though the President had said nothing to him – he had recognized in the President that night one who embodied all the hope and ambition and faith and devotion and admiration that Leonidas had in his life.

In the morning he started work. An official Mercedes arrived at an early hour, and swept him purring through early-morning Athens. He was a trace disappointed to find the Ministry a smaller building than he remembered, plain, looking like any well-to-do mansion turned into offices. He smiled to himself: what did he expect, a palace? He was greeted in the shady vestibule by the secretary to the Secretary, a thickset man with a deep-drooping nose who knew his way to every corner of the Ministry, and nosed ahead of Leonidas, introducing, directing, conducting. He gave him a guided tour; and again Leonidas was a little disappointed, for the Ministry was an old building, and not well lit, in any direction you soon came to the end of it; you could call it dingy. And so to his office: the schedule of the day, and certain recent reports, were set out on the ancient, massive desk. There the secretary left him, to settle in; he would be seeing the Minister at half-past ten.

He sat down. The office was plain and not big, the desk had a rich veneer but was old and cumbersome; any lawyer would have a smarter office. And the view did not inspire him, for somehow he had come to assume he would face a large window, with Athens spread below him, and instead he faced a stairwell, with shut windows opposite, some with rusty electric light and some black.

He took out of a folder the papers he had brought with him, and stirred them with his fingers; he felt a trace flat. Then, from among these papers, one slipped out that had got there by mistake. Picking it up, he saw it was his page of notes to do with Vangelis. He sighed: poor Vangelis! Vangelis and he were far apart now, a chasm was between them. He remembered times in the past when they had been at odds, arguing in cafés: and, remembering, he grew irritated, for Vangelis didn't understand friendly argument. Leonidas himself spoke with passion, from his fears for Greece: and yet Vangelis did not listen with respect, but with a face that was closed,

155

dismissive, a blank wall face, and a contemptuous jutting of his lower lip. It was a rude face, insolent. And when Leonidas had argued with all his heart about the need to put the unions down, for the good of Greece, Vangelis only laughed, remarking, 'Oh, I thought you believed in free market forces.' What was clever in that? Leonidas was infuriated: why should labour be traded freely just because goods were? These little retorts added up, Leonidas smarted again as he recalled them: he felt more indignation now than he had felt at the time.

The smile he had seen at the Government reception, the smile on every face, brightened in him: he shook his head, and sighed, then he screwed the paper small and chucked it in the bin.

As to Vangelis? Tomorrow perhaps, he murmured to himself, knowing that tomorrow he would say 'tomorrow'. He turned to his schedule, his zest restored: he was a busy man, and he must be well primed when he saw the Minister.

3

Once more Michael stood at Chryssa's door. He had announced himself at the grill below, but still, after he heard soft feet padding, there was a long pause. He realized she must be bending down to peer through the little glass eye in the door. Then she unlocked and unchained; the chains too were new, it was like visiting someone in New York. And still before loosing the last chain she paused, and part-opened the door to look at him. Over the taut chain he saw a pale blank face he knew but hardly knew, cold, guarded. Seeing her so, his words failed, and she didn't speak. The door closed blank again, and she unbolted and opened.

She stood small in the large doorway of the old flat, bare-foot; she had on a kimono. She looked at him still with those strange eyes, which were large, bright, as if with fever or sleeplessness. She murmured his name. It was less than a year since he had seen her; but years of events had passed since then.

His arms were full of irrelevant gifts, flowers, books. He fumbled with them insecurely.

'I'll come back later, Chryssa, but take these now. I can't carry them away.' He tottered towards her, his cornucopia was about to give way. She started to take things from him numbly; but as he passed her the flowers and the massed pink bells glowed all round, a smile grew in her face falteringly, like someone tiptoeing back into a shuttered house. The flowers surrounded and lit her while their scent enveloped her; the smile glowed for as long as surprise could last, and faded beneath returning worry.

'Come in, Michael.' The flat was almost dark, for she had all the blinds down. His eyes still ached from the dazzling streets, he waded blindly through the amber shadow, stumbling on furniture. Gradually he saw the disarray: clothes hung on the furniture, used coffee cups glimmered from the shadows, on the floor papers lay in sheafs and fans over the rugs.

'I'm sorry for the mess. I haven't cleared up since the police last came.'

He stood embarrassed too. 'Chryssa, I wish I'd been here for the trial. I wish there'd been *something* I could have done.' He looked at her anxiously; his failure to have helped hung on him like an awkward body.

'You tried earlier, Michael, we were grateful for that. Once Vangelis was arrested, no one could stop them . . . Sit down, I'll make some coffee.'

He moved some papers and sat, taking off his jacket. Though the room was dark, the air was dry and hot. Among the papers on the floor stood mounds of books: he realized they must come from her study in the university, she had told him on the phone of her dismissal. Opposite him was a wide, bulky armchair with crumpled cushions: a spindly art nouveau standard lamp cast a circle of brown light over it, and round it were laden ashtrays and huddled coffee cups and a folder of papers hastily closed. This was Chryssa's nest: even in her home, her living had retreated to here. His hearing, stunned by street noise, woke to the silence of the flat; from the kitchen he heard the tiny distinct sounds Chryssa made, a clink of spoon on china, a frothy pouring of coffee.

She brought the cups and set them down, and climbed back into the armchair, in the way in which evidently she had become used to sitting, her legs curled up under her, her body crouched. They were silent for a time, he could tell she needed to get used to his being there; then he asked whether she had seen Vangelis.

'Michael, I can't find out where he is. They won't tell me.'

'But surely, they have to tell you where he is?'

'There's no "have to" about it with political prisoners. They told me he was in a prison in the Peloponnese, but when I went I found he wasn't there. Another time they told me they couldn't say where he was, because he was being moved from one prison to another. I suppose they play games with me. But the fact is, Michael, I can't find Vangelis.'

She lit a cigarette and smoked tensely, gazing in front of her. After a pause she said, 'I'm sorry, Michael, I should have told you more. But the phones are dangerous, and also . . . I haven't been wanting to talk . . . I don't see people.'

He looked round the flat; what she said was obviously true.

158

Across the room, in the dimness, the massive carved suite of black furniture rose from the strewn papers like crags out of snow; the giant chairs were set to the empty table like a banquet cancelled; almost that fruit-bulged furniture *was* the banquet of this house, frozen black, and never to be eaten. He looked at her crouching in her chair, gazing ahead and seeing nothing. He was moved: for in his mind she had always been active, spinning through the world finding bargains, friends, new demands she brightly faced. Briefly in England he had glimpsed another mood, lightless, despairing, the cellar of her life: now she was in that bitter place.

'But you see your friends, Vangelis' friends?'

'Friends, yes . . .' she trailed. She mused, and then snapped, 'People steer clear, you know.' Suddenly he had all her attention: her eyes shafted looks like iron bars at him, her face was tight, she was coiled like an animal alert for the foe.

From that look his spirit fled: what could he say, the man who lived safely so far away and came only late, after all was done. Absently he swirled his cup, and hid his sight in the crawling coffee fingers.

He looked at her again: she was no longer looking his way, she was gazing hard in front of her, as at some object or creature, which he couldn't see, set down on the floor. The smoke from her cigarette corkscrewed upwards; her eyes did not move from the thing in front of her. He saw, she was gazing at a thought. What was it – the isolation of courage, the betrayal of friends? Everything that had been soft in her face was hard now: hard as he had never seen it, pulled tight, handsome. A handsome bitter face, closed to him, and miles distant though just across the room.

She presently looked his way. 'I don't know if I'm good to talk to, Michael. My thoughts about people are very black. And not just the people I know, or the dictators. But . . . anyone. You're very alone when you're in trouble. And if you're unhappy for a long time, you can get jealous of the happy people. As for *them*, if I had one of the gaolers here, what I would do, the things I would do –' But her voice broke, she had to stop, in a dry convulsion. Eventually she said:

'All I have is the fact that I haven't got Vangelis. How can I not think of him every day? And yet, it's a long time since I saw him. And I know he's changed. You see that folder, I've got all our photos there. I look at them often, and not just to remember old days. I look at them, Michael, because – sometimes, when I try to think of Vangelis, I can't see him clearly. I lost him once when they arrested him. Now, I am afraid I will lose him in another way.'

In a dry sob that still was not crying, she stopped, and only gazed at Michael or through or beyond him. All he could say was nothing that could help her. Suddenly his mind filled with the recollection of a song she used to sing, the Macedonian song of Yerakina. Yerakina was the rich girl of the village, one day she tripped and fell into the well, and as she cried for help from the bottom of the well all the golden bangles and bracelets on her arms clashed and jingled. The sound of their jangling made the chorus, while she argued, argued with the village blacksmith who wouldn't haul her out unless she would marry him. Michael remembered her rich lively-sad voice drawing out the long silky Oriental tune, tripping up and down the runs and returns of notes ripplingly; as she sang she waved her arms to make the imaginary bangles clash. From his memory but as if from the deep well where Chryssa now was this song came rippling; but he was not her blacksmith, and she was in a deeper shaft than he could haul her out of. There was no way, while Vangelis was removed. He sat there like an awkward hospital visitor, waiting inadequate beside someone too absorbed in pain to speak; and she gazed away, into the heart of a trouble that smoked blind all other sight.

He looked yearningly across to the blank windows, where, round the edges of the blinds, two or three streaks of light slipped in and raked the wall steeply. At the least she should have light, air: he longed to make some bold act of liberation, to stride across the room, pull open the blinds. Let sun and breeze come in, colour break out in the carpets, the papers stir on the floor. Gestures only; and she needed her protection, her safe place, yet too he must get her outside.

He stood up.

'Chryssa, let's go out to eat. I'll take you to that restaurant we went to before, by the beach.'

She didn't answer, perhaps she hadn't heard; he thought, she'll stay in her cell. But, abruptly, she looked up, with the smile of pleased surprise that he had seen before, and 'Thank you very much, I'd love that,' she said.

She went to dress, they left, and emerged suddenly in blinding sun: Chryssa blinked dazzled, and Michael noticed only now all her gold-brown colour gone, she was pale-sallow, hardly Greek.

By metro and bus they travelled through the suburbs, and didn't stop till they came to a taverna beside the sea, so far from Athens that the city was no more than a slight browning of the sky like a rusty dawn in the wrong place.

It was hot still mid-afternoon. The diners had left the restaurant and gone home to siesta; the waiters desultorily gathered plates and screwed up paper table-cloths. The white beach was nearly empty, a boy meandered back from the sea carrying flippers, taking high hopping steps on the burning sand. The blue sea slapped rocks sleepily and lapped on the sand. Very slowly Chryssa stretched out in the sun, and relaxed gradually to the rays like a person gingerly uncoiling in a too hot bath.

The waiter brought some dishes far from hot, and wine, and left them to eat as slowly as they liked. Only the old proprietor stayed, dozing beside the till. The beach was quite empty; the sky had not a speck of cloud; far out to sea the tiny white block of a ship moved slowly. Michael had brought Chryssa here for relief, escape. But whatever they spoke of, Michael was presently aware that he was no nearer to Chryssa than he had been. She was as much shut in her thoughts out here in the open as she had been in her room, and on all the huge calm sun-world of sea and sky her eyes scanned constantly, looking for something that was missing everywhere – seeing, every-where, only absence.

Michael was with Chryssa much of the time while he stayed in Athens. Sometimes they talked indoors, but as often as possible he took her out. She began to emerge; they considered what they could do. Michael suggested – Chryssa hoped – that if there were publicity about Vangelis abroad, this might help towards his freedom. She was afraid that the Junta kept his prison a secret partly so there could be no news about him. They would be disappointed. It was true that Michael would not have new news till she had found where Vangelis was, and seen him. But in the meantime she helped him bring his notes up to date, in a cryptic shorthand of his own manufacture. He would walk out of the country with Chryssa's knowledge of the Junta carried in tiny caches on his person. For certain things he noted only clues, he had no need to write them out, he would not forget them.

Chryssa described events interruptedly, as they came to her, and often there were lulls when she only sat, stuck; there weren't words for what she wanted to say. But even when they didn't speak of Vangelis, he was still beside them in their thoughts, so much so that afterwards Michael remembered these days as if Vangelis had been there. He saw clearly his friend, with his moustache, his jutting features, his passionate eyes sparked with irony that frowned from a cavern many distances away – there was a gaze in the flat Michael hardly could meet, a courage, a trust, a demand for fight.

Chryssa didn't sing Yerakina; but late one night, when they were sitting at a small restaurant built out on stilts over the sea, she did sing. The song began at another table, and with his limping Greek Michael missed many words: but it was a kind of soaring lament. The voice would rise and fall, but again and again would rise, as if its grieving were something it must climb to. Other tables came in with the chorus, so did Chryssa, he heard the quiet rich ripple of her voice. Then, for one stanza, the original singer's memory failed and Chryssa's voice sang clearer, substituting for him; and it was a new voice again to Michael, with a vibration or catch in it so that the curious weaving and climbing and dipping song seemed to play on the rim of a huge invisible emotion. The chorus continued, the various tables sang, and the rippling of the song mingled with the plash and slap of the sea on the wooden supports of the restaurant. It was one of the rapt moments of Michael's life; he could have sat years looking at her, hearing the song.

Now Michael had gone, Chryssa thought more about him: it seemed her preoccupation had grown so dense that when people came to see her, she realized their visit after they'd gone. And Michael anyway was hard to know, because he was foreign, and also because he kept much back. Even in England she had found it hard to fathom him. He was keen-eyed, kind, pensive. Occasionally he had bursts of exhilaration, as when on an impulse he took Vangelis and her to the racing dogs – an unheard-of phenomenon. Also, sometimes, a violence showed: when he racing – drove a sofa regardless through the streets – or of course on his motorbike. These things seemed interruptions of the person he was.

Now he was different – though he had not changed in the way she expected: but what he was had grown more distinct: as if this quiet, sinewy, young-figured person, who could slide through life like a lean knife unnoticed, were someone he had taken a decision to be. His quietness now, it occurred to her, was the quietness of the interviewer, biding, perhaps insidious. But she was touched by his resolution to take on the Junta in his journalism, more deliberately than before now Vangelis was imprisoned. It was also quixotic, of course – yet he seemed aware of the small chances he had of making a difference. In her mind's eye he girded himself for battle: he was spare and long-limbed, with a long-nosed, slender face, like one of his running dogs upended – or like a young Quixote, and no match, to look at, for even one burly soldier. She was grateful for knowing him, he was a large quiet presence of goodwill, that would visit her occasionally and then recede again round the curve of the world. His going left a gap.

Others too had gone. Simos and Clio were away for weeks in the islands. They had urged 'Come with us!' but she had put off joining them for the same reason that she put off going to see her parents. Her mother especially was often on the phone; and though Chryssa talked at length with her, she discouraged her mother from coming to Athens, and at the same time delayed going to Salonica. 'Do come, Chryssa, a rest at home would do you so much good – come.' 'I'm coming,' Chryssa said, but she didn't go. Though she made slow progress – or because she made slow progress – she felt she couldn't leave for a day her quest to find Vangelis. Also, she could not leave her home. She clung to the flat, even to the furniture, as if she herself were now no more than a memory of the life that had been there; as if, if she left even for days, the past itself would go.

She felt at times that she was tied to Athens just because it was a place of such unhappiness. If it had been a good place, she would have gone away cheerfully, but instead she stayed there, waiting for things to come right that would not now come right for years. She had also the task of finding work. She began applying systematically to colleges, schools, cramming schools, libraries; she received various forms of refusal, some curt, some apologetic, some patriotic and abusive. It all came to the same thing, the doors were closed.

Unemployment left her at least more time to seek Vangelis, and to visit every office that might have information. Still they put her off. Their records were out of date; he had been moved to Crete and then moved away again; she should go home and wait, they would let her know whenever they had news. Before his trial she had taken it for granted that once he was sentenced she would be able occasionally to go and see him: it was too ridiculous that many weeks later she still did not even know where they kept him. All she could do was persist.

She seldom saw their old acquaintances. It was not that these friends did not sympathize, for they told her they did, and also she heard it in the tremor and throb in their voices when they spoke to her. Yet, she noticed, it was less often that they did speak to her; she got no invitations. She did not believe there was an agreement to isolate her; rather, she imagined, each friend would suppose, without thinking too hard on the matter, that someone else would doubtless be seeing her. Perhaps also they let her be from respect for her grief, for her desolation. And what could they say to her? She and they were not in the same world: she knew from their disquiet that to them her eyes, her face, were a window into a furnace of trouble. And they saw in her someone who had a claim on them, and, for all their good nature, it chafed that this claim had no end in sight. And she remembered the cant she'd heard in Athens cafés about 'the figure of the survivor': she thought now, yes, people are 'survivors', and what that means is that when someone you know becomes a disaster area, you move quietly to a distance that is safe. And, for her part, she wondered, did she want to see people, and sit and talk?

Yet there was contact: when the interval stretched to a certain point, people would ring to ask how she was, and they told her on the phone that they cared for her and loved her; but they still stayed the length of a telephone wire away. When she came home once, she found a letter had been left for her: she recognized the handwriting of their friend the solicitor Cosmas Matziris. Why write? she thought, as she tore it open

164

and saw it contained money, many thousands of drachmas; there was a short note of sympathy and *bon courage*. The note was so brief, she could not tell whether there was in it any embarrassment or not. And she was grateful since, even with the help she'd had from her parents and sister, she needed the money. Cosmas asked her to be in touch if she needed more: but of course she wouldn't do that. And somehow she knew, from reading that note, that she would not see Cosmas again – and it would be as if she were avoiding him.

When she met her acquaintances, they spoke of the Junta, of the need, more than ever, for indefatigable resistance. But her own thoughts were more pessimistic. They spoke of striking blows, but what blows could anyone strike? If she thought of action, it was not of such protests as they spoke of, rather she would have ripped her guts out, or set fire to herself like the doomed Czechs. What else could be done? She knew in her roots that only with bloodshed would the Junta go: and she could not see who would oppose them.

The resolution and hope, which they all had at the start, she saw now in a different light. It wasn't hard for professional people, together and confident in the group they belong to, to protest and strive against tyranny, and face real dangers in doing so. But once you are outside such a group, everything is darker and more doubtful. And the lone person in misery falls through holes in life, and once they start falling they fall only lower, through levels of hopelessness where the state of the nation, civil freedom, the question of who has the power and money – where such matters are no longer topics of thought, and even if things wrong in those areas have caused their trouble, they stop seeing connections and only fall further out of life into cut-off unhappiness. She saw that underneath each person is a pit they can fall down, it is just wide enough for them and it has no bottom, and those others who stand round the brink in a ring can holler down about rights and wrongs and causes and hopes, and it is nothing but dying echoes to the person who is falling.

The weeks passed to months, cold autumn came on, the weather grew harsh, chilly, unpredictable. She seemed no nearer to finding Vangelis. She wondered more, what were the authorities afraid of? Did they really think that if she and Vangelis saw each other, they would pass secret messages, dangerous to the regime? Whatever they thought, they gave her no clue, but only continued to refer her on from appointment to appointment and from office to office.

These efforts, and the job hunt, had her walking all over Athens; and on days when she had no appointments she still strode the streets from sheer restless exasperation. On a dull September day she careered down the waterfront near Faleiron, hardly seeing the people she fought her way through. But she saw a policeman shouting, like a little dictator, in the centre of traffic, and a point in her head exploded in fire. And she saw a mother stuffing chocolate down her eldest son: he would be a dictator, every Greek family spoilt the eldest son. Across the road was a bustling, banging, shouting restaurant. She thought, What am I doing here? None of this is me. People say that Greece is suffering, but I can't see that Greece is suffering. She thought: It isn't only the Junta that's bad, everyone's complicit in what's happened to Vangelis. In the whole country, how many people actually care if you have dictators or not? Why did we bother? We destroyed our lives for nothing, we were fools fools fools.

She strode on, her bitter thoughts welled, it was a relief to her when an autumn *bourini*, blowing up in minutes, caught her protectionless out on the seafront. She had been so consumed, she had not noticed how black the sky had grown. Now, as the wind increased, she looked up and suddenly felt giddy, as if the world had turned over and she could fall off it. A pit, a huge shaft, had opened in the clouds; it was lined with ragged edges of cloud, turning and coiling, boiling, lit up white from inside – eerie white light in streaming rags of cloud, it was a sky of Judgement. All the sky was fleeing, looking out to sea she saw a blackness from earth to heaven, a wall of darkness, sweeping in towards the land.

The wind became furious. The few people round her were running for shelter, hunching in doorways. On the balconies of apartment blocks women were racing in with tables, chairs, potted plants, while husbands cranked up canvas awnings.

Race, race, you won't make it, she thought, the Apocalypse is on you!

But the people now had all disappeared, the balconies were

empty, the only movements were the sharp little wind-waves that rippled simultaneously down all the fringes of the rolled-in awnings. The buildings were dead, except that now, in the black windows, she saw the pale faces of the families pressing close to the glass to watch the storm. She realized some of them were looking at her. Go on, she thought, watch the storm in safety, behind plate glass, still be frightened! The buildings were lit in a white freezing ghost light, making them bright against the black sky.

The only thing that seemed kin to her was a young palm tree on the sea front, its long leaves a fistful of blades all threshing. The tree flung back and forth, back and forth, as if mad with pain.

The wind increased, and looking up she noticed the same frenzy at the tops of the buildings. High on the rooftops were thickets and forests of television aerials, on long slender stretching stems, swaying and tossing, jerking between their strings, whipping back and forth wildly; on one, the thorny crosspiece tipped up and down rapidly, in a mad seesaw signalling.

A gust nearly had her off her feet. The spray off the sea drove spiking into her. The sea had changed completely since she looked at it moments before. Now it was lost to sight at a very short distance in the white smoke of spray: all she could see were wave-humps, dirty grey-green-khaki, rising and falling quickly, making white crests that blew apart in steam. An empty dinghy appeared on the crown of a sudden wave-mountain, balanced there a moment, then swooped into a trough of hollowing water. All disappeared as a wave smashed vast against the sea front, and a geyser of spray shot up to the sky: for a moment a white cliff stood beside her: then all that water, blown forward, crashed down on the road, flooding it, bursting over her, soaking her.

There was a pink glare, and right overhead thunder sizzled sharply, crackled, cracked, and receded in echoes of explosion. In another flash she saw a jagged root shape of lightning slant to the sea: she had a momentary sight of boats further out tipping at their moorings. Then all sight cut out as the black wall, which had all the time been driving nearer, reached the shore. Its shadow came over the wave crests and veiled them, and now it arrived, it was rain, it fell in fury, torrent on torrent cascading, pelting, the big drops hit her like stones. They drove at the ground with such energy that each drop, on impact, jumped up again like a jagged dancing silver figure; for a moment she was surrounded by these tiny molten dancers as she staggered in the downpour, then all the road was awash. The lightning flashed, the thunder rattled, the clouds lit up, and water poured from the sky and the sea. Chryssa stood in the deluge sodden and battered; she wished the storm to destroy the city.

The rain continued cataracting down. On the sea front geysers towered. The drain-grids flooded, the road became a river. Chryssa strode slithering, almost swimming, almost dancing: oppression lifted, her body felt free, she felt a biting joy, then was happy as a spoilt child.

Eventually, slightly, the downpour slackened; the first vehicle passed, a lorry that ploughed through the deep water sending up great wings of wave. Later a car passed, sleek-shining as a seal, in a bow-wave of tidal swell. Chryssa stared at the strange road-fish.

The sky lightened, through a white veil she saw tankers and freighters, anchored far out to sea. They looked strange, for they did not sway at all, while the dinghies nearby hurled and trembled.

The veil thinned, the rain slackened to a pattering. The far sea shone, and over her also the sky was bright, just plain white with grey rags and tatters and torn shapes trailing on it. There seemed white things everywhere, the gulls reappeared, and a white pigeon that looked like a dove flew past her: she followed its progress up the grey front of a building, till it settled on a television aerial: for all those aerials that had tossed in frenzy were stationary now, sharp slender frozen rods. The rain had stopped, colour came back into the buildings, bright red returned to all the red-painted olive oil cans which served for flowerpots on the balconies. People emerged from their living rooms. Long rolls of thunder came clattering back from the far side of the city, where the sky was dark purple.

Chryssa's feelings lightened as the storm passed. She felt purged of a fury: as if her desire at the height of the storm for all the city to be razed had actually been accomplished in the furious onslaught; yet the city was there again, and she could feel differently now.

Shivering in sodden clinging clothes she hurried home and dried and changed. When she came out on her balcony the look of the world had altered again: now, beyond the buildings, she could see tiny fishing boats on the puckered grey-silver sea, under a sky lined with soft puffs and furs of pearly cloud strand. And beyond the sea a distant limb of land was clear, she could see separate fields, white towns; and far beyond these she looked through air washed clean to tiny sharp-edged mountains. It all was bright and calm and still. She saw it with an odd bewilderment: for her troubles were not resolved. She felt obscurely deserted. From the balcony she looked at the calm scene wistfully, at a great distance from what she saw: as if she saw the sunlight through a small window in a wall that was metres thick.

As the light fell she went in, and closed the windows, and let down the blinds, and went back to the door to make sure it was locked.

4

Chryssa went at last to see her parents, realizing as she travelled how long she had delayed. Time had seemed to pass so slowly, but she felt, looking back, that the weeks and months had darted by. Her conscience about not seeing her parents, which had hardly troubled her when she was in Athens, grew steadily stronger as she neared Salonica.

As she rose in the dark lift, in the building where her parents lived, she had the sensation that in returning to them she was returning to the weakness of a child. Her strength ran from her, a black sadness waited to engulf her, she felt brittle, on the edge of collapse.

She heard surprised, familiar voices when she rang the bell; then the door opened.

'Hello mother,' she said.

Her mother gasped, and knew her: with bewildered, intense, almost angry affection she blinked at Chryssa, and stared at her, ready to be in tears, ready to be cross, ready to hug her almost to death.

'You came, my daughter,' she said, with a frog in her throat; her jaw munched, her eyes sprang with tears. Chryssa, still cold and dazed, felt odd strings pull at her as she gazed at the snub plump affectionate-combative face of her mother; and her body moved forward, though she was lost, and the two women fell into a strong hug. And behind her mother now her father appeared, lean, nervy, his eyes wide, holding out his hands to her as he walked towards her exclaiming, 'Ach, my child, is it you? Have you come? How are you, how goes it? Good to see you, my daughter!'

When her mother had done, her father hugged her. Chryssa felt like a brittle vase, with one tap she'd smash.

They went into the living room and sat down under the spreading curved limbs and the skew yellow bulbs of the candelabrum. Chryssa was oddly caught, she had so much got out of the habit of talking that now she could not speak: her thoughts locked, nothing got out. And at the same time she had to talk, her parents' home was a place where all the family, all the time, had vigorously harangued. A hundred things there tugged at her: the pictures, her mother's embroideries, the furniture, even the little icons on the wall, as well as her waiting parents, all said to her 'Speak to us!' But when she did start, only broken thoughts got out, now an odd joke, now a reminiscence, now a stray enquiry about a relative she didn't care about. Her parents could make nothing of what she said.

'Our daughter, *how* are you?' her mother burst out.

'I get by. I'm okay,' she said bitterly, knowing that to her parents she sounded offhand, rude, they would be hurt as well as worried.

Her eyes focused on the embroidered mat on the small coffee table in front of her: it was a new work of her mother's. She noticed that, as always in her mother's embroideries, the counting of the squares had gone slightly wrong, so that the lozenges that ran round the edges met at square one with half a lozenge to spare.

'Do you still count wrong, mum?' She meant to be affectionate, playful, but her voice was jagged. Her mother flushed and blinked, wounded. Chryssa coiled in a worse knot of cold.

Her father sat staring at her hard: he had his elbows on his knees, his hands clasped, he frowned with concentration. She saw, he was working hard to attend to this strange meeting, though, since nothing was said, his mind kept running elsewhere, business tugged at it.

Her mother served an elaborate meal, dolmas, wine, zadziki, meatballs: they ate without appetite, almost in silence. Afterwards Chryssa insisted bleakly on clearing up: What is this? What's the matter with me? she was thinking. Her parents went out onto the balcony, and sat in the darkness over the brightly lit, noisy street: she heard their quiet voices, conferring anxiously.

Her mother made up a bed in her old room, and she went there thinking that lying down, or even sleeping, would make no difference to the null state she was in. But as she rummaged in the wardrobe, looking out hangers, she pulled out some old yellow papers. One was the draft of her first public lecture: she leafed through it absently. Then she saw in the margin a comment by Vangelis. She remembered, this was the first thing of hers she had given him to read: and as she read his comment which, typically, was humorous but terse even to her, she heard the words, she heard him say them, she felt his breath on her ear, just as she had in the past when he spoke to her closely in a warm whisper, a vibration of deep voice muted. He was in the room with her: she looked round, and he had gone. She shivered. The wide log jam that held her grief began to sway and give, timbers loosened, then the barrier broke, she began to cry silently then the first sob shook her and now she couldn't stop herself crying helplessly, she was borne away.

Her parents came hurrying in: her father fumbled uncertainly, agitating in panic, but her mother took her in her arms and soothed her and held her like a big girl and let her cry.

Her mother held her while her crying quietened, and lay down on the bed beside her and enclosed her as she had when she was small. As her sobbing slackened she only nestled closer in to her mother's large warm slowly breathing body, to her mother's smell from childhood: slowly her gasps sank into the breathing of sleep.

For the first time in many months, Chryssa slept late and woke slowly. Through a doorway she looked into the living room, where the shutters were open and sunlight poured in. And in and out of the shafts of sunlight her mother moved. With each foot set on a large duster, she was shining the parquet, a broad-built woman moving lightly, in a slow graceful skating, a sliding dance. From childhood Chryssa remembered her doing this, and for a long time, in a warm drowse of pleasure and love, she just lay and watched as if this were the happiest dream of the night.

She got up and in her nightie ventured out on the dazzled balcony. The air was still, the low autumn sun was hot on her skin. Her father, with his glasses on, glanced up from his briefcase and acknowledged her absently as though she were always there. Then he resumed peering and delving in his papers, while she sat and enjoyed yawning in the sun. Her mother came onto the balcony with a *briki* of coffee.

Then her father was up and all over the flat, finding and

losing his things, his wallet, a contract, a bill, his jacket, more cotton wool for his shaving cuts. Eventually he was ready, his jacket brushed, his hair sleek, his briefcase at his side, the smart businessman. He briskly said goodbye to his girls, and left. Then her mother sat down on the balcony, and chatted.

The day was quiet, mainly they pottered in the flat and rested; but in the following days her mother was active, and took her in tow all over Salonica. The handle of a small metal tray had come off, so they sallied into the metal-working quarter. In a grimy cramped workshop chock-a-block with iron bars and machinery, her mother haggled sharply with a gigantic figure who waved a blue welding torch as he bargained, whose face was invisible behind a square metal mask. Strong as the iron, she bargained on till she got a good price.

Then they went to the meat market, where every stall, with its section of tree trunk set up for a chopping-block, was dazzling red and white under the large electric bulbs, which hung down on slender metal stems. From there to the fish market, where the fish sellers seeing Chryssa would shout, '*Ah*, what lovely whitebait I've got here, what sweet plump lovely little whitebait I've got for sale to you, madam.'

Her mother frowned, and slapped the fish wetly to this side and that, inspecting them.

With all this activity, she slept well these days. Sometimes they sat quiet in the flat, her father peacefully absorbed in his paper. Then her mother would come, and Chryssa knew from the deliberate way her mother sat near her, and applied herself to her embroidery, that she had some family gossip in view. And abruptly she would lean forward and the embroidery would rest now untouched in her lap as she spoke quietly, closely, urgently, telling Chryssa the latest successes of an aunt who had the evil eye.

These scandalous gossipings Chryssa loved, not because she was moved by the evil eye, but because they carried her back to the abandoned world of her family life in Salonica. It amazed her to see how that life still went on, as if the bad things that had happened were still in the future: she was back in an earlier world. At times she found herself simply standing still in the flat, and gazing at the old things she knew – her mother's 1930s liqueur decanter with its crescent of black lacquer on the side; the little paintings in faded pinks and blues on the crockery

173

in the cabinet; the battered yellow-fingered piano (what a caterwauling Patra's singing lessons had been, and what an elephant stampede across the keys her own early efforts to play appassianato) – on these things her gaze would pause, as if she would gather them all to her breast; while an overwhelming feeling she had no name for rose, and slowly put her together.

She thought now gratefully what a marvellous oasis her mother had made their home, in the centre of their father's business rush. He always raced in a fury of dealing, and even when he was home his thoughts were not: it was her mother who got them the piano, and also made them read books, at a time when her father believed that a woman's eyes would go blind if she read two pages together. Through the war, the Civil War, the failure of their father's business, she sustained the home. Now she was tired, she had a host of little tubes and packets and ampoules of medicine; once a day she would set them out on the kitchen table, and she and Chryssa would pore over the directions, wondering which of them did more harm than good. One cause of her tiredness was clear to Chryssa: it was her father. He never tired, but his endless activity and fret would, if it went on, wear her mother out.

'And there was the hotel he was going to open, and the holiday beach, and the factory for ballpoint pens,' her mother told her. 'Ach, ach, my child, how far in debt we are!' And however little Chryssa wanted, in this rest of calm, to hear of old troubles, her mother would go on, one tangled calamity leading to another.

'He *must* take his pension!' Chryssa insisted.

'He won't do it, Chryssa. He'll never retire.'

'Ach, mum, he has to sometime.'

As a kind of quiet homework, Chryssa resumed the task she had begun before of trying to work out her father's affairs. How did they stand? Just what must be done before he took his pension? She wondered beforehand whether she had the nerve, now, to face such a tangle. But she proceeded carefully; and she was his daughter, she had merchant blood, a head for money: and the figures, now she saw them, shocked her awake. Her long sunk acumen rose to grapple with his wild accounts; she counted and calculated, began to plan savings.

Still it was cautious work. He was grateful when, as they sat together over a mound of invoices and bills, she helped him chart clearly money owing and money due; but he did not want to confide in her more than he had to. And, with time, he grew more uneasy. She would hear him up in the night, moving round the living room where the bank books were stacked that she might have been looking at. With time also Athens called her, she knew she must return, she had been too long away.

She had a good last day, gossiping with her mother, then her father saw her to the airport. He was quiet in the taxi, but as they parted at the barrier he gave a sudden small laugh and said brightly, 'So, you're back to Athens, Chryssa, and I'm back to business!' As she receded he waved goodbye decisively, and walked away with a spring in his step. Her alarm stretched out for him, but she was borne away into the sky.

Chryssa returned to her empty flat and to empty days, but not for all that to her old despair. Without being clear just at what point things had changed for her, or why, she knew she was emerging from a trough. She felt herself once more an alert sturdy body, as her mother was; also, during her labour in her father's accounts, her sense of her own capability revived.

On her return, she did not waste time applying for jobs in institutions where she was obviously blacklisted. It had oc- curred to her in Salonica that she might turn to account her skill with language, and she now sought work as a translator. She had thought first of translating English-language plays and novels: but, she presently found, the commissions available were not in that area at all, but in technical literature, in instruction manuals for tractors and fridges. As best she could, with a technical dictionary beside her, she squeezed into Greek the obscure lists of parts and instructions for repairs, hoping the imported tractors would be strong enough to survive any mistakes she made. She also found work translating Greek into English, labelling halva and tinned dolmas for export. At a different angle from her father, she was entering business.

The absorption in her father's business affairs had a further result. Oppressed by his tangles, she had wondered how Greece ever could change when everything here was business deals and money grabbing and money under the counter. Then in Athens it struck her, if everything was business, would the

Junta do business with her? As soon as she had this idea, she saw all the stonewalling of the officials, when she went to pester them, in a different light. It was not that they would *never* allow her to see Vangelis: probably they would let her see him in the end, but before they did so they would see what they could get out of her. Hot tears of indignation stood in her eyes when she realized that all the prevarication might be, for them, a way of haggling and trading. But it was better to face mean traders than to be, where she had come to think she was, in a senseless malignant Kafka-world where she would be shunted for ever from official to official, and never would trace Vangelis. Of course they would ask for more than she could give; but she was a merchant's daughter, a bargainer, she should manage something.

The Captain of Police brightened as this more practical Chryssa stepped into his office. In response to her enquiries he stalled as usual; but when he found she no longer pressed him with earnest legalities, his eyes grew slightly smaller, his voice a little warmed, and he said, 'Believe me, Mrs Tzavella, I should like to help. I ask you, why should we Greeks be always at odds, always at each other's throats? We should all work together for the good of the Fatherland! Can't we help each other?'

'There's no help I can give,' Chryssa said.

'Mrs Tzavella, you're too modest. You could make a contribution.'

He paused, and looked at her questioningly. She looked back at him with level hard eyes, cold eyes, stone eyes: he felt a tingle of pique and thrill.

'There are ways you could help – there are things we'd like to know, just to get our records straight. It wouldn't hurt anyone. And certainly, Mrs Tzavella, it wouldn't hurt your husband.' He gave her a gleaming look of emphasis. 'For instance, I feel I know very little about you, Mrs Tzavella. I know where you live, but I don't know your "circle". I'd like to know what people you see.'

'There's no mystery about that,' Chryssa said; she mentioned several names she knew the Captain would know of already.

'Mrs Tzavella,' he moaned, with a screwed-up face of pain, 'let's leave the obvious. We're not talking about the people you go to the bouzouki with.'

176

He persisted, and it became clearer to Chryssa that he was pressing for further information about the members of the resistance group Vangelis had belonged to. His voice was urgent but agreeable, and a quirk of smile hovered at the corner of his mouth, telling her that if she gave this information she would see Vangelis soon.

'I'm sorry, I never knew those people,' she said, truly enough. She saw he didn't believe her. 'Anyway, I've been out of touch with everyone since my husband was arrested.'

'Mrs Tzavella,' he cried, wincing as if he were hurt in body and soul by the disappointment she gave him, 'What do you take us for?'

He pressed, she still denied, realizing as she did so that this negotiation must be futile, because she had altogether underestimated the extent of his suspicion. The Junta mistrusted everyone who was not a friend: she saw it was not possible for him to believe that she was not involved in a plot.

Their discussion collapsed, and they parted curtly. Yet she continued her visits; and they didn't now rebuff her as harshly as they used to. Even so, the weeks were passing, and a winter of sleet and snow arrived. She ignored the winter, she lived from appointment to appointment, and finally she was sent on by the Captain to see 'The General'. This, now, was progress: she began to have hopes.

She told herself, I must dress for the part. She had got into a way of wearing whatever old clothes she had on when she went to see them, and she knew now this was bad tactics. She must wear confidence, and be attractive too, and impress them while she asked their help. She tested colours in front of a mirror till, seeing how long she was taking, she thought, how grotesque, dressing up like this for Vangelis' gaolers. But it was necessary for the bargaining that when they saw her they should have a shine of interest in her.

Of the colours, she chose black: black was smart and black was serious; also it would remind them of the widow, whom they shouldn't abuse; and also black suited her – with her dark hair and dark eyes, she glowed in black. But, jewellery for the General? Obviously not, the General shouldn't think she had dressed for his benefit. So, in a black top and a black skirt with glints of white, she surveyed herself. The black was good, it showed her figure, her waist, and it showed that she meant business: as she turned different angles in the mirror, she breathed in, eased her shoulders, took again the taut-sprung stance she used to have. She studied her face: her eyes were lustrous from sleeplessness plus make-up, there was light in her skin from her stay in Salonica. Not bad, she thought: she had forgotten she was attractive, she must remember it, for strength, when they harassed her.

The General, for his part, seemed dressed for a royal inspection. His uniform was hard and smooth as a breastplate; brand-new snippets of coloured cloth were stitched in lines on his chest; the stars on his shoulders and lapels glistened like a clear sky. She thought he must be the Junta's shop window: as if it were their main aim to show that military government had more smartness and chic than any woman.

'Mrs Tzavella? Be seated, please. How may I help you?'

'I have applied to see my husband –' she began. 'Right!' he said, cutting her short, making it clear he had no time for long performances. He looked at her keenly, with his brown eyes that had brownish whites that looked quite dry, then said abruptly, 'Mrs Tzavella, I understand you know foreign journalists.'

Her heart thudded: she was taken off guard, and his dry eyes, in his dry face of supple leather, recorded her alarm.

'For instance, there is this Englishman, a friend from the old days, I believe?'

Snatching for *sang-froid*, she pressed on to the main matter. 'Mr General, it is six months since I first asked to see my husband –' Again he interrupted her, 'I try to keep up with the foreign press, Mrs Tzavella. But what I read often pains me. We do not get justice. There is much propaganda.' His voice rose, 'You know, it would not hurt for affairs in our country to be reported *accurately*. Bombings, strikes, resistance – our troubles, they report. But we have our achievements also, and who reports them? We deserve a hearing!' He rapped the desk top, finishing firmly.

She nodded, businesslike. 'You would like reports in the foreign press giving credit to the National Government . . .'

'*Exactly*, Mrs Tzavella. If your friend, and his friends, were to report not slanders, but some of the *facts* about Greece today . . .' He hesitated to say what reward he would give, but she pressed him, 'If he did this, Mr General, then . . .'

The dry eyes studied her. She saw he was wondering, *Did she mean business?* – and she realized that though he had ventured this proposition, he was not optimistic. But he said with energy, 'If we were fairly reported, if there were *just* reports . . . Well, I'll tell you something, Mrs Tzavella. Your husband's sentence is what? – sixteen years? Puh! Three years, Mrs Tzavella! Three years, and he'd be home.'

She started, shaken to the centre: she had supposed she was bargaining to see Vangelis, she had not guessed they might offer to release him. Could she believe it? The General sat now smiling like a sated cat.

Making her voice cool, she asked, 'How can I be sure of that?'

'Mrs Tzavella, you can trust me!' He sat at his desk with pride, his stars shone, all his insignia asserted themselves. Now she understood why they had sent her to a general: the word of a general she would not doubt, nothing need be written down.

She sat enigmatic, allowing herself to enjoy the General's suspense: at this moment, she had power over them. She had supposed that in their truculence the Junta cared not an atom for what the world's press said, and she saw now that it wasn't so: they also were politicians, and they had any politician's anxiety – or greed – for a friend in the newsrooms. She saw she could get better terms still: if she could promise to give them, through Michael, the reports they wanted, she could have Vangelis back not in three years but in three months. And at the same time she knew that this deal also she must reject completely: nothing could be salvaged from it: any ghost of such a report, put out by Michael, would destroy in a day all of their work. She knew also that she would now have to wait even longer to see Vangelis, because she had disappointed them, and because she had made a general jump through her hoop.

'I can't do anything like that,' she said decisively.

'Good morning,' he said, shortly but not rudely; he was not surprised, and he had his self-respect. She left.

So, in the dead of winter, she thought she had come to the end of her hopes. But she didn't give up; and on a further visit to the Captain she found that they might still do business. But the terms they were offering now were poor. The Captain was annoyed with her, as chilly as the snow outside.

'Mrs Tzavella, you have family in Salonica. Why don't you go and stay in the north, up in the mountains. You need a break. Go and stay there for a year or two.'

'You want me out of Athens? For how long?'

'For three years at least.'

'Three years!'

'Don't you understand me, Mrs Tzavella? I said for three years.'

'This is crazy. How am I going to live, up in the mountains? Let me stay here, I give you my word I won't be involved in any "activity".'

'Mrs Tzavella, you're wasting my time.' Behind his desk, he swivelled from her.

Sitting in the chill office, she saw there could be no profit for her in trying to do business with them. That had been obvious from the start, only mad hope had let her think otherwise. She had only made things worse: sooner or later they would have let her see Vangelis, but now, because she had tried to haggle, they were going to make sure they got something out of her, even if it were only her absence in exile. She couldn't flatter herself they really cared whether she stayed in Athens.

The room was white-ceilinged, and lit bright by the snow outside: the still figure of the Captain was distinct. She looked at this green decorated bulk of man, who sat so primly in his show of indifference; at the cropped fur on his box-shaped head; at the shiny plastic-looking skin where he'd shaved himself close; and all she saw infuriated her. She said, 'Look, what is all this, are we in a bazaar? If I go north, I can see my husband. If I give you names, I can see my husband. If I become your press officer, my husband will go free. I want to see my husband, but you're asking for things you know I can't give. So I know a journalist. Do you think I've such influence on the world press that I can give the Junta a clean bill of health? You want information. But what information have I got? I'm completely out of touch. Yes it's true, I could go and live on the edge of Albania for three years: but I'd starve there, and what would it achieve? I'm not a political figure. How can you afford to spend all this time, simply not telling me where my husband is? Ask me to do something I can do, and I will.

You don't want me to join a resistance group? All right, I won't. You don't want me to send information against you abroad? All right, I won't do that either. I'm not doing those things anyway. That's all I can offer. Now tell me, where is my husband?'

He sat pulling his cheeks as she spoke. She thought, they won't stand for this, it'll be the women's prison now. But at the end he simply said, 'Oh, don't you know where your husband is?' and mentioned the name of an island.

She couldn't believe it: that suddenly, just like that, she knew Vangelis' prison.

'How do I know he's there? You've told me he's in various places.'

'He's there, he's there,' the Captain said offhand.

Strike while the iron is hot, she thought: she took a breath. 'I want to see him.'

He gave his largest shrug, 'Ach, Mrs Tzavella, that's quite another story.'

'Oh please God, not another round of it all,' she murmured in a convulsion of sob; and, for the first time, she implored, 'Please let me see him.'

Over the wide plain of desk, his chin on his cupped hands, he inspected her appeal; and glanced at his watch.

'You made some remark on the way we spend our time. Well, Mrs Tzavella, I've no more time today. Corporal!'

The door opened, she got up: she saw that the Captain felt high in virtue, nobly generous, he would give her no more on this visit. In due course he would give her a pass to see Vangelis.

She emerged from the office into frozen streets; the police guard at the doorway shivered and hugged himself. Yet she felt warm, she felt like spring: for the unbelievable had happened. In that vast concrete wall she had made a crack: and through that crack she saw Vangelis.

From the distant edge of cloud a yellow shaft of sun lit a tank bright khaki. Reflected in the wet road, it looked weightless, like a strange snub barge resting on the still skin of water. She walked past it smiling, and people stared at her: she smiled like a person who had found a blessing in this shortest, coldest day.

5

Vangelis' eyes flapped open, he lay panting in darkness that pulsed. The dream. The worst thing in it was his own wish come true. He must think of other things fast.

The nights were his worst time. The warders, the other prisoners, the building itself: all these he was used to, they were solid to him now, yet they counted for nothing when he lay down to sleep. In the night he was in another prison, and he knew it was the true prison, its catacombs ran underground everywhere. They took him to different cellars on different nights, but these changes made no real difference, just as again it made no difference if on some nights he had gone back in time to before his trial, and knew that the trial would not come, but only interrogation would go on for ever; while on other nights his trial was behind him, but they had new information, so they brought him to a new worse round of interrogations. In the dream he accepted these changes, just as he accepted that pig face and dark glasses had started to look like different people. In the first dreams they had always been themselves, but now for instance dark glasses might come with no glasses on and a thin face, and at once Vangelis knew him: he was an old shadow-eyed judge of the law courts with whom he had once had bad dealings. Pig face, another time, wore a tin hat, he was a soldier from the war, bivouacked in their village, who had terrified Vangelis as a child: here he was again, he had not aged at all, just so he could catch Vangelis and come at him now. Even he himself had begun to change: in some dreams he was outside himself, watching Vangelis, and the man he saw was the old Vangelis, dark-skinned, jet-haired, with small black eyes that glanced and darted, moustaches like black wings. But another time the Vangelis before him was a haggard, bony, dagger-faced man, years older, and he said at once 'prison's done this to me'. His face melted and changed as he watched, he realized he was a different prisoner again from the man he had thought he was.

Also, with time, the tortures changed: at first he was again tortured in the penis, or smashed on the soles of the feet. But now he might be asked to put on, of all things, a pair of winter gloves: he watched his broad, big-fingered hands disappear in the fur. The gloves looked soft and pleasant, but inside them were metal devices that started to close, and he saw when he looked close that they were animals consuming him. Another time a door was opened, he was to be shown the instruments, and inside the obscure cupboard-sized room there were just three things, an old lectern, a sack, and a large old iron clock. These objects were obviously nothing but lumber, yet there was something in the way they waited, in the small room that was swept quite bare, that filled him, in his dream, with paralysing terror.

But what most scared him, as he lay awake, after dreaming, in the long hours of dawn, was the fact that he himself was producing these nightmares. He wanted to forget, to get his suffering behind him: and instead, with these dreams, he was digging the groove deeper.

The faint light seeping into his cell reminded him also how cold he was: he had woken sweating but he froze now, in spite of the blanket huddled round him. He crossed to the window, but all he could see outside, far below, was a dim boiling of foam. The water between the grey-white scuds looked black as pitch and freezing cold; he returned to his mattress, and tried to hug himself warmer.

He must get his thinking onto a fresh track. He tried to conjure up his new friends: the surgeon, Stamatis, who had given him a cigarette when he first arrived; the agriculturalist Christoforos, stooped, sardonic, jesting, like Karagiozis in the puppet-play; the student Andreas who had been his client. But they would not come, and he realized now why they seemed so remote: it was because, even when he was with them, he was absent, not listening. He hadn't in the past been an absent-minded man: on the contrary, in the old days, he didn't feel he was properly awake if he wasn't attending keenly to what happened in front of him. But now he could not attend, it was like a physical incapacity, his thoughts were abstracted all the time in recollections and bitterness, weaving day nightmares out of his torture.

So he came back to his dream of tonight, just the effort to sink it made it surface more strongly: one cannot look at a nightmare and kill it. And it had seemed at the start different from his other dreams, and not a nightmare but the opposite: for he was in a large garden walking down a path with pig face. They didn't speak, but they were not at war. The path sank into a deepening gully, the bushes grew taller and closer: then, while they turned a corner, pig face slightly tripped and his head sank into a thorn bush, and he rose exclaiming anxiously with his hands over his face, 'Are my eyes all right?' but Vangelis could see his eyes weren't all right, for studying them and wanting to comfort, he saw the yellow jelly standing in columns from the punctured eyeballs.

As soon as he woke, he thought: this is my wish, this is what I want for them. He recoiled from the wish, but he knew it was there, it was generated in him by the torture itself, it was born of the pain that did not stop, and of the eagerness and thrill with which they hurt him, of their excitement which he watched, helpless. That was when the infection caught him. His priorities were changed; he still prayed for the Junta to fall, but above all he wanted them to suffer. He knew now that though people say revenge is futile, to the man who has been hurt beyond a certain point revenge is something that he needs: it satisfies and fills the veins, it is something he must have to get his own life clear.

He kept these feelings secret from his friends, for they cast him as the man of justice, and revenge ran counter to all they believed. They must not use the methods of the Junta, or feel the emotions the Junta felt. But the only result of burying his feelings was that they hardened inside him till he felt he carried solid boulders in his chest. 'No, they must suffer,' he said curtly to himself, sentencing them privately; then his throat hurt as if the skin cracked, and abruptly he remembered his father – his round glasses hung crooked, his learned face was deformed with rage that harped on endless as if all the killing and maiming and pain, which he saw in the Civil War, had got now inside him.

When he saw his own rage as his father's rage, he saw it as his fate: there was no escape, he swam in black blood. The old Vangelis, the advocate of Athens, the Vangelis that Chryssa knew – that man of briskness, zest, assurance – he was dead, gone, he twanged his rhetoric where the angels sang. Even from Chryssa he felt cut off. Occasionally, in good dreams, she was close beside him, they embraced; but in the sterile daytime she was far removed, in a world he couldn't go back to. His memory was closing. If only he could see her – but he knew, she wouldn't be allowed to visit him here.

6

Michael was glad of the need to put all of his energies into his Greek reports. With Vangelis and Chryssa he had felt the pull of his young, disconsolate, serious self. Since those days he had slipped far in the headlong hopping and racing of the news world, grabbing temporary stories and throwing them to others who threw them to the public who threw them away, while he jockeyed to keep up in the crowded fast lane of competitive careering. Now these anxieties died, for he was engrossed in the task. It must come from his youth, the energy he found now. It seemed to him that he had only *thought* he enjoyed his news service spinning, really he was tired of it, jaded, he needed the change.

He worked fast. From the London office of the news service he dispatched down wires threading England and the world all the news about the dictatorship he had. He translated Vangelis' speeches and essays, and began to get them published in England and America. He himself wrote reports and features, and took all the advice and help he could get as to placing them. He relied partly on a saturation attack: the particular stories might be butchered or dropped, as they fought their way through sub-editors' hands; but he knew the value of persistence, and any story that did not appear he pressed on other hands till at last, somewhere, it was taken. He knew too that there was room for stories, for in these hard times the newsrooms of the nationals did not hum as they used to. He made his way through a half-acre office, low-ceilinged, open-plan, crisscrossed with half-height partitions: and the huge room was not crowded and racketing, but half empty and quiet. The staff did not rush in with new scoops, but frowned as they sifted other papers and teletype, looking for items that would fill the space. He was able to place his consecutive articles about Vangelis. Who read these reports Michael did not know, they were missiles fired into darkness: but still he had an optimism that kept his energy hot. The twentieth century was the age of news: the nations of the world had drawn very close, the walls between them were glass walls now, and the best work of people like himself was precisely to make people in one country give interest, sympathy, imagination to what went on elsewhere. Dictatorships had lost the privacy and secrecy they needed for their work, especially in Europe, where the countries leaned over each other's fences, looking in. And with Greece above all this was so – Greece, the nest of democracy and civilization, all the Western world watched what happened in Greece.

He had this work so constantly in mind now that it was hard in retrospect to believe he had stayed these last weeks in England. His attention was abroad. Casting for words, he would pause by the draughty window; red buses stood high in the droning advance of patient traffic. Yet he felt he had only to turn where he stood, and he would see parched sunlit mountainsides, writhed trunks of olive trees, yellow buses in squealing streets by voluble cafés; and tanks, soldiers, prisons. Above all, the image of Vangelis in prison possessed him. Vangelis now *was* obstinate freedom, shut up. And he was outside, striving to help Vangelis; also, in imagination, he was inside with him, working to push back walls. His senses in England were dominated by this, as if, while he walked in the free country, a magnified cell was around them all; almost he saw in the clouds, on the hills, through the sunk city, and in the night, a gigantic Vangelis cramped in a cell as big as the world.

Writing with passion, Michael feared for the consequences of some things he said. Yet these pieces were published easily enough: he could not complain that they were suppressed, or that anyone gagged him. Confidently he awaited reaction, correspondence at least; it took him time to realize he had no effect at all. More cruelty and injustice in the Colonels' Greece? Bravery, endurance and freedom still penned, kicked and trampled on? There was nothing new in that: it happened in many countries, all the time. Yes, it was bad, but what could one do? At least it was different at home. The Junta, he saw, didn't need to worry. Let their critics fuss, the storm would die, it made no difference. So the nations had glass walls, wrongdoing could be seen: it was observed with sorrow and allowed to continue.

How much the world cared he could easily gauge, for later that autumn he was often abroad, recommending the advantages of the news service to editors in other capitals. He was kept so mobile in these days that he was sometimes confused as to which city he was in, or which city he was remembering. The cities had similar municipal buildings, and especially, everywhere, they had the same shops: and shops are where the people go. It might just be travel blurring, but he felt that differences were disappearing, the cities of Europe were converging, growing into one city. Always in the middle was a broad slow river, sluggish, brown, like the painful fluid drag of history, one broad stream of trouble, dancing lights on its surface and cold underneath. On the banks of this river were empty balustrades, where the past had promenaded and the traffic now dashed, and beyond the embankments were always small streets, and grim closed buildings with flaking ornaments, pilasters, cornices, pediments on the windows, as though all the cities were engaged in acting out in a gloomy show of grandeur a memory of ancient Greece, so they all seemed long-lost children of Athens, adrift on their rivers: only Athens itself, riverless, stood still in the sun.

In these cities, this city, the image of Greek freedom seemed as dim now as the ubiquitous Greek pediments. Speaking to journalists, editors, publishers, he realized how secure the Junta were – they need not fret while it pleased the European governments for Greece to have dictators (provided of course that as the years passed there was some glimmer of cosmetic improvement). And the governments would not change their view while NATO was pleased with the job the Colonels did: they guaranteed the eastern flank, the eastern Mediterranean, they deserved congratulation. This contentment was not confined to military strategists. He met at a London reception some well-known scientists and civil-servants, newly returned from a conference in Athens: and these distinguished men had been very courteously and properly treated, and they had observed how well actually things worked in Greece now, and they saw no misery but quite the contrary, and the President, whom they had met, was an officer of some presence and dedication, and actually a firm government was the only sort of government that worked in a place like the Balkans – it had always been so, as it was so also in Latin America and

Africa and Asia and indeed in many parts of the world.

So his optimism had faltered: but he did not stop, and as he continued with his stop-go foreign travelling it became clear that he could not have the satisfaction of a clear pessimism either. For there began to be a political response to the general tide of criticism of the Colonels: European hearings, formal condemnations, restrictions on trade. Such measures would not dispose of the Colonels, but they were more than Michael had expected to see. The Junta released certain prisoners, and it seemed they made some change in their civil practices. It became clear that his big mistake had been in supposing that his individual effort could have some consequence that he could perceive. His effort could not count like that, but still it mattered because, in an invisible way, it augmented and swelled that force of opposition, which had proved to be so much gentler than he'd hoped, but which still was a power.

Then a crisis at the newspaper, of which the news service was a limb, took all his thought. Tasks were reorganized, he had to go to New York: he found himself recommending the service to executives in stetsons who had in their pockets whole chains of papers in Dallas and Nevada. He hadn't at all their executive style, but they weren't interested in that, only in the service, and he was practised now in making the case for it. He was busy adjusting, and simply busy, and on the Greek notes he'd brought with him dust gathered in his hotel room.

He emerged from his room one evening near Christmas: he had been so absorbed in European news all day that he had forgotten how far from Europe he was. He gazed at the world he had returned to: across the road a line of skyscrapers receded, identical plain blocks, darkly shiny, not like human buildings; at the base of them the crowd streamed while from cracks in the tarmac, from gratings and manhole covers, from a ship's funnel sunk direct in the street, steam gushed under pressure in clouds the wind tore. The siren of some ambulance or police car nearby made a weird high plastic-metal howling like something in pain yet like nothing alive. In the interval of orientation he felt he stepped to another planet, he could nowhere be further from the Mediterranean.

But he continued walking, towards the Rockerfeller Centre,

and looked down into the white lighted pit where the skaters spun and threaded. Continuing, he thought he heard a Spanish voice; then an Italian voice; then really he was hearing Greek voices. 'Coulouria for sale!' Street sellers shouted, Greek families promenaded, chatting contentedly, as if on the sea front. It seemed all the Mediterranean communities of New York gathered here at holidays to meet and stroll; he sauntered among them, dissolved in a happy nostalgia for Greece.

Quite distinctly he heard her – perhaps only two words, but he knew Chryssa's voice, a low voice, many toned, lively. She was here. But doing what? – seeing relatives? – seeking help for Vangelis? He looked round eagerly, and through the crowd he glimpsed her – her clear-boned face that was elegantly square, her gleaming eyes, as she cheerfully turned. Then she was cut off by a movement of the crowd, and when he saw her again she had changed: the woman still wore a coat like Chryssa's, of fur-trimmed suede, but seen from close to she had a round face, a high Armenian nose, and a too clanging voice. He was confused: had he been mistaken? He moved faster through the crowd, urging inwardly, Let it not be a daydream, let Chryssa be here. But he did not find her and with pain he admitted: he had not seen her, it was a slip of the eye. Then he realized the Chryssa he had seen was not Chryssa as she was – as he had seen her in the summer – frozen, disillusioned, hollowed out by loss. It was the old Chryssa he had glimpsed, Chryssa before Vangelis was taken. He had seen a ghost. This thought wrenched his heart, he walked quickly away from the Mediterranean.

He returned to his hotel unsteadily; with time he felt only more shaken by this odd non-meeting. He knew now what it was that had troubled him so when he visited her in the summer: it was the thought that in her suffering Chryssa had lost not only Vangelis, she had lost a part of her former self. He remembered how she used to be, she had a special bright zest, a freshness from childhood, even her own character seemed something she performed, amused, pleased, while her spirit danced outside herself enjoying the self she played. That quality had gone. Perhaps always her life had a black possibility, a gift for despair as great as her excitement. Still she had a strength, he met in her desolation something concentrated, hard, a strength at her roots, a bitter strength, biting;

it almost scared him as it moved him. But her bright self was gone, as if part of her soul had been ripped out. Since then he had kept her out of his daylight thoughts. But with the sight of this spectre of Chryssa, he saw something further he had hidden till now: that it was Chryssa he cared for, more than Vangelis.

Now he thought of Chryssa, he thought only of her, his past sightings crowded his thought: they all came at once, a large bright family of her selves. He remembered her being Dr Zhivago, Julie Christie and Garbo by turns, in someone else's swaggering fur coat; he saw her braced mobile stance turning this way and that as she argued politics with several people at once, and kept them all at bay. He saw her serious, insisting face, arguing with him about *King Lear*, till it occurred to him that Greece was more like old England than modern England was. To him Chryssa was Greece, he remembered her showing off the statues of the kouroi, with a bright wide-eyed smile like theirs, plus the yellow light in her eyes that couldn't be in stone eyes. And he remembered, years ago, her eyes darting to greet him as she sped past on her bike, flushed, bright-eyed, vigorous, scarf flying, hair flying, coat-tails flying, a brown southern figure riding the English north gale; and out of that whirlwind vision of speed, for a moment, her brown eyes fixed him. He admitted now the shock and thrill it was to him each time those gold-brown eyes met his eyes directly. He remembered her seizing his hand once, when they went out walking in England.

What was he discovering? – that here was the slow-on-the-uptake man, waking after years to the fact that he loved Chryssa? Were these his motives: my friend's in gaol, so I fall for his wife? He didn't know if this was love, infatuation, a sentimental storm. He had thought his heart was seedy with newsrooms and airports, and embassy parties floated on cheap diplomats' booze: and here he was whirled on this cataracting love storm. All he could say was: I'm far enough away, she's safe, I can't betray Vangelis. And it was human, in nature, that care should turn to love. But he ached, he hurt, at the base of his lungs, all through his body, with a solid pain of love, desire.

New York itself had a new aspect: bright, pleasant, surreal. Under a Renaissance palazzo made twenty storeys high, he watched an elegant space car, with fins like folded wings, materialize as if by a miracle out of a dazzling globe of steam. As he warmed his hands at a chestnut seller's brazier, watching Central Park in the clear winter light, it came home to him that these solitary, dislocated days, where he was caught by surprise by Chryssa, and in the freedom of distance wandered happily alone with her, were the good moments his life contained: the rest could be forgotten.

After several days, and a new burst of appointments, he ceased from thinking each moment of Chryssa. Gradually, sad now, the lovestorm retreated behind some large hill of his landscape – would it rise again in lightning and danger to seize him? Now his life was hectic, and his official work was remote from the Junta. Late at night he revived his writing on Vangelis and Greece. But he needed more information: he needed really to do more work in Greece, if he wanted to help. But when could he go there – and what was true help now? What would the good friend do?

7

Leonidas did wonder at first, when he started at the Ministry,
whether the work he was given was altogether worthy of him.
For he had taken office to fight communism and save the
nation, and he expected to begin at once on the reform of
Greek industry. Instead he found himself wading through old
regulations and other people's memoranda; and the particular
tasks he was given were small things. He had to reconsider the
dates of national holidays: could any days be scrapped? –
should new holidays be introduced, to celebrate the advent
and the achievements of the National Government? He was
then asked to consider the institution of the siesta: should it
be abandoned, so people worked one shift instead of two each
day, and Athens had only two rush hours instead of four? The
more he worked on this proposal, the more important it seemed
to him: it would be such an economy in man hours and fuel.
And he had dropped his own siesta, why shouldn't everyone?
He worked hard on this project; and in the meantime he was
given responsibility for vetting new trades union officials.
Now, he felt, his skill would tell.

True, it was at first an embarrassment to him that he had
no great expertise in political science. Indeed, though a man
of political passion, he had for some time scarcely turned the
page of a political book, other than the odd memoir. So he
turned again to that library of books on political and economic
theory which he had recently bought, and which he had now
had bound in black leather with his own name embossed in
gold on the spine. The Ministry kept him so busy, however,
that he found that in practice he hardly had time to do more
than turn the flyleaf of a volume; and then he realized with
relief that it was not actually necessary to read the books, since
in reality the job of running the country was a quite different
matter from issues of theory. It was a practical job and he was
a practical man. And a change began in his political views,

whereby arguments as to whether Greece needed a National Government or democracy no longer seemed the vital issue. There simply was the country to be governed: they were the people appointed to govern, they must just get on with the work.

He was indefatigable, he worked all the time; and yet his relations with the Minister did not grow cordial. The Minister did not seem pleased that Leonidas worked so hard; there was an edge to his thank-yous, and he rolled a wild eye when Leonidas handed in yet a further report. So Leonidas slowed down a little, and yet even so, however hard he laughed at the Minister's jokes, and however much he complimented him on his speeches, still the bright bead eyes of the Minister looked at him askance, without complete trust.

Leonidas was hurt by this, for he liked to be liked; he became irritated also with the constant necessity of agreeing with the Minister, when, as he found increasingly, his own ideas were quite the contrary. On the subject of trades unions they were repeatedly at odds. The Minister believed it was the purpose of the National Government to do away with trades unions in any form and anything less would be a betrayal, though he admitted that this action must be taken by stages. But Leonidas took a different view, arguing that there must be strong trades unions, with real control over their members, and all that was needed was firm government supervision of union appointments, so that only true patriots, and men with the national interest at heart, were appointed presidents of trades unions. In practice they did not differ so greatly, since the Minister agreed that in these early years trades unions did still need to have presidents and general secretaries; yet still they fell out on the nominations, for it seemed that the Minister could appreciate the merits only of men so senior in industry that they were going to retire in a year or two, while it was as clear as day to Leonidas that what they needed were young men in their forties like himself, men of experience who still had some fire and activity left in them.

When the Council of the Union of Textile Workers forwarded two names for president, the Minister held the paper taut and crackling in his nervous hands.

'Of course it must be Vassios!' He stared hard at Leonidas, braving his disagreement.

'Of course, Vassios,' Leonidas said with emphasis, seeing he had no option. The Minister continued to stare at him, not quite believing it, not altogether pleased.

Leonidas sat back, inhaling smoke thoughtfully, scratching the silver-socked ankle that rested on his knee. Since the Minister, delaying, gave him a chance, he said, 'Of course, the other man – what's his name – Demetriadis, he's not so bad. He's a man of principle; and he'd have a longer run ahead of him.'

'He's a boy!' the Minister snapped. Leonidas saw he would insist, so he shrugged gracefully and let it go. But he blazed inside as this 'boy' of fifty – a vigorous, dancing, hunting man, who could turn a factory round his finger – sank from sight. Leonidas saw what a handicap to him, in the eyes of the Minister, his own youth must be: it was only because the job of a secretary was the job of a servant that the Minister allowed him in.

'I must get back to my office,' Leonidas said drily, and slid from the room, while the Minister crouched at his leather-topped desk, a spider of a man, staring after him with tight eyes of misgiving.

Back in his own office, Leonidas quietly raged. And such frustrations multiplied, as he found his feet in the Ministry, and came to be sure of what he wanted to do there – what he wanted to do, and couldn't.

So presently, in what was still a short period since his accession to power, Leonidas took stock again. For the thought was coming clearer in his mind, like a dawn light growing to day, that if there were one man who could take that Ministry over and give it direction and achievement, that man was himself. This idea he insinuated into the air, let it crackle quietly in the static electricity of the department, so it might crop up in anyone's mind, who happened to be thinking over present troubles and likely remedies for them. It was becoming known – Leonidas could not gainsay it – that in many ways the Minister made the Ministry's work harder, he did not fully appreciate the needs of the present. Leonidas laboured still to please the Minister, and would be defending him loudly when he came into the room; but still he tried now to please other ministers also. He prepared quietly and waited, biding his chance.

The Minister, perhaps unwisely, had given certain powers into Leonidas' hands. For he was not easy in social situations, and was at first grateful when Leonidas offered to represent the Ministry at receptions and businessmen's parties in Athens. Later, he was as uneasy away from these gatherings as he would have been at them, but by then the practice of asking Leonidas and Mrs Patra had become established. And Leonidas improved each such occasion. The particular proof that he was gaining ground in important eyes came when he was invited to a special party that was to be given on the island of a shipowner: at this party, he was advised, there would also be a meeting of a discreet group of officers and officials who had a particular concern with foreign policy. Both the Minister and Leonidas sympathized with this group, to which also Leonidas's cousin Kostas was attached; and it was Leonidas, not the Minister, they wanted at this meeting. In the Ministry, in the following days, Leonidas had a smile quiet and deep: this could be the crucial meeting of his life.

They prepared elaborately. Patra shopped, and brought back shimmering dresses for all occasions. Inspired by her example, Leonidas took a taxi into Athens and on his own initiative bought a set of shirts – shirts suited to his distinction, shirts covered with gold lozenges, spotted like ermine, striped like a tiger, all manner of shirts, and ties to match, which Patra, with a glance, peremptorily sent back. She replaced his set with others which he, the Secretary to the Minister, accepted in ill-willed silence, in dour and dignified misgiving.

The day came. Spruce in their light white travelling clothes, their new bags packed, they bade farewell to Alexis.

'Goodbye mother,' he muttered, enduring her kiss.

'Goodbye, Alexi,' Leonidas called – and his son ignored him, he sullenly looked at the paper.

'Alexi!' Leonidas started to shout, through all his elegance fury burst, but Patra caught his arm at one.

'Leonida, we must go!'

She hurried him clear; and so, hot, hurt, flustered, in sudden ill humour, they left. But reclining in the taxi, as their home fell quickly away behind them, they relaxed into the glow of anticipation.

★

They were flown out by seaplane. They turned once over the tiny green island, and saw the streamlined knife shapes of several large yachts anchored nearby; then they landed in a fan of spray, and waited rocking on the glassy sea.

At once there was activity ashore, and a company launch hurried towards them. White uniformed men stood up in the boat, like sailors attending the arrival of an admiral. The launch collected them and, slapping and jolting on the hard sea, raced for the harbour as though it raced for life. Leonidas and Patra held hands, and gazed at the island in exhilaration.

They wheeled into the harbour and docked, seeming now, for all their sailors to attention, modest among the tiered pleasure boats that slightly swayed there. Beside them was a boat built up in three storeys: the plush cabin on its lower deck had French windows at the rear, like a penthouse apartment set down on the sea, and that apartment all bar; on a deck above an estate car was parked; on all the decks were potted palms; and bristling on the mast were antennae and aerials and radar bowls slowly circling, and a silver battery of hooters and klaxons to squawk lesser vessels from its path.

Leonidas gazed at the unseaworthy vessel, 'Ach, Patra, *that* is a pleasure boat!'

As he spoke, the ship-to-shore loudhailer of that boat crackled, 'Which top is it you want, woman? There are twenty here.' From the terrace overhead a soprano voice hallooed a long reply; the loudhailer crackled with muttering static, and switched off.

From the quay they faced a gentle climb upwards from terrace to terrace, between palms and shrubs, and walls dripping with bougainvillaea; but even this mild exertion proved unnecessary. One of the sailors, chatting deferentially, led them round the harbour, and into a cave filled with gentle light and cool air; at the end of the short tunnel was a lift shaft. As they whisked upwards, Leonidas sighed for the lift he had failed to build on his own cliff, and looked at Patra with wolfish eyes, as if to say, 'See, you narrow-gut, how the rich really live.'

From the lift they stepped into a marble-floored lounge, like the lobby of an Athens hotel without the kiosks. A stout balding shining steward, who might have been the keeper of a Turkish seraglio, unctiously showed them where their cabins were, and then led them across the terrace, over a lawn kept emerald by perpetual sprinklers, between bikinis and flowing dresses, to the thickening party beside the pool where, from the centre of pulsing, laughing silks, a plump brown arm shot up like a periscope and a robust voice called out, 'Hello Mr Secretary! Hello, Mrs Patra! Welcome, welcome, wonderful to see you!' The silks peeled back like the petals of a luscious flower, and from the centre their host, Polikarpos Polikarpou, manager of the shipping line, strode to greet them, and gave a hug to Leonidas, whom he hardly knew, and a warm kiss to Patra, whom he'd never met.

'Great that you came! The Government is welcome here!' he cried; and walking between them, shorter than either but embracing them both, he took them the rounds. Politicians and millionaires, with slack bellies, in bathing trunks, were momentarily before them, and were dropped as soon as introduced. He pulled down delicate blooms for Patra to sniff, and himself gave her a nosegay of orchids. He showed Leonidas the glowing radio room, and pointed out to him the booster station, with its giant aerial like a giant ear, on top of a nearby mountain on the mainland, that relayed his messages to the ends of the earth.

Leonidas was silent, this was his heaven; and yet it gradually came clear to them that though they were meeting here business, politics and films, and Germany and America as well as Greece, they somehow were not meeting any members of the family who owned the shipping line, and the island too. Patra asked Polikarpos where they were. For the first time his good humour failed, he made a face, 'Uh! Them! I wouldn't bother with them, Mrs Patra! They stay on their yacht all the time, they haven't been here since I did the place up. Look at them!' He pointed out to sea, where a long white ship basked like a floating sword, too far away for a soul to be seen. His face contracted, 'What people! Stingy! You've no idea. Steer clear of them.' Displeased, he led them in another direction, announcing that it had cost him twelve million drachmas to redecorate the island; while Patra and Leonidas cast long looks out to sea, dismayed to find that their entrée after all was only to a vulgar outhouse, and that a higher-class party was taking place next door, to which they weren't invited. Even as they gazed, they saw the tiny white dot of someone else's launch arrive at that serene and distant yacht.

'It's hot here,' Polikarpos said, 'let's go below.' He led them down a long staircase, which presently gave way to steps cut in the rock itself, and they came out in a large cave with a low opening to the sea. At their feet was a pool of clear water lit by underwater lights: Leonidas watched girls swimming like plump fish through the channel to the sea and back again. Round the wall of the cave was a long curved bar: here Polikarpos fetched drinks, and they lay back in easy chairs sipping slowly and watching the light from the water dandle shimmering lines on the cave roof.

Polikarpos talked for an hour. Leonidas had shrewdly supposed that the purpose of all this hospitality, apart from their shared interest in foreign affairs, was some particular boon Polikarpos wanted from the Government on behalf of the shipping line; and in the long run this was so, but Polikarpos had no intention of coming to the point without taking every chance of recommending himself first. So he told them of the ships he bought and sold in Brazil and Switzerland and England, and of his helicopter fleet, and of the factories he owned in North Africa and Ireland, and of his expansion in passenger traffic such that the only uncertainty he suffered from at present was whether the new service he planned, which would crisscross the Mediterranean and leave it trussed like a chicken, would be hydroplane or hovercraft. Leonidas said in jest that all that remained for him was to open a transworld passenger service with vertical takeoff jets, and even this idea Polikarpos revolved in his mind like brandy in a glass before swilling it out. He spoke without end, his face shone. Patra knew the condition he was in, it was the condition that overwhelmed the Greek male when successful, it was the condition of her father when his fortunes were high, it was the condition of Leonidas when he arrived in government: Polikarpos was just drunk and inspired with swelling of ego, with ecstasy of power, he was possessed, he could not stop. Success ran through his veins like adrenalin, he could only work harder and succeed more and soar from height to height and spend and brag and shine until he burst. He stopped talking only when he had truly exhausted everything about himself he could praise; and only then he broached the business he intended with Leonidas, as to certain concessions and arrangements he hoped to see included in the provision of port facilities for the

Greek and NATO fleets. When, following this, Leonidas in his turn started to expand about the responsibilities of government, Polikarpos shifted restlessly, and, taking advantage of a pause in Leonidas' talk to get them new drinks, he remained standing, reminded them how tired they must be, and then remembered that he had an ambassador waiting upstairs. Shouting greetings to the other guests, casting waves and kisses about him, shouting welcome to Mr Secretary one further time from the cavern entrance, he departed.

Leonidas sprawled back, elated and unsnubbable, sharing the exaltation; while Patra felt the full force of the headache that had developed while Polikarpos talked. But even the headache needed only a plaintive moan to the bar, and a chalice of fresh water, and a packet of Panadol, came to her on a silver tray.

The hours at the party passed slowly and lusciously. Of the political purpose of the visit Leonidas heard not a whisper, but that would come, and in the meantime there were many activities. He was taken on a speedboat trip which passed not far from the shipowner's yacht, and had a momentary glimpse, which made a snapshot in his memory that stayed for ever, of a thin balding man who sat in a deck chair wearing simple shorts, and a fair-haired boy who leaned on a rail and chatted, or not, to a handsome dark-haired woman lounging nearby: obscure pictures of a rich life he would never reach. He realized, with chagrin, it was easier for him to become a Minister than to join them on that yacht.

In the evening there was cabaret and gambling, and more introductions. The following morning they met, with cries of surprise and pleasure, their friend Manolis, the textile industrialist, who had invited them hunting on his mountain, and introduced them to the Minister. But Manolis, though tough and macho still, was a shadow of his former self. He was taciturn, morose, and gave them no clue as to why he was so. They sat together, Leonidas doing all the talking, as he was pleased to do when Polikarpos was not there, yet it was clear that Manolis was not listening; he opened his mouth only to say with biting vehemence, while contemplating a girl at the party who danced dazzlingly, 'Women are whores.' Leonidas did not disagree, but he glanced apprehensively at Patra: she however ignored Manolis.

It was only later, when they were alone, that Manolis told Leonidas of his misfortune. It had begun with the new prosperity of his factory – for which all thanks to the National Government – but with the new money they had moved to Athens, and had entered the milieu to which by rights they belonged, and not a weekend went by which did not see them at one or another island, yacht or casino; but while this new life should have been pure pleasure and just reward, actually events took a different turn, for their new rich company had an extraordinary effect on his wife Anoula. Manolis had all his life been unfaithful to Anoula as was proper in a man, and Anoula had in the past accepted it and stayed faithful to him; but some devil of Athens had got into her now such that not only had she started being unfaithful to him, but she was unfaithful so far as he could see every weekend, on whichever island, yacht or casino they were. The change had astounded Manolis and destroyed him: his spirit was crippled, his sex had withered, he could do nothing with other women now. He didn't have balls any more but shrivelled walnuts. Leonidas listened with solemn sympathy, and several times he said with emphasis, as he nodded and pondered, 'Hm!'

And then the meretricious Anoula appeared beside the pool, not obviously contaminated but if anything more radiant than of old. She and Patra kissed, and the two of them sat on the edge of the pool gossiping. There they met a playboy, who offered to teach them water-skiing, and presently they were to be seen, the last shreds of their dignity gone, crossing the bay in splashes, tumbles, and three-point squats upon the water, while from time to time their cries and laughter wafted up to the two husbands who sat smoking slowly, watching them darkly.

Some personal consolation Leonidas later found in the company of the tall sprightly wife of a Swedish company director, a woman with eyes that flashed ice while her face flushed, with a spun wavy floss of blonde hair, with a slender rippling undulating body, and with longer legs than he had seen on a woman before. She enticed and teased him, and though she mocked him poutingly she wouldn't let him be; and he, unused to ice eyes, and unused to everything about her, he was drawn, and filled her glass as he met her look, and held his cupped hands to her cigarette as if he were raising a goblet to her lips. The director husband was not in evidence; they sauntered through the bougainvillaea, Leonidas glad at least to be assisting the increase of foreign investment in Greece, and the long-legged wife evidently glad for her part to cement the good relations between industry and government.

Manolis, left, drew little pleasure from seeing his friend prove his theory, and sat back smoking hard, watching the party with a prowling crippled fury.

It was only on the second evening, when a number of guests had gone and others had arrived, that Polikarpos drew Leonidas aside and, suggesting to Patra that they men had some night fishing to do, led Leonidas down the terraces, remarking as they strolled that they were heading for a meeting on another yacht that anchored there that evening – a meeting of patriots.

'At last,' said Leonidas.

'We'll hear the war plan,' Polikarpos murmured, for the first time himself completely serious.

They got into a small dinghy, where other men also were waiting, and to the high-pitched spitting of the outboard motor they sped out to sea, approaching indirectly the large lead-grey ghost of a great yacht.

In the timbered saloon of the yacht, a handful of men were waiting for them. Among them was Leonidas' cousin Kostas: he hurried over and shook Leonidas' hand fervently. Quietly, though there seemed no need to whisper, he said, 'Cousin Leonida, you don't know how proud I am to see you here!'

'It's good to see you, Kosta. I didn't see you on the island.'

'I have been busy,' Kostas said discreetly. Another man approached and stood inspecting Leonidas. He was lean and long-limbed, very upright, with a sparely handsome, hollow-cheeked head and close-cut hair.

Kostas introduced him: he was a Major General.

'You serve in the National Government, Mr Argiriou? It is an honour to know you.' His testing eyes fixed Leonidas', his sinewy hand held Leonidas' hand hard.

'I thank you, General,' Leonidas said, respectully and a trace uneasily: there was a severe ardour in the Major General's scrutiny.

Cigarettes were passed round, and small glasses of liqueur. The separate twos and threes of men talked intently, guardedly. Polikarpos, across the room, was as subdued and serious as the others. He was talking to a vigorous, muscular, loud-voiced man, whom Leonidas recognized as a General – General Vouros – though he wore sports trousers and a blazer here.

The Major General remarked to Leonidas, 'I understand that foreign policy is one of your interests, Mr Argiriou.'

Not to waste time, Leonidas said at once, 'I believe in the Idea.'

The Major General eyed him keenly, pleased. Leonidas went on, 'How soon the Idea can become a reality – that I don't know.'

'Oh it could be soon – it depends on you and your colleagues.'

Leonidas nodded slowly, not fully understanding and taking therefore an opaque expression. 'True, true. But still, an attack on Turkey. . . .'

'Oh, there's no problem. It could be done at any time.'

'Yes?'

The Major General seemed to inspect and enjoy his astonishment. Cryptically, as though it were a proverb, he said, 'The dawn comes to Turkey an hour before it comes to Greece.'

Leonidas wanted to know more, but the Major General was silent: he would leave the details to Kostas, who said in his cousin's ear, 'Our airforce will cross the Aegean by night. When the sun comes up, we are over Turkey, and we hit them – every airfield, every barracks, every camp, every city. And then, from the islands, we launch the land attacks.' While Kostas explained, the Major General looked at Leonidas with emphasis, as though Kostas' words were his also.

They were joined by an emaciated, raw-skinned man, evidently another officer, but in a black suit. As he listened he grinned, with overt, almost angry contempt; his upright body gave jerks of irritation every few words. Then he interrupted, 'Yes, yes, captain, we know this "plan". You don't mention the odds. The Turkish army is several times the size of ours. Of course, we say in the barracks that one Greek is equal to ten Turks, and if you take that view there's no problem, but on the other hand –'

But he was himself interrupted by the Major General, speaking loudly and distinctly so everyone in the room attended to him.

'The point of the plan is speed. We copy the Israelis in the Seven Days War. The Turk will be in confusion, his communications will be dead, he won't know what has hit him. And while that is so, we drive deep in. Of course, if the war went on for long, the Turk would counter-attack. But do you think NATO would let it be a long war? Do you think the Americans would allow war in the Eastern flank, war between Greece and Turkey? They would come in with everything, they would stop it in hours. But in that time, we would have gained ground.'

The emaciated man was not satisfied. 'And the Turks will let us stay there? They will make us at home?'

'Of course, the moment hostilities cease, we begin to negotiate. And we make concessions. On the coast we retreat. But the negotiations about the northern front – the negotiations about our retreat from the Hellespont – those negotiations drag on, they are not conclusive, and in the meantime we reinforce and fortify, and there we stay.'

Leonidas murmured, 'Constantinople will be Greek again!'

The emaciated man heard him, and said at once, 'We retake Constantinople. Gentlemen, I think we are risking very much to get back Constantinople.'

'There are risks of course; there must be. But it is not a matter only of Constantinople. Gentlemen, let your imaginations dwell on it, if Greece retakes the Hellespont – the Dardanelles – if we control that channel, do you realize the power that gives us over Russia? Our hold on America? The *strength* we would have in the eastern Mediterranean? Gentlemen, I tell you, if there is one thing that Greece must do, however long it takes, it is to regain the Hellespont.'

In support of him, a stout, soft-voiced man now spoke. He had been quiet before in massive assurance, and he spoke slowly, with oriental complacency.

'There is another matter also, which the Major General has not mentioned. Oil. It is certain that there is oil in the Aegean. Any day we will find it. The Turk will want to share that oil, but not a drop of it must go to him. The oil in the Aegean is

Greek oil. But if that oil is to be defended, Greece will need to be stronger than she is at present.'

'She will be,' the Major General affirmed. 'The eastern Mediterranean will be our lake.'

Leonidas also nodded sagely: the oil was the point. They were not fighting only for the Great Idea, for a dream. They were fighting for oil, for real wealth and real power. Looking round, he saw that Polikarpos' face was aglow, and more tense and serious than before. He permitted himself the thought: yes, oil is good for Polikarpos' patriotism.

They looked at the emaciated man, thinking he would be quelled. His flushed, raw, jagged-boned face was hard to read. It struck Leonidas that he was if anything more impatient than the rest of them for military action by Greece, but was for that reason more tormented and exasperated by the risks and the costs. He said now, 'Good, good, but will you tell me this. What do we give up?'

Give up? What was he driving at? There was a new annoyance with him. One man said, 'Give up? We give up nothing.'

'It's very clear, you know. If we want to keep the Hellespont, we must give up something else. Of course.'

The Major General and the soft-voiced man exchanged looks; evidently they knew what was in his mind, but didn't want it drawn into the light. The soft-voiced man said, 'I grant we would have to make concessions. I have said that. We might have to give Turkey – I suppose – an island. . . .'

'An island. Yes. And which island, do you think?'

The room was very still. Sharply, a little nervously, the Major General said, 'Who can say? How can we possibly anticipate?'

But the challenger wouldn't be put off. 'Which island?' he asked again, and others murmured the question, though they hardly needed to, for almost at once, from several voices, the answer came.

'Cyprus.'

The name was repeated. One man said vehemently, 'We will never give up Cyprus!' The word '*enosis*' was repeated. Looking round, Leonidas saw that though the threat to Cyprus was news to some, there were others to whom it was not news at all, and they for the present stayed quiet. Then abruptly, harshly, with a kind of brutal humour, General Vouros cried,

'Cyprus, Cyprus, we talk a lot about Cyprus. In the name of God, what have the Cypriots done for Greece? Do you believe the Cypriots want *enosis*? They want to go on making money out of the English.'

Another said, 'And there's the Archbishop. Is he our friend? He does nothing but call us names to anyone who will listen.'

'We will deal with the Archbishop,' the Major General said quietly.

'Deal with him!' General Vouros said loudly. 'We should throw him to the Turks. They'll deal with him.' He laughed.

The Major General called them to order. 'Gentlemen, there is one fact we should admit now. If ever we are at war with Turkey, this is certain: there is no way we can defend Cyprus. It's too far from here and too close to Turkey. We could not do it.'

Discussion of Cyprus faltered; a different question rose. 'What about the Americans?'

'*What* about the Americans?'

'Will the Americans let us go into Turkey?'

'They will not know. They are our good friends, they have helped us in the past, but this plan is not for them.'

'Uh! How can you keep it secret from the Americans? They're everywhere.'

'Listen to me. Of course they know we have a war plan against Turkey. We always have a plan of what we would do if we had to go to war with Turkey, with Yugoslavia, with Albania, with Bulgaria – with all our neighbours – of course they know that. And we have exercises according to this plan. But that the plan will be put into effect – this is something they do not know, and they will not know till it happens. My intelligence unit works only on this. It isn't only the communists we watch, we watch every CIA man.'

There was a gratified silence, while they took in what he said; presently he resumed, speaking with more gravity than he had before.

'Gentlemen, there is much that could be said, but we are all in sympathy here, even Grigoris' – he motioned to the emaciated man – 'I will come to the main matter that brings us together this evening. As some of you know, the plan we have outlined was not made last week. It was one of the aims of the National Government, when it first took power. At least, that is what they told us. And what has happened since then? Nothing. Some of us wonder what the President is doing. Well, we shall learn, we are making arrangements to see him. In the meantime, every one of us must work to ensure that the Government remembers its duty. There must be no more delay. I ask you, gentlemen, will the Fatherland once again be great, and great among the nations? For this cause we all must work, for the Great Idea, for the greatness of our nation. The fate of the Fatherland rests with us.'

The spontaneous murmur of the audience grew to a noise of assent. Leonidas' heart swelled in him, he felt his face, his body, burn with pride. Looking round, he saw Polikarpos solemn-faced, transported; his cousin Kostas, General Vouros, even the emaciated man, were the same. He could weep with exaltation: he was among such men! His mind still reeled with the things he had heard, shock on shock, the risk, the cost, Cyprus lost to the Turk. But to think of the Greek troops marching through Constantinople, and the Greek navy at the gates of the Black Sea. His mind was full with rising warplanes, and jets swooping from the sun, and warships and troop carriers closing on the coast, and all across Turkey fires burning and smoke rising and through the smoke the Greek battalions advancing, and Greece once more great, and the Greek Empire restored.

He had found his life's work: to be minister in the government that laboured in this cause – he could ask no more of history.

8

Chryssa continued relentlessly her visits to the police offices, and at last, in late spring, she achieved her purpose: she was given permission to visit Vangelis.

On a cool, gusty day in May she took the boat to the prison island. There were few other passengers in the steamy saloon: a peasant with empty produce boxes, a widow in black, two burly men in T-shirts who might be warders returning from leave. They lounged back lethargic, resigned to the long boredom of the voyage, and not trying to see out of the misted windows. A priest in a dusty cassock, with a wire tangle of black beard, lay like a felled tree on the torn bench, snoring.

It was so murky there Chryssa went outside, and sat among the clean, white-painted ironwork at the back of the ship. For hours the boat ploughed steadily on, and she sat in pent excitement as if she would hold her breath till they arrived. The wind flapped and ripped, and whipped sharp gusts of spray in her face; the clouds overhead streamed past continuously, with a white glare coming and going within them. In the distance the grey silhouettes of islands, some smooth like whales, some bulky like rough shapes covered in palls, slid past gradually.

At last a low mound appeared on the horizon. For a long time it did not change, but eventually it grew to a brown rock of island, jagged with promontories, bony, pitted, hacked, almost split in two by a long gorge. Now she made out, on a rough cliff, brown as the rock, an old Turkish fortress, with long embattled walls, sprawled like a curled dragon over a brown village, and the grey still pool of the island's harbour. The fortress had low turrets with odd black hoods on top like heads facing inwards. These were lamps, she saw, this was the prison: her heart started to thud and swing as if it would tear out of her. She could see no one, it looked utterly dead, it was a place where terrible things happened.

They landed in front of a single café where distributed policemen, sitting on several chairs each, and a handful of old men with scorched faces, gazed fixedly at the new arrivals. Impatient, anxious, Chryssa hurried up a narrow street. Away from the harbour the village became a dingy maze of tight alleys, where bony cats picked their way between stones, their thin shoulder-blades sliding jaggedly up and down as they stalked; where roofs sagged and balconies and shutters lolled from their supports; where in the black insides of the houses wrinkled ill-willed old women's faces would advance from shadow, peer at her, and withdraw when she looked back.

Chryssa felt suffocated, she didn't know the way, but she kept climbing and so came out in a rocky waste area picked and pecked by chickens, where a donkey raised its head to greet her with a long gasping bellow of idiot misery. The old fortress stood clear now, still looking deserted, on the far side of the harbour; she worked her way over the rough ground to its entrance. What struck her most, as she saw it clearer, was not so much the terror as the meanness of the place. The stone walls had fallen apart here and there and been patched up with rough jumbles of brick; the strands of barbed wire along the top sagged in tangles, a goat could have escaped. The gate itself was just a big sheet of old iron, paint-peeled, rusted by the sea; some sort of disused wooden kiosk or sentry-box was falling apart beside it; on the bald rocks were shreds of plastic, watermelon rinds, old Coca-Cola bottles, tin cans, general refuse. It all seemed small, run-down and above all mean.

She still had seen no one, but evidently an eye was watching, for a little semi-circular flap in the iron door slid open, and a man looked out and seemed amazed to see her.

'What do you want?' he muttered, full of dislike. He was sun-baked, scrawny, with deep-sunk glinting eyes: he seemed to her like a withered woman-hating monk, warning her away from a monastery gate.

'I'm the wife of Evangelos Tzavellas.'

The man stared, mistrustful; she passed in her papers, and he disappeared again behind the flap. Presently she heard him shout, 'Hey, Prokopi, come here.' Eventually a door was opened in the iron gate, and she stepped inside.

She was in a tiny whitewashed courtyard, where the gate-keeper stood muttering over her papers with another warder in grey, who was young, tall, bored: he didn't look the prison type, he held the papers absently and stared at her. 'Get Captain Vartharkas,' he said. Presently a high-ranking officer arrived, a fat man with a hard belly like a cauldron, with broad unshaven jowels and a fiercely curled moustache, who spoke to the other warders in a deep guttural snarl. He put on his glasses, and snatched the papers and frowned at them, breathing noisily; then he glanced up and said, not roughly, 'Please follow me, madam.'

She followed, through passages, rooms, little courts. The prison looked large and spacious from outside, but inside it was a close warren of small lean-to buildings stacked and jumbled on top of each other. She was led into a white-washed room, and asked to sit down beside an odd dark window, which evidently let light into some sort of storeroom on the other side: there she was left. In the distance she heard the officer tramping through the passages, snorting.

She looked absently at the window, which was smeared, greenish, like the wall of a glass tank: then a light switched on the other side, the shadows disturbed – and the world swooped, her eyes went blind, as the dark crophead figure sat down in front of her, very close. It was Vangelis: or was it him? For moments she could only gaze. The plumpness had gone from his face, his nose was thin and sharp, the bones of his head showed clear: he almost looked younger, the young Vangelis had a sharp head. But there was some other way also in which his face looked different. It was not just the bareness, now his thick moustache was gone. She hung for moments searching, and then she saw: what were missing were all the small curves and curls and puckers in the skin that made the *expression* of his face. For all his frowns and sharp dartings, his aggression, he always had some trace of humour, zestful or shrewd, and a kindness in his eyes for her, whether he was angry, sad, or however he was. These things made the face she knew, and the man she saw now looked so stark and hard he scared her: she knew and didn't know the tense, staring eyes that grabbed her.

His mouth was open, she realized he was speaking: and she heard nothing, there was soundproof glass between them. She blinked tears of frustration; and then she heard a distant crackling voice that called her. It came from a piece of bakelite lying on the bench below the window: it looked like an odd telephone. She picked it up, seeing Vangelis hold a similar device on the other side of the glass. So now she heard him, though his voice buzzed like a person calling from a distant city.

'Vangeli?'

'Chryssa –' Several times over he said only her name. Then his voice cracked and he looked for a moment brittle as a glass man, 'I can hardly believe that you're here.'

'My love. Oh, I've died to see you. They wouldn't tell me *where* you were. Oh, my dear love, my love –' She shook her head, blinking.

In stops and starts broken questions reached for each other, as their hands made vain moves towards the thick glass. A guard and perhaps a tape recorder were listening to what they said: let them make what they could of it, they weren't exchanging secrets. All they wanted to hear was voice: she caught his timbre through the crackles, and clung to the sound as she would have clung to his arm.

'Vangeli – oh, why can't we talk properly, why this ridiculous telephone? I should break the glass with it so I could hold you. Love, tell me what happened. Don't tell me things you don't want to go back to, but otherwise . . . tell me.'

He nodded, his face went hard again, and tersely he told her of his interrogation, the trial, his imprisonment afterwards. He left much out but, even so, at the points of pain she would gasp, her eyes closed slowly, she stooped as she half turned away wanting him to stop or pause: but his terse acid voice continued, as though irony were all that could speak of these events. At times it seemed that, when he thought of them, he no longer had feeling either for her or for himself.

He left much dark, but still he was in great tension when he finished, his face like scorched stone, his eyes blinking sharply. They must move on: and he started then to ask how she had been. She noticed that he let into his voice, as he enquired about her, just that sympathy and love which, offered to him, he had seemed to repel. But the bad things she told him of, such as her sacking and blacklisting, moved him to a rage that slowly worked stronger: she thought she would lose him in a cloud of fury. It seemed for some moments as if pain had given him an appetite for injustice. But evidently it was a fury he was used to: in the way of a familiar passion, it presently subsided, and he was as before. He asked about money, what she made from translating, what help she got from her family: they discussed how she'd manage with an odd cool practicality till she said, 'They won't last for ever, Vangeli. They're – petty people. They came from nowhere. They'll go away.'

Bitterly he said, 'Do you believe that, Chryssa? I can't any more. They're in charge, and they'll stay. Yes, some people resist them, but they don't get anywhere. Did we make any difference? I don't think so.' His voice was metallic and inward, he was biting on a bitter truth for his own benefit as well as for hers.

'My love, don't say such things, don't think them. What you did wasn't nothing. You did very much.'

'It achieved nothing.'

'There are people in Athens who are grateful to you, Vangeli. Don't call it nothing, just because you didn't bring the Junta down.'

He looked up, both stung and touched; and for the first time the taut skin of his lean face cracked into a rueful smile.

'I'm bitter wine now,' his distant voice said.

Then she smiled, 'I'm the same, my love – and not just because of what the Junta do. Sometimes I look round Athens and I think: people let this happen. So what if there's a dictatorship? – they keep their heads down and get on with business. Then I ask why we bothered. Was it worth what it's cost us? That's what makes me bitter, Vangeli. We have suffered very much, for people who don't care.'

He looked up, startled. He had seemed completely toughened, but she saw now he was vulnerable, hurt: he counted on her to deny his bitterness, if she confirmed it his own strength slid. Quickly she said, 'My love, we're both bitter wine. What else could we be? But your work has told, you should hear what Simos says. They know of you abroad, Michael has helped. And there *is* more resistance, they can't flatten everyone. You did good work, love. The work doesn't stop.'

She spoke with emphasis, her voice low and steady, she realized she was not telling only him, she was telling herself also a truth which in bad times she denied. She heard her confidence gather and brighten.

He listened quietly, his eyes feeding on her words, nodding

shortly. Then he shook his head, laughed, and suddenly said full-voiced, 'Chryssa my love' and lavishly, vehemently, kissed his hands to her through the glass. She kissed hers to him, their hands pressed towards each other against the cold glass.

'Chryssa, tell me how things are outside.'

'Let's leave outside, it isn't good.'

'I don't mean serious things. Tell me gossip, something stupid – it would be water in the desert to me.'

She began slowly, thinking she knew only grim things. For a long time she did not mention Leonidas, any thought of him now was too bitter: but then she came to his villa, she recalled how they strove to make a road to the sea, but ran out of cliff. As she imitated Leonidas demon-driving his hapless driver downhill, while the bulldozer foundered on the crumbling brink, they started laughing. Blessedly, as if it came from nowhere, laughter took hold of them: from joy of itself it grew, their eyes streamed, their ribs hurt, laughter touched them with electric wires all over. At both their doorways stood bewildered warders, leaning in.

With weeping eyes, with hurting sides, they collected themselves: they were in a gentler terrain. She heard in Vangelis' voice the old affection. Then he spoke more urgently.

'Chryssa, they'll come soon. There is one thing I must say: Chryssa, you must have your life, while I'm in here. Don't just mope for me. You know what I mean.'

'Vangeli, I couldn't –' But she heard footsteps coming closer; while in her ear Vangelis was saying in a tender hesitant voice, 'Chryssa, your visit has taken me out of a bad place. I've been in an oven. You don't know. I thought I wouldn't see you again. My love, thank you for coming. . . . My dear love, I can't bear for you to go.'

The shadows beside him darkened, a uniform and belt buckle came into view. He kissed his hands to her, then as he got up and turned from her she saw all the affection that had come into his face disappear, not as though it died, but as though it sank inwards into him, leaving him, on the surface, keen, bleak, hard. He'd gone.

The snorting officer returned, and conducted her through the corridors: but as she walked she heard, within the sound of boots and doors from other parts of the prison, the sound of a known voice speaking with a crackle inside her ear.

9

They took Vangelis back to his cell, but for once the heavy clang of that door was not like despair closing its lid on him. He was content just to sit, remembering Chryssa's visit: he was almost in pain from the happiness it brought him. He had been in such blackness that her coming felt like a supernatural event, almost as if she had descended in a beam of light, had let in air from another world. Every moment of the visit was clear to him, and clearer than it had been at the time because his memory removed the glass wall. He still saw her sweetly square face, pale perhaps with the shock of seeing him; her brown eyes reached for him; her tender mouth was slightly open; he saw her neat small jaw that he loved. Her voice, which had been so distant in that telephone, spoke clearer now as memory repeated everything she said. He heard its low vibration, its rustle of tones, it was a soft voice that could speak to a theatre. Still hearing it, he heard her voice from past times also, as if that telephone wire had connected him not only to her, but to their past as well, so their lost life spoke.

As summer advanced and the days grew hotter, the prisoners were more and more put to work out of doors, digging land attached to the prison or repairing the stonework in the walls that shut them in. The work was hard but mechanical: Vangelis was in an odd still suspended mood: and he found these days that Chryssa's visit had the further effect that it allowed him to remember the past. He had thought it would involve straining and cracking of all his muscles for him to turn himself round and look at the old life; but while he was heaving a barrow loaded with stone, or half following an argument between the prisoners, or sitting tired in his cell, he would find events from his past life with Chryssa approaching unbidden to meet him again. He remembered the first time he saw her, in England, peering in some odd perplexed elation out of smoke and red flame, like a flower that had unfolded in a smithy. Then she left; and he remembered, years later, a large declamatory gathering in Athens, where his friend's speech, which he had helped write, faded in his hearing to distant waves as he registered a girl who had just come in, late but unembarrassed, and was making her way by smiles through the hall. She slipped through the crush with such lightness, radiance, she seemed like a fresh tune people turned to hear: the crowd parted for her, a space appeared on a bench for her to sit, just in front of him, and he saw for sure that the girl was Chryssa. At intervals in the speech she whispered with animation to the person next to her, who was evidently a friend: Vangelis found himself dismayed, and watched, annoyed, to see how close the friendship was. Chryssa *seemed* free. Vangelis heard no more of the speech.

It seemed to him now that he had been in a prison of his own inside this prison, so that there was extraordinary release just in being free within his own past. Once he had started remembering, he did not stop: it was as if memory were a live creature that, reviving, needed to try each recollection to be sure it was whole. He remembered their wedding, which had taken place, at family behest, in an ancient beehive church in Salonica: he remembered the ripple of exclamation that entered the church just before Chryssa did: 'Kukla! What a doll!' and she in the doorway shining amid her veils like an angel through a cloud, holding in both hands a small bouquet, looked too beautiful to be marrying him. Stiff in his suit, he had felt himself the peasant, down from the mountains, made urban and intellectual by dogged unnatural effort; while she was all the good chances of nature and of city life together in their sweetest form. Then the solemn face of the priest filled their sight: steadily he married them, while the chanter beside him sang the responses. In a happy trance, like a person under faulty anaesthetic half aware of an operation taking place, Vangelis had watched while slowly this strange alteration was made to his state. After the ceremony he felt that, for all their loving before marriage, they glowed still with the new light of bride and bridegroom. Uncles who were tired in their marriages seemed moved by the wedding to a new impatience to be alone with their wives. Gently in the hotel room their own familiar loving and their new bridal aura joined.

On their early marriage he dwelt a certain time, then, lightly

215

as if he were borne in a balloon from one country to the next, his remembering moved of its own accord to other events, and to their conflicts too. At the start of their marriage they often fought. In a crowded restaurant in Athens they found a disagreement which grew as they discussed it into a passionate war quarrel that dragged up from the abyss all their exasperations with each other. She reproached his obstinate one-track fixity in egoism, his lawyer's pedantry and bullying, his heavy furious peasant jealousy: there was rudeness in his head-tossed 'no'. What could he reproach? Her family had been only briefly rich, but still she had a rich city girl's blythe assumption that life was wonderful, and she was the centre of what was wonderful in it, and whatever she did was right because it was done by her: she had self-love, she thought she was the actress, she talked too loud, she hadn't grown up, she saw things black and white, she haggled in shops and counted the drachmas like someone mean, but also she was careless, she lost things, she never arrived at a rendezvous on time, she couldn't shut a door, she never put the lids back on her shampoos and bottles in the bathroom so every so often they all went over in a pool of trouble. He didn't remember now what he had said to her and what he hadn't, but the quarrel went on, the restaurant attending, till they had turned each other inside out. They finished their argument in the street, then he strode off. She had been so unjust: when they quarrelled, she was a different person, she saw only poison in their marriage and in him; he was a bully and stingy, a ranter, a snare, a shrivelled soul: a black figure, the mistake of her life. She allowed nothing good in him or his motives. He smarted, writhed, she was so unfair: but her words lodged, he half saw his motives now as she described them: his own bad wishes and his cruel words echoed stinging in his head.

He turned a corner: and by chance she was behind it, dawdling by herself. She looked up, startled, then, eyeing him slightly askance, smiled – a rueful smile – she evidently, like him, had been thinking of the bad things she had said. Her smile offered truce: he smiled acceptance. Then she said, 'my love'; they came together and kissed.

Late at night they walked home along the coast, with its racket of bouzoukia and discotheques, its dazzle of neon and too harsh lights, its lit up pucker of sea, in a deep friendly calm of understanding, embracing, smoking, talking, kissing, deeply together, loving as never.

These were blessed days in which, alone in his cell, or sitting in a corner of the yard talking to no one – the other prisoners respected his withdrawal – he wandered up and down his years with Chryssa. He had never before thought about their marriage in the way he did now, for in Athens he always had at the front of his mind new emergencies concerning his court cases and politics; and when he got to prison he was tangled in torment. But now the obstacles that had blocked his thought thinned and melted and with no noise or trouble slid out of the way. Looking back with detachment, like a man seeing life mistakes when it's years too late to do anything about them, he saw that cloud of anxious urgency in which he had lived as a protective smoke that saved him from seeing that the best thing in his life was his marriage to Chryssa. He had wanted not to see this because he was ambitious: what he would achieve in his life would be, it must be, the most important thing in it. Her ambitions he had treated as secondary, without admitting it. And where now had all his work brought him? He could have done no other thing: but his main grief now was not for the treatment he'd had or his long lost hopes, but for the years he was losing from his life with Chryssa.

He thought of her laughing, arguing, dancing: she could say things that hurt with the pain of truth, and she could say things that made his world turn over. He thought of her bargaining, finding in the bric-a-brac beautiful things that she got for a song: her father's skill, but not his profiteering. She was quick to make these fine discoveries because she had an optimism Vangelis did not have. Chryssa, he thought, where are you now? He didn't mind her being free while he was stuck, he wanted to think of her in freedom, it gave him also a connection with the free. With a feeling between a prayer and a blessing he pictured her to his mind's eye: an energetic, graceful figure confronting the roaring world. Let her be protected: wherever she went she had about her the invisible wings of his love.

Sitting in a nook of the scorching yard while the sun crawled overhead, watching the sweltering guards yawn on the walls,

Vangelis was overcome by a weariness of the rage that had held him for many past months. He wanted only to lose the burden, to be of no more weight than some fibres of rag he watched stir on the ground in the slight burning breeze. He felt starts and quakings inside him, as if under the tight surface something rock hard were breaking: he had an odd inclination to weep that startled him just because he had been so parched. From the strange oasis that Chryssa's visit had brought him to, he looked back at the anger that for months had filled him. It was a just rage yet he had suffocated in it; and all his life, like his father's, had been veined with anger. Behind them both was the large anger, nurtured by hundreds of years of foreign occupation: it was the live coal at the base of everyone's spine. In war after war, and in the Civil War, it flared, as it flared in Greece now. Both sides blew the flames hot. It was a cruel anger; it was an engine of justice; it had scorched him.

'Why are you always angry, Vangeli?' Chryssa had asked him once, before the coup, and it was true he had lived all his life in ready indignation, almost as if he expected the dictators. Anger had stepped between him and Chryssa, it had invaded their bed: when they were side by side at night he had lain rigid with the red serpent of anger coiled round him, separating them. He had fed that anger till in a way it became a safe place where, even in their marriage, a part of him hid from Chryssa. He realized now there was some secret treaty between the anger and his sense of his importance, his ambition, his jealousy. And in all the country it was so – the frantic grab society: fired with old anger, each individual clawed in a rage of ego. Fighting it made you mad with anger, till you fell into the machine of anger, and were shredded by men who fed anger with sex: but the torturers were only the extreme, they were the bad wishes of many people come real as men with claws.

Vangelis started to rock where he sat, he groaned from the base of his lungs: as he remembered torture, the fury he had been thinking of revived as a feeling, grew, heated, dug its spurs into his heart. But exactly as this happened he saw in front of him, in a scorched corner of the walls, a gust of hot wind suddenly whip up dirt and sand. A smoke of dust spun in a funnel, now bits of wood and scraps of paper went whirling in the air, and spun round in the hectic shadowy column that had appeared from nowhere. About a man's height, it wove on the spot as though a tormented spirit were tethered there. Vangelis watched the dust devil with fascinated eyes. He felt at this moment more kin to it than to any person in the yard: he knew it was a part of himself, it was his anger, whirling there outside him. Now it began to move steadily away from him, beside the wall: and he knew as he watched that the part of him that was in it was leaving. He saw his anger receding, as if a spirit that had possessed him now took its leave. In the end it moved very rapidly, whipping up a new cloud of sand, and climbed the prison wall. Open mouthed, glassy eyed, quite still, he watched it go.

The lifting of his rage was not permanent – at even small brutalities he would still descend into the poison trough – but he was displaced from the single bitter groove which he had been in before Chryssa's visit. It seemed to him now that not only he but the prison itself had changed. He had chiefly felt previously its dead-end sterility, but he noticed more now the activity around him. In the times when they were together, Stamatis, Andreas, Christoforos and the others talked and argued: they would not be silenced, they would not be dejected. Stamatis had developed a new medical practice, and had almost become the prison doctor. He was given the run of the small prison pharmacy, and on the occasions when Vangelis could visit him there, he found him occupied in calculations and tests. He watched his balding head bend, precise and absorbed, to a thin glass slide on which he carefully smeared a drop of blood. Alternately the two of them peered at the cells through the ancient prison microscope, with its brown surfaces of tarnished brass. Patiently, testing and clarifying his ideas as he talked, Stamatis explained to Vangelis his theory on the origins of thalassaemia.

More often, Vangelis worked with Christoforos. The agriculturalist had reorganized the prison garden, and also, to the contempt of all the criminal and half the political prisoners, had started a flower bed. Captain Vartharkas however was taken with the idea, and allowed Christoforos the seed he wanted, and also extra hours in the cool of the evening. In that pleasant time Vangelis helped him, reducing the hard clods to a dry powder of soil while the low sun lit the fortress walls

with yellow light. Among his pots and tools and fertilizers and
weedkillers, Christoforos had a supply of *zippouro*, village ouzo
bought from a warder, which he disguised as Paraquat; and as
they sipped, he explained the changes he wanted to see in
Greece. These were not the views that had brought him to
prison, for they found it hard to talk politics while trapped in
the works of the political machine. These were his agricultural
hopes.

With a quizzical nod, with self-irony on top and complete
certainty underneath it, he said, 'And there's one thing we
need above all, Vangeli. Bigger farms! I don't care what
they are, they can be private farms, state farms, collective
farms, village commune farms, but we just have to have
bigger farms, instead of what we have now, which is that
every man has a tiny plot, one in this village, one in the
next village, and his aunt's husband's cousin's olive tree
over the mountain.'

Vangelis nodded. He enjoyed listening: his village childhood
returned to him, and the truth of what Christoforos said came
home – and the difficulty, 'How will you make the villagers
let go of their land? They're planted in it.'

'Yes, it's a problem; but they let go of it for money, when
they go into the city.'

Christoforos moved on, discussing the new crops Greece
needed to grow: salad crops for the Common Market, not just
the endless cargos of watermelons.

As he got into the way of these quiet conversations, Vangelis
came to feel that prison life was like life anywhere. People
hang in a void, the past lost and the future blank, but nonetheless they draw together and make a life, and they can't be
stopped from doing this while they have life.

He began visiting the prison library, and with the paper and
biro he was given there he made notes. For at the least he had
leisure, and he decided he would try actually to write the
book he had planned before the Junta: a speculative work on
boundaries and property. When he was arrested, he abandoned
speculation: it seemed, in the interrogation centre, an idle
charade. Yet now, like dead bodies magically revived, his
forgotten arguments began to stir, raised to him distant pale
faces in the dark of his cellar.

He had none of his old notes with him, but he found when

220

he sat to it that his arguments returned. His first chapter was speculative. He began with a territorial dispute he had once seen between two café owners in a village, where it was clear that the array of tables and chairs outside each café had an invisible boundary running round them as sensitive as a skin – these boundaries overlapped, and this goaded the café owners to fury. Their passion seemed to him the clue to politics. It is the mark of the human creature that it projects its life beyond its body, and into other objects: if you use a stick to reach a fruit, the stick becomes your longer arm. So with property: people put roots and nerves into the things they have, letting them go is like letting a limb go. Perhaps this was the reason for the Government's savagery on the *bodies* of 'communists'. For groups of people are giant creatures, whether they are families, classes, armies, nations: so their boundaries are important, for a boundary signifies *this* far I extend, my nerve endings are here, an attack on the edge will be resented as bitterly as an attack on the heart. And when boundaries overlap suddenly, when the creatures are inside each other, when a limb of a nation tries to swallow a nation, the result must be a nightmare of suspicion, fear, cruelty, of insecure megalomania, its own people resented as a disease inside it, a madness of boundaries and creatures twisted inside out.

He paused: was this his original argument, or had he begun to develop a new one? But he wrote on, he saw his subject in the things round him – even in the prison he was in, in the way the warders felt free while the prisoners felt trapped, though they were both shut up together. The warders felt the prison was theirs, an extension of them: they could feel as free as it was big, and as confident as its stones were solid. There was an odd marriage of flesh with stone and iron, of the living with something dead: and the prisoners were germs within this organism, helpless like microbes suspended inside the body in a paralysing fluid.

He recalled an earlier horrible thought, that part of his torture was in the way his body had been treated as a live body and as dead meat at the same time: the shadow of death falling on life. The machine they had inserted into his penis had seemed, as they held it up in front of him, both a dead implement and a hideous metal tendril of their bodies and their will. His old erased arguments stirred and extended, like clouds shaping to creatures. Guardedly, apprehensive of inspection by the warders, he wrote.

He enjoyed working in the dusty hot room of the prison library. At least it was quiet there. The only books on the shelves were religious books, which the political prisoners never looked at though the criminals sometimes did. Oddly, it was in the library that Vangelis got to know the criminals better: outside, in the yard, the two groups seldom mixed. But, knowing he was a lawyer, they would visit him in the library from time to time: and when they came they would insist on interrupting him, taking it for granted that since it was paperwork he was engaged on, he must be bored by it, and glad of company.

A criminal called Legs Sarakinos would come and gossip about his lawyers. Garrulous himself, he seemed pleased by Vangelis' curtness. It seemed that at one stage or another he had employed half the legal profession of Athens: he had even employed a member of the Government.

'A member of the Government? Which member of the Government?'

'Petros Yiannopoulos, the Minister of Transport,' Legs Sarakinos announced in a loud voice. The thick hide of his stubbled face looked too inert to show expression, but some sort of pleasure, amusement, triumph glinted in his wrinkled eyes.

'What's that about Mr Yiannopoulos?' the library guard asked, sauntering in their direction from his desk near the door.

'He works for me. The man's my lawyer,' Legs shouted to him. 'I was one of his big cases.'

Small-eyed, concrete-faced, the guard studied him, then called through the door, 'Hey, Lefteri, come here if you want to hear something good.' Another guard came in, then the two guards came and stood over Legs, arms akimbo, hands on their clubs. Across the room a younger criminal looked up from the bible which he had previously been reading in a quiet slow voice.

Taking note that he had an audience, Legs made himself more comfortable. 'Yes, he's a good lawyer, I tell my friends to go to him. This last time, when the police were on my track, I rang him up. Come round, he said. What, to your home? I said. Never mind, he said, come round. So I went. I said, They're after me, Mr Yiannopoule. You must give yourself up, he said. Well all right, I said, but I can't do it here. Why not here? he said. Oh I couldn't do it here, I said. The last time I was here, the police chief told me what he'd do to me next time. What's that then? he said. I don't like to mention it in company, I said. Uh, mention it, he said. Well, I said, with your sympathy, he told me that next time he saw me he'd have my soul out of me from behind. Oh, he said, if he's going to have your soul out of you from behind you'd better give yourself up somewhere else. Where then? In Larissa, I said. The police chief there is soft as yoghurt. Larissa? he said, no problem. But it'll cost you money. I can pay, I said. You'd better, he said, because if you don't I'll have your soul out of you from behind. Ach, what a lawyer! He's a bastard.' It was the word the guards were waiting for, their truncheons came down and there was a sound like stones dropped on a table. Legs reeled, but in a moment he sat up, shook his head vigorously, and though tears stood in his eyes he continued to Vangelis, ignoring them, 'So he drove me to Larissa, he was my chauffeur, and I gave myself up. It didn't do any good, of course, the police chief there was the same as the other. Still, he took me there, and he defended me in court. Afterwards of course I got the bill. A million drachmas. Well, where would I get that sort of money? He's a bigger thief than I am. You don't get money like that in my line.'

'What *is* your line?'

'What? I'm in the import line.'

'What do you mean, "import"? You're in drugs, are you?'

'Of course drugs, there's no money in anything else. But anyway, I had this bill to pay and I was inside. So Mr Vangeli, what was I to do?'

'How should I know? What did you do?'

'No problem. Because Mr Yiannopoulos had this new Rolls Royce car that he took me to Larissa in, and when he picked me up I saw where he kept it. And do you know, one night that car disappeared, and I don't know where it went, but the next thing I heard was that there'd been a Rolls Royce for sale in the main street of Ankara.'

Vangelis frowned. 'You stole your lawyer's car?' Across the

room, the young criminal suddenly shouted, 'You arsehole, Legs!'

Legs ignored them. 'Well, did Mr Yiannopoulos lose out on the deal? No he didn't, because that way my bill was paid, and it wouldn't have been otherwise. I said I'd pay him.'

He paused some moments, enjoying their attention; then he said vigorously 'So, Mr Vangeli, and who was your lawyer? Not Mr Yiannopoulos, then?'

'Of course not. He may be your god, he isn't mine.'

'Go on then, tell me, who's your lawyer? Ten to one I know him.'

'You can see him now. I did it myself.'

'What do you mean, you did it yourself?'

'I conducted my own defence.'

'Huh! You did a good job, didn't you? You should have had Mr Yiannopoulos. You wouldn't be here now.'

'Why not? You're here.'

Legs paused. 'You're right, Mr Vangeli. He didn't get me off, did he? Ach, the bastard!'

The guards again descended, but Legs seemed made of rock. He presently shook his head again, and said with shining eyes of pain and admiration, 'Ah, but what a lawyer he is!'

Every few days Legs would drop in at the library, telling the guards it was for devotional purposes. He would sit down, and talk to Vangelis about the law; and though Vangelis cursed the interruption of his work, he was interested to be borne by Legs' thick words through the plains and mountains of Anatolia, past deep lakes to Iran and the East; trekking and driving by night, or being pursued at sea by a customs speedboat, plain grey, armour plated, that shot through the water like a spearhead, inescapable however they dodged. With a friendly interest Legs enquired after Vangelis' torture, and insisted that the politicals were privileged; the same and worse was done to his friends and to him when they were interrogated, and even when they weren't, and no world press made any noise in their defence. Ah but what the hell, what can you do, it was in a day's work. He mainly talked and sometimes listened; he had limited interest in Vangelis' opinions, and Vangelis didn't see any point in trying to argue. Vangelis was grateful for these talks: he found it made the tight world that he was trapped in bigger, when he talked to people who had been through the same mill that he had, but for utterly different reasons.

One afternoon, after some legal advice Vangelis gave, Legs quietly passed him a small transistor radio. The gift changed Vangelis' imprisonment. Alone in his cell, his ear close to it, he tuned through atmospherics, catching faint music and occasionally voices.

Late at night, or in the early hours of morning, Vangelis continued still his new remembering. It seemed that, involuntarily, he was slowly recovering all his life. He recalled times with Chryssa, and still earlier events which he had not thought of in years. In the end, in these quiet times in his cell, he found himself dwelling on things which he had not even seen – which he could not have seen. His imagination hovered tenderly over his father's first meeting with his mother. He visualized clearly that young father, whom he knew only from photos, with his robust village physique, his smart high-buttoned city suit, his trimmed moustache and thin-rimmed spectacles. He was walking up a stony track, and round a shoulder of the mountain came a woman riding a donkey. She too wore city clothes, she was young and had a serious beauty: such a person he had never seen here. He made his enquiries and found she belonged to a village high in the mountains: she had studied as he had, and now she was doctor there. A woman doctor – she was more remarkable than a Salonica-trained schoolmaster. He devised a purpose for the trip, and in his smartest suit took a donkey himself, and at the slow pace of the donkey travelled up through the hills, above the olives and chestnuts and through the sweet pine forests, to a high village that clustered in a small bowl of soil between the peaks. In the distance he saw her, carrying her doctor's bag through the village.

On that trip they met, and exchanged courtesies; later he visited her father; they married, and she descended from her mountain to be the doctor in his village. Ahead of them, but out of sight, was invasion, war, a chasm of pain; and death, and lonely hands smashing on a table. But Vangelis' thoughts turned away from these later events and kept returning to his young father riding through the mountains in uncertainty, hope, in a premonition of love, in new-changed sunlight, as if life could have moments that made up for everything. Then,

225

from thinking of his parents, and thinking also of Chryssa, he suddenly thought, quite at odds with the possibilities of the moment, We should have children. What have we been doing? Why have we delayed? This thought was such a light switched on in the dark place he had been in that he simply rested on the prospect.

'Don't lie, you shit. Where did you get it?'

All his body tried to shrivel together in one wincing coil of movement trying to avoid – but he couldn't avoid because the uniformed men held his arms rigid – the hand with the iron ring round its knuckles that drove into his stomach so he felt it would come out the other side, so that now however hard they held him they couldn't prevent all his body rolling together in the hollow ball of a single unending gasp to swallow air.

'Don't you worry, bastard, a radio doesn't come from no-where. Oh, you're going to tell me where you got it.' Captain Vartharkas shook his head slowly, giving a grunting snort as he eased the metal on his fingers; then all his fat body, his big belly, seemed to go hard as he swung his arm back. Vangelis also tensed: but nothing he did could help as the piston fist transfixed him and again he folded over it.

Even after many blows had landed, Vangelis was still amazed. Though at first, after his trial, he could not get the interrogations behind him, he had with time come to be so sure that they were over that he found it difficult to believe he would be tortured again. Yet he should have guessed that sooner or later they would find the radio, and that when they did they would not rest till they learned where he got it. Could he resist them? He was an old hand now, as to torture. But still he felt paralysed, falling into nightmare, as they unlaced his shoes while one of the guards picked up a rifle, which he held in both hands by the barrel.

The cell door opened while Vangelis still lay on the floor. He didn't look round because he hurt too much, any movement would make his pain peak; but he knew from the creaking shoes that approached his ear, from the heavy rustling of large clothes, from the thin sour smell of sweat, from the slow snorting grunt, that Captain Vartharkas had returned to his cell.

'What now?' Vangelis murmured; he waited, eyes closed, poised for the blow. But the blow didn't come, and instead a new heaving and panting, and a straining as of stretched canvas, told him that Captain Vartharkas was sitting down. There was a clink of metal on stone right in front of him. He wondered, what new instrument would this be? Opening his eyes he saw on the floor a metal tray with a frothing briki of coffee on it and two thimble sized cups. Blurrily he registered the mass of Captain Vartharkas seated on the bunk bed beyond, but immediately he just stared at this strange coffee tray materialized from nowhere. The briki was a piece of battered copper; the little cups were delicate, though one was cracked; an elaborate pattern was incised round the edge of the metal tray. What are these things doing here? he wondered: everything else in the world seemed to step back to a safe distance while the coffee tray and its cups slowly grew harder, till they looked solid as stone.

It's the old trick, he thought. He'll give me the coffee, chat a bit, let me go soft, then start again. They won't let up till they get their information. And presently Captain Vartharkas leaned wheezingly down and poured out the coffee: then he took a cup for himself, and sat back again. Vangelis took a cup, and sipped the thick drink, bitter and sweet at once, that ran like nectar through his awakening body. He murmured, 'The coffee break, eh?'

Captain Vartharkas finished the sip he was taking, wiped his moustache, and sighed. In his guttural, heavily breathed voice he said, 'Uh, Tzavella, don't take it so seriously. We know politics, eh? Now we are doing this to you. In a few years' time, we'll be doing it to them.' His eyes glinted, a spark of harsh humour showed deep inside them.

Vangelis raised his brow; in spite of all, he smiled; and shook his head; and took a slow sweet sip of coffee. Before him sat the heavy dark mass of Vartharkas, draining his cup: Vangelis noticed wryly that he raised his little finger in a small fat hook as he held the tiny cup. The Captain lowered his cup, and wiped his moustache again.

'And besides,' he growled, slapping his thigh, 'what we do to you is nothing to what we do to recruits!' He had done his business: he got up, and without more ado creaked heavily out of the cell; the door closed.

So the further blows did not come. In an odd pause, ignoring his bruises, Vangelis sat, tracing the curved lines that crossed each other as they ran together round the edge of the gleaming metal tray.

10

The summer following the visit to Polikarpos and the meeting on the yacht was a time of desperate impatience for Leonidas. His head burst with knowledge of the great secret plan, but he was forbidden to say anything of it to anyone, even to Patra. His colleagues at the Ministry he could not tell, and the Minister, though he knew something of the plan, was not to be told more: he was not thought completely reliable. Leonidas was racked: he had to speak.

Since the visit to the island he had taken to seeing, now and again, for a drink or a quiet exchange, that long-legged wife of a Swedish businessman who had charmed him at the party. His blood effervesced when he was with her: and she too, it appeared, found his company something she could not do without. He rented an apartment for their stolen hours, one far from his home, and removed but not too far from the Ministry. And though she teased him and sometimes mocked him and was always late at their rendezvous, still he felt that she and he were close, and had an understanding. Yet after all he had to allow that she was not discreet, he watched what he said to her even at the best of times: so of the great secret bursting in him not a word, not a whisper, could he pass to her.

The only people with whom he could discuss the plan were those who knew of it already, and them he seldom saw. The secrecy hurt so, that one afternoon at the Ministry he did something which he had not done for over twenty years: he wrote a poem. As a student he had sometimes written poems, about Greece and about love; he had only ever read them to Patra, who admired them as he throbbed them to her, lustrous-eyed, his moustache and hair like the young Clark Gable. With mature years he put such fancies by; he thought all that survived of that taste was an appreciation of the lyrics of fifties love songs, which he and

Patra would drive for kilometres to hear at a concert. Yet under the pressure of his new secret passion the old skill returned: the words flowed: he put in the poem all his hopes of the National Government and the Greater Greece, all his trust in the heroes of the new Greek dawn. The poem began with the Empire of Alexander, and ended with the tragic betrayal by the Allies of the Greek armies that invaded Turkey in 1919: let that betrayal not recur. All the nation's history led to the triumph that was rising now. He read the poem over to himself several times, murmuring the words in a sonorous voiced whisper, his heart large and hurting; and eventually, reluctantly, with great gravity, he slipped it softly amongst the most secret and important papers of his office, and closed the safe, and sadly spun the lock.

Perforce he found patience, and waited: and soon enough the day came on which his hopes, and the future of the nation, rested: the day when the Major General and other officers involved in their group went formally to visit the President, to demand of him clear answers as to how the plan stood. Leonidas could not be there but his cousin Kostas was: from him he learned by hints what happened, his imagination leaping to hear each word they had said.

Tall figures, fit, upright, their uniforms spotless, their braids and insignia shining, they were led through the hall, their feet tapping sharply on the marble floor. In the antechamber of the President they were kept a short while waiting: they heard his high voice in the room next door. They waited stiffly, unused to waiting; then the secretary returned, and led them to the office of the President. The President was alone: he got up from his large desk that was bare of papers, and came round it briskly to shake hands with them: a short stocky man, stub-nosed, with a bald high-domed head, with prominent eyes, a small but toughly smiling mouth.

'Dmitri! Good to see you!' He gripped the hand of the Major General; and each of the others he greeted promptly by name, vigorous and curt.

'Gentlemen, sit down,' he said, and sat himself not at his desk, but in another armchair like their own. After a few moments' courtesies he asked for business. The Major General then spoke, summarizing the war plan and stating their anxieties. The President listened with unsurprised, concentrating eyes, nodding sharply from time to time. At the end, he looked round at all of them and said, 'Gentlemen, you are true patriots.'

The Major General said at once, 'Mr President, we are impatient to show it.'

The President studied him shrewdly, then, looking fierily round at them, he said, 'Gentlemen, we shall play tavli in Ankara!' It was a slogan he had used before, among brother officers.

One of the generals cheered, and seemed ready to leave. But the others sat quietly, pressing questions, and eventually the President said:

'I see, gentlemen, you want to know why we are not yet at war. I shall tell you, though it is not easy for me to say this. You, gentlemen, are patriots – we should all of us lay down our lives for the Great Idea tomorrow – but can we say that all in our army are patriots?'

At this they sat up, such words they never expected from him; and he continued.

'Gentlemen, your loyalty is a rock. But can that be said of all our officers? Do you know how many we have had to retire? Do you know how many our military intelligence have under surveillance? And the navy, gentlemen? Will any of you tell me that the navy would lay down its life for the National Government?' He was speaking louder, his voice was rising high as it did in his public speeches; but he contained himself, and said in a slow, biting voice, 'Give me a loyal army, gentlemen, and we shall make real the Great Idea.'

Finally the Major General was shaken; the purge of the army had been great, none could deny it. Were they ready for Ankara?

The President went on, 'Gentlemen, we are fashioning a new army. We are training. We are making ready.'

Then suddenly Kostas, who had spoken no word so far, being overwhelmed with the privilege of being here, said in a clear voice, 'Sir, once war is declared, every Greek will fight. That will be our army!'

The generals turned to him, surprised, approving; the President nodded towards the young aide-de-camp, as recognizing a spirit strong as his own.

'True words!' he said, 'but the army must be ready too.

Gentlemen, I look to you. Give me that army, and that day we march.'

With that he stood up sharply, showing a trace of stern impatience. The meeting had taken time, and his time was of great value.

The Major General, rising also, had more to say, his poise recovered now; but the President clapped firm hold of his hand and shook it strongly, saying loudly, 'Dmitri, it was good to see you. The next inspection will be at your division. There we shall recall old times.'

He moved on at once to the others, shaking hands and bidding farewell. Hearing the movements, his secretary came in and held the door open for the officers to leave. The President detained them a moment, saying with a smile, 'Remember, gentlemen – not a word to the Americans!' He put his finger to his lips. They laughed, and left: some with eyes of molten ardour, and others, who had listened but not spoken, with faces still contained and thoughtful.

Leonidas heard of the meeting when he was invited by Kostas to dinner at the officers' summer camp near Athens. There were present both several of the officers who had seen the President, and others also of their group, like General Vouros, whom he had seen on the yacht. After dinner they strolled down through the olive trees to the sea, and sauntered along the beach. One of the generals had his summer cabin beside the sea, and under the broad awning there they sat over cigarettes and brandy.

'Well, gentlemen,' their host said, 'and where shall we play tavli – here, or over the sea?' He gestured to the east, and they laughed together.

'He is still a soldier!' Kostas said, in clipped awe. He meant the President; and one of the officers nodded, but the others were incalculable. Leonidas had been about to propose a toast to the success of the foreign policy of the National Government, but seeing these faces he held back. Then he realized that they were all waiting for a lead from the Major General, who sat not smoking and not drinking, gazing in quiet and severe thought at the blue-black sea. He presently said, 'Ah, my friends, and when do you think we shall see Ankara?'

232

'Oh, come on, Dmitri,' their host said, 'you're a dry stick!'

'You're right, I am. But still, let's put a year to it. This year, next year? No! Two years hence? Three perhaps. . . .'

'Get on with you, Dmitri! When the army's ready, we let fly. You don't question the word of the President, surely?'

'I question no one. If the leader of the National Government says that we will go to war when the army is ready, I believe him absolutely.'

'Well, you don't question the army, I hope?'

The Major General paused, and surveyed a gnarled olive tree, and waited till all of them hung on his words. Then said, 'Do you call this an army? I call it the auxiliary police.'

The others started. Leonidas looked round, he expected General Vouros at least to explode in military pride. But the lion face of Vouros was perfectly still.

Hesitant, hushed, Kostas enquired, 'Do you think, sir, the President may not have meant. . . .'

The Major General stayed silent; Kostas petered out.

A quiet voice from among them said, 'You realize, Dmitri, where this could lead? If we question the President. . . .'

The officer next to Leonidas stood up. 'I want no part of this. My hearing is poor, I did not catch what you said. But I have heard enough for tonight.' And he turned and left them, strolling through the olive trees; yet with something hard, gripped tight, in his strolling.

The Major General sat forward and in a voice like stretched wire said, 'Has anyone else bad ears? Is anyone else ready for bed?'

Leonidas also had wondered: should he leave? To be involved in a group that not only sought war, but might be seeking, in the interests of that war, a new president – he was in deep waters. But to leave now, to arouse suspicion, when he was one of *their* men in the Government. . . . He stayed, in a cold sweat.

The Major General spoke on quietly, carefully, firmly. He was facing danger, but he had an iron courage and the others were under his spell. He believed in one thing, the greatness of Greece: without hesitation he would die for it. It crossed Leonidas' mind, perhaps this was the man who should be president of the War Cabinet, when the war with Turkey came. But if others had that thought, they did not mention it now;

all they talked about was the need to ascertain loyalty to the original aims of the National Government.

A stillness descended on them, as they sat listening to the clear voice that talked in the darkness. The Major General spoke an old-style, formal Greek, his voice was like the voice of the Greek past, and like the voice of the destiny of Greece. In his pauses the sea lapped.

Eventually they broke up, and Kostas escorted Leonidas back to his car. Leonidas wanted to talk, but he was cautious, as Kostas was also. They only said goodnight, and Leonidas drove away through the winding earth tracks of the camp.

To be involved with a group that might try to change the Government – he was on dangerous ground. Yet he saw too why they had wanted him, and not the Minister, on their side: for in any change of government, the Minister could only lose, but Leonidas could rise. And his heart was in their cause. He went cold at the thought of the risks he ran now. But also, this was history: it was the thrill and danger of history that touched his skin like freezing steel, so his blood thrilled from top to toe.

11

Summer cooled to autumn, but Chrýssa was still not allowed
a second visit to Vangelis. When she had gone to see him
before, she took it for granted that this was the first in a series
of trips she would make to the prison island. But it was made
clear to her now that political prisoners were not to be visited
except at long intervals. The officials she applied to were rude,
and if they spoke to her at all, it was only to remind her that
she had got what she wanted: she had been allowed to see
Vangelis, and she knew he was uninjured. She shouldn't expect
to see him again in less than a year, making a noise about it
wouldn't help.

She accepted this now: and her one visit to him had made a
difference. She was bleak but calm, she had no choice but
patience. Her quieter pleasures revived: she saw Clio and
Simos sometimes – but not often, because they were all three
watched, and she guessed also that Simos had some resistance
involvement now, which made it not wise for him to be seen
too often with the wife of a prisoner. The domesticity implanted
by her mother reawoke, so she tidied the flat often, though
there were seldom visitors to disturb it. The nearest she came
to dancing was in polishing the floor, skating on two dusters
as her mother had taught her. She was used to isolation, and
also had found new companions. Each time she went out,
she would buy a plant – not to return empty-handed to the
emptiness. Now the flat was crowded. Every day she took a
flower-patterned island jug she liked, and proceeded from
plant to plant, carefully pouring water in the bowls in which
they stood, in a quiet greeting and communion with them. She
considered their health, and polished leaves that were clouded
or furred. It seemed she had a jungle inside the flat, with
shining leaves, budding stems, and the brown thin fingers of
aerial roots reaching for the light. She moved among them,
aware of her forest secretly growing.

Michael hadn't come, and he seldom rang. She realized she had been looking forward to his visit: she wanted friends from outside Greece, who would bring with them free air. He wouldn't ditch them – but yet, where was he? She had a spasm of mistrust, then thought in old bitterness: well, why should the foreigners care? We take it for granted they do, but why should they bother? We're not them.

Then he came. He rang to warn her: he was sorry for his delays. And one evening a little later she heard his voice, that seemed permanently slightly hoarse, relayed upwards from the grill down below, and presently his rap on the door. There he stood in her doorway, the elongated Englishman, ever active, alert eyed, his features drawn to a point. She surprised herself with her pleasure to see him: he had arrived like a lorry loaded with good memories.

Of its own accord her voice said warmly, 'Come in, Michael, it's good to see you.'

She was aware of his leanness stalking through the flat – was England some sort of rack that stretched its people out? She followed his movements as he stooped over her plants and flowers, feeling that something too foreign, too tall, with too great a kindness, had entered her home. She must see people more: this arrival was a ridiculously overwhelming event.

He sat, folding his long limbs at skew angles; he seemed nervous, but also pleased and excited to see her. He apologized again for his delays, and asked her several times how she was. He looked round the flat.

'You've made changes.'

'You mean, I've tidied it?'

'No, I don't mean that, I mean all these plants – it's a tidy jungle, if it's a tidy anything. But I like the way the plants go with the furniture – I like your Balkan Baronial because it's full of plants, and now it's as if there's *so much* vegetation in the carving that it's overflowed in real plants, as if the woodwork's come to life. It's really a garden, this flat.'

He looked about him with pleasure; and the afternoon light came into the room, so the furniture with its carved plants, and all the green plants growing about it, seemed rich, calm, a warm abundance. She hadn't seen her flat like this, though this perhaps was what she had been wanting: affected by his pleasure, she looked round the familiar room, enchanted.

'Anyway, I've done my reports,' he said, 'and people talk about Vangelis, you know, quite apart from anything I've done. Amnesty International does. How is he? Have you seen him again?'

'No, I can't yet. But thank God he isn't injured.'

She told him of the obstacles to her seeing Vangelis again. 'Oh that's wicked,' he muttered, almost voiceless. 'You manage very bravely, Chryssa.'

'I manage as I have to. And I've pulled in my horns, in a way. Before I saw him, it was different: then I didn't know where he was or what had happened, I was looking for him everywhere, I would look out for him walking through Athens, sometimes I thought I saw him and at the same time I knew I would never see him again. Or I'd simply be out in the street, and I'd remember being in that part of Athens with him, at a happy time, and then I'd miss him – so much, as if he'd been taken just that day. Now it's different, I know he is all right, I know where he is. But there's a very terrible thing, Michael. Part of you gets *used* to – disappearance.' She paused, and her calm seemed fragile, fractured, close to tears. 'I feel now he's very far away.'

'He will come back.'

'He'll come when the Junta falls. It won't be sooner.'

'When will that be? They *can't* last.'

'I don't know how long they'll go on. They aren't loved, but many, many people prefer the quiet life. But yes, even so, it must be true – with time, more and more people will come out against them. There *will* be an explosion. They *will* fall. Vangelis and I always said that.'

But she hesitated, on the edge of a doubt she didn't want to voice: and Michael saw she had lost the conviction, which she and Vangelis had at the start, that their movement was part of a tide, a current. She had a measure of faith and trust, and hope for change, but these things were maintained now by resolute private effort, against the apparent odds, while what she chiefly felt was isolation.

He set to work, occasionally going out with her, but otherwise working in his hotel, or doing his researches on his own: her secret advice guided him. He toured Athens, seeing people she suggested, or people whose names she had obtained from Simos. He had thought he was calloused by too much reporting

237

of pain, but the things he heard now, matter of fact from the people he spoke to, made him writhe, coil, made his eyes smart, his mouth dry as if he bit sand.

In the evenings he reported to Chryssa: she'd assess what he'd gathered, and propose other lines for him to pursue. She was sharp in telling him what not to believe: her remarks worked for him like x-ray spectacles, so he could see how dictatorship comes home. But also he was elated just to be with her. He felt he could dissolve in the sound of her voice: it was low, confident, with a timbre like rustling cloth, now taffeta now calico. His skin tingled, he wanted her to speak on for ever. At these times, the passion he felt in New York would rise to overwhelm him. How had he ever supposed he had suppressed it? – and still he must act the quiet good friend. In this, his reporter's training helped: for years he had interviewed, being pleasant faced, interested, while behind his mildness he sifted and planned. He had become a good hypocrite.

Most times they met, she would speak of Vangelis. After the first evening she didn't talk about his absence, her missing him: she recalled him in action, heroically obstinate.

'How is he in court?' Michael asked. 'I've never seen him there.'

'Oh, he has his own style, you don't know the impact he made when he began.'

Preparatory to describing Vangelis, she described the law courts as they used to be. Her bent for mimicry and burlesque revived, describing the old style advocate's eloquence. 'If you knew, judges, the sufferings my client has endured, if you knew his remorse . . .' She switched then quickly to the client himself, became for some moments the rubble-faced reprobate in the dock.

'Like a Daumier lawyer,' Michael said.

'*Just* like a Daumier,' she said, slipping instantly out of role and then back into it. She had come to life, reminiscing: now she was all the parties concerned in another courtroom dispute she had seen, where the judge stood up and harangued the advocate, the client joined in, and another lawyer, they all expostulated at the tops of their voices.

'But Vangelis had a different style, right from the start. After the banging and rhetoric, he was very quiet.' She recalled his first case. Even then there were expectations of him, the newest lawyer, who had studied abroad, but at first he seemed an anti-climax, for his address to the court was almost comically brief and plain, and otherwise he seemed to place all his faith in a few curt questions shot off at the witness. Then it became clear that the witness could not answer them; and then it became clear that the witness could not afford to answer. Now the court woke up, the judges in a row attended, and Vangelis continued, giving nothing it seemed but the bare bones of his logic. He spoke quietly but distinctly, he was energy compact, even his silences pinned the court. As she spoke, Chryssa's eyes sharpened, the asiatic fold on her upper lids tautened; her voice became hard edged, curt, dry. As he looked at her, Michael saw Vangelis also, tense but pleased, nimble, aggressive. Michael gazed, both spellbound and in pain, seeing the two people one. Vangelis-Chryssa won his case, and Chryssa's own wide smile surfaced as she relaxed from the role.

'Congratulations!' Michael said to both of them.

Then Chryssa and Michael were silent some moments in reverie, as if really, for a short time, Vangelis had joined them.

'Michael, you must talk to Simos.'

Chryssa spoke to Clio, who invited her to bring Michael the following weekend: the occasion was to look as much sociable, as little like an interview, as possible.

Michael called for Chryssa in the car he had hired for his circuits of Athens. He had chosen, out of chauvinism or economy, a mini, which seemed hardly equal to the city's torrent of large German and American saloons: but he drove adroitly, threading the crush, slipping fast through temporary openings. She glanced at him, leanly concentrated forward: he didn't quite conceal that he meant to impress her, the diffident foreigner who was still a suave international driver. She was amused, remembering his old thunderings on his motorbike.

But his aplomb was interrupted. They both jumped at a sudden frantic hooting, far behind them but rapidly drawing closer. Chryssa glanced round: it looked like an ordinary family car, though it made as much racket as though it owned the city. 'Pompous . . .' Michael muttered, and held the centre lane.

The furious hooting continued. Chryssa turned again: the

239

car was very close, almost bumping them, she could see clearly the silhouette of the man at the wheel.

'I'd let him through if I were you.'

Michael looked again in his mirror. With a face of annoyance, and still taking his time, he moved aside. The other driver, overtaking, had the merest contemptuous head toss for the foreigner: already he was busy hooting other cars in front that blocked his way. Through the back window they saw clearly the shoulders of his uniform, his officer's hat. He was alone.

'That's not a staff car,' Michael mused.

'He's probably shopping for his wife. This is a military government, Michael.'

He registered her reproof: he had displayed a fecklessness, blocking so long the officer's path. The cars ahead were not so innocent, they scooted clear quickly.

Chryssa guiding, they drove now through side streets to the apartment block where Clio and Simos lived.

When the door opened, Simos filled it. He was dressed for the weekend and wearing shorts, which Michael had not before seen a Greek man wear. He embraced Chryssa, appearing to lift her an inch from the ground, and held out a broad-spread hand to Michael, while his soft, gentle-giant voice said in careful English, 'How do you do, I am pleased to meet you.'

They entered a large, high-ceilinged room. With his journalist's camera-eye Michael scanned the furnishings, which were modern, fragile, with caprice: a slender aluminium lamp standard, with a square metal shade on a long elbow; even, on a glass table, a glass-stemmed table lamp with a glass bird attached. Clio had come, speaking vivaciously in Greek like a peal of bells: Michael found it hard to keep up with her, and mainly watched the passions flicker in her small-featured, beautiful face. He had not before seen anyone so elegant, delicate, fluttering, neat. Chryssa, talking to her, was immediately animated, her arms moving freely and gracefully. Michael watched from the outside their bright foreign-to-him feminine rapport.

There were further voices, a door banged open, and a child, a daughter, danced half into the room, saw them, and dived back laughing. Simos raised his head.

'Sophia!' The words were a kind of quiet shout. The child stopped, returned shyly to pay her respects.

'Good day, Mrs Chryssa.'

'Hello, Sophia.'

She was fair haired like Simos, petite like Clio. Michael now saw the furnishings in another aspect: like the aluminium lamp they were slightly dented, slightly on the skew, from the passage of children. Their elegance, and Clio's, was something continually retrieved, perfected momentarily, before being eroded by a new child-burst.

'To business?' Simos enquired.

'Please.'

Simos led Michael to the balcony where, while discussing a referendum the Junta had held, he picked up two beach chairs by the neck and lightly flapped them open.

'The figures were fixed, of course, but in an odd way. The vote was ninety-six percent *before* they added the vote from the army. They had to invent a lower figure, so it wouldn't be ridiculous.'

'What was the real vote?'

Simos shrugged, gave a ponderous jut-chinned pout, 'Who's to say? In the villages, people would vote for the Government whatever the issue was. I know, as a lawyer I had to go and invigilate. The old women would come in shouting "My vote is yes" just for the policeman and me to hear. In the cities it would be another story, but there's no way of knowing the actual figures. There would be false votes. The tellers would put in figures to please the mayors. The mayors would put in figures to please the nomarch. The nomarchs would put in figures to please Athens.' He laughed, a slow subterranean cough.

Michael had come wanting information from Simos about other trials that had occurred since Vangelis'. Screwing up his face in the autumn sun, Simos pausingly but steadily recalled names, dates, appeals. Michael jotted, and in the pauses wondered at him, extended at ease, his limbs too large and tree-like to feel the cool. They were covered, as was his large, boylike head, with soft-curled sun-bleached hair. Enormous, tanned, motionless, he sat as though summer must linger where he was.

They heard in the distance a shock of sound, a faint dull bump. In a quiet, suspended tone Simos said, 'There's a bomb gone off.' He stirred his limbs, moved to the balcony, all his face puckered as he scanned the city.

'I think it's the Ministry of Labour.'

Standing beside him, Michael made out, near the distant brown block of the abandoned Parliament, a tiny ball of white smoke climbing, slowly distending.

Simos turned away sighing, 'I don't know what bombs achieve.'

'Bombs aren't the way,' Michael agreed definitely.

Simos glanced at him, his face furrowed more. In his gentle voice he chided, 'Well, you can't just say there shouldn't be bombs. I don't believe in bombs, but when there's a dictatorship, people will protest in the ways they can. Some will use bombs. Of course.'

When Simos had completed his list of cases, they moved indoors to eat. As Chryssa and Michael were ushered to the table, Michael suddenly thought: they're entertaining us like a couple. The drop in Clio's voice, as she passed him a plate, seemed to acknowledge that he and Chryssa were a twosome. Simos' friendly smile, as his large arm, like a crane, reached over the table with the wine, seemed to say the same thing. Then they began talking: and at once it was clear, she was their friend, and the wife of their friend Vangelis: he, Michael, was the foreign guest. Anything else was unthinkable: he should blush for what he thought – and he did, his skin burned. But no one noticed, the meal advanced cheerfully.

Later, the general attention turned to him.

'What are the British doing?'

'Taking their holidays elsewhere. There are protests and condemnations of course, it isn't that people are silent. The trouble is, those things don't have much effect even on our own government. And people say stupid things, they'll say "Uh, the Balkans, what do you expect?" Or they say, "Well, the politicians were probably corrupt", as though soldiers were incorruptible by nature.'

Simos gave his coughing laugh, 'The brothers of these soldiers do well enough. So, do you get a response to what you write?'

'It's like your referendum, Simos, it's impossible to say. Some days I think reports do tell. Other days, I think you can talk in the world's fat ear for ever, and the world may listen, and agree with what you say – and in the end he wanders off, to hear some other chap tell him a different story.'

242

Chryssa said, 'That's a black picture, Michael.'

Michael bethought himself: he was speaking too much from his own disappointment. 'Yes, and that's wrong. Because it's true, there is a *tide* of protest, everything that joins it helps. You mustn't look for quick or obvious results.'

Simos nodded, 'The fact is, other countries won't make the Junta go. It's our work or no one's.'

The talk slipped into Greek and moved on from Michael. He still participated, intermittently venturing his Greek. Chryssa attended: for his Greek was not bad, he had found a good rhythm, neither mimicking Greek stress, nor foreign and flat. It suited his composure, as he sat there at ease with his arms folded or his legs crossed – inhibited English postures which Greek men didn't easily use. He looked a trace the dandy, in the light suit he had on for the occasion, even though, with his leanness, he seemed all made of bones and bumps. His blue eyes jumped quickly from speaker to speaker, keen, amused: she could read the conversation there. Then his eyes turned to her – and snatched at her, seized her, as if some hot message would jump out of them at her. For a few moments her friends, the conversation, disappeared: she thought, I've known Michael years – and what do I know about him? He's totally the foreigner. She was perplexed; but a second later Michael was talking to Clio, answering her questions, as the good-humoured conversation resumed.

The curiosity about Michael hovered in her mind when, after coffee, after thanks and goodbyes, they left. All Athens was shut for its siesta. The sun was very bright but not over hot, she suggested they stroll before driving home: so, in after-lunch good humour, they sauntered in the dazzling streets. They had the city to themselves: shops had their grills down, the bars had no tables but only stacks of bright-coloured crates outside, scooters and small cars were parked on the pavements of the narrow streets as though they had pulled off the road to rest. It was like midnight seen by day.

She said, 'How did you become a journalist, Michael? That wasn't your idea when we knew you in London?'

'No, no, it was by a roundabout route. I'd studied all those languages, then I was researching them. After a time I

243

wondered: where have my languages brought me? Is it the be-all and end-all that I study them in England?'

'So you decided to be a foreign correspondent?'

'No, I got a job teaching English in Germany – it was the only job I could get. But I felt cut off and I started to write – bits on wine and Oberrammergau – and sent them in to English papers. I moved on to other things, industry, politics, that's how I drifted into foreign-corresponding. I'd thought it would be difficult to get started but it wasn't.'

They came to a small square, where pink oleander blooms surrounded a pillared stump of antiquity. As if weary of his travelling, he sat down on some wooden fruit trays which evidently survived from a morning stall. She sat on the next pile.

'Then I changed to the news service, which is different work. I do some reporting, but mainly I prepare news to send to other papers elsewhere. It's not full-scale news-hounding, and it does give me some time – and I wanted to be in London, it gets harder as the years pass to put down new roots. Though I'm away so much, I feel I'm a foreigner in London as well.'

'And is the news service the answer for you?'

'No it's not, but I don't know where else I'd go.'

He stopped. He had spoken lightly, but Chryssa felt sad. She had a vision of the solitariness, the unsettledness of his life. What did he have? No roots, no home, no wife – no future perhaps, she saw only further wandering ahead. And he was not drifting, he was moving clear-eyed down the line of his decisions: he met the void with quiet self-irony, no loneliness would be allowed to show. She felt she was noticing, for the first time, the person that he was. She looked at his hands, resting on his knees: slender-wristed, sinewy, fine-fingered.

They got up, continued walking. They came presently to another square, where a large area had been cordoned off. A policeman kept a small group of onlookers at a distance. Coming closer, they saw a weird curled shape: there were pieces of metal like giant torn petals, black, round the collapsed chassis of a car.

'The bomb,' Michael murmured.

They paused by the cordon. The ground near the wreck was strewn with small broken objects, and chalk circles had been drawn round some of these. Two men in shirtsleeves stooped over the wreck, discussing it desultorily: evidently the important evidence had already been removed. The buildings in the square had their windows blown out, except where knives of glass lingered in some casements. The wreckage was eerie in the sunlight, the silence.

Nearby, the onlookers questioned the policeman. 'Were they fascists? Were they communists?'

'No, no,' he said, 'they were terrorists. They were in the car when it exploded.'

Chryssa shuddered, they moved closer together. 'Let's go.'

They walked on steadily till they were a distance from the square. Chryssa was silent, her head down, in thoughts about her country that hadn't a place for Michael. All the city seemed disfigured. One building was shrouded by sacking, long folds ran down it from top to bottom, and slightly stirred in the hot breath. The head of a tall palm tree seemed exploded to rags, just a few green spikes above a thick bunch of tatters.

Chryssa surfaced only when, returning towards the car, they paused by a small furniture warehouse. Over the door, the stone bust of a nineteenth-century statesman was set up on some sort of metal tripod, so it seemed to hover in midair, like a nineteenth-century Big Brother, or like the Wizard of Oz.

'It's open,' she said, 'let's go in.'

They entered the shop, which was a curious ramshackle building, half a shed, opening into bigger sheds further back. The proprietor wasn't to be seen; there was a noise of television from the depths of the shop. The goods were of all sorts, piled up on the furniture: imitation classical figures, carvings, icons, old crosses, Turkish swords, mountain pistols, ships' brasses, a Nazi helmet – all heaped up in the dimness as though this were the place where the country kept its memory. Chryssa looked up, her face dusty, her eyes brilliant.

'Michael, this reminds me of the warehouse my father had.'

He saw she was not only seeking bargains, she was also wandering in memory, touching her childhood in touching the old goods and chairs. Still they were not challenged, they worked their way back, Chryssa holding by now an armful of potential bargains, till finally they arrived at the proprietor and his associates. An aged man of colossal paunch lay back in an armchair with, beyond him, another old man, and an old woman also, of identical kidney. Whether they were two brothers and a sister, or a husband, wife and brother, or even a menage à trois grown venerable in age, there was no knowing: they were watching an American soap opera on a flickering television that stood on a pile of carpets. They were too absorbed to haggle.

'What's the price of this?' Chryssa held out a small fruit bowl.

His eye barely moved to it.

'One hundred drachmas.'

Chryssa blinked; but from habit, from training, she must bargain, she'd be ill if she didn't.

'I'll give you fifty,' she said.

Without a glance at her, he held out his hand.

She gave the money, but still was not happy, now she had conscience, 'It's worth more than that, Michael.'

'All right, give him more for something else.'

They moved back through the shop, but still she kept finding more things, and returning to the shopkeepers. Michael saw it was the shop of her dreams, it was not a shop she would be able to leave. He was moved to see, after her troubles, her entrepreneurial zest revived.

Near the entrance they discovered, under a pollen of dust, an upright piano.

'You used to play?'

She nodded.

'Play.'

'Oh, it's years, Michael, I can't any more.'

'Play, play; your hands will remember.'

'It won't be Rachmaninov.'

'Who wants Rachmaninov. Come. I want to hear you.'

'I can't play here.'

'Uh!' he said Greekly, 'they won't mind.' He walked back through the shop, and called out in his distinct foreigner's Greek, 'May we try the piano?'

They looked up, shrugged quickly, and returned to the soap.

Chryssa still hovered, reluctant to begin, reluctant to retreat. They found a piano stool: she eased her shoulders, flexed her arms, waved her fingers, pressed the pedals. She slightly stooped to the keys, her arms raised as though poised to pounce: then she glanced at Michael, took a breath, both hands plunged

246

to such music bursting from the old wooden box: rippling, reverberating, booming, rapid. What had he expected? A plaintive ditty? She played like an orchestra all suddenly switched on at once, with verve, with emotion; her face forward to the piano though there was no music to read. She frowned oblivious of Michael, the old piano tinkled and jangled, she played with unstoppable rhythm – till the tune stopped, and she sat back, sighed, beamed, laughed.

'It was full of wrong notes.'

'It was wonderful,' he said: his ears still rang, he was stunned, irradiated, at all this music stored up within her and suddenly released.

He imagined her years since, in the prosperous family bosom, some music teacher visiting and putting her through her paces: all her young energy and expectations marrying with the music, so that years later when she played not only the tune returned, but all that feeling, her youth itself, before ever he met her.

She stopped exhausted, abstracted, in a lovely relaxed happiness. They had too much to carry away with them; Michael went to get the car.

She was in no hurry for home, he took a wide loop through the city. In the green suburb of Kifissia, Chryssa pointed out, among the mansions, the squat new block where her sister lived.

'Do you see her at all?'

'No.'

As he drove, he snatched glances at her. She was pleasantly drowsed with the motion of the car. Her eyes, half-closed, gazed gently out: the fold of skin over them, which gave them a Slav look and also a keenness, was smoothed, relaxed. She had a slight, calm smile, her mouth had indentations at the corner as if it wanted to dimple. This still, full expression was not one he had seen before, it must have grown in times of quiet love in her marriage with Vangelis. It was good that it had stayed, like a memory in the body, and could surface now.

Though the traffic, ever busier, hooted, he continued snatching looks. He had developed a habit, these days, of snapping her: when they glanced at each other while talking, just as people do to hold attention, all his energy of sight had jumped through those glances, to take a clear photo he could gaze at later. Now she looked his way, and caught him looking: he quickly looked back to the swerving road. He thought, she's caught me spying on her. Everyone spied now, watched, eavesdropped, listened in: the police, the military, the secret service. Am I just another spy – like the plain-clothes police, like the ears on the phone-line, like the dictators? But he was love's spy – masquerading as the friend. That was insidious too.

Lights and car lights sparkled: stretched away between apartment blocks, the night city was emerging from its haze like a galaxy from dust clouds. Chryssa stirred, looked out of the windows innocent-eyed.

They arrived at her home: he helped her ferry her purchases into the lift. She insisted she'd manage now. She thanked him warmly, wearily.

'It was a very good day, Michael.'

He took himself off.

Upstairs she unloaded, and shepherded her buys into her flat. It was dark inside, but she did not want light. She shut her eyes also, they dazzled from the day, and felt her way through the room: certain in the dark like a blind person. The security of home was close as her skin. She touched the edge of her armchair, and sat back easy, recollecting, amused, the huge-paunched shopkeepers. She opened her eyes and could see things now, in the glimmer that came through the slats of her blinds: a dim shine on the surface of the table, the silhouette of her plants. They seemed to grow everywhere, as if she were present at night in a still intimate garden.

She reached out and cupped her hand round the curved shade of her art nouveau lamp. One push of a finger, and its brown light would flow back dimming to the walls of the flat, while the green plants came forward. But even that light she did not want. Sitting in the soothing dark was like enjoying already the rest of sleep, while in a kind of clear dreaming her thoughts collected. But Michael confused her. She had been startled downstairs when she turned round from unlocking the door, and found him behind her unexpectedly close, unlike himself, haggard, his blue eyes looking black. He changed at

248

once to friendly goodbyes, but she was unsettled. Often his eyes disconcerted her. Behind their kindness they tracked her: she did not know what other eyes through his eyes watched her. Are we alone? she wondered sometimes, alone with him. Then she felt his kindness: Why was she mistrustful? He had seemed the good man, far away: now, so close, he disturbed.

Her thoughts moved back to a safer distance, and to one of their evenings in England. He had taken her to a party in the country on his motorbike: the ride was exhilarating, rocketing down lanes, she felt safe hanging on. When they arrived he was glowing, perhaps with pride of the bike, perhaps with pleasure of taking her: his skin was tanned with sun and wind, he shone like a slender, long-nosed bronze, his eyes were very blue and clear. All his guardedness and tension were gone: he was confident and easy, a relaxed tender touch and kiss. It was an isolated evening, one of her good memories of England.

She was tired, sleepy, relaxed in the dark: yet not only tired. It grew, in quiet waves, a feeling she'd thought dead: it was desire. Clear as words in the dark, after all this dead time, I need love, I want love, for *my* self, for my life. She stretched back in the dark.

When she switched on the light, the whole room swung to her, her plants gave her greeting. She got up to give them water, then retired, tired, to heavy sleep.

Shortly before Michael left, they went out in the evening to have a meal in Plaka, and afterwards walked in the little streets under the Acropolis. As they paused in the light from one of the small tavernas there, he looked at her seriously: he was going soon, his eyes looked older and very tender. She knew her own eyes had changed. She thought, it happens at this moment or never. She stood paralysed, her arms at her side, all she could do was gaze. His touch grazed her hand.

She lay on her back. Light as mothwings his fingers alighted, traced her belly, touched her breast.

She lay on her front. Gently the fine pads of his fingertips traced her back, her shoulders, her neck. She wanted only to be a flat wing of bone, forever outlined by patrolling fingers.

They lay side by side, facing: in the brown dimness she

made out his open eyes. They looked enlarged but calm, she had not seen them so quietly open.

Clear light came in, she looked up at Michael who was looking at her. His lips were firm in a gentle serious smile of love, then she saw a question grow.

'Chryssa . . .' he began. She raised her hand, rested her fingers on his lips.

'This is a stolen time, Michael. It's outside normal time.'

He nodded; his face clear in steady love.

12

Contact with those working for the Great Idea had made Leonidas rethink his politics. It seemed to him now that his earlier views had been too negative. True, there had been the huge danger of communism, as the nation collapsed in riots and anarchy while the King and his prime ministers bickered in deadlock: from that nightmare the National Government had saved them, it had disciplined the nation. But this still was holding, checking, negative work: it left unanswered the question – where, after all, was the National Government leading Greece? On what clear road was it marching? Was it marching at all? He could see the bad side of military government, that too many of these disciplinarian soldiers were willing just to freeze things as they were, or even try to take them backwards, and he knew that wouldn't work. In the early days he hadn't worried: Greece had been on fire, out of that fire the National Government rose like the phoenix that was their emblem, huge powerful bird growing as it climbed till its wingspan of beating muscle covered Greece from end to end. Yet now it hovered, its wingbeat had faltered, it rose and fell unsteadily on turbulent airs. The economy was weak; the wreckers and bombers were still at work. Their new constitution had been approved by referendum, but it was still not put into effect. The blind Greek people were worse than ungrateful. Where were they heading?

The war plan, the Great Idea, had come as the answer. Here was purpose, here was the road. They would smite Turkey, and regain Greater Greece, and be rich with all the oil in the Aegean. He could not desire a greater mission.

As he saw this, he saw that he must take strong action, but also that he must think well first. For the mission was clear, but the road was hard. They were forced to suspect the President and his cronies: were they in the pocket of the Americans? Did they dare to go beyond what NATO wanted?

The President was at risk on several counts. He had spoken of introducing more civilians into government, and Leonidas' new friends were strongly against this. And just here Leonidas had to be careful, for though he was ardent to work with the officers, still he himself, after all, was a civilian. It would be easy for him to be nothing to them. And he was part of the President's government, if the President went it would be easy for Leonidas to be swept away with him.

He must find a right way to ride the storm: even in the Ministry he stood in danger. For it grew ever more clear to everyone that the Minister was too reactionary, too blinkered, the Ministry was not working well: and he was the Minister's second-in-command. Sooner or later the Minister must go, whether or not the Government changed, and Leonidas must make sure he was not sacked with him.

One thing was clear, he must secure his own ground. He must dissociate himself from the Minister, and those above must know it. And he must get such control of that Ministry, he must become so indispensable to it, that if and when the changes came – if the Minister went, or even if the President went – he himself stayed. For he had powerful friends: he might, in a new national government, be promoted, he might be the one civilian minister in the new war cabinet.

Now, as Secretary, he changed gear, accelerated, he would make quite sure the Ministry was his. Of late months he had a little relaxed, savouring power, enjoying being chauffeured, and being buttered and flattered as he toured the shipyards. The soft period was over. He summoned aides and officials, drew up plans, rounds of visits, schedules of legislation; every opportunity that came of negotiating with the bigger business-men he reserved for himself. He had them come to see him, he talked to them shrewdly and at length, he laboured to lodge in their minds the knowledge that *he* was the friend, the patron, the man who got things done, the man who had a decisive say on which projects got government backing.

These contacts served Leonidas in various ways, for they not only put him in good standing with business, they also gave him pretexts for seeing other ministers. He apologized for troubling these great men, but their opinions must be sought; and at the same time he flattered them, and also advanced the tentative idea that he himself could do much more in his ministry if he were not perpetually impeded by the conservatisms of the Minister. In candour, but modestly, he touched on the many plans he had.

He gave more time also to trades union officials. He summoned them to the Ministry, and when they arrived was affable to them, and took time understanding their point of view over a quiet glass of brandy. Here too he established understandings, so that *if* they had questions, uncertainties, worries – for even between the best willed of national governments and the most patriotic and loyal of government-nominated union leaders, there may sometimes arise a conflict of interest – they knew he was the man to whom they could talk, and come to some good agreement.

So with new energy, at all hours of day and night, he improved his connections. He introduced policy initiatives, which he recommended to the Minister by telling him these measures were inspired by his ideas, while to others he made it clear that the measures were children of no brain but his own. And these proposals, with some modification suggested by the Minister – Leonidas made a point of including suggestions by the Minister, so the Minister should feel a commitment to them – went into effect. For he concentrated on plans of a kind that could be put into effect. He sounded out the relevant officials beforehand; and indeed it was said by some that Leonidas' initiatives were not actually his own idea – still less the Minister's – but simply measures which a number of officials had been pressing for for years. This in turn meant that Leonidas' measures now were not the radical changes he had dreamt of in early days. Still, it was necessary for him at this stage to have initiatives coming to fruition, and if actually they were not so radical, this did after all make them popular in the offices. And if none of these measures had any real effect on the problems of the economy, still it was early days – give Leonidas time, and give him power, and the nation would see what he could do.

In the meantime, too, simply being in motion was a form of power. For his political philosophy was changing, and he saw now that power in politics often consisted just in riding events in a prominent posture, and pretending to steer them the way they careered. But there was real power too: when he was Minister, then he would steer.

The Minister himself was an intractable problem. Leonidas
had tried to be friendly, and even to confide. He had sought
the Minister's advice in the matter of Vangelis, as to getting
him released if and when the time were ripe. And here the
Minister said he would help: he understood the claims of
family. But in other matters, though Leonidas might exert
himself to be never so obliging and courteous and smiling, still
the Minister only suspected him more. The man's paranoiac,
Leonidas said to himself, and he worked with yet more
humble abasement to show himself to the Minister as the
Minister's slave, and to apply to that man's hectic neuroses
his smoothest balm and lanoline of flattery. His extremity
of effort had some success: for though to the Minister's
discerning eye he might look a stout and rapacious wolf
concealed by the flimsiest wisp of fleece as he crept on
tiptoe towards him, still nothing so blears and dazzles the
discerning eye as gold drops of flattery dripped in without
ceasing. If the Minister hadn't a wife, he might just have
been lulled, for all his anxiety. But he had a wife who, from
the other side, reinforced in the Minister a resistance that
Leonidas would never surmount. The wife met Leonidas
when he first came to Athens, and from that moment it
never occurred to her that Leonidas had any other motive
for all the work he put in, except to be Minister as fast as he
could.

Consequently, work and try as he might, Leonidas could not
prevent the Minister from constantly returning to devouring
suspicion. The more work Leonidas did, the more alarmed the
Minister became, for he saw that Leonidas could make him
superfluous. He must slow Leonidas down, set him harder
tasks. He began placing traps in Leonidas' path. If only he
could get him out of the country. Alone in his office, clenched in
thought at his large desk, he had a brainwave. The Government
needed a negotiator for a team going to a communist country:
and he would send Leonidas. The Minister chuckled harshly
and cracked his knuckles: this would stop Leonidas in his
tracks – the man lost control at the mention of communism,
his hatred of it was like a madness, even he, the Minister, did
not hate communism as much. His lean fingers drummed the
desk top as he waited for Leonidas.

And Leonidas blanched, his eyes glazed, at the news. This

254

was not a commission for him, he deeply disapproved of the National Government's negotiating at all with communist countries. The pounding engine of his great ambition missed a stroke.

But he must go. He kissed Patra farewell with tears in his eyes. As he took off, a storm blew up over the mountains, and the sky was blocked by a purple misty wall: lightning flashed in it, the tiny plane drove into peril.

Yet the Minister's plan did not work as intended. Leonidas landed in the same sunlight that scorched Athens. Deferential staff led him to a limousine. He thought, is this communism? He met his opposite number, and the Balkan communist was far from being the rigid puritanical commissar he expected; he was an enormous laughing man, fat, florid, he at once poured Leonidas a glass of rich sweet deep-yellow wine: an export wine, available also to notable people. The man chatted and joked, then they drove up into the hills, and dined on a terrace grown round with vines, where for hours while they waited for the pork to be cooked they did nothing but knock back spirits. So far as Leonidas remembered afterwards, and his recollection was far from clear, the man made not one remark which Leonidas could construe as an attack on his personal property. In a haze of spirit, chewing sweet pork, gazing at the mountain peaks, Leonidas developed a certain fellow feeling: they had common ground, they were both men of power, running a country.

When, the following day, they came to negotiate, they haggled in good part and concluded an agreement to mutual advantage. Afterwards Leonidas toured the city, and saw with pleasure that the shop windows were meagre.

And so Leonidas returned to Athens, in good spirits and in triumph too. The Minister was disarrayed, the more so because of Leonidas' habit of keeping an extraordinary number of people posted on how well any of his negotiations were going. The Minister saw he had little chance of hiding Leonidas' light. But at least this episode made him sure of his purpose: he must stop Leonidas as soon as possible. Systematically he began to test the loyalty of his staff: he made remarks about Leonidas, and then watched needle-eyed to see which way people would jump. And Leonidas, with all his confidence, had inspired dislike: the Minister identified these dissidents and drew them to him, and gave them special charges. In his office now he wove a web.

Which Leonidas sensed, and he began to mobilize his own loyal forces. He promoted new programmes, of specific advantage to civil servants. Down all the filaments of command in the Ministry the two men sent investigative signals, and mentally circled each other. They did not meet more often than they had to, and when they did they were clipped and elliptical, keeping however a certain formality in front of subordinates.

On the question of Vangelis, it grew clearer that the Minister was giving no help. He would tell Leonidas to leave the matter with him, and then do nothing: and in a sudden illumination, Leonidas saw the point of this tactic. The Minister wanted Vangelis to stay in prison; with such a handicap Leonidas could not rise higher, he depended entirely on the Minister's patronage. It left him bitter: he had failed to help Vangelis, and now he saw his folly, he had hurt himself. He must make moves elsewhere; and Vangelis had suffered much, it would be an honourable deed to set him free.

Cautiously Leonidas began his moves. In the Ministry itself he had stopped proposing new measures, for nothing he proposed could get past the Minister. The Minister thought only of hindering him. They must pass this point quickly, for they were holding each other down: and this was dangerous because in the deadlock the Ministry suffered, and if that became known they might both be discarded. Leonidas saw, he must strengthen his hand quickly. And he knew where he must look for further strength, it could only be the army. Since he first took office he had a growing sense of that shadowy body of army officers – the new colonels, the new generals – to whom ultimately the National Government had always to answer, for they had the tanks. The generals were the men who mattered most: and thanks to his loyalty to the Great Idea, he was personally acquainted with generals. He must strengthen quickly his connections with them, for with them was his future, and the future of Greece.

The next step he must take soon came clear. On a windy day in early summer, he attended a presidential inspection of the navy: he was there in connection with some naval contracts in which his friend Polikarpos had expressed an interest. They stood on the deck of a destroyer: the air was fiercely clear, the separate fields stood sharp-edged on islands tiny in the distance, the white horses on the sea were acid white against the sharp blue water; from a disturbed sky thin showers came down, swept sidelong by the wind. An old naval sergeant, with a hatchet face and drooping moustaches like a hero of the Revolution, barked orders that the wind blew half away at a shivering line of young marines. Taking the salute, the President and his senior ministers stood huddled inside thick coats, that were reflected in the wet windswept deck, suddenly screwing their faces as a gust of spray drove into their eyes. They had come in force because of a recent attempt by the navy to mutiny; but, remembering the mutiny, and seeing this handful of middle-aged men, once his heroes, grimfaced now, shivering in the wind, Leonidas felt, for the first time, a frailty in the National Government. They were men with worries, and exposed: they did not look like great leaders of the nation. He wondered, would they last? and said to himself: Think well, Leonida!

Afterwards, as they waited to leave, while the President's helicopter lifted over them in a whirr of blades, Leonidas heard two of the ministers, who had previously been colonels in the army, shouting to each other over the engine noise.

'Ach, the army – do you think the army's more reliable than the navy?'

The other nodded wryly and shouted back, 'Where does Vouros stand?'

'Ask him!'

Evidently it was a bitter joke, they both laughed harshly.

As his helicopter tipped and swung clear from the diminishing battleship, Leonidas nursed the remark with rising spirits. The ministers hung on the loyalty and power of men like Vouros. And Leonidas knew General Vouros. He was in their group; and he and Leonidas had had several bluff, brief conversations, in which it seemed they had a rapport. If Leonidas could make a true friend of Vouros, then his ties with the army would be strong indeed. For Vouros was not rash or zealous, like some men in their group: he was canny, shrewd, powerful in the army and interested in power. And Leonidas had the perfect chance of making friends with him. He knew from a previous conversation that Vouros was interested in buying land on the promontory where he and Patra had built their villa. And that villa, at last, was truly finished. If they could christen it by inviting General Vouros to come for the day – what an opportunity it would be for ambition! Ah, Leonida, he thought, as the blades overhead throbbed round in the blue and the landscape slid beneath them, you'll be the friend of generals – this is your coup!

13

Michael sat at Heathrow, waiting for the Greek flight that would take him to Chryssa: they would meet on an island far from Athens, where they would have a better chance of evading the spies. Still he was amazed, hardly believing it. When they had made love, it had been so much what he had hoped for, and never believed would happen, that he felt he had slipped into a different world, part dark, part blest. Immediately afterwards they didn't talk of meeting: but they had to be in contact, for his reports if nothing else; they couldn't keep talking and not think of meeting; and the meeting couldn't stay in the past. But even after they had made arrangements he would some days be overcome with amazement.

The flight delay stretched interminable. He had hardly believed he'd go, now it seemed he wouldn't. A turbanned waiter moved solemnly between the tables: beyond the slanting windows, in the centre of the sky, a wide-winged plane, homing, stood solid and still like a rock. Time stopped: and should he go? In this delay, all the voices against the trip spoke together: you're going in order to betray your friend, betray his work, your motives are bad, you shouldn't go. The white-robed waiter arrived at his table, and, stooping, swabbed the tacky rings clear of the formica. In the shining table Michael watched him: a cloudy figure, white as a cloud, pausing and withdrawing.

The flight was signalled: in that instant he felt Chryssa's pull, she pulled like the Pole Star, he knew he'd go, he had less chance of resisting than of crawling up the jet engine against the jet. He murmured a stupid imploring 'Vangeli . . .' – a prayer for forbearance? He was hurrying for the plane as though that way he'd leave sooner. Outside a tiny plane slanted steeply upwards, against the sliding Himalayas of the English April sky. Below the crammed jets queued and fumed. He prayed they'd leave quickly.

Over the Alps, he looked down on soft billowed landscapes of cloud, which themselves covered smooth-mounded landscapes of snow: unbelievable whiteness, dazzle of light.

The green island turned on its mountainous axle: while the transit plane from Athens swung on a falling curve to the jarring runway.

He took the stifling stand-up bus to the village of their rendezvous: under the plane tree he saw Chryssa at once. She hadn't seen him, she looked shadow-faced, solemn: his heart missed beats, misgiving. Her delicate square face looked up, blinked, her eyes black moths. For a moment her face trembled, as if a shadow of birds flickered back and forth over it. Then he knew her wide smile.

They barely kissed, in the public square, for old men sat in the shadows and watched them: Chryssa led them quickly away from there, up a steep street to where they'd stay. He could murmur only bits of nonsensical travel talk; and she didn't try to talk, didn't even, he was disconcerted, often look to him, though each time she did a smile would surface, extraordinarily young, shy, gleaming-eyed. His steps hurried, he felt he couldn't exist till he'd held her.

Chryssa woke disturbed, momentarily unsure where she was; but as she opened the shutters and gazed out over village roofs to the lagoon of clear water below, her worry eased and an extraordinary still happiness invaded her. The water was glassy, just one small boat made a slow progress to the sea, the fisherman standing and stooping slightly to push the oars; the ripples of its wake parted in a wide fan. There was, otherwise, an enormous stillness, the radiance of early morning seemed to lie even everywhere, filling space. The yellow goat, that sat on stones in the next door yard, turned its strange eyes towards her and bleated. In the distance the fisherman greeted someone on the shore, he might have been calling to her. She remembered how she had felt in Athens: there was turmoil and storm outside, she must lock herself away from it. Now she felt differently, beyond her trouble was a wide clear space of light: she could open the hatch of her tight box of trouble, and step forward into that day.

She went downstairs and walked in the yard, while Michael

came out on the balcony. Moving freely, breathing the fresh morning, talking across the space to Michael, she couldn't keep back the excitement, elation, that rose in her like a clear spring. As they walked down the steep alleys to the quay, she wondered at herself, at her irrepressible happiness: it was as if her vigil for Vangelis had been so long and steady and loving that she had been vouchsafed without guilt this strange brief holiday with someone else.

They sat at a café, and looked round like young tourists: Michael watching amused, ironic, the village priest and the village policeman walking past arm in arm. Squatting fishermen chatted quietly as they stitched holes in the yellow nets spread out on the quay; their boats rocked behind them, red, yellow, green; steadily came the unpleasant wet slap as a little boy walloped an octopus on the stones.

Every so often he would turn and look at her, as if her simply continuing to be there answered a prayer.

He said, 'Pinch me, Chryssa, so I know we're really here.'

And she did, she reached out, gave his arm a playful pinch that turned violent, he yelped. She crouched at the table, gleam-eyed, dangerous, then, satisfied, released him.

'Love!' he murmured, rubbing the sting.

They got up and walked along the quay, passing the priest and the policeman, who had been joined now by a third man, in a light loud suit, evidently a local businessman: all three linked arms, the businessman working his worry beads fast.

Chryssa looked after them. '*There's* Greek politics.'

They paused at a shop hidden by dresses, hung out in the sun like banners.

'Let's look,' she said. They went inside, where she moved attentively down the racks.

'Do you know, it's ages since I bought a dress!'

He had privately resolved he would buy her the dress or dresses, the shopful if possible. She was unhooking them now, measuring them against her: the shopkeeper had arrived, a broad-beamed suntanned powerful old woman, with long fine hairs on her chin, who still wore, in the shop heat, a dark thick cardigan.

'Try them on, madam.' Chryssa was directed behind a curtain, into a tiny back scullery and loo combined.

Michael wandered among the dresses, which were mainly

light loose cones with arm holes, with bold zigzags or sun shapes stamped on them in a tarnished gold colour.

'What do you think?'

She emerged in a deep maroon dress, a rusted brown-gold sun on it: slender within its looseness, and with her slender arms, slender neck, delicate square jaw showing outside it, she looked, he thought, beautifully elegant.

'It's marvellous.'

But she didn't like it. She tried another, then another, asking his advice but going her own way, till it seemed a dance, in and out of the dresses: spinning within them she was young, exhilarated, graceful. She seemed to try a new role with each new dress: he watched entranced, feeling he was seeing hundreds of her. The shopkeeper attended, nodding, urging, not insisting, seeming sage on these dresses so different from her own. She shrugged and didn't argue when Chryssa criticized: and Chryssa did criticize, the dresses she abandoned accumulated about her on chairs, on boxes, loosely strewn over the dress racks. She was long past the point where Michael would have felt he had to buy something, or would have awkwardly skulked from the shop: but she was unembarrassed. He was amazed, he disapproved, he began to be awed. The shopkeeper was stoical, and at leisure gathered in armfuls the dresses that didn't answer.

And in the end she chose none. She said sorry to the shopkeeper, who shrugged and began phlegmatically hanging them again.

They continued down the quay. Michael thought she would be strained, depressed, from all this testing to find nothing at last. Again he was wrong, this plunge and bathe in the world of dresses had given her excitement, elation, pleasure. She moved now with a walk he especially liked, with a certain sway of her body, her arms moving free with a neat turn to the wrist, her head slightly cocked.

He said, 'You swagger when you're feeling good.'

'That's right,' she said, with a flourish of her fingers as though they played arpeggios, and a sidelong look, superior, from under her eyelids.

'I don't know what to call your walk,' she said.

'It's called the tall person's saunter.'

'Yes, it's like a streetlamp walking.'

262

'I don't care, I still want to be seen out with you. So would anyone.'

She clicked her tongue and teeth, added swerve to her swagger.

They stopped at a garage to rent a motorbike: there were only scooters, however, and low c.c. bikes that Michael disdained; they wandered among them, neatly lined and shining red and blue. In the end, perforce, they took a scooter. Chryssa watched him test it, turning sharply, standing in the saddle to ride it over the stones as though it were a fractious bronco. He was adroit at this, an unexpected cowboy: he even, standing, waved. She wondered at the free life these machines seemed to bring him. She'd never scooted. With hospitality he invited her aboard the ridiculous vehicle, and steered them steadily over the slippery stones.

The clear sea lapped quietly, small clusters of people dotted at intervals the wide beach; the spring sun was hot, not yet at summer's scorch; and they lay separate. Nervously they touched, but each hand met a foreign hand, unwilling to fit to the other: their fingers twined nervily and prized apart, like slender lovers who disagreed.

In the last days there had been times when Chryssa was distant; and today the silence hardened between them. They shifted and turned on the sand like a couple in bed who had had bad words and couldn't lie easy.

When he next opened slit eyes to the sun, he saw she was sitting up, faced away from him.

'Chryssa, what's the matter?' he asked, knowing the answer.

She didn't reply.

'We should talk.'

'No we shouldn't, it's wiser not to.'

He moved round to see her better: her face was red; she hugged her legs tight and slightly rocked. Then she turned her large black sunglasses to him.

'I was thinking about islands, Michael. I thought, Vangelis is on one island, we're here on another. He's shut in prison on his island; and me, on mine, why I'm sunning myself with someone else.' She took off the shades: her eyes were bloodshot, and accusing. 'Why did we come here?'

263

Squatted on the sand, Michael watched his knotting fingers, tried to pick words. 'I came – right or wrong – because I love you – and I hadn't the strength not to come.'

She kneeled up tall in the sand, flung her head, cried out loudly, 'What *am* I doing here?' Across the sand, a stout woman, lying down, shaded her eyes to look their way.

He sat quite still. He couldn't argue; nor special-plead; nor demand. His inside caved away: he saw that at any second in their love, things could tip, he could lose her.

A nearby family, in silhouette against the sun, stirred and attended.

She gazed about her at the beach, at her limbs, as if each sand grain irritated, her body irritated, an inflammation through and through she couldn't escape. Abruptly she stood up, shook herself sharply: sand stung his eyes. She took uncertain steps, then stood straight and walked quickly down the beach, hurled herself into the sea, and, her arms big paddles, swam. Michael standing watched her. He felt she was tearing a part of him after her: and he must let her go, be stoic, not chase after begging as helplessly he wanted to. Across the beach, from level bodies, heads rose erect like skittles, watching after her, glancing at him.

The clear cool received her with no shock. Flailing her arms, hardly pausing to breathe, she drove from the shore, while a seabed of rock and black weed and darting shoals sloped downwards beneath her, darkening into endless blue. The sea grew cooler, cold. She paused and looked back: at the white blade of sand, olive trees shimmering, behind them the land climbing upwards to peaks, like alps set down in the sea. If only she could swim on through these cold waters, till she swam out of her body, till she left it in its torment drifting empty on the swell, while she swam clear without it, free.

At first Michael didn't follow, he knew she didn't want his pursuit. Then, as her sleek bobbing head passed out of sight behind a promontory, he suddenly worried. He began swimming after her, but by the time he reached the promontory, she had disappeared.

Near the coast, a fisherman bobbed in a dinghy; Michael swam to him.

'Good day!' Michael called, in awkward Greek.

'Hello!' the fisherman shouted back, in masculine curtness.

Swimming alongside, Michael pieced his words together: he was worried, could he engage the fisherman's services?

The fisherman grunted and nodded; intrigued by this foreigner with his element of Greek, he helped Michael climb in, started his motor, they began to putter along the coast. Michael's eyes scanned keenly, out to sea, along the shore. The fisherman watched also, and at the same time talked: he had been to England, Liverpool, when he worked on ships. He was not old now, though his face had deep lines from screwing up into the sun; his cheeks and forehead were patched with dark brown sunburn.

They passed a fantastic coast, made of slabs, boulders, tunnels, caves: a weird pitted landscape of spiked and curving limbs, gnawed and whittled out of brown stone. Round the next point was a small perfect bay, a half-moon of even sand. A figure sat there.

'Can we go closer?'

It was Chryssa. Michael swam ashore; she sat as she had on the other beach, her face down and lined with tear tracks. She did not look up yet.

He waited, not far off. Now she looked round, and smiled to him: a tired smile, tender, clear, as if they were at a great time and distance from when they last met: it seemed to him of heaven, a smile he would always see.

'You brought a boat.'

'I was worried.'

She shook her head, slightly sighed. Some way from them, the fisherman cast his line.

'What should we do?'

'I don't know, Michael. We need love. I do. Also, Vangelis is in prison. I don't know what I want, it changes every day.'

Michael nodded: it must be so, placed as they were.

She stood up, the fisherman took them back to the village. Michael watched her as they travelled: the wind blew her hair back from her forehead, all the curves of her features were clear, tender. He thought: I don't know whether we're going back in order to part for good; or whether we'll be together

265

longer. He didn't at this point fear: he was too glad simply being with her again, returning to harbour in the spring sun.

The fisherman chatted about Liverpool; at the harbour they had ouzo with him, a quiet lunch. It was late in the afternoon when they returned to their lodging, stepping with deliberate slowness up the steep paths.

'Shall I leave?' Michael finally asked.

'We'll both leave very soon,' she said. She took his hand.

In the dim light that came through the shutters they stirred and eased, dozed entwined. Outside, a man's and a woman's voices rose in greeting: a handful of words, then the slip of hooves and boots on stones, and the slap of sandals, receded opposite ways. There was a low rustle of sound, somewhere a family was talking in a garden.

Chryssa unhooked the shutters and in her kimono went out on the balcony: couched in bed he watched as she slowly stretched, and yawned wide like a cat, then rested her hands on the balcony rail. The sun was low, she was looking at the village waking for evening, while he was looking at her.

He put on his trousers and came onto the balcony. She was seated on one of the chairs there, that had a seat of woven plastic piping: he stood where she had, looking at the rooftops receding downhill, their flat grey stones crusted with lichen, furred with moss, with here and there a stone replaced by brown metal. Voices rose quietly from yards and balconies, of which all he could see were clustered leaves, and the odd glimpse of red-painted oilcans in which flowers grew. Beyond the rooftops was only sea, in a sheet of light.

Chryssa made coffee; they sat in the leaning chairs and sipped. She was quiet for a long time; he looked at her concerned, but her face, gazing over the village, was calm.

Quietly, to her cup, she said, 'It was a mistake coming to a holiday island. It's furtive – and worse than that.' She looked up. 'But also, I'm so glad we came – and I'm glad you're a stranger, a foreigner. I need to get out of the world I live in.'

She paused, reflecting, then said, more warmly, 'Athens is a nightmare now. When I'm there, all I can see anywhere is spies and bullies and thugs on top, and then just a horde of *egos*, dashing and grabbing and snatching – houses, villas, cars, money, food, power – grab grab grab, the grab society. I know why it's like that – Greece was very poor, everyone's trying to catch up fast. Sometimes I think *all* the good people are shut in prison, they've really got the lot. I don't know what connection I have here any more – I feel I should either be in prison with Vangeli, or outside it altogether, with the exiles. And you come from outside it all, Michael, and I connect you with very good times, in the past – and more recently. I've very tender feelings for you. For me, you're a different world from the world I'm in, in person. I'm just trying to say why, even if I shouldn't have come here to see you – oh, but it's important to me, to have this time with you.'

She stopped, gave a dry cough. He held her, wanting to ask, 'But does it stop here – or do we go on?' But he couldn't ask it, and anyway his own throat was dry as straw. They both looked seawards.

For coolness, they had started at dawn this long climb up the slope behind the village. They clambered up the stone walls of a steeply terraced olive grove, and paused for refreshment in a cluster of thick-leaved trees that carried small bright yellow fruit. Michael picked one, and saw it was an orange: he had only ever, before, seen them on stalls. The small oranges were sharp, fresh, rich with taste, aflood with juice: they ate several, then continued, climbing up an uneven ramp of rough woodland, where every so often they would find a ragged path or track, and think they could follow it, and then lose it in stones, or in a twist of the hill. When they looked down, the village was a grey freckling among the silvery olive trees: the sea had become enormous, as though they were on a flat planet where the level water receded in all directions for ever. The sun was hot, they panted and streamed sweat; they had stripped to the waist, and carried on with their clothes tied round their middles like tangled pantaloons. They had never guessed, on the coast, how high the mountain was: they climbed on till they felt they were on a dream mountain which had no bottom or top, but only was one endless uneven slope athwart the sky. The sun scorched, they rested often, collapsed breathless creatures, then clambered only a few steps more.

The slope eased; and then, all unexpectedly, in a sheltered

lap of the mountain they found a green meadow. Evidently there was a spring here that fed the grass: Michael had not seen such green in Greece. The grass was long, and still damp with dew. Pine slopes and crags stood over them, but here they rested; sweltering from the climb, they stripped completely, and lay and turned in the damp luxurious grass.

Michael opened his eyes, and raised himself on his arms. Some way off he saw Chryssa returning from the rim of the meadow: she was unaware of him, and trod casually, with dragging steps, enjoying the touch of the damp grass on her feet. The spring sun had tanned her lightly and against the rich green her skin glowed. She moved naturally, as if it were her way to go naked. Then she saw him: her hands moved to cover herself, she made a shy face, then smiled and continued walking. He rubbed his eyes; the thought went through him, feeling as if it were not his thought only but a vibration of the grasses and trees, 'How beautiful: nothing can spoil Chryssa.' He shook his head bemused, as if something which could happen only in an afterlife had come real now.

Not far away was a clump of late spring flowers: he picked them and took them to her, and the two pale figures in the fresh emerald field joined and clung in one.

Dressed, they continued along the flank of the mountain, between clumps of pine tree and outcrops of stone. The climb was gentle, they lingered in clearings where Chryssa gathered herbs.

'We can make mountain tea.' She moved, crouching, from clump to clump, bending and sniffing.

'You look like the bee of the mountain,' Michael said, stringing together the leaves she gave him.

'I feel like the frog of the mountain.' She stood up stiffly. They pinched and sniffed together the dry, musty leaves.

Climbing a new promontory, they arrived at a small chapel they had read of in their guide book. The paintings in it were perhaps a thousand years old: the doors, notwithstanding, stood open. The walls of the small building had lost shape with layer on layer of whitewash, it could be any age, the stark dazzling hive on the mountain.

As they entered, they collided with another couple, coming out: fair, lean, handsome, Scandinavian or German. Chryssa was shaken: she turned in the porch, and watched the couple's identical long red legs walk them rapidly up the sunlit slope.

Michael had gone, she followed, and as she grew used to the darkness she began to make out the ancient, simple, blood-coloured murals. Rigid figures with steady eyes gazed from a millennium ago into the present: but whether it was from the sun, or tiredness; or from the stuffy air in the tiny chapel; or from the odd shock of meeting the foreigners, Chryssa felt light-headed, dislocated from herself. She thought, I'll faint, yet all the time she heard her voice talking about the figures in English with Michael. The lean brown figures stared: she had a moment's uncertainty who she was. She thought: if I'd stayed in England, if I hadn't been pulled back because of my father, I might have married Michael. She had wanted to stay, see the world, not always live in Greece. She had a sudden vivid picture of a child in a house in England: herself at home there, watching from a distance Greece's pain. Curious moments, dislocated, the other side of life.

When they returned to their lodgings at dusk, Chryssa made her mountain tea. She put a few leaves in a saucepan of water, and presided over their boiling.

'Won't it be stewed?' he ventured.

'This is how you make mountain tea.'

As she stood over the seethe, she tried to describe her sensation in the chapel. Michael listened pale-faced, as though what she told him was conclusive.

'What will we do – after now?'

'We don't know what will happen.'

'I'll come again – or we can meet . . . outside Greece.'

She decanted the brown liquid into glasses. 'I can't leave Greece. I'm too far from Vangelis already, and if I left Greece as well, and they cancelled my passport so I couldn't come back. . . .'

'But we should say what we'll do.'

She sat down, silent.

'I love you,' he said. In the low light, his face was pale as if his blood had drained, but intense, bright, solemn-eyed as the figures in the church. His statement was a question also: I love you – but what are your feelings for me? *Is* this a love affair?

269

'Drink the tea I made you.'

He sipped the dark tea, with its unfamiliar tang: it warmed and soothed his tiredness.

She said, 'Don't let's talk about the future. We don't know what will happen, we're at the mercy of events. If we can have good days now, that is very good. We don't know what's coming – Vangelis may come home, Greece may blow up, there's no knowing. Let's live just in these days now, if we try and do more than that, we'll be lost in a cloud.'

He nodded, and sipped the bitter tea. Chryssa presently went to bed, but Michael could not rest. At the end, as she spoke, he saw the choice of his life: his head was still ringing.

He left their lodging, walked down through the steeply winding streets, and began walking from end to end of the quay. Beside him, strings of fishing boats put out to sea, their large lights, dazzling like acetylene, mounted in hats at the stern. From the tavernas came chat and laughter, clash of plates, bouzouki music amplified. He couldn't attend to these things, he was grasping his purpose. Of course she could not leave Greece, he must come here: he must give up his news service job and, trading on all his experience, try and patch together commissions to be an Athens correspondent. Then he would live here: though nothing was certain, Chryssa promised nothing, if they were together there would be violent ups and downs. The plan was perhaps crazy, and also bad – he'd be coming here for one purpose mainly, to love Chryssa while Vangelis was in prison. And they'd have no future: as Chryssa said, Vangelis *would* come home – and would Chryssa then leave Vangelis for him? He couldn't see it. He thought, how strange, all these years I've kept moving on, God knows what I thought I was hurrying towards, and all the time it was this – that I lose what I've got, and act badly by a friend, in hopes of a love which will probably end painfully, with someone who won't love me as I love her. *This* is where I put my life: a drastic decision; and he felt for the first time at home in the world.

He climbed the zigzag alleys back towards their lodging. In a tiny square, with a single tree and a single bright lamp, he paused, surprised by a sudden shouting: a chase of children, skittering down the village. He smiled: in England they would all be tucked in bed, here they played till they dropped.

270

With shrill yelps a bony-legged boy ran in the square, paused a moment noticing Michael, then ran and hid behind the tree. Now his pursuers appeared, tumbling out of the mouth of an alley. The boy jumped from behind his tree, held his arms before him, and shouted hu-hu-hu-hu-hu-hu-hu-hu-hu-hu, slowly sweeping from side to side. The others stopped in their tracks, shrieked, and staggered and dodged back; now one of them stuck his head into sight again, held up his fingers, went bang – bang – bang, but still the other stood in the path, hu-hu-hu-hu-hu-hu-hu, still he sprayed them. A lull; then they reappeared, holding their arms before them, now they all had machine guns, hu-hu-hu-hu-hu-hu-hu-hu-hu-hu-hu-hu. The boy nearby turned tail, scooted down the path, while the others followed yelping, shouting, in a shrill of excited happy voices playing in bursts of gunfire down through the village alleys to the sea.

14

They returned to Athens, where Michael took his flight to England, and Chryssa went back to her flat. In the following days she resumed work on an old article by Vangelis which she had recently found, and which she was putting into English to send to Michael. She opened out the dry, slightly yellow newspaper clipping, and ran down the text to the point she had got to: beside that paragraph was a photo of Vangelis, blurry in dots. Pausing between sentences, her eyes would linger on it; and then she realized the photo was seeking her. It was a poor picture, old, out of focus: but still she knew Vangelis' real face was drawing closer to that odd speckled window.

She studied him as he stared, slightly frowning, at the camera. So often he had that look, a slight pinching of the brows and eyelids: at home he used to take it in fun, when he chose to express astonishment at things she said. What struck her now was that even on this serious occasion, fronting the camera, there was still just that touch of deliberate emphasis, a slight pleased-amused exaggeration of his gravity. His full-lipped mouth had a curl of self-irony. He too was an actor, she thought with amusement, as in the courtroom he had to be. He could accentuate his feelings because he knew what they were.

She held the photo at a distance, his eyes still looked back: with that slight pucker of the eyelids as if he found it hard to see her. And he did, he did, he could not see her: that was the sadness, he was there in the frame but through that window he never would see her. And did she want him to see her? And was he still that Vangelis? She remembered his scorched face, expression gone, when she saw him in prison. She had to stop work and screw her eyes shut; she rested her forehead on her wrist, collapsed on the table top, every few moments shaking.

She looked up, said loud in the flat 'Vangeli!' Her voice

sounded to her hollow, forlorn. She saw her plants drawn round her like children, their big leaves blank faces. The brown aerial roots reached mutely for nothing they could touch.

Her gaze fell on something she had not put away. It was a necklace Michael had given her, on the island: a thin silver chain, with a small blue globe set in silver, and a dark dot in the centre. It was an eye, to protect her from the evil eye. As she looked at it and thought of Michael, she felt a sharp point of pain right inside her in the centre. She had thought Michael and Vangelis lived in different dimensions, which she could keep apart. But from that small point she felt the flaw run, she felt a tearing begin and continue, as if she were a piece of paper like the sheets in front of her, which two hands held and slowly pulled.

15

Leonidas shook his head, sighed, and patted his stomach, for his plans and efforts bore fruit now. He had issued his invitation and the date was fixed: General Vouros would come to visit their villa.

'A general for our friend!' he murmured over. 'Oh, Patra, if the army backs me, where will we stop?' His eyes misted: true power approached.

The day came, and General Vouros. They had wondered whether he'd bring a convoy, for when he left his garrison he was liable to travel in a squad of armoured cars: it gave him protection, gave his lieutenants an outing, and assured him as nothing else did of a clear passage down the hectic streets. But on this radiant Sunday, as they scanned from the villa, all that drove out of the low burnt hills was a single crimson Mercedes, large, long, shining on the dusty yellow ridge like a capsule of blood. They saw it, tiny in the distance, turn a bend in their track, and buck and wallow towards them in a billowing smoke of dust.

He was earlier than expected: in the villa was panic. Leonidas hopped between trouser legs, complaining loudly to Patra for being uncertain about what he should wear, while Patra, her dripping body wrapped in one long towel while another turbanned her new-hennaed hair, her face new washed but peevish from strain, followed the maid round the house chivvying and nagging, and in exasperation with the maid's slow progress – for this was a new maid who could absorb any volume of nag without either worrying or speeding up at all – swept bits of floor, darted at cushions and hit them, and swung little low tables from one side of the room to the other and back again. Alexis sat on a carved wooden bench, still in the eye of the household storm, reading a book with an intent face: at regular intervals, in a perfunctory way and without doing more, Patra snapped at him to lend a hand. The engine noise grew, they heard outside the slushy squeezing sound of wheels on damp grass: in which moment Alexis disappeared, and Patra was everywhere, and in and out of the bathroom, and in the blink of an eye her towels changed into an elegant dress. With hair-grips clamped to her lips, and eyes like steel balls, she back-brushed her hair in the Lollobrigida swirl that always became her; while Leonidas completed his last sleek combings. And so to the door, Leonidas at ease in immaculate leisure wear, and Patra in elegant languor, while welcome, youth and beauty switched on her face at the moment she stepped outside.

Their guests still sat in their car, gazing nonplussed at what they had arrived at: for this was a villa! A cantilevered balcony shot out towards the sea; sliding glass doors were sheets of light; trellises of yellow chestnut wood came in and out at different heights between projecting walls which seemed to exist for no other purpose but to have large archways blasted through them; two grand staircases climbed round the house on either side, and little capricious sets of steps connected each terrace with every other. General Vouros had his exuberant side, just like Leonidas, but it had not occurred to him before that anyone would build such an exuberant house. He sat and gazed, caught at a loss between mockery and envy.

But he must move: for, arm in arm, like a young loving couple, their dear hosts bounded to meet dear them. The General surged from the car like a rising wave, and from the car's other side, presently, at her own convenience, climbed a plump woman with her hair dyed blonde. She stood at a distance looking round indifferently, while General Vouros introduced himself, and made no move to introduce her. Patra vaguely remembered meeting Mrs Vouros at a Government reception, and knew this was not she.

The car was not yet empty; for the General turned, and shouted at it, and out of the back seat and through the window loped two black lion-sized dogs that sprinted to him, and yawned panting at the company with long crimson mouths of fangs. At a word of command, they bounded away on thumping pads, yelping and barking, turning and snaking as they leapt in midair, receding loudly into the scrub.

Leonidas and Patra smiled their guests indoors: and General Vouros, all hard muscle, hard vigour, hard bullet eyes, and clipped hard jovial voice, stepped ringingly over their flags like an officer of occupation. Leonidas was immediately, busily, the host: 'You'll have a drink, General? Aphrodite, at once! A scotch for the General!' But Aphrodite was paralysed, gazing slack-mouthed at a living general; Leonidas brought the drinks himself from the cavern of dressed stones that served him as a bar.

'Loula?'

Desultorily the plump woman announced what she would drink. Leonidas poured it frowning, for though excited by her he was not altogether flattered. He appreciated that the General's bringing his mistress meant that he saw Leonidas as a friend; and yet he knew too that the General would have brought his wife, and not his mistress, had he thought he were visiting a true minister of government.

'A fine house, Mrs Patra!' the General cried, fiercely brusque in emphasis of wonder, as he surveyed the large living room with its stone floor, its chrome furniture, its wooden chandelier with artificial candles, its bulky gleaming television. But what most caught the General's eye was, in a corner, a brand-new miniature football game: Leonidas had it specially imported from Italy. The General strode up to it, gave it a slap that sent all the little footballers spinning head-over-heels, and cried to Leonidas, while the whisky danced in his glass with enthusiasm, 'Ach, Leonida, we shall have a game, eh?'

But the game was not yet. Leonidas lured them through his arches and halls, suave, cajoling, like a stout spider winding in its prey. And he was not only sly: he was so flushed and happy with pride of ownership that a huge hospitality fountained within him, beamed in his eye, and gave a warmth to all his diplomacies. He must give them every pleasure at his command: his best chairs and all his drinks.

Too soon he had shown them the apartments, and led them out on the cantilevered balcony, where in a large gesture he presented to them, as his grandest possession, the Aegean sea – a white liner in the distance, and beyond the blue sea dim mountains at the world's end. It was his showpiece and he let his guests rest, in the long beachbeds on the terrace, while he held to their hands pieces of cheese and salt fish, and wafer-thin tissues of smoked ham. After him came Aphrodite with mussels and oysters, and little saucers of crisp fried tentacle to crunch. It was the merest snack, to carry them through mid-morning;

276

when he had filled their hands he sat back, and admired his domain.

'Good fishing, eh?' General Vouros said.

'Fishing?' said Leonidas. 'Mmm,' and he closed his eyes and waved towards the sea. 'It is my *bachze*!' – he used the Turkish word, a garden of sweet fruit, a garden of delights.

The General's girl friend hardly answered Patra, and volunteered nothing herself, but only lay back in a sunbathing posture, occasionally murmuring requests of her little General in a mild soft alkali voice.

This rest was the merest breather and snack, for Leonidas and the General were active men, and the women wanted sun and sea.

'To the beach!' said Leonidas.

They went to their apartments, and in a moment Leonidas was out of the white creaseless trousers he had so recently put on, and back in his swimming trunks: a fat, brown, energetic body, with curling black hair on arms, chest and legs. And presently the General emerged, another brown body, but squarer, broader, deeper, more muscularly stout. Leonidas gave him plastic slippers and a straw hat like his own; and when the General called for Loula and she didn't come, the two men set off for the sea. They scrambled down the crumbling earth path, Leonidas apologizing to the General that he had not as yet installed a lift (he kept quiet about his plan for a road). The General made light of it: they would walk off their whisky, and be free to swim when they got to the bottom. He whistled shrilly, and two black dogs leapt suddenly out of the thorny scrub, nearly knocked them over, and hurried ahead, loping with ease down the sheerer parts of the cliff. Below them was a small sandy cove, with translucent shallow sea.

On the shore the General hurled driftwood out to sea to get his dogs wet, while Leonidas unlocked the rusting chains that secured his beach hut. He rooted in the shadows inside, and presently – for there could be no question, for men such as they, of merely using the sea to swim in – he lugged out from between his boats and rafts, and the outboard-motor that clung by its teeth to an empty oil drum, the gear they needed. So, muttering like old friends, not yet approaching politics, they strapped oyster knives to their calves, and fastened round their waists net bags for their catch, and sprung the tridents in their harpoons, and pulled on flippers and masks. Snorting to each other, they made a flapping progress down the sand, and with sudden fluid movement launched fast into the sea.

Loula picked her last careful steps down the rough path, spread a towel on the sand, and affectionately rubbed herself with oils and creams. And now, like beasts of burden, Alexis, Patra and Aphrodite arrived, precariously laden with salads, watermelon, bottles, a portable fridge. They piled these in the shed, and Aphrodite settled herself beside them in the stifling shade. Alexis walked up the coast, and resumed his reading in the shade of an overhang of earthy cliff. Patra brought out a giant beach umbrella, and planted it so that she and Loula could both lie with their heads in the shade. They had not taken to each other, but the hot rays they basked in slowly melted their dislike. They grew bored with silence, and when it next happened that they both at the same time turned on their fronts, Loula poked a small twig of driftwood into the sand, and asked, 'Tell me, Mrs Patra, how many stremata of land have you got?'

'Oh, it adds up, I suppose to . . . seven. . . .'

'Seven? Good. That's very good!' Loula warmed with friendliness.

'And you, Loula?'

'Uh! Tst! Nothing! A flat or two in Larissa, nothing. Nikolaki, now (my little General), he wants some land, he wants to build a villa. He says it would be for me. He says the best way for me to be sure of that, is for me to put some money into it. But I don't know if it's for me.'

She had suddenly become frank; she rolled on her back and gazed out to sea. Along the coast, far apart, the shining backsides of Leonidas and the General moved like slow dolphins among the sunken rocks, to occasional spumes of white from their snorkels. Patra saw that Loula had broached a sensitive topic; she stood up, 'The sea looks good.'

'Yes.'

They pinned up their hair, walked down the beach, and then wincingly, standing tall in quick shudders, they walked into the glassy sea. There they flapped a few strokes, then stood on the bottom with the water just up to their chins, and continued chatting.

'This is very good for our tans,' said Loula. 'Do this,' and she splashed water on her face, so the bright beads stood out on the suntan oil.

'You should keep the flats, Loula.'

'Mmm, well. Nikolaki now, he says I should sell the flats, he says now is a good time to sell. But I don't know if it's a good time to sell.'

'I wouldn't think it's a good time to sell,' said Patra. Presently they waded back to shore, and lay down again on new patches of hot sand, enjoying the burning prickle on their wet skin. Loula did not stay long on property. It turned out that she had a child, which her mother looked after. Her husband had been a brute, but men were all the same; she still slept with her husband occasionally, to keep Nikolaki in his place. From the bulging plastic sachet she had of lotions and creams and ointments and juices, she produced the photograph of a pretty, well fed child, laughing to someone outside the picture, and another picture of the child proudly held by her. In the picture she had her hair in a loose bun, she looked affectionate and tired, and older than she did now.

They talked on, absorbed, not minding the delicate tickle they felt when a sand ant ran busily over them. In Alexis' ears, as he tried to read among the rocks, it seemed there was now no pause whatever in their light silvery musical chattering, though sometimes when he looked up they were again standing up to their necks in the sea, and at other times they lay at different angles on the hot sand.

There was shouting out to sea: his father and the General stood waist deep out of different rock formations, their masks on their foreheads, discussing their catch. Presently the two slowly rose from the water, converging as they tramped ashore. Before the women they disgorged from their bulging net bags a cargo of stuck fish, oysters, mussels, dragon fish. 'Bravo!' the women cried, and shuddered.

But Alexis, as they arrived, himself put out to sea; he dragged out of the hut a long plastic raft, and paddling with his hands, keeping his book dry, he drifted out into the millpond sea.

The General looked up from his efforts to unpeel a squid from the barbs of his trident, and observed Leonidas watching, frowning, while his son deserted.

'Not a fisherman, eh, your son?' he said, in commiseration and irony.

'Ach, my son,' Leonidas muttered, and shook his head.

'Our sons, our sons, they're the curse of our life!' the General cried; the two men got down to some expert gutting and washing of fish. Alexis meanwhile sailed out to a point where the difference between sea and sky could no longer be seen, where there was only a long white band of white, and, floating in space, the small silhouette shape of the boy on the raft.

The men summoned Aphrodite from the hut to gather driftwood, and made a fire to cook the fish. But the smoke from the fire blew in their faces wherever they stood, and they decided, having hunted, to excuse themselves from cooking; and Loula and Patra shuddered away from the slithering fish guts; so Aphrodite squatted down, and screwing her eyes into the smoke watched over the cooking, taking morsels continually so as to be sure when the daintiest parts were cooked. The men retreated to the rocks, and lit cigarettes, and while this smoke blew more pleasantly into their brine-tanned faces, they prepared the ground for their later talking. Leonidas touched a little on the war plan, but, even at his ease on the sunny beach, the General was cagey; Leonidas realized that though they were in the same secret group, the General would never confide in him as he would confide in fellow soldiers. Leonidas drew back, and discussed more generally the Government's policies. To engage the General's curiosity, he let go some snippets of Cabinet gossip. The General was intrigued, and asked for more; and Leonidas enquired then what view was taken in the High Command. The General told him with force that the High Command was far from pleased. Leonidas listened keenly, for the General was speaking now not only for their own group, and for the Great Idea, but for the army as a whole. For the National Government had been the army government: and now Leonidas learned how far apart the two bodies had grown. Above all the army were disturbed by the President's plans to return more power to civilian politicians.

'Ach, he has to do it,' Leonidas said. 'The Americans, NATO and so on, they press for something that looks like that.'

'Bah! That's not his reason. He wants a civilian government so he can set it against the High Command, and the police:

then he can sit on top of everything, the Mister President –
President for life! He was a soldier, he was one of us, when
we began.'

Leonidas drew his smoke in deep, as he tested now and
tasted the General's words.

'Well, well,' he said, 'a civilian government – it would be
controlled. It would be supervised.'

'It would be a betrayal of the Revolution! We didn't do all
we've done to see at the end of it a government of *politicians*!'

'Yes, General, yes,' said Leonidas, 'but then, the new constitution did allow for politicians of some sort . . .'

'Fuck the constitution!' said the General.

'Well yes,' said Leonidas, 'that's true too.' He spoke with
some coolness, finding offence in the remarks about civilians.

The General retrenched a trace. 'Eh, Leonida, I don't deny
that when the work of the Revolution is done, *when* it's done,
then perhaps there can be some form of government with
civilians – under the council, of course, under the military
council. But the Revolution's work is not done yet. The
President said he would smash the communists, but he hasn't
smashed the communists. He said he would smash the old
guard – and he hasn't smashed the old guard. He said he
believed in the Great Idea – but do you think he believes in
it? Will we march into Ankara with politicians at our head?
Uh! Poh! Great hopes of that!'

Leonidas nodded sagely. 'So what do you think will happen?'

He asked too eagerly: the General glanced sharply, said
curtly, 'What will happen? Who knows what will happen?'
Abruptly he left, and strode over to the bonfire.

'And so now, Mrs Aphrodite – how's our dinner?'

'Mmmmmm! It's just at the point, Mr General.'

Leonidas hurried after, for the General was ruffled, he must
soothe him quickly. All courtesy, all host, he bent quickly
among the embers and burned his fingers picking out fish. He
opened the large ones, and started giving best pieces to the
General: roe, strips of fillet, and glasses of ouzo with ice
smoking in it, snatched from the portable fridge. These tenders
were accepted: General Vouros did not waste time standing on
his dignity, on the contrary he accepted every morsel he was
offered, so Leonidas presently discovered that not only the
best fillet, but all the fillet, had gone down the General's throat.

That put a damper on Leonidas' hospitable passion.

When he had done eating, the General, with military decision, lay down on the sand, closed his eyes, and quickly began to snore. Leonidas sat smoking, reflecting with satisfaction that his repair work had succeeded; but his ambitions developed a new complication. He did not know whether it was a result of the fish roes he had eaten, or of after lunch relaxation, or whether it was simply his natural virility, but he did find himself dwelling with growing interest on the deliciously, the lusciously plump gold limbs of Loula, lounged on the sand. It was no part of his plan that he should seduce not only the General, but the General's girl friend too; but General Vouros now was a tranquil snore, unwarlike and unaware; and Patra walked away down the beach calling to Alexis, a dot far out to sea, to come and eat. And what could Leonidas do, the others defaulting, but bestow his hospitality on Loula. She needed attention, for poor she, in her languor, had not troubled to eat much: so for her Leonidas drew his knife, which caught the sun like a scimitar of the Turk, and waded among the inshore rock pools, a brown glistening sealion shape: till he returned bearing oysters, which he loosened in their shells, squirted from a cut lemon, and tipped in her mouth. And not only oysters, but again he fished, and returned with a pouchful of glistening reddish-black knots of spikes, which he laid out before her. He pointed at the sea urchins, 'This is your dessert.' She shuddered back from the spiked horrors which lay there drying, their tiny spines feebly waving. But with his knife Leonidas split an urchin, and with tough brown fingers impervious to thorns he opened out the brittle shell, and scooped out the long fat strands of roe, and dipping the handful quickly into a rock pool to swill it clean, himself put to her lips the shining soft sweet orange roe. And, 'Mr Leonida, you're right,' she said, she found them tasty: so presently, and at some pain to himself, he fetched her now new handfuls of thornballs.

Which Patra returning saw; and though he did not look her way, Leonidas felt her return as though a giant had stood up in the next cove to study him. His pleasure was spoiled; for he was aware of old of her smallest vibrations, and he knew that just those things that so drew him to Loula – that sweet little too much of plumpness, those radiant empty eyes, that tremble of pout, that touch of piquant insolence in her, that took it for granted that others would serve – just those things, which seemed to him so feminine, which so made her a creature for him to subdue, which set such a quick inflammation of desire dancing like fire all over his skin – that just those things would set a very different inflammation at work in Patra. So, amiably but briskly, he asked his wife if Alexis were coming; and toughly and tersely she answered that he was. And Leonidas now had his work cut out, as he laboured still with guarded glances to make it clear to Loula that his flattery was sincere; while trying to make it clear to Patra that he was working to advance his political career.

General Vouros was roused by the talk of sea urchins, and sat up blinking, wanting his share; and truly now Leonidas had to work.

The oven heat of midday slowly passed and the sun came down from its blinding height. Alexis paddled in, and skirting them put the raft away and went up to the villa. But they were not left alone, for presently they heard voices far above them, and looking up they saw a family slowly making its way down a grassy flank of the cliff: a big family with large mothers and aunts that took a long time arriving, and talked loudly up and down the slope. Patra and Leonidas stared at them displeased, for they could tell from their voices that they were not top-class people. And there was nothing they could do: the beach was not private.

The family arrived, and, as if they could not see the large beach hut and the rigid adults in front of it, selected a good site and prepared for the sea. The women chatted vigorously, the children shouted as they hopped on the beach changing; the father of the family took out a piece of cork wound with fishing line, and bawling the children clear flung the line out to sea.

Having failed to chill them, the Leonidas party could only ignore them; but that did not work, everyone was cramped. Leonidas was flustered, here was disaster: he had to act quickly. So, since he could not beat the interlopers, he joined them. In a strong voice he called out to the fisherman, 'What have you got for bait?'

'Worms,' the man answered.

'I didn't find many here,' Leonidas remarked, walking over.

'Huh! You didn't look well.' Having asserted independence,

283

the man laid down his piece of cork, and taking one of the children's spades went down to the waterline, and with several quick scoops dug out a mound of sand worms, and showed them to Leonidas.

General Vouros came over, 'Good bait, eh? These worms are something.' The three men spoke vigorously, laconically, then withdrew to their camps. Now they could coexist.

It was the hour for fishing. Small boats came puttering along the coast, and stationed themselves out to sea while, distinct in the raking rose late-afternoon light, the men in them prepared their tackle. Beyond them, a line of fishing boats proper, with lamps standing high at the back, made a slow progress to the fishing beds. There was a great peace now: the water lapped quietly on the beach; on the horizon, as the air grew clearer, a long grey tanker appeared, ghostly, remote, seeming not to move at all.

The women took their last swim; then Leonidas and the General loaded them with the few items Aphrodite couldn't carry, and dispatched them perilously up the earth path. They themselves were staying, for now was the sweetest hour of the day. They laid strips of driftwood on the sand, and with great shouts and heavings pulled the large fibreglass boat out of the shed and down to the sea: then, running in mincing hops because of their weight, they carried the outboard motor to the boat and attached it. After several yanks at the motor the engine fired, and they put out to sea.

The bow rose high, they rode smoothly the dimpled sea. When they came in line with the other boats, Leonidas throttled down the motor, and handed the General his best fishing line: a beautiful line, the silver hooks shrouded with long white hairs. The General carefully let down the hooks, watching to see they didn't tangle as they sank through the green dimness, while Leonidas prepared for himself a line with more modest, more tatty hooks, and paid it out. They lit cigarettes and then just sat, holding their lines, gazing with slit eyes at the low blazing sun.

For the first time that day they were truly alone, in enormous privacy: now each could attend to all the other might say. But for the present their thoughts only followed their lines, which had become, lightly held, taut, long tendrils of nerve with which they felt what was happening at the bottom of the sea:

284

the lead weight bumped on stones, slithered in weeds, dragged in sand. They waited, all alert, for the slightest real tug.

For a time the only movement was the swing of their hands, up and then down, as they tested their lines. Then the General sighed and shook his head, 'Ach, you in the Government, you know how to live! The lap of luxury!'

Leonidas made a wry face, 'Ha! Is that what you say?'

'The lap of luxury!' the General roared.

'We have our problems.'

'Huh, what problems does the Government have?'

Leonidas alerted, this question was one of the General's hooks; and he was not going to oblige the General too soon. 'I don't know about the Government,' he said, 'I know about the Ministry.'

The General grunted; he didn't care about the Ministry, and fell to studying the distant coast. 'That's you is it?' he exclaimed, nodding to a jagged brown box that stood on the cliff top, and was the villa. Leonidas barely nodded. To make conversation, the General said, 'Bit of a trial, that minister of yours, eh? I've met the man. A thorn in the arse, I'd say.'

Leonidas nodded quietly, 'He *is* a thorn in the arse.'

'Still, Leonidas, his heart's in the right place. He's for the National Government, all right. Oh yes! Phew!' The General shook his head, whistling – even he – at some extreme remarks the Minister had made.

'For it!' Leonidas allowed himself to lose all patience. 'He's for it in a way that turns everyone against it. It's like having a scorpion for the National Government! What's the good of telling the heads of the Labour Federation that you want to shoot them?'

Leonidas cried this out strongly, for the Labour Federation was a conservative body; but he reckoned without the General, who only sat back, roaring his laughter and rocking the boat, 'A lot of good! That's very good! That's the best thing he's said.'

Leonidas adroitly joined in laughing, but said at the end as he wiped his eyes, 'Well, that's very good. But still, why shoot them? They're a good kilometre short of the communists.'

'Ah, you politicians – you and your diplomacy!' The General shook his head.

'Seriously, General, I've good men on my staff, very good

285

men. It would all work well if the Minister would just let us be, if he'd just let us get on with it.' Once started in this vein, Leonidas continued with all his seriousness: he would make it clear to the General just by weight of persistence that if any man could run the Ministry, that man was himself. He felt a fish pull at his hook, but he let it go: he mustn't interrupt. And eventually the General, borne down, cried, 'Mister Leonida, you should be the minister!'

'Me? Ach!' Leonidas said ruefully, 'I don't know that they'd take me.'

'Oh and why's that?' the General asked, then screwed his face slyly. 'Do you mean because you've got some relative in clink?'

Leonidas' eyes widened appalled. Did the General know of Vangelis? But in any event the General wasn't worried. 'Uh, forget it, Leonida, every family in Greece has got its black sheep, it's been like that since the Civil War.'

Leonidas nodded, and shrugged the matter off; but still was uneasy, for Vangelis was a problem. Quickly he went on, 'No, no, General, I meant nothing like that. It's just that the President and the Minister *are* very close. And I don't mind, I'm perfectly happy with the job I've got. I just wish the Minister would let me get on with it, and spend his own time opening roads with the President.'

'Yes . . . hm . . . the President's for him, eh?' the General mused; and then with a sly, sidelong look he asked a question that might only be a joke, 'Well, and tell me then – who *is* for the President?'

Leonidas showed by his gravity that he took the question seriously. He gave the General an informed look which said: I know the answer, but it's risky to tell you without more guarantees. After a pause he said, 'You know, General, what would help very much, in this time of uncertainty, would be – if we had clearer guidance from the army.'

The General returned his subtle look, and seemed pondering whether to answer his question. Suddenly, he jerked his arm up sharply, and began to pull in fast. Hand over hand he hauled in the slicky green plastic line which heaped up in loose coils on the bottom of the boat. Both men leaned over, and saw a flash in the dim, a thin white shivering, then something large that jerked and shook silver in the green, and the General

286

swung out of the water and down into the boat two large fish, writhing for life.

'Let me, General,' Leonidas cried, and snatched tight hold of a chilly slippery sharp-finned fish which pulsed in his hand, its eyes wide wheels, as he extricated the barb from the fine, tough, glassy jaw. The General grabbed the other and tore it from its hook, and the two fish fell to the bottom of the boat and arched and jerked among the bare feet and tangled line. The General started separating his hooks: they were slippery and free moving, it did not take him long. Now Leonidas felt pulls on his line, and jerked his hand hard up, to sink the barb deep into the fish's mouth. Evidently a shoal of fish were swimming beneath them. Leonidas had three fish on his line; and now the General had another catch. They cast and hauled in till the bottom of the boat was alive and slapping with slithering fish. Then, no more: the shoal had passed.

The General returned to the topic. 'So. Clear guidance from the army, you say?'

'The Greek army should do more than just sit in its barracks.'

'Oh it will,' the General said quietly, with menace, half to himself.

Leonidas fastened on the words: he was sure, from all they'd said, that the move the General spoke of was a move against the President. So he knew: the army would intervene. But immediately afterwards the General looked troubled, and Leonidas saw he must shift the conversation quickly. He said excitedly, 'The army, General, the army will save us – with the conquest of Turkey.' He hurried on feelingly, conjuring up the Great Idea, leaving their previous words behind. And it worked, he drew the General to him just by the ardour of his patriotic passion: they moved to discuss the invasion. Perhaps the sun helped and heated their mood, for it had lost its dazzle and was a globe of blood: across the black iron sea it lit red splinters and blade shapes.

Leonidas paused, 'I am still worried, General, by this question of numbers. The Turkish army is big, they have very many troops.'

'Uh, Leonida, never mind! I say to my men, "You know, men, that one Greek soldier is worth ten Turks?" "It's true!" they say. "It's not true!" I say. "Any one of my men is worth

287

twenty Turks!'' at that, they cheer. And it's true, Leonida, it's perfectly true.'

'Yes indeed,' Leonidas nodded, with strained eyes. The General watched him slyly, and then said, 'However, Leonida, I'm not a fool. And the point is this. The Turkish army is big, as you say. It's what? Ten times the size of ours? Right. And it's in three places. Some of it is down by Cyprus. Some of it is near us, on the Hellespont. And the biggest chunk of it is on the border with Russia. Would they pull reinforcements from the Russian border? I don't think so. But what I say is, make them go the other way. I say, when we start this thing, let's shoot some rockets into Russia – not a lot, just enough, down in southern Russia, so they think they've come from Turkey. And the Turks, then, they won't be heading our way. Because you're right, Leonida, there are a lot of Turks. But, my God, there are a lot of Russians. Oh yes, a lot of Russians!' And General Vouros sat back, bellowing huge laughter, so the whole boat swayed and tipped.

The sun sank behind a distant mountain which, invisible before, stood sharp against the red disc like a black tooth, and ate it away. Across the horizon a hanging spread of purple light slowly dimmed and shrank and fell in after the sun.

With a tremor in his voice, Leonidas said, 'It will be a great war, General. I hope – I only hope – the Government will have the courage.'

'What government? This government? Puh! They're fingers of America! They've got goats' milk in their balls, not spunk! What we need, Leonida, is a government of men.'

In the falling light, Leonidas said with his deepest urgency, 'General, there are those of us in the present administration who would give their lives to see Greece led by such a government.'

The General observed him, and then said, laconic but vehement, 'You're our man, Leonida.'

Leonidas sat absorbing the words, warm in the cooling dusk. One by one round them, with a cough and a chug, the outboard motors of the other fishing boats spat into life, and thudded off into distance. They were alone on the sea: a gull settled on the water and, white and eerie in the twilight, watched them with a staring eye.

The General said, 'Ach, Leonida, we have had good talk.

Tell me now – there's something else I've wanted to know. What do they say in the Cabinet, about the army? Who do *they* want to see as chief of staff?'

The question took Leonidas by surprise, but he had to answer, for the General had given him much, and pressed him now by lowering his head and so obviously listening. Leonidas passed on the opinions he knew. The last thing he saw, as the light died from the sea, was the General's face, all puckered and curved in shrewdness, listening hungrily. It left Leonidas uncertain. Who was this man he had risked all confiding in? Was he truly a patriot, committed before all else to the Great Idea and the Greater Greece? Surely he was, he was a General of the Greek army, that was modelled on the German army, devoted to the Fatherland. But the opaque shrewd face disappearing in darkness reminded Leonidas also of some old bandit chief, a klepht, a brigand from the mountains, concerned only to line up with the stronger side so that, whatever the turmoil, he carved out gains for his men and himself.

Leonidas shivered; and both men now felt the cold on their bare backs. Overhead the stars were appearing, along the coast the lights of villages sparkled. Leonidas started the motor, and headed for shore. In a dim white flapping the gull departed. Huddling down, they drove fast for the coast, the spray stinging cold on their arms and legs.

They beached the boat, and by the light of a hand torch gutted the fish on the edge of the sea: quickly, for the mosquitos were out and at them. Then they plunged in the water for a quick last swim. It was warm now on their chilly bodies, sliding smoothly over them in a faint phosphorescence. Then they clambered out, grabbed the fish, and slithered as quickly as they could up the path.

And so stepped into the bright-lit villa, huntsmen returning, laden with spoils. The women shouted to greet them. The General's dogs leapt at him, prancing, leaping, baying loudly. One dog danced round him, half on its hind legs, sniffing at the catch and wagging its tail, the other rolled on its back and squirmed, while he, stooping, vigorously scrubbed the short tough hair on its front. Then he decided to ring his family. Oblivious of all of them he roared down the line, 'Stassa, how are you? No, no, it was a difficult day. I spent the whole of it looking at land. The farm? Bah! It was worthless, a garbage tip. Not what we want. Keep well, my Stassa. Hello, Lianaki, how's daddy's dear love? Be good now, look after your mother. Give me your mother again. Stassa, look after yourself, I won't be back till the day after tomorrow, military conference. Bye, bye, kisses, kisses, bye.'

The women cooked, the men were at a loose end; then the General's eye caught the football game.

'A match, Leonida! I'll be Athens, you be Belgrade!'

'Thank you,' said Leonidas, with a frowning smile at the General's doubtful joke.

'Right! The kick off!' cried General Vouros, and he whisked the handle so all the forwards spun like a lathe. Leonidas returned the ball. And now on light feet like boys the two men sprang round the trembling table, pulling and pushing all their handles at once, so the players spun like tops. 'Back to the centre forward!' roared the General. The football table danced on the flags, the whole villa echoed to the shouts of the men. The General was in high good humour, and Leonidas too: they had cemented a connection, they had new allies now.

Athens beat Belgrade; but both were pleased.

16

Leonidas returned to Athens in pride of success, in the ease of a man with the best connections. He watched the Minister grow depressed at his new bright confidence: and in other regards also he exerted himself.

Chryssa picked up the phone: it was her sister Patra – but why so excited?

'Chryssa, Leonidas has done it. He's got a pardon for Vangelis. He can come home.'

For a terrifying moment she felt no emotion at all – an odd blank surprise – then her heart thumped as if it would break her. 'Patra, what? Say it again! Tell me it's true!'

Patra repeated what she had said; Chryssa could only shake her head, caught by odd gasps, neither laughs nor sobs. Still she could not believe it. She wanted to know more, but couldn't ask, her voice was breaking.

'Come round, Chryssa, we'll talk here.'

Chryssa gulped, agreed, put the phone down: she must hurry there, but she could hardly move. Her eyes were tight shut smarting, she was shaken in a slow long shudder of sobs. Through tears she blinked at their flat, which was all changed, and a home again: she, the flat, she and Vangelis, floated up on a rising sea of pleasure, gentle, sparkling.

She collected herself and hurried to Patra's, her excitement streaming from her. Let it be true, let him come home, she murmured; the thought crossed her mind, would there be conditions?

As Chryssa arrived Patra opened the door, and the sisters fell into each other's arms, and swayed from foot to foot, hugging each other, and kissing and crying and laughing at once. They went inside, and there in the middle of the living room, radiant in his silver-thread suit, large, benign, stood Leonidas. Even as gratitude welled in Chryssa she slightly jibbed at the plump way he stood and beamed, presuming thanks: the lord of the family, who had stretched forth his hand and saved. But he *had* saved them; she embraced him so seriously that he too was shaken from his vanity of benevolence, and blinked moistly, modestly, receiving thanks.

They went out onto the balcony. Patra brought brandy and they toasted Vangelis, soon to be with them. Chryssa smiled, they all smiled in one broad smile that curled back in the clear late summer sunshine through all the city round them.

So, to details. 'Tell me, Leonida, when can I see him? Are there conditions?'

But Leonidas would tell her first how he secured the release; he related blow by blow his visits paid, his politician's tricks, his cajoleries and wangles. The officials concerned were not over difficult, for it seemed that Vangelis had begun to be known abroad as a martyr to dictatorship: that was not fair, but still they let Leonidas persuade them that they would be glad to be shot of Vangelis. Leonidas concluded, looking down at his brandy demurely, 'So, Chryssa, you can go to the island at any time. Vangelis can sign himself out, and he can come back with you. You can go as soon as you like.'

'How do you mean, sign himself out?' The sunlight shivered.

'Uh, Chryssa, he must sign himself out. The usual thing. It's nothing.' He brushed it aside.

'Well, but what is it he must sign?' It hurt to ask, but her wheel had faltered.

'It's nothing at all,' he smoothed soothingly. 'It's just, you know, a statement . . . gratitude for clemency . . . loyalty to the National Government. It's just – words on paper, it's nothing.'

Chryssa gazed hard at him; he resumed, with a touch of impatience, 'Chryssa, it's a formality. Of course he must sign a loyalty oath to get out. There's no question! I grant you, it's not a paper Vangelis would like to sign. But it'll get him out, and once he's out, well, Chryssa, then he can do what he likes. Who's going to care then what the paper said?'

'What does it say?'

But he didn't hurry to tell her what it said; he frowned at the Parthenon in the distance, being hurt now, and dignified, at her ungrateful harping.

'Is it a confession?'

'No, it's not a confession!' He heaved back, irritated. 'It's very general. It's as I say – a loyalty oath. Look, Chryssa, he

292

can sign it or not, he doesn't have to. It's up to him. If he
signs it, he can be out at once, and be as free as a bird. That's
what I've arranged, I can't do more. If he doesn't want to, he
needn't, and he can stay there, and I should tell you, Chryssa,
that if he stays there it will be for years, that's the choice you
have –' He was starting to hector.

'All right, Leonida,' Patra said quietly. Chryssa sat upright,
very still; she said, 'Please tell me what it says.'

'Well, it says . . . it says . . .' Leonidas heaved about,
couldn't find the paper then found it, couldn't find his glasses
then found them, then briskly read the declaration, snapped
off his glasses, and looked at her big eyed. 'Well, that's all
right, isn't it?'

Chryssa was blank to them: taut, white, her eyes blinking
sharply. Patra urged, rubbing her hand on Chryssa's knee, 'My
sister, don't give up everything because of this paper. It's what
everyone signs, getting out. Just bring Vangelis home, that's all
we want.' Both Patra and Leonidas gave her serious liquid looks,
urging her to take in her stride this little obstacle, which was
nothing; and she felt the kind pressure of their urging, and the
pressure of her own desire. But she knew Vangelis.

'Chryssa,' Patra said, more seriously, with a burr of menace,
'after all our trouble, you are going to take this paper to
Vangelis, aren't you?'

'Of course I'll take it,' Chryssa said, but numbly. 'Thank
you, Leonida.' Patra saw her to the door, and returned frowning, shaking her head.

'Uh!' Leonidas reassured her, 'Once she gets there, and
Vangelis has the open door in front of him, and the pen in his
hand . . . there's a limit to how stupid he is.'

So again Chryssa took the boat to the prison island. It was this
time a summer voyage, but out at sea they found a sharp
breeze; she sat cooped in a white-painted nook of the ship's
superstructure, sunlit but cool.

Now the voyage had started, she was locked in confusion.
How could she meet Vangelis, how could she face him? Yes,
she had told herself, 'I shouldn't be ashamed, I've my life too,
I need some love.' The fact remained, while he endured in
prison, she was off on an island, making love. Should she tell

293

him, and hurt him – or be silent, the traitor? Then she wondered: was it thanks to Michael that they had this pardon, because he had helped to make Vangelis known abroad? That had been one purpose of Michael's visit, so something was achieved – and now it was poisoned, because they had been lovers. How bitterly compromised Vangelis' pardon was – secured by Leonidas, and his own wife's lover. Surely he must be told all this? And how could she tell him, how could she bring him, in the same bouquet as the news of release, such serpents? She rolled her head to and fro on the white ironwork: how could she even meet his eyes?

The sharp breeze blew spit of spray; the disturbed sea was black; the low brown humps of distant islands slid by slowly. As the hours passed and the prison drew nearer, her feelings changed, and she thought more simply: all that mattered was bringing Vangelis home. Her guilt was something else. Even the fate of her marriage, of her relations with her husband and Michael – that was secondary to the release of Vangelis. Now she was near, she thought: it cannot be I am making this trip for nothing. She said over to herself the declaration he must sign. *Could* he put his name to that? The words cancelled their work, made all that they had done and suffered pointless. She knew Vangelis. What was she doing even bringing this message? But she thought, life *can't* be so cruel, to let me come all this way, to build my hopes – and then send me back without him. As the cloven island appeared on the horizon and slowly grew towards her, all her questionings silenced and shrank to the simple urging: *let* him come home, *let* a way be found. Now the brown fortress itself appeared, curled on its promontory. Abruptly she asked herself, *Do* I believe Vangelis will come home? She tried to visualize the return voyage, herself on the boat and the island receding to the stern – did she see Vangelis beside her? But she saw nothing.

She made out a guard on the prison walls. He seemed a restless man, his dark shape moved back and forth continuously at the entrance of his sentry box. She thought, if he leaves his box before the boat docks, Vangelis will come home. She watched intently: the dirty village swung close to them; the sentry stuck in his box; then quickly he came pacing clear of it, out along the walls, and only afterwards the boat struck the quay with a juddering scrape. 'Oh thank God,' Chryssa sighed; she felt a great relaxing and relief. She had a sign.

Knowing her way – her thoughts locked – she hurried up through the village to the prison gate: where the surly monk studied her through his flap, and let her in. The large snorting and wheezing officer, with the big moustache and the protruding cauldron of hard potbelly, approached to inspect her papers. He had a different manner this time.

'Good afternoon to you, Mrs Tzavella!' Evidently she was expected: he barely glanced at her papers, and again led her down passages, leaving doors open behind him as though it made no odds to him which prisoners came or went.

She was shown into the room with the glass panel, and there she sat, clutching the small telephone mouthpiece, till the shadows moved on the other side.

'Vangeli!'

He sat down opposite her, smiling – a strange, pleased, young smile: he was surprised to see her here, evidently they had told him nothing. Her starved sight darted over him, attending to his eyes, his nose, his level mouth, as if they were words, each of them saying to her, 'This is Vangelis.' He was changed since her last visit: then he looked snatched from a furnace, his face expressionless. Now he had a curious quietness, shyness. His eyes, so often fierce, were moist. His voice on the phone was so soft she scarcely heard it.

'Chryssa – it's a blessing to see you.'

'My love.'

Their voices caressed. For precious moments she held back the news: trouble attended it. But he asked gently, 'What is it, love?'

She found, as soon as she started to tell him, that just the ability to say she had brought his release filled her with happiness, whatever the snags.

'Vangeli, something has happened that may be . . . very wonderful. There's a pardon . . .'

He blinked, a shimmer slipped through his face: they stood poised by an opening door. The news called up such hope, he looked fragile.

'Tell me.'

'Leonidas got it.'

He glanced down at the desk, otherwise he didn't move.

'What's the catch? Do they want a testimonial from me?'

She read him the words of the oath.

'What do you think, love? Can I sign this?'

'You say, my love.'

He sat behind the glass opaque as a stone; his face was hard-skinned, bleak.

'If I signed that, they'd use it.'

He paused; she waited.

'What do you think, love?'

'I don't know, Vangeli. I know you have done enough, you have suffered enough, you have a right to get out, however you do it. We've both lost very much. We have a right to our life.'

His black eyes hung listening on her words.

'If you were out, you could work again.'

He paused thinking, then quietly gave his 'tst' – no. 'I couldn't. What could I do? A prisoner fresh from gaol? They'd watch me every second, and you too. And besides, if I put my name to this, I'd have lost something – my backbone most likely.'

She was silent: she couldn't urge him to compromise, but she couldn't bear to see him set himself against signing.

'Vangeli, I can't say what you should do. I know that if you don't sign, I won't have you home for – a very long time. We must ask ourselves, if you stay here *years*, is it worth what it would cost us? It's our lives we're talking about. Yes, if you signed, it would be a lie. Well, we've told lies in our lives.'

'Oh, I know that, I'm a lawyer after all.' He smiled to her with great affection. 'But this isn't the same, I'd be lying my life away. I suppose my pride is in it, as well. Do I give in to them?'

'Pride? I'm glad you're proud, Vangeli. Do you want to stay here? Oh, I'm sorry, my love, I'm tired, I'm stupid. It's just that – I want you home, Vangeli.' She gazed at him, tears in her eyes.

He opened and shut his mouth unspeaking, and rubbed his neck hard as if a noose were chafing it. In the corridor outside they heard feet approaching. Chryssa said, 'Don't say now, Vangeli. Let's rest on it. Let's try and think of a way. I'll come back tomorrow.'

The doors opened, the warders clattered in. They led Vangelis away, and led Chryssa to the gates.

She returned to the village and easily found a room to stay

in; she spent the evening sitting at the café at the waterfront, eating and drinking nothing, her face numb, gazing up at the crumbling fortress while its black walls and blind windows faded into darkness. She felt she had said little, she had said nothing at all; and the saying nothing was a kind of lying.

It was only as he returned to his cell that the thought truly came home to Vangelis, I could be out of here, I could be free. When Chryssa had first told him, he was stunned; and when he heard there was a catch, a difficulty, he was not surprised. The news had been too good to be true; he knew at once, by instinct, he would not be able to sign this oath. It had hurt to discuss the pros and cons: and when he looked at Chryssa, at her strong sweet face with just a pane of glass between them, he felt the sawing of a knife blade continuously severing them. But he knew the oath was like that pane of glass: it seemed a difficulty you could hardly see, yet it was a wall, you could not pass it.

Now he was again cooped up close in stone, but the talk of freedom had freed his thought. As he moved to the small window, he felt that inside his body was another person, who flung up his arms and sailed clear: over empty seas, hillsides, fenceless plains. He was in the bow of a ship, holding Chryssa; he was in Athens beside her, in a yellow tramcar full of cheerful people that swung down a curving road.

He paced. He thought I'm mad, mad, mad to stay locked up. Why throw my life away, just for a principle? The oath was only words. He had said the Junta would use it, but would they? What capital could they make out of it? Probably people had forgotten who he was. No one would notice, he could sign and have done. And yet it was true that once he was out, there would be nothing he could do. He would be disgraced, and watched: he would be free and impotent, a useless person. But what use was he here? And to remain here and fester, and do nothing and come to nothing, where they drugged the food so their minds were dull and their sex dried up – His thoughts grew into a darkening maze, with passages leading to crooked corners while the right course steadily receded from him.

It was dark outside, for coolness he rested his head on the stone: and while he stood motionless, and the hard cold stone seemed to enter his temples like a drink of freshness, he thought, 'I'm arguing very hard to keep myself here.' He remembered Chryssa's asking, Do you want to stay here? He had hid that question, or hid from it, but now he wondered, was it so? Had he grown so acclimatized to prison that he was nervous of leaping free? Then, with a feeling of some wall collapsing, he admitted a thought that had lain in wait at the back of his mind like a bear behind a door. Was there something in his life, in him, which all along had been driving him here, a will to anger, enclosure, separation from Chryssa? For a moment he looked from outside at the shape of his life; then it tangled, he must leave these thoughts. He would have to tear himself inside out by hand to find the truth.

He retreated from questions: they weren't to the purpose now, for a different thought of its own accord came clear as words. Whatever my different motives may be, still I must do what I must. Blurs resolved, a wide space cleared in his mind: with a steady eye he saw the road ahead.

With this thought, the weight of his tiredness descended on him; he consigned himself to it and sank to sleep. He dreamed he was at home with Chryssa, sitting on their balcony in Athens, they were chatting and laughing. But even in the dream he thought, is this the past, or is this the future? When he woke, stiff on the cold bench, he was still asking, Was that dream a memory of the past, or was I seeing how things will be? He had momentarily an image of, in each human couple, an eternal cycle of separation and joining.

Outside dawn slowly grew, but no birds sang to greet it, there were no trees outside.

From the long voyage and from strain, Chryssa was tired: she slept deeply but woke early, and before sunrise was patrolling the shore. The houses slept still, with their shutters closed; the sea lay completely calm, merging with the pale sky. She walked out along the low concrete mole and looked back at the island: up on its promontory, behind a thin veil of haze, the prison fortress looked only like an ancient disused fortification, peaceful, brown, part of the hillside. There was a stillness, a radiance, a dawn spell on all the island. Did it mock her anxiety, or in some way relieve it? She thought of Michael,

298

and Vangelis; and couldn't make her thoughts connect: she was two people. The sun had appeared now, an enlarged red wheel like a sunset but rising; the wind dropped to nothing; sea and land hung between night and day. It was the still moment before choice: the wheel had paused: soon it would turn.

Now, tiny but clear in the sun, the owner of the café appeared in his doorway, yawning, stretching, blearily beginning to sweep up from the night before. She must have a coffee, slowly she walked towards his establishment: then she had a new thought. She realized that she had just been thinking, oh let Vangelis sign and come home, and now abruptly she asked herself, Do I *want* him to sign? What will I think of Vangelis if he signs? For a moment she stopped where she stood, feeling her wishes divide.

When she arrived at the prison she was met again by the snorting officer, but was taken a different route this time. She was brought to a small barc windowless room, whitewashed and clean, with a table and a couple of chairs in it. Here, puzzled, she was left.

He was gone some time. A young warder sauntered in, and leaned on the wall, glancing at her occasionally: presently he offered her a cigarette, and started to tell her about the island. There was no work here, but the pay in the prison was all right. She couldn't listen, all her ears were for steps approaching. Then she heard them, echoing footfalls: she knew it was Vangelis, her heart started to hammer and bang like the clapper of a crazy bell. Let there be a way, let him come home! This was the turning point: if he came now all their life would take one course, and if he didn't – she felt they had both fallen far into a pit: for a moment, with the light still in sight above, they clung to a ledge: if they let this chance go, they would drop to the bottom.

The steps paused: in the doorway was Vangelis. Though she saw him yesterday, at the sight of him now with no barrier between them everything swam, her sight came and went in waves while Vangelis grew broader to fill the room. Those black bright eyes were so close she could fall in them, his arms clasped her and she hugged him banging her head on his chest, Vangeli, Vangeli, Vangeli, hardly able to believe they were holding each other.

Eventually they stepped back, and held each other at arms length, looking at each other close, still holding hands tight; while the guards stood by benign, looking not like gaolers but like doctors who had brought Vangelis through a difficult illness.

She looked her question.

'I can't sign that paper.'

As soon as he started to speak she knew what he would say, and knew too, with absolute certainty, that all along this had been what he would say. She accepted it at once, it had always been so. She looked at him, as he looked ahead with level eyes, and saw his courage.

The fat-bellied officer stood near the door, listening to them, breathing heavily; abruptly he shouted, 'Sign the damn thing and go, man!'

The couple stared at him; he roared at them ferocious, 'For the love of God, sign the thing and get out of here! Are you an idiot?'

Vangelis smiled at this encouragement, sparkled with zest, just as in the old days.

'Madam, he is an obstinate man. Tell him to be sensible, tell him to sign.'

Chryssa smiled at Vangelis with love. She said agreeing, 'He is an obstinate man.'

The officer snorted and walked out, muttering and cursing, they heard him banging doors down the corridors.

There was sudden quiet in the room.

He took her in his arms, and they held each other as if they would melt in one. Their hands moved slowly, as if carrying all of them: they passed out of consciousness and back.

Footfalls grew in the passage; they parted. Chryssa was led to the gate by the young warder who had given her a cigarette; he was depressed and cold now.

In the front yard the pot-bellied officer was scowling and grunting, exclaiming angrily to the monkish gatekeeper. She saw – as he listened – his narrow face sour. He muttered to himself as he opened the gate, and as soon as she was out he banged it shut on her heels. As she picked her way over the stones she heard the large lock cranked shut with passion.

*

In their living room, Leonidas and Patra listened seriously as Chryssa told them what had happened. Their son Alexis sat at a distance, listening in the shadows, pale and intent.

Leonidas heard Chryssa out with difficulty, his head down, his face tense, his hands gripping his knees. At the end he said, in a voice that throbbed, 'Chryssa, he should have signed. You must go back and make him sign.'

'He won't sign it, Leonida.'

'He must sign it!' Leonidas sang, his voice rose and he rose too, 'Chryssa, what he did was very wrong. He was very stupid not to sign!'

'Leonida!' Patra called. But Leonidas could not stop, he was injured and enraged – the folly, the ingratitude, after he had moved heaven and earth to make escape possible. 'Oh no, Chryssa, what he did was a big mistake.' He sighed heavily, then slowly nodded to himself. 'But I know why he didn't sign.'

'Why then?' Chryssa demanded quietly.

But he wouldn't say; he glared at her, enigmatic in fury.

'Why, Leonida?' Chryssa insisted.

'Well, I'll tell you why, Chryssa. He did it for his career.'

Chryssa stared; Patra exclaimed, 'What garbage is this, Leonida?'

That tone of hers always cut him to the quick. Helpless, exasperated, he cried out in justification, 'Of course he did it for his career! He is a man of politics, I know how he thinks. He believes that one day this government will fall, there may be elections, and then it will be very good, oh yes, to have been a "prisoner of conscience" all the time of the National Government. Then, who knows, he may be a minister. That's what he thinks. You shouldn't let him do it, Chryssa. This government will not fall.'

Patra in her harshest hiss, her face a jagged dagger, said, 'Drop it, Leonida. Leave it.'

Glaring yellow in chagrin, he fell silent. Disgusted – but locked, because he had helped – Chryssa left in silence. Alexis watched all saying nothing, a hungry-eyed dazzled face at the back of the room.

17

Alexis, Leonidas often felt, was the cross he had to bear. And of all those innocences in his son, which got under Leonidas' skin and inflamed there, the most infuriating was Alexis' way of constantly asking how 'Uncle Vangelis' was – at a time when Leonidas wanted to think of Vangelis as very far removed from himself, and a more distant connection than any uncle. But once Vangelis had refused the release that Leonidas had secured for him, Alexis did not any more mention the topic.

He was almost totally silent at home. At times Leonidas tried to persuade himself that Alexis had given up his weak resistance; but steadily it grew clearer to him that his son was very far from being at his side, and that the space between them was not a crack but a chasm. He smarted in irritation, deeply betrayed. Before all things his son should look up to him, and revere him, and beg to learn more from him; and when he had so many important duties to think of, it was not right or fair that he should have to take time off to worry about his son. And again, when the National Government and the great cause had so many enemies in the nation, at least his own family should be a citadel of safety, he should not have to fear for loyalty there. And yet it was true too, he thought with unease, that even in the family of the National Government – in the cabinet and in the chiefs of staff – there was division. He was involved in the division. These were difficult times, things were not clear as they should be any more.

As to his son, he must have things out with him, and put him right. But he delayed the encounter, feeling nervous: he did not like to think what insects, serpents, scorpions, he might find in his son's mind. Hurt, impatient, he bullied Alexis at home, suddenly sending him to fetch things for the table, and then receiving them with displeased grunts. Alexis was, as ever, obedient and mild: yet sometimes Leonidas would look at this maturing young man, moving into his late teens, who within a year had grown broad as well as tall, and good looking though still with those dark, liquid, too soft almost feminine eyes – yet after all with hairs springing on his chest and arms, and a fine black down on his jaw – Leonidas would watch him with alarm at the incalculable, irresistible force of change which, so fast, was drawing out of his gentle son this tall dark brooding presence he was unsure how to control.

Alexis for his part froze to his father whenever he saw him. He wanted to shut all doors in his face. He had passed the period in which his father's beliefs and habits and pleasures, and the roll of his voice, and his enormous shadow, and the scent of his body and his talc and aftershave, surrounded him in a cloud that became a close smother through which he groped. At one time, he had been so full of his father's views that, when he opened his mouth at school, he would hear his father's words come out as readily as if they were his own thoughts. Later, the same process had happened in reverse, and at home he would hear the things the other boys had said come out of his mouth, all unbidden but with devilment driving them, raising in his father storms of spat crumb and indignation. There was a miserable period of transition, when by an odd constant twist of perversity he echoed his father at school and the other boys at home continuously: he felt that he himself was nothing at all, that he had no self, that he was as his father said feeble as a girl. Whatever he said, his voice was a thin reedy half broken hard pressed nothing in his ears.

But that was a stage only. As his father had grown more busy in the Government, and was away long hours, and preoccupied when at home, he had almost stopped speaking to Alexis. And at the same time, at school, Alexis heard a new kind of story. Some boys had fathers who were for the Government, but they said little, these days, while the stories that ripped through the corridors and dormitories were the stories from boys whose relatives had been arrested. In a little time there were few means of torture that Alexis had not heard of, from the phalanga to shoving a Coca-Cola bottle up your arse and breaking it. These stories ran through the boys sickening and thrilling, they stuck hurting in Alexis' mind, jagged images he couldn't get out like the broken glass caught inside you, lacerating, tearing. These things, mixed in odd ways with his father's shouting, recurred in his dreams; they'd spring to

303

mind suddenly when he saw his father wolfing food, while losing temper with the nation's traitors.

Though the school was supposed to be a respectable academy, books and papers started to circulate, pamphlet versions of Marx and Trotsky. Alexis began to have a secret library, and developed not only disagreement but a contempt for his father. For though Leonidas was in the Government, he knew nothing of political science, his mind was a jumble of slogans and prejudices: if they tried to argue, he would hector and browbeat. At one with these things was the revulsion Alexis felt for his father's physique. In the morning Leonidas would be hours shaving, tilting his head back to stretch his jowels flat, and something in the way he did it, and in the silly vain look in his tipped up face, irritated Alexis extremely; his flesh would itch when he saw his father carefully smarming a curl on his forehead. Even the way Leonidas sat over his papers, his brow slightly puckered in conscious intelligence, some touch of old film star in the way he composed himself, inflamed Alexis. And when Leonidas lost his temper with him or with Patra, and his face went set and brutal and his nostrils were big holes and he was helpless with fury: then everything in Alexis locked, he burned all over in freezing hatred.

Now, after this general had been to see them, he wanted to speak about politics too; but his politics had gone harsh, he couldn't talk economics, he was only interested in things which would be serrated knives to stick into his father. Not free enterprise, unions, monopolies, but torture, and the terrible things done in the past – such issues as arose when one of the boys brought to school a photograph which he quietly showed to Alexis. It seemed torn from a book or magazine: it showed a mound of heads – heads of guerillas cut off by Royalist troops during the Civil War. One of the heads, he said, belonged to a cousin of his mother's. The photo was faded and crumpled, and it was hard to believe what it showed: the heads looked so like normal heads that it was hard to believe they were not still attached to bodies, the eye kept thinking they had simply been poked through holes in some sort of board.

All afternoon the photo ate into Alexis' mind. He carried the knowledge of it home with him as a bloody trophy for his father – 'There – that's what your friends do.' At dinner he remarked that his friend had shown him this photo: coldly,

304

factually, he described it. Patra winced; Leonidas listened with yellowing eyes – and at the end, he denied it, he denied it all. Furious, he shouted, 'Do you hear this, Patra? Do you hear what he learns in that school now? He says the Greek army cuts off heads. Look, Alexi, you should not believe just what you're told. My son, you are very immature. You shouldn't believe what schoolboys say.'

'But I saw the picture; it was a photograph.'

'Uh! It was a trick!'

'It was real; I saw it.'

'It was a trick! They did not cut off heads. What do you think they are? Barbarians?' Leonidas' face flushed, he spat in his anger.

Alexis only stared: how could his father deny it? Did he really believe it hadn't happened? Could it be a trick photo, a fake?

'But it was his uncle,' he said. 'He showed me the photo.'

'What was his name?'

Alexis gave the boy's name. 'No, no,' his father shouted, 'the name of the uncle.'

'Ioannou.'

'Ioannou! You are at school with a relative of Ioannou! You did not tell me that, Alexi.' His father stood now, towering forward, crimson.

'He showed me the photo, it was real.'

In a huge shrug of exasperation Leonidas protested, 'But of course, Alexi. Ioannou, yes! He was a leader of the communists!'

'But you said it didn't happen.'

'It didn't happen! But to the *leaders* of the communists, Aris and the others – of course!'

'You said . . . barbarians . . .' Alexis' words broke in pieces.

Leonidas opened his hands and closed them, helpless in passion. 'No, Alexi, excuse me, for the leaders of the communists it was very necessary. Because the people in those parts were just peasants. If someone said Ioannou was dead, someone else would say he wasn't dead, he was still up in the mountains, still fighting. Of course they had to see the heads! It was necessary!'

At that point Alexis could not speak more; and his father could not stop. Standing over the table, waving his arms,

appealing about the house to wife and walls and pictures for
confirmation, his round face swollen and hard, the brown skin
of it flushed deep red, his eyes rolling, he cried out about the
Civil War and what the communists had done: they killed,
they stole children from the villages to bring them up in the
east just as the Turks did. Alexis must learn this, it was time
he woke up: he was weak, in a dream, he must face the truth.
His roaring face coming close to Alexis, quivering, filling his
sight, he shouted how he saw two communists shoot an aunt
of his, he was a child, she stuck him in a cupboard, they
banged into the room and knocked her around and then kicked
her and shot her and shot her again: she was a woman lawyer,
she was disapproved of in the village. Leonidas got more
wild-eyed as he spoke, and shouted higher and was not far
from tears. Alexis suddenly could take no more: he felt too
hot, he couldn't breathe, the room swam, he keeled over and
fell on the floor.

There followed a furious row between his parents, all night
he heard their voices rising and falling, he heard his father's
exasperation alternating with fierce pleading and protest, and
his mother's voice stabbing and shrieking in retort.

That was the last conversation that he had with his father
about politics. In the following days father and son didn't
speak, and avoided each other's eyes. Patra maintained communications: Alexis had always been closer to her and they
worked together as he prepared for his university exams.
Leonidas did not want to know, he feared even worse things
if Alexis went to university: madness reigned there. So Patra
helped test him on what he must learn: her interrupted education revived, and as they worked over the textbooks, they
chatted sometimes almost like boy and girlfriend.

It was Patra he told one day, as they sat on their balcony
revising, 'I go to Party meetings.'

The textbook she was leafing through fell to the floor; in a
gesture of her mother's not used in years, she crossed herself.

'Alexi!'

He tried to reassure her. 'It's all right, mama. We're careful.
We keep quiet.'

She could only gasp still; tears stood in her eyes; she was
too shocked. Eventually she said, 'Alexi . . . but you're still
at school . . . it's banned, illegal, they shouldn't let you . . .

you can't, not yet . . . you don't know how dangerous it is . . .'

He quietly insisted there was no great danger, it was a student branch of the Party, they were very careful. She would not be comforted; but he, for his part, would not be dissuaded.

She agreed to keep his secret. She gave no sign to Leonidas, and Leonidas did not ask about Alexis.

18

Leonidas, for his part, had new hopes and new convictions. His friends in the army wanted change – so did all the nation. To himself he admitted things he had not dared admit before. For it was true: the National Government in its present form had run into the sand. The economy only worsened, for all their reforms; the profits and prosperity, that were supposed to come as a result of strong discipline, had not come; and, in the meantime, the cost of that discipline steadily grew. Their expenditure on security was a third of the national budget. What a waste! Leonidas thought. If they had found their way to the heart of the nation, this would not be necessary. And for all the cost and the cruelty, the discipline did not work: still there were bombings, still new resistance groups formed – however many the police cracked, new ones came into being. They had more enemies now than they had at the start, and sectors of the nation had to be written off as hostile; and not only students, who were now all communists, but factory workers, farmers, many businessmen even, were disaffected. Outside the nation the enemies bayed and howled: the Council of Europe, the international bodies, the endless wail of accusation in the foreign press. In the east the Archbishop of Cyprus denounced them continuously, and intrigued against them, and was a rallying point for the Greek opposition. This was not triumph, Leonidas must admit it: this was failure.

Change must come, he could not doubt it. And just here he stood well, for he was strong in the Ministry – latterly he had almost *been* the Ministry – and he had powerful connections in the army. His abilities were known to the people who counted. He must hope and pray – and work to make sure – that when change came, he would survive. And oh it was risky, it would be difficult, a leap across space to a higher ledge almost out of reach. But one must take risks. And if he succeeded, if when the army brought in a new government, he was in it – if he had a portfolio, if he were a minister – then he would not stay long in the Ministry of Coordination. For if this new government would lead Greece to greatness, and secure all the Aegean oil, and reclaim the Dardanelles, and tell the superpowers what to do, then he must be nearer to the decisions on foreign affairs than the Ministry of Coordination amounted to. Foreign affairs were his passion and his gift. And if his star rose now, if he snatched each opportunity, where might he stop?

As he sat one day alone in his office, his elbows on his desk and his fingers pressed together and pressed to his lips, as if he were locked in a prayer to himself – as he sat so, motionless, a large space cleared in the centre of his thoughts, a hush descended, and he said to himself, 'If things go well – I could – be premier.'

It was a far thought: it depended on many things falling right: such luck he needed! But it was the goal, he should aim at nothing less.

He emerged from this thought slowly, like a man unbending after confession: he knew he had been in communion with his fate.

He had, in the next days, a new calm in his dealings with the Minister: he must bide his time, and play his cards carefully. He laughed again at the Minister's jokes, deferred and was easy, and became once more a quiet smiling obligingness hovering at the Minister's desk.

After the tense pushy Leonidas he had recently been at odds with, the Minister found this new quiet servant more disquieting again.

'I have the report of the mining union, Mr Minister.'

'I thank you, Mr Secretary.'

As he accepted the neat report, presented as usual ahead of schedule, the Minister swivelled tight eyes at his underling. He could see the man was in some excitement, his adrenalin flowed, he sat on some deep secret that thrilled him; and Leonidas only smiled back with a suave grin of teeth, like a shark waiting and smiling from the bottom of a shallow clear pool.

One afternoon Leonidas' telephone rang. He was in conference at the time, and picked up the receiver with a mild annoyance that his secretary had let the call through. 'Hello? Yes?'

A firmly curt woman's voice – not that of his own secretary – said, 'Mr Argiriou? Please wait a minute. The Secretary to the President wishes to speak to you.'

A great space hollowed inside Leonidas. Putting a hand over the receiver, he begged his visitors to leave; then sat back in his chair, melted, trembling, hanging on the phone.

A busy, slightly weary voice came on the line. 'Leonida? Afternoon. How are you? I'd like to see you. Can you call this evening, when you've finished at the Ministry. Say, nine o'clock. All right?'

'Yes . . . yes . . .' Leonidas murmured uncertainly. 'You mean . . . at the office of the President?'

'Yes of course. See you then. Bye.' The phone clicked dead.

Leonidas breathed brokenly, he felt he would faint. Slowly he hauled together his shattered thoughts, which had shot off to the ends of the world. 'Oh, this is important,' he repeated to himself. The call was so momentous that he hardly dared ask what it meant.

A huge event was coming towards him. What could it be? He had a spasm of fear. Did the President know of his disloyal thoughts? But no one knew; and if they did, it would be the police who called, and not the Secretary to the President. No, this summons could only be good news: it must be – a promotion.

Yes, he was clear, it had to be promotion, his wish of the old days at last come true. The President had seen the Minister's incompetence, and he was going to offer him the Minister's job. Another portfolio? But his experience was in the Ministry of Coordination. Perhaps the President had decided already on the civilian government he had spoken of forming – and he, Leonidas, would be in it.

But what then of his recent plans? Would the army tolerate a civilian government, or any government led by this president? If he joined them, when their days were numbered, he would disappear with them: that would be the end of him. Yet, to refuse a ministry, to turn down *such* an offer! What a choice to give him! The cruelty of fate!

He writhed in anxiety: but the minutes passed, and his thoughts circled, all his wheels spun. And then he thought: what substance was there, in this talk of change? What, after all, did Vouros know? The man had been pumping Leonidas for tips. And that stern major general he had met on the yacht, who had lectured them in patriotism with old-fashioned rhetoric – was he really in touch, did he really know what was going on? For of course there were officers in the army who would not be pleased when they saw the President, who had once been one of them, rise so high. They were older than him, of course they would intrigue, and want to see him fall; of course they would talk about changes, and new governments and new presidents under their influence. Ah, but the President was shrewd, his police were everywhere: would he be caught napping? He was a great man, and a clever man, and a strong man. He had power.

Leonidas sighed, and thanked his stars. He had nearly made – a terrible mistake. If he had declared himself for the malcontents – Vouros, the Major General, the disappointed men – what disaster! Promotion had come just in time.

And the difficulties of the Government? Of course there were complaints, and the communists conspiring, but the President was choosing a new team, a team of younger better men, civilians with dynamism like himself. They would save Greece, and the National Government, and the goals of the Revolution.

So Leonidas mused. His visitors went away. He gave instructions that he was too busy to be interrupted further. He needed to be free to think: but he could not think further, he could only pace in his office, in agony of waiting.

Should he ring Patra? He must talk to someone. Yet she was far away. And he should not talk: state secrets!

The sky outside darkened, he put on his light but still only paced. Then his door opened, and the Minister came in: he too was excited, his nervous eyes glittered.

'Evening, Leonida. How goes it? I'm off now.'

'Uh – evening, Mr Minister.' Leonidas blinked: the Minister did not pay him social calls.

The Minister rocked on his feet. 'I have to go early,' he said. 'The President has asked me to visit him this evening – to have an ouzo.' Leonidas gazed, open-mouthed: he was too surprised to control his face. The Minister was pleased with this, it was the face he wanted Leonidas to make. Exhilarated, he took his leave.

Leonidas pondered. What now? Why the Minister? Ouzo

with the President? *What* was going on? He spun in panic. But he dealt with it soon. Of course, the President would let the Minister down gently; he would need an ouzo. Poor old man. For the first time Leonidas felt sorry for his superior. For the man was human. And he felt a new respect for the President, for his consideration.

The time came at last. Leonidas walked down bare corridors, descended in an empty lift, and with good wishes to the guards left the darkened Ministry lobby, and stepped into streets that were busy with lights. He would walk to the President's office, it was not far: he would walk there quietly, just like any citizen.

He crossed the bright-lit crush of Constitution Square, passed in front of the Parliament building, and took a few paces down a sidestreet to the plain state offices – it was not a large building – where the President worked. Introducing himself as he went, he entered the courtyard, climbed the stairs, and passed through a handful of rooms to a not large office where a plump, sallow middle-aged man, hard worked, wearily smiling, stood up behind his desk, and reached forward to shake hands with Leonidas.

'Good evening, Mr Secretary,' they said to each other. 'Leonida, good to see you. How are you? What will you drink, scotch?' The Secretary to the President poured Leonidas a drink, then, motioning him to one of the armchairs in the office, sat in the other himself. Leonidas looked round critically: the office was high, but dim and dingy. But then, he thought, secretaries do not get good offices. With an impulse of confidence he sat back and made himself at home: and as he did so, his glance caught the big photograph of the President on the office wall: the high-domed forehead, the piercing eyes. He was a leader, Leonidas backed him.

The Secretary studied thoughtfully the whisky in his glass, as it slowly swilled round in a syrupy wave, then said, 'Well, Leonida, I don't know whether you will have heard this, but a number of ministers have been called here today. Your own minister saw the President a little while ago. And the news the President gave him – well, it was good news for Greece, and yet it was not good news for him, for he will have to give up the ministry. The President deeply regrets the painfulness of the decisions he has had to take.' He paused, and shook his head gravely.

Leonidas sat fixed, in agony of impatience: in two seconds, in half a second, he would hear his dream come true. He could hardly believe it. Deep in his brain a worm of question curled, Is this going well? But he saw, almost, the golden chariot waiting, to sweep him to power.

The Secretary resumed, 'Yes, the President is seeing the members of the cabinet, and I am seeing some of the Secretaries. For you see, Leonida, and this is confidential, it will shortly be announced that the President has asked a civilian, one of our leading politicians, to form a government. He is considering the portfolios at the present time, and will announce his cabinet shortly.' He paused, and looked very seriously at Leonidas. 'As I say, this must remain confidential, until the public announcement.' Then he stopped, as though he had said everything.

Leonidas only gazed, in a thrill of bewilderment. What was he being told? Was the man hinting that one of the portfolios was for him? But he had a terrible fear. And yet – things could not, simply, stop here.

'I'm sorry,' the Secretary said. But why sorry? thought Leonidas. He died to ask 'and my future?' but the Secretary was looking at him with such grave sympathy that he did not dare ask. As he studied that serious face, Leonidas felt that invisibly, outside this room but just next door, the whole high edifice of his ambitions and plans and hopes was slowly collapsing, slowly crumbling, like a slow-motion film without sound, slowly disappearing in a billowing smoke of dust, which disappeared, and left nothing.

He must stop this, there must be something he could say, some magic right words if only he could find them, he must say them quickly, for nothing final had been said yet: everything was possible still. In frozen, yearning hunger he cast for those magic words.

The Secretary stood up: evidently business was done. Leonidas got up too. Then he thought, of course, there's nothing the man can say – he doesn't know who the new ministers will be.

Just then the door opened, and the President himself walked in. He held out his hand and greeted him seriously, 'Good evening, Leonida.' Leonidas shook hands strongly, and his eyes fed anxiously on the President's face. And the President

313

spoke to him, 'Leonida, you have done great work at the Ministry, excellent work. I know how much service you have given us. It has been most highly prized.'

The President said more, praising his services; and all the time Leonidas wondered, What does he mean? What is he telling me? Then the President stopped, and his firm eyes expected a reply. In panic Leonidas cast, what should he say? He knew he was being discharged, but there must be something he could say, some special words which would retrieve everything. This was his chance, he was closeted with the President! But instead of the words he wanted, he heard his hoarse voice saying what the President expected, 'It has been a great honour to serve in your government, Mr President. A great honour.'

Immediately he had said it, Leonidas cursed himself. You fool! he had signed away his career.

The President nodded curtly, seriously, with a grave face of military self-discipline. He shook hands with Leonidas again, with eyes of candid respect and friendship. Then he withdrew.

Through his weariness, the Secretary beamed at Leonidas, as if a great honour had been given him with this visit. And with that honour given, he stood waiting for Leonidas to go. Leonidas delayed, his mind milled, he thought, If I go now, I go for ever. But he had to: he said only, 'I must be going,' and shook the hand of the President's Secretary, and left the room.

He paused in the next room: but there the eyes of a presidential aide rested coolly on him. So he resumed walking – but he should not just walk away from power – but that hall brought him to the stairs, he had to go down them and into the courtyard: there a guard watched him, and all he could do was continue walking, and walk out of the archway, and into the street. Another ministry stood across the road, its pillared doors shut. It wasn't for him; and the short road brought him to the crowded avenue, dazzling and teeming, and there he could walk anywhere he wanted, like any citizen.

When he closed the door of their home, Leonidas let his last restraint go. The face he showed Patra was exhausted, collapsed, it looked ready to cry.

'Leonida, what is it?'

He crossed the room with drugged movements, and dropped

into the sofa. 'Patra, get me some aspirin. My head is split in two.' There was a certain bad headache he always got, when he was failing to have his way in a business negotiation.

He swallowed the aspirin Patra brought. 'Leonida, what has happened?'

He told her; she burst out in a fury of commiseration. 'Oh, Leonida, after all you've done! You've run that ministry, you've done everything for them. What thanklessness! The bastards! Oh, the donkeys!'

Her passion gave him comfort, they were together in indignation. Eventually they talked about the new government: who would be in it? 'Who can they bring in? Who is there?' Patra wondered.

In a weak voice, like a furtive creature, Leonidas ventured, 'I suppose . . . it's still possible . . . when they come to the Ministry of Coordination, when they ask *who*'s the man. . . .'

She looked at him with eyes of pity, 'No, my love.'

'What do you mean, no?' he asked, weak-voiced, hurt.

'You think they may still ask you? Don't think that, Leonida. They would have said.'

He was annoyed as well as hurt, now. 'It's not *so* sure, is it? Why are you *so* sure they won't appoint me?' His voice became accusing; her face went stony.

He got up and prowled the room.

'I *should* be minister!'

'Leonida, you *should*!' she said with vehemence.

They embraced tight, in furious grief.

He had some days yet, working at the Ministry; but they were dead days. It seemed the staff knew he was finished, for now when they saw him, they agreed with all he said, and ignored it. He realized that a politician only has power while he has a future: once his end is in sight, he is finished already.

Yet still he could not kill his hope. The new government was still not announced, perhaps they were stuck, looking for good people: his mind invented devious schemes whereby the new prime minister, after trying out many people, would come back to him. Of course, by the theory he had a few days ago, he should not want to be in this new civilian government at all: General Vouros had told him that the army would not stand for it. And he had said to himself, he *should* be out of power now, so he could come back later. But his friend General

315

Vouros seemed far from him now: perhaps he and the Major General still dreamed and planned for the Great Idea, but Leonidas felt himself dropping fast from any place in that scheme. His connections with the army felt to him like far stretched gossamer, spider's web thin.

Leonidas waited for Alexis' reaction in a nervous terror of what he would say: he felt disgraced and vulnerable, he was ready to knock his son down if he were cocky, or denounced the President, or tried to make political capital out of it all. But his son did none of those things, he did not mention politics or his father's career at all. Then Leonidas realized, his son was sparing him; and when he realized this, he wanted to weep.

Unmanned, paralysed, he lived on his nerves; he was still waiting. Every time the phone rang, something in him said: It is the prime minister, wanting me.

The School of
Architecture and Engineering

Boots scuffed gravel, the policemen and soldiers stood sharply
to attention as the President emerged on the terrace of his villa,
a short plump figure, blunt nosed, hot eyed, his small mouth
pinched. His cavalcade was drawn up before him: the outriders
stood at the salute beside their motorbikes, the police beside
their cars; his own car waited open to take him, large, comfortable, black, shining. He snuffed the sharp dawn air: it was late
in the year, yet a keen, clear morning – propitious for the new
government which today he must announce.

'A fine morning, gentlemen.'

He settled himself in his car: there was a moment's pause
while engines started, then, all together, the entire procession
slowly moved forward, emerged onto the main road where
other guards saluted, and gathered speed fast. For there was
nothing to bar them, the road was empty. There were no boats
on the calm, quicksilver water; the stony hillside was distinct
and bare; and all the way there was no one to be seen except
for the police, in their green uniforms, who, at every road
junction, at every turning, at every large rock or building on
the road to Athens, stood waiting, alert and braced, saluting
briskly as the procession passed. Once an assassin had waited
by the road; but with the guards they had now, not even an
animal could get near his route: all the way, to the heart of
Athens, was clear.

Alone in the car he sat upright and officer-like, his black
suit tight on his fat hips, his eyes staring hard ahead and only
momentarily darting to the brown frieze of rock that blurred
past his window. Every so often he grunted impatiently, as
though there were someone else present whose speaking annoyed him. He slightly shook his shoulders, he was impatient
with his own anxiety. This government must work, it had to
succeed. If it did, he would have triumphed: all would be
secure, and he would be secure. The government would depend

on him to keep the army at bay, the army would depend on him to preserve its privileges. The world would not love his government, but it would accept it, and would trade with Greece again. And he would be in charge, the Revolution would go on, all would be well –

But would it work, would his government be accepted? He worried, he feared, he had so many enemies. The country was riddled rotten with communists; other countries never stopped attacking and damaging him; even his old comrades, his allies in the coup, were his enemies now. But he had had to make a gap between himself and them. And he had done it shrewdly, he had made them ministers, bringing them to Athens and cutting them off from the army and their tanks. Now, as he moved higher, he must dispense with them completely: it was necessary, but they would hate him. And the army mistrusted his civilian prime minister, and disapproved of his own gains in power: the generals could not be his friends. He took on more police, for he had to know who was loyal to *him* – and the more he did this, the more they complained he was becoming an autocrat. The higher he rose, the more opposition and danger he faced: but it was his fate, he was the steersman of Greece. And the new plan, the new government, would make everything good – if, if, if the nation, the army, accepted its rule. This was his biggest risk, the most dangerous step he had taken yet: but it must work, it had to, for the nation's sake.

In the last stretch of bare countryside before they ran into Athens he closed his eyes. All his thoughts converged on the single urging: let this plan work, let my government succeed.

Houses passed the windows, while the police, in greater numbers, lined the road like a fence: each policeman at the salute, like the same man repeated endlessly. He ran through the plan again: the generals worried him, he must check them again with the Brigadier in charge of Military Intelligence. At least he had the Brigadier, his oldest friend, his one good friend. And the Brigadier was the best friend, in all the nation, to have: he knew all that went on everywhere. And yet, even with the Brigadier, relations were not as they had been – oh he must be alert, even with him.

The procession drove fast through the Athens streets. He glanced at the royal palace, visible through the leafless trees, a white bleak bulk, black-windowed, empty. The King had betrayed him – but the King had gone. He breathed in, sat firmer: he had a protection, history ran his way. His plan would work.

The announcement was made: a civilian prime minister had been appointed, and was at present considering the distribution of portfolios. Shortly afterwards, the names of the new ministers were announced: they were heralded in the press as distinguished parliamentarians, experienced statesmen tried and tested in their commitment to the nation. They were, it was true, somewhat elderly, their fame was not recent: but their credentials were good, the President was satisfied, he shook heartily their thin dry hands and commended them with confidence to the nation's trust.

The nation heard him, bewildered: the announcement was sudden, what was this new government? The new names, suddenly, were on a million lips: slipping with misgivings between tiny coffee cups in Colonaki, between men talking closely across office desks, between half heard voices shouting hoarsely in the deafening strobe-dazzled sea front bouzoukia. The names rippled quietly, urgently, through cinema audiences, while their eyes scanned the subtitles of American films.

Who were these men? Slowly their characters rose through reminiscences into the light. Some of them were veterans of other governments that had fallen long ago. Such senior politicians! Each of them was older than the minister he replaced.

When private with friends, Leonidas mocked them: what a set of old greybeards, what a government of pensioners! He thanked his stars his name was not among them.

It was said they were nothing but fingers of the President. And it was said they were an interim government, caring for the nation till elections were held, till freedom was restored to Greece.

In the prison itself there was change, a new atmosphere. Vangelis noticed when, out in the yard on a cold autumn day, a guard who had treated him with a particular tight impatient brutality took out a packet of cigarettes, took one for himself, and then stuck the packet in Vangelis' direction. Vangelis was surprised, puzzled, but he took the cigarette. The guard then looked his way and, seeing him with a cigarette, held out his lighter. Vangelis took the light, and inhaled slowly down into the cellars of his lungs. For a few moments they smoked side by side, gazing across the yard. The guard glanced his way with a furtive twinkle, but Vangelis kept his face passive, wondering what it was he wanted.

The guard stirred the gravel with his boot and remarked, 'Winter's on the way, then.'

Vangelis nodded slightly, and waited to see what else he'd say.

The guard glanced round cautiously, sighed, and said, 'Life's a funny thing. Why must Greeks be at odds?' He looked at Vangelis' large set face, on which a frown slowly knit, and then said, 'We're human too, you know.'

'I don't doubt that. I know what the word means.'

The guard shook his head, and said as if he were chaffing him, 'You're a hard man, Tzavella.'

Presently the guard walked away; and Vangelis was moved, in spite of himself, by this new friendly feeling.

The next day he saw another guard joking with Stamatis.

'Did you see that, Vangeli,' Stamatis said afterwards. 'The bastard winked at me.'

Vangelis nodded, puzzled. 'Has someone given them happy pills?'

In the following days, each of the guards seemed to want, privately and in his own way, to make his peace with the prisoners. They chatted in whispers; showed photos of their families; they seemed to be saying, they only did what they had to. The prisoners began to understand: the guards knew there were changes in Greece, more changes might come, the prisoners might be released. And these men were political prisoners, who knew but what, in the seesaw way of politics, some of them might be in office sometime? And then, well, it would be no harm to have them friendly.

While autumn grew cooler and the wind only sharpened, the prisoners enjoyed, in their conditions, a mild Indian summer. It was hard to believe they would really get out; but still they made plans, as to what they would do, back in Athens.

320

Old party disagreements began to reappear. Vangelis wondered: could it really be, he might soon see Chryssa again? He had been shut away so long that he could hardly bear now to think of the life they'd had; but she visited him in dreams. It hurt sharper than the knifing wind, to start again expecting and yearning. In spite of that a hunger to see and hold and have her swung and swept up through him.

Behind other fortress walls, also, the change was felt.

'It's the end. He's sold the Revolution!' the General said, swilling and spilling brandy as they left the regiment's dining table and walked to take cigars.

'Shut up, Vouro, you fool!' a major beside him said bluntly. 'Where the hell do you think you are? You're not in your own barracks, you know.'

A trace tottering, his eyes not fully focused, General Vouros drew himself up rigid, and breathed in loudly so his barrel chest expanded further. Slowly he said to the Major and another friend, 'Gentlemen, when a comrade of ours becomes – a dictator –' He spoke almost clearly, he was extremely drunk.

The Major caught his arm, and said to him urgently in a slurred voice, 'Be quiet, Vouro, for God's sake. It's the brandy talking, isn't it? You shouldn't let the brandy talk here, man. The walls have ears in this place.'

Vouros eyed them both. Eventually, in a choking voice, with a timbre like a boot turning on glass, he said, 'Gentlemen, your pardon. It is a great day for the Revolution. Gentlemen, I give you – the civilian prime minister!' Unsteadily he raised his glass in the air; all three slightly rocked, they had all drunk heavily, bitter and depressed at the new announcement.

'So my friends,' Vouros said more quietly, 'and what about foreign policy now?'

But even this topic, or especially this topic, they would not permit him. 'Shut up, Vouro,' they snapped, sharper than before. 'Here's the Brigadier!'

All three were now silent and unsteadily still, as the Brigadier who commanded Military Intelligence came over to join them: an austere figure, a lean head, sharp-nosed, shrewd as a hawk. If he had drunk as they had, he gave no clue.

'So, gentlemen,' he said, in a dead level voice, 'we have a *new* national government. I say, good success to them.' But he said it like a knife scouring ice. His eye fell on Vouros, whose body, though he did not speak, seemed slowly to be growing larger, and his face slowly reddening like a winter sun. 'You share my sentiment, General?'

'Yes indeed, Mr Brigadier!' Vouros barked savagely, like an old sergeant-major taking orders from a junior officer; and he frankly glared, he would go only so far in his efforts to contain himself.

The Brigadier laughed through his nose, and it was hard to tell whether he was pleased or displeased with the slow-mounting apoplexy of Vouros. To the other two he remarked, 'You may have heard that the President has made me an offer.'

'We weren't clear. . . .'

'Yes, gentlemen. He has invited me to join him in Athens, as his military adviser.'

'Excellent! Congratulations!' they said. 'It's an honour you deserve.'

'That's as may be, Major. At all events, it's an honour I declined. I told the Mister President that I believed I served the nation best by staying with the troops I know, and by staying with Military Intelligence.' His bright eye sparked at each of them – a hard glance.

A younger officer had joined them, and stood at a slight distance, evidently admiring the Brigadier.

The Brigadier turned to him, 'Ah, Kosta. Gentlemen, I don't know whether you know Lieutenant Colonel Kostas Hadzikiriakou, a colleague of ours from the Pentagon.'

Kostas shook their hands, then the officers resumed talking, while Kostas listened to them with the dry face of the wise observer. He was excited to be here: he had done better, after all, than cousin Leonidas, who was nowhere now.

He listened to them speak; but his eyes kept returning to the Brigadier. He studied that bald but fine long-nosed head, with its dry eyes, its taut-lipped mouth. It was the head of a Caesar. Before leaving he said, 'We hope, Mr Brigadier, it will not be long before you visit us in Athens.'

For reply the Brigadier gave only the slightest nod, as briefly he shook hands, like a man under tight constraint – pent-up, frustrated perhaps, but patient too, and determined.

While the army worried that the National Government was betrayed, the students in Athens had the opposite fear. In the cafés where they met, Alexis heard one cry only.

'This is not democracy,' a student urged. 'This is not civilian government, it's a front for the army. This is the deal they've done. This is the government NATO wants, to keep Greece safe. The Junta moves out of sight, but it stays in power.' He looked round at all of them; he had pale blue eyes which in his dark face glared emphasis of what he said.

'Yes, Vasili, right. But what do we do against a government?'

A girl student answered ahead of Vasili, 'We protest, of course; we demonstrate. And we have to do it now. If it gets established, if people accept it, if they get used to it, here and abroad – then there we are, tied up for ever. There will never be elections, there will never be change. The Junta will run everything, behind the scenes.'

'Bravo, Rena! You're right,' the students said.

Alexis heard the same thing, wherever he went: the new government was a mechanism to prolong the dictatorship. The students spoke and argued about the form of protest. An earlier demonstration had been crushed by the police. The students retreated from barricade to barricade, in the end they retreated to the roof of the Law School. From across the street, Alexis had looked up at the tiny, waving, shouting figures, standing in a line along the classical parapet. Then the police, in their green uniforms, appeared on the roof. For a time the parapet was ragged with people, but gradually it cleared and emptied, and the students were bundled downstairs, and driven away in vans to interrogation.

'It mustn't be like the Law School,' they all said now. 'It must be a proper demonstration, it must be so big they can't cart us off. We must march through Athens. Everyone must see us – foreigners, newspapers, everyone.'

They began to discuss how to get loudspeakers. For several days they were busy, making contact with other students who also planned demonstrations. Alexis was in and out of school, and seldom at home, hovering on the rim of the students' activities.

Then everything was ready: the following day there would

be a demonstration, it would be so large it would overflow the campus and progress through Athens. It would be peaceful but overwhelming: it would defy the new government, and the dictators, and NATO in the background. Alexis was transfigured, there was one passion in all of them: it flickered and darted throughout Athens, tomorrow it would blaze so the world would see.

In the café their talk was dominated by Rena. Now the plans were ready, the other girl students sat like wives behind their boyfriends, chinning their shoulders, nodding, approving, making a chorus: but Rena still argued, in a clear, energetic, musical voice. Alexis and his friend Petros sat at the back, admiring her: she was a cousin of Petra's, it was through her that the two schoolboys had come to know this group of students. She had a mobile, handsome face, with a mass of dense, very dark frizzy hair tied together at the back of her head, but bursting out behind the ribbon like the tail of a black comet. When Vasilis, the blue-eyed student, started saying what he wanted to do with the dictators, how there was a particular bare rock in the Aegean where they should be staked out, she broke in, 'What garbage is this, Vasili? You're as bad as them!'

He turned on her, rising, his blue eyes glaring white, 'How dare you say that, Rena? How can you say that to me?' He had already been arrested, and questioned by the police.

'What do you mean, how dare I? Why are you so sacred? I said, staking them out on an island is the sort of thing they do. You're just like them. If that's your idea of the social solution, well bravo for the young Greek politician!'

Eventually Vasilis said, 'You think these people deserve humane treatment, Rena? After what they've done, they *aren't* human beings any more.'

'Not human beings? Oh great, Vasili, a great analysis!'

'All right, Lady Marx, let's have the ideology then. What do you say they are?'

'Well, we know what they are. They're a part of Greek society. They're not the old families, and they're not the proletariat. They're the sons of shopkeepers, and the sons of peasants. They've got middle-class ideology, and peasant ideology, mixed. That's how they're blind. But still, their "revolution" is a *sort* of revolution. So you tell me what good it is, staking them out on an island. They need to be educated, they need to be taught.'

'Educate them? Are you joking?' Vasilis exclaimed, and in the background Alexis muttered, 'Educate my father! Phew!' He whistled with amazement at the thought of his father being retrained. The students stared at this amazed schoolboy; and the conversation turned from educating the Junta.

They stayed hours at the café, elaborating plans. Afterwards Alexis and Petros went back with Rena to the students' lodgings. Vasilis had a large room, the walls lined with makeshift bookshelves and huge posters: blown up photos, heads of Marx, Lenin, naked girls loving.

The lighting was low; they ate souvlaki and cheese pies they had bought on the way there, and reviewed again the plans for the demonstration. Later they started to dance. Alexis and Petros watched with yearning, elated eyes as Rena and Vasilis danced to each other. Rena moved proudly, rippling and shimmering through the room at great speed, clapping her hands with decision, whirling on the spot. Vasilis danced in the manner of a proud islander, head back, blue eyes glaring; with a touch in it all of exaggeration, deliberate swagger. Then the music gave way to samba, he grabbed Rena, and with head held proudly, swinging her suddenly at extreme angles, marching from room's end to room's end, they danced an exhilarated caricature samba.

It was late when Alexis got home. He heard his father snoring; his mother stirred uneasily, her voice called him and he spoke softly, identifying himself, soothing her to sleep. He lay down, but for a long time he could not sleep, his mind whirled through imaginings of the demonstration.

He woke early, and before his parents had got clear of their slumbers he had left the house and was hurrying through the empty fresh early morning streets. He called for Petros, and together they stopped at the hostel where the students were still falling out of bed and shaking themselves together. They had coffee there, and headed in a group towards the University, walking briskly together in something between a march and a run. Whenever anyone started to hum or sing, the others took up the tune, they wanted their voices all to make one voice: the song swelled till excitement broke it, their cries cut through it.

325

'There they are!'

They turned a corner, and saw in the distance the University buildings, classical pediments and long rows of yellow columns. They were oddly quiet, they had expected banners flying, people on the roof. Ahead of them in the road was a dark crowd of students, milling confusedly.

'What's happening? Are they inside or outside?' they shouted. But as they came up behind the others, they understood. For all the length of the long yellow frontage stood a close row of policemen, one long green fence barring their way. On their own side of the road, more large platoons of police moved down the pavement, telling them firmly the University was closed, assembly was forbidden, they were blocking the road, they must move on. The students shouted to them, but the police did not argue: they moved steadily forward, repeating their instructions. The crowd pressed this way and that, at cross-purposes. The demonstration was stopped.

They withdrew from the University. There were continuous scattered shouts, bitter, disconnected. Vasilis kicked the road as he walked, muttering, 'Bastards! Bastards! Bastards!'

More police lined the road, watching their retreat. They moved into backstreets, unwillingly walking down alleys tight and crooked as their frustration: till the narrow road opened into a square. They stopped dead.

'God! Look at that!'

Round the edge of the square was a line of trees, which had grown big and crowded the buildings; and it took them a few moments to make out that the dense shadow under the trees was a huge troop of police, standing still, waiting, green themselves in the dapple of the foliage. Among them were police buses, also two armoured cars. The heavy boughs overhead rustled, and the police, standing close packed, shifted and murmured in low voices: they stirred slowly, like a large animal, waiting.

The students stopped, their blood froze: *so* many police, they had hardly known there were so many policemen in Greece.

★

There followed bitter, sterile days, in which the students met in frustrated groups, and made plans and gave them up. What could they do, against an army? The people of Athens didn't care. No one would help them.

Rena hurried into the café, her dark eyes staring. Alexis was disturbed, he had never seen her look worried before: with all her passion she'd seemed steady as a stone. She said, 'Vasilis has been arrested!'

Vasilis had spent the night at his mother's house, in a small village outside Athens, and had been arrested in the early hours. His mother was in a taxi outside, they must try to find out where he had been taken.

The students headed off in different directions, Alexis and Petros got into the taxi with Rena. A large-built elderly woman sat there sobbing, all in black, in the dress of a village widow. Rena hugged her and tried to calm her, but she wouldn't be soothed: she only lamented, she was poor, she had no family, no connections, she didn't know where to go.

They went to a police station in the centre of Athens: Rena insisted, her handsome face shone, the policeman at the desk tried to answer her. She persisted and pressed, and eventually began to make headway. But Vasilis' mother despaired: she began looking round desperately, she was evidently thinking, 'Students! They'll never find where my son is!' and she was casting for other allies. Suddenly she shrieked, 'Murder! Murderers! They have murdered my son!' She shouted this at all the people in the police station at the top of her voice; she grabbed hold of an elderly man and shouted at him, 'Help me! Help me! They have murdered my son!' He stared at her blankly, solemnly, he couldn't make sense of her, he evidently had his own grave worry. Presently she abandoned him, she started collapsing against other people shouting, 'Help me! Murder! Save my son from the murderers!' Rena, Alexis and Petros all tried to calm her, the police were probably not murdering her son. She didn't know, they didn't tell her, the things that probably the police would be doing to him. She seemed to decide then that they also had deserted her, and she walked out of the police station, and collapsed on the pavement moaning and lamenting. When they said they should go back into the building, she refused, but stood in the street, shouting at the building and denouncing it while the crowd gathered round her.

They took her home and cared for her; and in the end she did relax, and no longer believed that her son was being murdered. But by then the day had gone, it was too late to discover more about Vasilis.

The following day they went to the School of Architecture and Engineering, which was still open, and where students from various parts of Athens were meeting. There they compared reports, and learned how many had been arrested.

'What do we do?' students were asking. 'We can't go out, the police are waiting. We can't go to the hostels, the police are there. We can't go home, the police will come and get us. Where *do* we go?'

'We march, we demonstrate,' others shouted. 'All in one group, one enormous group, we march through Athens.'

'How can we? The police are there. They'll film us. They'll stop the march. They've got armoured cars. And there just is – so many of them. They're armed. What can we do?'

They went round in circles, there was no course of action, there was nowhere to go. Only as he listened to them talking, in the densely crowded room where students squatted cross-legged and knees-hugged on every inch of floor, and leaned on every inch of wall, and blocked every doorway, in a stale smoky atmosphere that had got so thick that the further students were brown silhouettes in the gloom, did Alexis realize that he would not be going home tonight: he was in a different world, his family was as far away as America. He swallowed, and shuddered, and felt a sudden kindling thrill, as he realized, none of them would go home tonight.

The day wore on in frustrated talk. Alexis went to the door to get some fresh air, and saw that more people had come. All the ground outside was covered with people squatting or lying down, and others advancing through them, picking their way between tangled legs. It seemed that all the students in Athens had heard of the gathering at the Architecture School, and had come. Alexis felt he could walk all day, and still not come to an end of the crowd sitting there, talking and waiting.

In the large hall, the frustrated talk about marches which the police would stop gave way to a different proposal, 'We simply stay here. This is our demonstration. We occupy. the building.'

'We *are* occupying it,' others said, 'and so what? Who

328

knows? Who cares? The police can put a ring round us and keep us here till we starve.'

'We can make more noise, we can make it known.'

More voices endorsed the idea, and those who had spoken for marches fell silent. It became clear that simply by gathering there to discuss demonstrations, they had occupied the Architecture School: and they could not march and they could not leave, occupation was the only choice. They started planning, they must get out flags and banners, they must get loudspeakers.

Evening came on: some students already had sleeping bags and provisions, others left to supply themselves, others again left to stay with friends in safe places they knew of. In the morning they returned to the Architecture school and remained there. It was clear that it had ceased to be a school, it was given over to them, they were in occupation.

They put out banners, the occupation was announced. Students could still come and go as they wanted, and the police did not try to enter the building or to seal them off. It seemed accepted for the present that the Architecture School was the students' territory, and the Government would let them stay there. Students arrived from further towns, and older people came with messages of support. But some of these visitors stayed, and seemed very keen listeners to what was said, and sharp-eyed watchers of the people who were there. The students became more cautious.

'We must shut the gates. Leaving them open means anyone can walk in, take down what we say, and walk out again and report to the police.'

On the third day they shut the gates, and only let people in after questioning. The occupation had become organized: there were stockpiles of provisions, sleeping arrangements were worked out. Loudhailers and radio equipment were brought in, the Architecture School began broadcasting on its own radio band so that anyone in Athens could tune in and listen. The speeches of the earlier days, which had complained about student rights, about the police coming onto the campuses, seemed far away: the broadcasts became a general attack on the Junta.

Alexis woke in the night full of vague trouble and fear. In

329

the first days he had been full of zest for the fight: even though they stayed still, they were going to battle. At night, crammed together uncomfortably on the hard floor, he slept soundly. But now he lay awake in the dark, hearing all round him the breathing of several thousand sleepers, and hearing too that others were disturbed, turning uneasily. He had telephoned his mother on the first day, that was the last word he had with any of his family. He realized, he was frightened: he must not let the students see this in the morning. They were older, they were strong, they were the example: he must be like them.

He turned back and forth, now cold, now too hot, unable to find sleep. Dawn began, a grey light grew: he crawled out of the large coat he used as a blanket, and with creaking limbs, feeling like an old man, he made his way to the door.

Rena sat outside smoking, she offered him a cigarette. Unused to tobacco, he lit the cigarette, and worked at inhaling it.

'What wouldn't I give for a cup of coffee,' he said.

'Coffee we've got. It's other things we need. And people. I keep thinking about Vasili.'

Alexis nodded seriously; but still he was glad to be sitting on the parapet beside Rena, with her handsome, her beautiful Greek-statue face, her dark-coloured eyes, the sunburst behind her head of frizzy jet hair. Even as he shivered, he lounged out casual on the cold stone, and tried to smoke with nonchalance: he thought, Let them see, here's a man smoking with a beautiful woman, evidently he knows her well. He envied Petros having such a cousin, Petros could see her any time he chose. It was good that Petros was still inside, somewhere among the sleeping bags.

It was the first time he had been alone with Rena; and he realized he had no idea what else he could say. His heart by now was thumping with nervousness; but his voice sounded to himself surprisingly mature when he presently asked her, 'What will you do after university, Rena?'

She turned to him, and he thought: What eyes! They were deep-set and black-lashed, serious eyes that were somehow able to look sad and cheerful at the same time. 'That's what I don't know,' she said. 'I keep making plans, I'm good at that. But the plans are all different. I don't see what I'll do.'

Alexis nodded understandingly – realizing slowly that he was nodding as he'd seen his father nod, listening – till she threw the question back,

'What about you, Alexi? What do you want to do?'

Then he faced the gulf, the chasm of ignorance: he wasn't even at college, he had no idea what he would do afterwards. He cast round quickly, but he was so busy thinking he mustn't be like his father that he couldn't imagine anything else. He looked round the three dim temple fronts that made a façade for the School; then his uncle Vangelis came into his mind, taciturn, frowning, with some crinkle of smile about his big jaw.

'Oh me? I'm going to be a lawyer,' he remarked.

'A lawyer?' Rena said amazed. 'What sort of cases will you take?'

'I shall specialize in labour law. I shall represent trade unions against the bosses.'

'Not under the Junta you won't.' But still, evidently, she was impressed: her black brows remained in a slightly raised position as she smoked her cigarette thoughtfully; mentally Alexis gave thanks to his uncle.

The light grew slowly. Round the courtyard the grey buildings grew clearer, till their pillars stood distinct like taller tree trunks over the tops of the small trees.

'Alexi,' Rena suddenly said, 'they've come!'

Between the trees they could see clearly now the line of high railings along the front of the Architecture School, and between these railings, half merged with them, they could make out figures standing on the pavement opposite: men who did not move at all. They seemed all grey at first, but as the light increased there was a glimmer of white belts, and the grey uniforms became green.

All along the colonnade other students stiffly unwound from their sleeping bags, rubbing their eyes, waking to this line of motionless figures opposite, who evidently were studying them.

In the distance they heard the squealing tyres of early morning traffic in Omonia Square. But along the roads round the Architecture School, no car drove, nothing moved. Evidently they had been sealed off. Days before they had been shut off from their meeting-place by a ring of police all round the University: now they had met, in another department of the University, and the ring of police was outside them.

As the morning advanced, more police came in jeeps and vans; high-ranking officers looped with white braid, and Intelligence officials in leather coats and leather hats, looking like detectives from an American film, conferred importantly. For all the efforts of the police, a crowd grew round the building: constantly they hurried it on, but it only grew, a gradual flow of people looking in through the railings. Parents and relatives arrived; there was violent arguing with the police, even rich fathers in light-coloured suits who began by tapping cigarettes on cigarette cases, and offering them round to the police officials, and nodding with puckered faces understanding the police worries, even they ended calling, protesting, taking officials aside and then abandoning them angrily, and returning to their wives with faces of fury, and so trying, as the poorer parents already did, to get closer to the railings, shouting out in high voices their children's names.

All the time more people pressed to the railings and the police moved them back. The correspondents of foreign newspapers arrived, they spoke into small microphones snugged into hands cupped to their mouths; discreetly they raised small cameras, quickly snapped, and moved on. The building was festooned with banners, 'Death to the Dictators', 'Down with the Junta'; loudspeakers mounted on the roof blared the same call. Shaggy-bearded students stared from the roof like sea captains searching for another sail.

The arrival of the police made the occupation definite, and made it news. Throughout Athens the story echoed: the students are holding the Architecture School. Good for the students! said some. Uh, the students! said others, what can they do, they'll get hungry, they'll come out! But on that day there was no change, and on the next day it looked clearer that the students were there to stay. The occupation of the Architecture School was appearing not only in all Greek papers, but in the foreign press as well; it was international news. The supporters of the Government, declaiming in cafés, were moved with indignation: the Government had gone out of its way to court the students, it had made concessions to them, it had raised student grants: now the students had betrayed them. They deserved all they would get.

'Don't say that, my son is there,' said Leonidas, arguing with his friend Manolis. 'Patra is in hysterics all the time. And I am very worried, I don't tell her how worried I am. They're playing with fire. This government does not joke.'

Throughout the country the occupation was the talking point. In cafés, in workshops, in streets, on terraces, on wharfs, rumour and conviction and passion and bias and fear and prophecy joined: voices shouted over raging machinery, and zipped down labyrinthine coils of wire. Prejudices, at odds, rebounded like cannon balls colliding in flight, passion pounded the table and the air, affront turned up the yellows of its eyes, and fear and sympathy blanched and waited. Through the gregarious, garrulous city alarm and hope together rose like the morning glare. Was it possible the students might succeed? They defied the National Government. As they stayed in occupation, the dismissive voices quieted and support for them grew. Everyone knew that the world knew: with every flight more reporters and camera crews flew into Athens, they roamed the streets. In newspapers in Japan and America and China and Russia, on newsreel films all over the world, there were pictures of the steep pillared façade of the Architecture School, and the banners hanging round it, and the students on top of it determined and exposed.

These papers and reports and above all these pictures came back to Athens and were pored over by Government eyes, which could hardly read the stories told in foreign headlines, but which filled in with alarm the words they didn't know – eyes which could read, at all events, as foreign eyes couldn't, the huge banners and placards reproduced in the photos: 'Down with the Junta', 'Death to the Dictatorship'. All the world was being told this. Messages passed from barracks to barracks: what was happening in Athens? The President, the new prime minister, they must stop this betrayal quickly, they must stop it now.

'Why aren't we there?' a major shouted, in the barracks where Kostas was seconded. 'We've the arms here, we could deal with them. Ring your friends, Kosta, find out what's going on.'

Others pressed round: Kostas, from the Pentagon, was

333

the man who should know. Importantly Kostas called the Pentagon.

'Couli? Kostas. Hello. Look, what the hell are you lot doing down there? Why is nothing happening?'

The voice crackled back from the Pentagon, 'Ach, Kosta, do you think we know? People are going mad down here, they want to bomb the place. No one knows what's going on. The new prime minister called us up, he wanted to know what was happening. Frankly, Kosta, if you want to learn anything, you'd better ring the President direct – or get the Brigadier to ring him. And that's assuming the President knows what he's going to do.'

Kostas found there was silence round him as he switched off the radio; turning, he saw that the Brigadier had arrived and stood right behind him, he also had stood listening. He was motionless, his face pale, in an extreme tension as if his skin would crack. In a dry voice that slid from him like iron scraps down a rusty chute, he said, 'All right, gentlemen. I have spoken to the President, but I see I must speak to him again. Get him,' he ordered the communications officer, who urgently snatched the microphone, pressed buttons, shouted down it.

'If you please, gentlemen,' the Brigadier said, and the officers withdrew. But from a distance they heard the Brigadier speaking curtly into the microphone. The President was his old friend of decades, but his tone was brusque, 'You need me down there.'

The President spoke at length, it seemed he was arguing that he did not need the Brigadier and his troops, it seemed he preferred for them to stay away. But presently, with sudden familiarity, the Brigadier snapped into the radio, 'Uh! Never mind! You need me there. I'm coming. I'm on my way.' Briskly then he put the microphone down and turned it off, and turning to his retinue said sharply, 'I've spoken to the President. We're travelling to Athens. Prepare.'

The officers moved, the Brigadier's order branched and spread. Throughout the camp were busy voices, quick men, excitement of preparation and movement: during all the years of the National Government, they had not been able to act; now their time had come. The courtyards thronged with men, packs were slung into trucks, the armoured cars drew up in a column, and from long shelters tank after tank emerged reverberating. The Brigadier climbed into an armoured car; at his signal all the engines revved heavily, the first armoured car started to move, and the next and the next, like the slack being taken up in an endless rope: and now in a rising turmoil of dust and smoke and noise the entire armoured brigade attached to Military Intelligence emerged on the road, and drove steadily towards Athens.

The announcement of the new government gave Chryssa no illusions. She knew it was a cosmetic change only: so the dictatorship had a new face, more comely to Western eyes – it showed only the dictator's confidence. Behind his elderly civilian façade he was likely to last for many years. Since Vangelis had refused their pardon, he would stay in prison for the rest of his sentence: she had not again been allowed to see him, though steadily she applied and reapplied. Michael had not returned to Greece: and how could she see Michael now? At intervals, from other suburbs, Chryssa would ring him; or, by arrangement, he would ring her at particular telephone offices. In these wary conversations which were probably monitored she gave him, quickly, her latest informations, while their tones of voice called to each other, like spectral lovers, voices on the wind, their bodies all gone into voice. A rustling voice with a low music; and a hoarse husk of tender concern; caresses of sound. As for the students, and their conflict with the police, she watched them from far off, as through a dirty pane of glass, with a sense of their bravery, and of the hopelessness of their attempt: if they pushed their effort beyond a certain point, the police or the army would descend on them in force.

But their protest continued, more and more their news reached her, like the words of someone speaking to her urgently to whom she hadn't been listening enough. She found the wavelength of their broadcasts, and left the radio tuned permanently to their station. Gradually, like a person surfacing from depths, she rose towards that thin voice, that called from a transmitter only streets away. She waited tensely for the next bulletin and the next. She realized all Athens and all Greece was watching the Architecture School, and the wishes and fears of everyone attended there, in climbing apprehension.

As the broadcasts continued, and the students did not give in, her own hope rose: there was reason for hope. The nation was stirring. She heard of other demonstrations, there had been a protest outside a ministry, the police had attacked with violence but the protest still went on. It was said the Greek farmers had risen in protest, they were driving into Athens on tractors. She couldn't make sense of that; what common cause had the farmers with the students? But she imagined with pleasure the tractors converging on Constitution Square.

As she sat beside the radio, trying to tune the signal stronger, she said to herself: I'm listening to this radio, as I listened to Vangelis on the prison phone. Then she had the strange thought: Vangelis is at the Architecture School; he is in prison, but he is there as well. A spirit couldn't be kept shut in prison: she had been wrong, so wrong, to despair, to let hope fail, to think resistance would end with imprisonment.

In the early evening, suddenly, a new voice spoke on the Architecture School's channel, 'We are being attacked! Please help us. Please help us in any way you can. We need doctors. Please bring any medicine you can, and food, and lamps. We are being attacked, please help us.'

As she sat alert, Chryssa started to tremble: what had she been doing, being isolated, torpid, shut away? She hurried to the bathroom cabinet, grabbed bandages, iodine, every medicine she could find. She stuffed them in a bag, put on a coat, hurried out.

Outdoors it was already dim. She ran down roads, till she came to a wide twilight avenue, which was filled with people moving towards the centre of Athens. She fell in with them. In the thickening dusk she could not see how many were there, but they were a great number of people, people of all ages, even schoolchildren. Many were carrying things: the man nearest her had a hurricane lamp, others were carrying bags of food. She kept thinking as she walked: I am going to join Vangelis, he is there.

There was a girl next to her who was perhaps twenty. Chryssa registered that the girl was her own build and height and colouring: it was curious, it was as if she were walking beside herself when younger.

'Are you a student?' she asked.

'I'm at the Medical School,' the girl said.

336

'Are the others here from the Medical School?'

'*Who* are they? I don't know. We started with a march from the Medical School, but we've picked up other marches on the way.'

It was dark now, they were close to the Architecture School, ahead was a dense, much larger crowd in which they merged: people called, shouted, somewhere a loudhailer crackled but she couldn't make out the words. They moved slowly, compressed between a high block of offices on one side, and on the other high pillars and railings. Then she realized, these were the gates of the Architecture School, they had arrived.

The girl beside Chryssa crouched to the ground, the people behind were stumbling over her. Chryssa stooped beside her, trying to block them.

'What's the matter?' she said, finding she had to use her strength to turn the girl on her back.

Several young men hurried over, moved Chryssa back, picked up the girl, and started carrying her away.

'What are you doing? What's the matter with her?' Chryssa called.

'The matter?' one of them shouted. 'Can't you see she's dead.'

Chryssa couldn't believe it: the girl's eyes had been open, it was a seeing face, moments before she had been alive, striding vigorously beside her.

The men carried her to the gates and shouted there: urgent faces showed on the other side of the gates, which quickly opened and shut again.

How could she have died? Chryssa had seen no police, she had heard no shots. But now there was confusion, groups of people moved in contrary directions, there was frantic shouting, Chryssa was knocked over. As she picked herself up she saw that a large space had cleared, and that in this empty area of road a number of people were lying. One of them was groaning, he was not dead. She could not understand it, still she heard no shots. Then a group of students passed her, shouting and pointing upwards: there were police marksmen on the rooftops. Chryssa looked up, but all she could see were the black windows of offices disappearing in the darkness.

She hurried to the large gates, 'Let me in.'

'Let you in? Who are you?'

'Let me in, I work here, I work in the university.'

'What faculty are you in?'

Surprised by the questions, she was momentarily at a standstill: in her mind's eye she had a glimpse of the library, the classrooms of the department she had belonged to. But then she saw the girl who had walked beside her, her own size, figure, colouring, the girl who had died more suddenly than a person can die.

'I'm from the Medical School, I came here in the march from the Medical School.' She brandished the medicines she had brought.

'Oh, let her in, for God's sake,' a student said; they swung the gate open a little way so she could come in, then closed it.

'Where's Casualty?' she asked, looking round blindly. She was dazed, she had no bearings, she was confusedly aware of high buildings with columns leaning over her on all sides.

'I'll take you,' a student said. She followed him over the grass unsteadily: she felt lightheaded, slightly dislocated, it was still, only now, coming home to her that people here were actually being shot dead.

She was brought into a large room with a blackboard at the end. It was filled with desks, and on the desks people were lying. She was led to an elderly man in shirt sleeves on the far side of the room: he was bearded, bespectacled, with a long mane of white hair all flying and awry. He stooped over a wound, busy but sure, he was evidently a distinguished doctor or surgeon. The student called him 'Professor', she gathered he was one of the Professors of Medicine.

'What can I do?' she began.

He looked up from his work, harassed and tired: he took some moments to focus on her. Then he reached out an arm, 'Take that side of the room, from there to the back. Do what you can.'

'Yes . . .' she said, unsure; but he had turned from her.

She hurried to the place he had pointed to, and stopped where a young student, perhaps only seventeen, was lying. And she made the same mistake as before: she glanced at his serious eyes and asked, 'Where are you hurt? Can you talk?' He didn't answer; she wondered what had happened to him, till other students, passing with a stretcher, called to her, 'He's dead, don't waste time on him.' She looked at the young face that looked back at her, not believing it was dead.

338

She moved down the line. Some students could describe their wounds, and help her with the bandages, even as they coiled with pain; others were in shock, and they just stared as the dead people stared. There was a horrible wound she could not begin to tend, where the bullet had shattered cheekbone and jaw. A student wounded in the back kept repeating the same name continuously. There was a middle-aged woman who whimpered all the time like a damaged and hurt animal. Between the cries and moans, a voice would shout in bursts, 'My God my God my God,' fall silent, and then shout again 'My God my God my God my God.' She had some medical knowledge, she had sometimes tended the wounds of Vangelis' clients, but there was little she could do here, it was mainly work for a surgeon. She comforted, applied dressings, bandages, shouted to the Professor about the most urgent cases; other medical students worked elsewhere in the room. And still they brought in more wounded and dead, till all the desks were covered and they were laying people on the floor. One of the students passing shouted to her shrilly, 'Do you know what's happened? Something terrible's happened. We've just heard there are tanks coming. They're coming in tanks.'

He gazed at her as he walked past, shocked at his own news: for the first time Chryssa realized fully that she herself might be killed here.

Then, no more wounded were brought. Someone shouted from the door, 'The army's here.' Presently they learned that the police had withdrawn, and the Architecture School was now surrounded by soldiers: there were three tanks parked in the road in front, and tanks stationed also at the other gates of the School. For the present the soldiers were taking no action: either the killing had stopped, or it was no longer possible to bring stretchers into the building.

The Professor, the medical students, Chryssa and other helpers continued to work with the wounded. Students who came into the room to see friends were bewildered, puzzled: they did not understand why the soldiers, the Government, were doing nothing at all. A student delegation had been formed, to negotiate, but the soldiers had not let it leave the School. One of the wounded had a small radio, which he tuned to the national service, waiting to hear what the news bulletin said now. And presently they heard, over the crackle, a clipped official voice announce: 'The Government has identified the ringleaders of the disturbances at the Architecture School, and by morning the matter will be resolved.'

That was all they said: it sounded a small issue, it would soon be over. Alarm spread in the white faces listening.

They paused in their work: they had for the present done all they could. Chryssa went outside for air, she was faint from her nonstop attending to wounds, her mind had nothing in it but different pictures of the holes that bullets make. She hardly remembered just what she had done; she had worked in a strange, automatic way, as if she had a nurse within her who knew what to do, how to dress wounds, tie bandages. As she sat on the parapet smoking, she found herself imagining that the girl who had walked beside her in the march had got inside, and had been working in the Casualty, and also was sitting there, resting and smoking.

She moved to the end of the parapet, where she could see, through the railings, the three tanks parked in front of the School. They had their lights on, and she could see, in silhouette against the glare, numbers of students who had climbed up the railings, and hung onto them, waving and shouting to the soldiers. Beyond them, bright-lit by the lights, she got glimpses of the faces and uniforms of the soldiers: they weren't lined up rigid and impassive as she had expected, their mouths were open, they were shouting and making gestures at the students. She couldn't get clear what the mixed voices shouted.

As she watched, the students on the main gate suddenly stood out sharp, in dazzling silhouette: a white blinding light had come on behind them. She realized that the tank at the main gate had swivelled on its tracks: now its lights were aimed directly at the gate. Then the white glare trembled, the students hanging to the gate all started moving, jumping down, but many were still hanging to it when the gate itself came down as the tank hit it: then she couldn't believe what she saw, for the tank continued coming, it simply drove on over the gate, and over the people caught under the gate. Now the tank was inside the grounds, and soldiers poured in after it, and everywhere students were running from the gates, but as they ran they fell. The soldiers who had come through the gate swung their machine guns to and fro, firing continuously. Chryssa saw the flashes as the bullets left the guns, but only

340

confusedly heard the rattle of shots over the shrieking. Now the students who could still run had reached cover, but the ground, wherever it was lit by the tank lights, was covered with bodies.

Shattered, in shock, Chryssa hurried back into Casualty. The new wounded arrived, terrible, pouring blood. A student who staggered through the door collapsed, crouching and curling down, he seemed to melt into the pool of blood growing round him. The sight sawed her brain: she must not pass out, she must help, be of use. With skeins of bandages she hurried in attendance; but almost at once two soldiers strode into the room, holding their machine guns ready to fire.

'Out! Out of here!' one of them shouted. He motioned them to move with his gun.

The Professor walked up to him, shouting furiously, 'Do you see the wounded? Do you see the dead? Can they run?'

The soldiers stared at him surprised. The one who had spoken before said, 'You've got five minutes. All out in five minutes.'

The Professor took his glasses off and started to clean them; he turned to Chryssa and told her, 'I've been in three wars.' One of the medical students interrupted him, 'Professor, Professor, they'll be back any minute.'

The Professor blinked, owlish without his glasses.

'We must decide what to do, Professor.'

He nodded, but didn't suggest; he shook his head, and murmured again to Chryssa, 'Three wars.'

Before they had decided on any course of action, the soldier returned, with a small squad of soldiers. He shouted 'Out! Out!' at them, as though he were beside himself with fury. This time, those who could move heaved themselves forward. The soldiers hustled and shoved them on, it seemed that the painful movements of the wounded irritated them extremely. A man who had been shot in the stomach held himself together with both hands, and limped forward doubled over.

They came outside: then, for the first time, the medical students saw the tanks, and suddenly one of them ran, he sprinted away across the grounds. A soldier began spraying machine-gun bullets after him, he dodged, a group of soldiers stood right in front of him, and he, weaving and turning, dodged again so that he ran straight into them. They closed round him as he went down, Chryssa saw them raising their guns and striking; they were using their machine-guns as clubs.

Dazed, stumbling, dazzled by the tank lights, they were marched to the main gate where, from all over the School, gangs of students were converging, limping, bleeding, being struck at random by the soldiers who shepherded them.

In the crush at the gate, Chryssa found she was stumbling and slipping. The ground was churned like swamp, when she looked down, her fear was true, they were walking on people.

There was a line of military buses outside, and they were kicked and punched into these. Looking round, Chryssa saw she had lost contact with the Professor and the medical students. Holding her arm behind her and twisting it hard, a soldier forced her down to the end of the bus, where he banged something hard into the side of her head. She felt a slit of pain as though her skull cracked. Everyone in the bus was staring at her: she realized that the object stuck to her head was a gun, a pistol. The soldier was shouting, 'If anyone moves, I shoot the nurse.'

A teenager squatting in front of Chryssa shouted, 'Let me take the nurse's place.'

Down went the soldier's hand, and the gun in his hand, so it tore open the student's cheek; he squatted upright again, trying to hold the deep wound shut. The soldier banged the gun back into Chryssa's head. 'If anyone moves I shoot the nurse.' The wounded and the students only gazed; the bus started.

By wild exertion of all the political muscle he had left, Leonidas at last got through the cordons and, in a chill of premonition, approached the broken front of the Architecture School. It was an aftermath of war: lights had been mounted, empty tanks stood in the road, one tank stood inside the grounds. A pair of soldiers came out of the shattered gates carrying a body and wearily heaved it into a large military ambulance, which he saw was already full. The only sounds were the quiet words to each other of the soldiers, as they returned for more. In the white glare of the lights it was an eerie silent scene of loading. As he entered the gates his heart stopped, just to see, all apart from the fact that his son might be here, how many bodies there were – bodies lying in awkward twists, trampled, some mangled together – he came to in the sharp night air, but started weeping as he started searching, there were just so many young dead. So many, he *knew* his son would be here. Searching, he covered the same ground over and over, his eye jumping all the time towards what it couldn't bear to see. He feared his tears would mark him as the parent, but the soldiers took no notice. The terrible rage in which they had done the killing was dead: now it had deserted them, they moved like old machines. They looked exhausted, on some of their faces was a shine of tears, which coursed steadily while they numbly carried on with their carting.

He didn't find Alexis. He knew he could be among the dead who had already been taken away, but he had stopped fearing that now. What he now feared above all was that his son was in the interrogation centre. He knew the means they used: he shut his eyes and shivered, he prayed, Let them not harm him.

From home he phoned person after person, he woke people in the night, he begged, implored, insisted, while Patra behind him, gnawed mad with anxiety and bitterness, muttered at him continuously, 'You and your Government, bastards, the bastards, the pompous cruel bastards.' At times she cried and at times in sheer bitter desperation she would coil her fingers in his hair and tug hard at it and torture him, even while he cunningly implored down the phone.

In the end, but it was next morning, his urgings worked: they drove to Bubulina Street. All his ambition had narrowed to one anxiety, his son, what had they done to his son. In the interrogation centre they were kept waiting: Patra was in a turmoil of hatred and pity for all she saw there; Leonidas shuffled while the officer on duty eyed him with contempt, the politician who was finished, the patriot whose son was a communist.

Eventually someone came round the corner, led by a policeman. Patra gave a gasping indrawn shriek: was this Alexis? He walked with difficulty as though his legs were different lengths, and his head was the wrong shape, it came out huge to one side. Perhaps he mumbled something to them, but they couldn't tell, he could hardly move his mouth.

343

Patra held him, shrieking at the same time to the policeman, 'What have you done to him?'

'Madam, madam, it looks worse than it is.'

'Are you mad? What have you done?'

'The students were fighting among themselves, madam, we couldn't help it, his jaw got fractured.'

'What fighting? You've broken his jaw!' Her voice shouted higher, piercing the building. 'You've broken his jaw!' She screamed at them louder, Leonidas started pulling her out of the building. She shook him off with loathing, then he led Alexis out, and she came with them.

In the street, his face streaming, he moaned, 'My son,' and wanted to embrace Alexis, but Alexis quickly knocked his arms away and stepped out of reach. His eyes withered, he couldn't look at his father.

They took Alexis to the hospital; later, in plaster and bandages, they brought him home. He had to be still. He couldn't speak and he didn't want to. He sat beside the radio.

The news came on: the problem at the Architecture School had been resolved. There were no casualties, no dead, though some students had been hurt in fighting between student factions. The Prime Minister congratulated the army on their part in solving the problem of the Architecture School.

Leonidas and Patra watched helpless as the broadcast tortured him and took him further from them. What of his face could move screwed up in pain; tears started in his eyes, but they looked tears of acid. Patra approached, but he was so completely oblivious of her that she drew back.

Afterwards he sat motionless, his eyes looked dead, as if they had been knocked out as other eyes were. He still could not bear to see his father: if he glimpsed him through a doorway, he turned away.

Alexis could not stop remembering the girl Rena who had been one of those clinging to the main gate of the Architecture School. It was a tall gate but the men students gave her helping hands, she climbed up over them, and by wedging her feet between the bars hung on to the top of it. From this point of vantage she joined in the shouting. 'You are our brothers,' they called to the soldiers, while the soldiers shouted back obscenities: her voice clanged high over the men's voices, a strong voice of passion not to be stopped.

With a slight giddiness she saw the tank in front revolve where it stood: the beam of its headlight lit the end of the street, then moved down the crowded railings, and grew to blinding dazzle. The light trembled, grew bigger, the shouting stopped, people were scrambling, jumping down, but she was high up and her feet firmly between the bars. A shock went through the gate, it started falling backwards, automatically she clung to it, the ground hit her from behind, her head felt split, other people were beside her, at the base of her sight something black and very wide climbed, the white searchlight jerked.

The students were everywhere, the crazies, all along the front of the Architecture School ran this low wall with railings and the students clung all over the railings and there were more behind, all their faces lit up, just open mouths shouting, 'You are our brothers, join us, join us,' but brother, no, he only thought fucking communists, he fingered his gun he wanted to pick them off, Fuck you fuck your mothers fuck the whores fuck you bastards he shouted, he thought what a rabble, hair all over, beards all over, old sloppy clothes, the communists, look they'd painted a hammer and sickle on the walls, they'd shot his grandfather, they wanted to take everything, there were thousands of them, again they shouted You are our brothers, brothers no you filthy fucking bastards, fucking students, they were sent here to study and what good did it do, it only made them communists, let's get in there and clear out the communist filth, why don't we get the orders, Oh fuck you bugger bastards fuck you filth we'll get you we'll show you, Fuck your sister, bugger.

The signal came, alert, the lead tank turned steadily, in perfect control, and oh you students, yes, jump down, now it's coming to you, the tank lights lit up the students on the gate, white, flat, like cut-out people, look at them gaping, girl up there still shouting, oh its coming to you now.

The tank hit the gate, it went down, and he saw the tank didn't stop, it carried on over the gate and students together, that was new to him, he hadn't realized that would happen, as he saw it his brain exploded, his body electrified, everything

345

changed, Bastards, Bastards, Bastards, he shrieked, he jumped in with the others following the tank, like a part of his body his gun came to the firing position, he started shooting, and oh he shot and shot and shot, he swung the gun round, it jerked in his arm kicking him, the shots rattled in his ears, the students were running all ways, animals in panic, down they went, he piled the bullets in, bastards, bastards, he shot and shot.

But they'd already gone, behind the buildings, fled where the light couldn't get them, but they'd be caught, they'd be found, where were they hiding? in cupboards, in the lavatories? oh they'd catch it, their time was coming now.

Afterwards it was different because the huge feeling that took him through the killing left him, it went away, and they simply had the bodies to clear, and the killing was done in a great blaze but clearing the bodies went on and on, and time after time but each time different he saw how part of the body was exploded by the bullet, and these things didn't make him sick but they took his mind in a funny way, everything shook, he'd never seen an actual battlefield. Another man was crying as he picked up bodies, there were bodies on bodies, he found this huge bearded communist, a monster like a shot whale, but he couldn't find the bullet hole anywhere, and there was another man shot in the guts who was all writhed and crouched and clutched together as if he were still alive and hurting, he felt exhausted as he collected them, he felt more tired than he had ever felt.

They returned to the barracks and he slept like lead; and the next day was just like normal, looking after the tanks, hanging around the paradeground. But it was very odd, being so normal, as if the business at the Architecture School hadn't happened, and first they didn't talk about it but later they all talked about it, some people were still in a daze but others were actually saying, It was terrible we had to do that, so they were communists – so what? They were only students, a fire hose would have been enough. And it was terrible, Greeks doing that to Greeks, the President should never have ordered that. One of the officers even said, 'Who's going to be next, then? How many Greeks must we kill for the President?' And he was an officer who had marshalled and dragooned them yesterday, and ordered them in.

'They were Greeks we killed,' other soldiers said.

In the Pentagon also, where Kostas had returned when the Brigadier brought his troops into Athens, officers and even generals were saying, 'Yesterday was terrible. It should never have happened. The President has gone too far.'

Kostas nodded vigorously, but still he was struck by the change overnight whereby the students who had been communists yesterday were Greeks today, and whereby the decisive action by the army, which so many in the Pentagon had pressed for, was treated today as all the President's doing. He found this odd because in all the gossip he had heard previously, the President had resisted using the tanks, while it was the Brigadier who had said, 'Mr President, we must act. It is an open wound, we are bleeding to death. The tanks are in position. We must send them in.' And at all events, it was the Brigadier who got the credit for it in the Pentagon: here was decision, here was leadership. And yet today, Kostas heard, it was precisely the Brigadier who was saying that the army should not have gone so far, and that the President's decision to send in the tanks was a cruel act of tyranny. The Brigadier would remark that the President had cut himself off from the people, and this was the bloody result.

'The Brigadier's right, you know,' colonels said in corridors, 'the President is not one of us any more.'

However these matters stood, one thing was clear: the intelligence services had not been as vigilant as they should have. If they had been, the disaster at the Architecture School would never have occurred: the President had been appallingly unwise in relaxing surveillance, easing discipline. The Brigadier would make up for that. In the days following his men arrested thousands associated in various ways with the universities; they arrested the farmers, and the other groups who had protested. It then became clear that a nationwide investigation was necessary, for other traitors had unmasked themselves in these days and must now be brought in; and many more citizens were under suspicion. So not only in the early hours but at all hours, the police or the military police arrived at

347

houses and flats all over the country, and roughly, angrily, indignantly, ordered hapless half-dressed men and women into vans and cars. Even in the barracks of the army they were busy, for there were many of unsure loyalty; and not only in the barracks but in the Pentagon itself the officers of Military Intelligence paraded. Two of them walked into Kostas' office, without knocking on the door, without any salute.

'Where's Missios?' they asked; they were curt, rude.

'Do you mean General Missios?'

They didn't reply, they just stared with assurance, waiting till Kostas obeyed orders and answered: as he had to. When he told them what they wanted, they walked off without a thank you, he heard their steps ring sharply down the corridor, and then, watching after them, he saw them walk straight up to General Missios' door, open it, and go in. He heard their clear voices, and then the thick voice of the General, indignant but confused and unhappy.

Later he heard them go; it seemed they hadn't arrested the General, they were merely pursuing enquiries. All that day they and other officers of Intelligence strode through the Pentagon, and from his window Kostas saw various colonels and majors being hurriedly escorted to jeeps, and driven off quickly in the direction of the Brigadier's camp.

'Ach, Couli, have you seen such a thing? Policemen running the army!' Kostas hurt with contempt: he admired the Brigadier personally, but he despised the military police, they were parasites.

'I'd be careful if I were you, Kosta,' Coulis said; and would not agree or disagree with any view Kostas expressed.

Afterwards, smoking in his office, Kostas reflected bitterly that there was this drawback to military government, that it gave special power to the military police. It meant that all of them, in the long run, were governed by Military Intelligence. The country was run not by soldiers but by spies, by spies and policemen. He was saddened. He had for years invested his ambitions in the officers devoted to the Great Idea, for sooner or later they would take over; and all the time, he saw, a different process had been working, and where those officers stood – the Major General, General Vouros and the others – he could not guess. And

348

did the Brigadier believe in the Great Idea? Some said he did. . . .

Later that day Kostas actually saw the Brigadier walking calmly through the Theatre of Assembly, clear, assured, giving orders; he moved with an importance, a bevvy of officers attended, and sped to do his errands. As he watched him, Kostas saw for sure where the power of the nation had shifted. For the crisis of the Architecture School had shown up the impotence of the President; and somehow in that whole process the new civilian government had ceased to be of any account, it had disappeared from sight. It was the Brigadier himself, head of Military Intelligence, who ran the country now.

'Hello, Kosta,' the Brigadier said briskly, in passing, with a slight nod that recognized Kostas' loyalty.

Kostas saluted: his misgivings expired: they all of them rested in this man's hand. Kostas watched after him, in admiration.

On the second day a warder came for Chryssa. She stiffly unwound herself from the narrow concrete bunk, and stepped into the corridor where she could hear, louder, voices, moans, somewhere an old voice shouting and a young voice arguing. She was led down staircases and corridors to a small, bare, dirty office, where, behind an old wooden desk with the varnish rubbed off all over, a fat man with a red vein-webbed face and protruding eyes received her.

'Ah, come in, nurse. Sit down, please.' He pointed to a chair and she sat, still shivering from the cold of her cell, though this office was warm.

'Nurse, I am Major Klathas. May I introduce my colleague, Captain Kalokyris.'

Chryssa looked round, and found behind her not the warder who had brought her there but another man, of middle height, nondescript, he didn't look like anything.

'So nurse,' the Major said, rubbing his hands, amiably popping his bulb eyes at her, 'Why, we haven't got a name for you! What's your name?'

Chryssa didn't answer.

'What? Oh, come on, nurse, surely now, you can tell us your name. What's in a name? No modesty now. Look, I'll tell you what, just give us a name – any name you like, make one up, just for our files. Come now, what shall I put down?'

She mustn't give her name. If once they found she was married to Vangelis, to a political prisoner, everything would be worse. They wouldn't believe she had come only at the end to the Architecture School, they would believe she had been there before, that she was an organiser, that she and Vangelis were involved in a plot. There would be further interrogations for her; and new interrogations for Vangelis, where he wouldn't even understand what was being asked. All this would follow, if they knew her name. To get clear of names she launched briskly into speech,

'Look, you're wasting your time on me. I'm not a communist, I'm not an agitator, I'm not even a nurse. I heard the students' broadcast, I heard them say they were attacked, they were being killed, they wanted doctors. What should I have done, go to the bouzouki? I took what medicines I could find and walked there. They let me in, I went to the casualty ward. What's wrong with that? Do you think I'm a political bigshot, a party leader? Ask the students who were at the gate – you've got film of them, I'm sure – ask them if they know me, if I'm anything to do with them. So I went there! Great crime! I went to put dressings on the wounds of the people you shot. What of it?'

'Nurse, have a cigarette.' The Major leaned forward, and lit the cigarette he gave her.

'Nurse, have we criticized you for putting on bandages? Have we said you shouldn't have done it? Of course, you're not completely right, you know. Actually it *is* a crime, to give aid of any kind to enemies of the state. You committed that crime. But do we bother about that? Uh! Forget it!' He blew out smoke, and watched it coil.

He sat forward. 'So there's no problem. Tell us your name, we'll check you out, and you can go. Do we want to keep you here? The place is full to bursting, and it's all work for us. When do you think I'll get home to see my family?'

'When will I?'

'Nurse, nurse, come on, do. Tell Captain Kalokyris your name, he'll go and check, and you can go today.' He held up his watch and tapped it. 'You can be out of here in an hour.'

Chryssa pondered, she was stuck. Fortunately, by chance not design, she had brought no identification with her when

350

she came to the Architecture School. She thought of various false names, but gave them up – they would only postpone the problem, the interrogators would soon come back again, knowing she had lied, asking why. Sooner or later they would identify her, she knew: her photo and name would be on their records, together with Vangelis', it was only because they had so many people to deal with that they had not yet traced her.

The smokes in front of her parted, the round red bulb-eyed face of the Major leered through them like a gargoyle, musing 'I wonder, now, I do. I wonder, nurse, whether you may be someone – more particular. Eh? What's your opinion, Captain Kalokyri?'

The Captain didn't say. Chryssa sat up, trying to look impatient, indignant, that they still kept her; but she was growing nervous.

'So, nurse, you were listening to their broadcasts. And were they good listening? Full of helpful information about the National Government? Good for the students, I say. Bravo!'

He spoke with heavy violent sneering, her sight clouded with blood, all the bodies she had seen swung back before her,

'Don't speak like that, not after you've – killed so many – shot so many – so many dead –'

Suddenly he stood up, short, fat, bulbing over his desk, and shouted in her face, 'And what should we do to communist filth, to treacherous filth, they got off lightly, we should have killed them all, the filth!'

Chryssa's caution snapped, 'How can you – how dare you – those students, the youth of Greece, the hope of Greece, they were brave, they spoke out against this filthy dictatorship, filthy murderers, for years you've. . . .'

She stopped herself, and sat shaking with passion, frustration. The Major sat back. 'I think, nurse, you knew a lot about the National Government before that night. I think you were in there with the students from the start.'

'Ask them! Bring them in, ask them to tell you if they know me! A fat lot you'll learn from them.'

His bulb eyes exchanged glances with the Captain, who all the time stayed behind her, out of sight; and at his leisure the Major said, 'Nurse, one thing is clear to me. You're not a nobody. No, no, please. Me now, I'm just a village boy, but I know education when I see it! I know character and fire when

I see them! You are a person with a role. Perhaps it is with the students, perhaps it isn't with the students. But I think you have to do with politics. Perhaps you have a husband, he. . . .'

At the word 'husband', Chryssa froze: she must betray no sign. But even that tiny stiffening the Major's huge eyes caught. He stared at her hard: horrible huge naked eyeballs in the big red head, she could not get away from them. The Major leaned across his desk, and suave as oil he gentled, 'I think the nurse has a husband, eh, Captain? I think she is somebody, and her husband is somebody.'

She tried to make sure she gave no sign, while the horrible eyes glimmered at her through the smoke.

'But was her husband with her in the Architecture School, Captain? Hm? I don't think he was. No – and somehow I don't think he is in Athens just now. Or is he, nurse? No, he isn't. And yet you know, Captain, I guess the nurse's husband – that he is of her mind, as to politics. And if she is busy here, perhaps he is busy somewhere else, eh Captain?'

All Chryssa's body wanted to tremble, she froze it rigid, but still there were tremors; she couldn't tell whether the Major saw the tremors or not.

Abruptly the Major stood again, and came round his desk shouting at the top of his voice, 'Tell us who you are, woman. We'll get there anyway. If you delay, it'll be the worse for you, and for your husband as well. Ah, that gets you, does it? Well, listen, if you don't cooperate, we'll do things to your husband which I won't describe. Because there are some things we won't do to you, because you're a woman, but we'll do them to your husband I promise you, and I wouldn't like to be you, the next time I saw my husband after that.'

Chryssa couldn't control her trembling longer, she shook in convulsions at the knowledge that Vangelis was more available to them than they knew; he awaited them in one of their own prisons, how could she keep them away from him?

The Major stood over her. 'Tell us your name!' he roared, his eyes looked enormous, great wheels, she felt it was his eyes that were shouting. Then suddenly she was hit, a blow on the ear like a bomb in her head, Captain Kalokyris was contributing at last.

'I'll tell you nothing,' she said.

352

'You'll tell us now,' the Major roared, his large hot-veined head almost touching her face.

'Tell us,' Captain Kalokyris said in her ear: it was the first time she heard his voice, it was a dry wheeze, hoarse to a whisper, a sound like dry straws crumpled.

'I'll tell you nothing, nothing,' she clenched. 'Come on then, hit me, burn me, do what you like, I'll tell you nothing.' The Captain obeyed, the blow on her ear knocked her to the floor, she sat up gasping, clutching her head which was full of iron hooting. 'Nothing,' she said again.

The Major and the Captain muttered to each other, they seemed out of temper; the Major grunted, tapped his watch, then abruptly he shouted, 'Officer!'

A policeman came in.

'Get her out of here.'

As she staggered up and out of the door, the Major called after her, 'I'd get to work on your memory, nurse. We'll have some reminders ready, when we see you tomorrow.'

It was after midnight when Major Klathas and Captain Kalokyris finished work for the day. They were exhausted but at ease: like everyone, they had good days and bad days. On bad days they might work for hours, use all their cunning, use all their resources of burns, twists, special blows, and yet learn nothing, perhaps discover there was nothing to learn – and for all these hours they must account to their superiors. It was – for they were both keen fishermen, all the thrill of their work was like angling in the depths, and drawing the catch in – like trawling a dead stretch of sea and getting no bites but only plastic garbage off the sea bed. But today had been different, today was the harvest. As to fishing, oh, fish after fish was dragged up by its tearing mouth up up from the safe deep till the water went glassy, disappeared, there was blinding glare, and vacuum, suffocating in tearing gasps and all its head agony as clumsy graspers tore its jaw to rags. There was a thrill in hurting, while tracking and catching. Time after time the catch was landed; nuisances like the nurse they threw back in the water, tomorrow, with more leisure, they would catch her. At the end of the day they were exhausted as they had never been;

353

but they had an ease and satiety, like late leavers from a seraglio.

They weren't ready yet to return to their wives; they wanted fresh air, rest, a drink in company. At the entrance of the building they met a good friend, another captain, and the three of them got into the Major's car and drove to a taverna they knew beside the sea; they met friends there from the civil police and the secret police, it was a good place.

They chatted in good spirits. 'This is action, this is what we've waited for,' the new captain said.

'It's about time,' the Major grunted. 'We should have had a free hand years ago. They've been pussyfooting, and look at the result. The Architecture School – what a mess! And you know who's fault that was?'

They waited for him to tell them, for he was the Major.

'It was the fault of the President. He started it.'

'Major Klatha, what are you saying?' the new captain exclaimed. 'I send men to Yaros for saying that.'

The Major swirled the ice cubes in his ouzo and crunched a dried fish; at his ease he said, 'The President started it with his civilian prime minister. It was too soon by far. Greece wasn't ready, and we've seen the result. It made people think we were losing control. It encouraged the students. I tell you, those students would be alive today, if he hadn't tried on this *civilian* trick. Well, we want no more mistakes. We want leadership. I give you, gentlemen, the Brigadier.'

'The Brigadier,' they repeated, clinking glasses, exchanging glances.

At other tables the toast was repeated.

The interrogators retired; but in a spartan office in a barracks near Athens a bald, sharp-cut man like a bayonet sat still at his desk, disciplined and upright as if a hundred eyes inspected him, his uniform with its stars and crown tight and sleek as it had been at dawn, his finger ends pressed together knife-point to knife-point while his sharp-lidded eyes stared beyond hands and through walls and barracks into distance. He sat so, considering his options. So much had come to him. The Architecture School had been his opportunity, it had brought his tanks to the centre of Athens. It discredited the Government, and the President too. It left all power with Military Intelligence. Everyone said now there must be change: and he was the man who could make that change. The machine was ready to his hand, well oiled, in working order, ready to move; and all the men stationed on it looked to him. This was the turning point.

His lean fingers, arching, seemed to cup a globe: he knew he held there the fate of Greece. He had never believed he would come to such power: the more he realized it, the more it took his breath away. A light descended round him, gathered into him: slowly the genius of the nation possessed him.

The future was dark; but who knew the future? The President was his old friend, but there was no saving the President now. At this moment, he could take control of Greece with a sentence, with perfect ease. And if he did not act, his power would slip from him, his chance would be lost. Was it possible for him *not* to take power? He knew, he had no choice.

The President paced, he could not find sleep these nights: if he did drop off, he woke within the hour, pitched abruptly in a cauldron of trouble. His plans had been so good, and had all gone wrong. He fidgeted his dressing gown, turning in the villa lounge. Those idiotic students, so foolish, mad, forcing the crisis when he was giving more freedom: what craziness, who could have predicted that? – and now all their bodies, he was called the murderer, and he was saving Greece, and he had so many enemies, and making him kill children –

He paced the large rooms. When he heard boots on gravel outside, and drawing the curtains saw soldiers advancing over the lawn towards the villa, it seemed only like one of his fear-dreams made real. These soldiers were not his guard, they were walking fast towards him.

He heard doors being opened, businesslike voices, boots now on parquet. They had two rooms to cross, to get to him: for the time that took them, he would still be President, the ruler. There must be measures he could take. But he took no measures, he only stood, and now they had arrived, they stood in a line, armed soldiers in his private lounge.

'Mr President, will you please come with us?' Their faces were taut, their eyes blank.

He found that at one and the same time he was not surprised, and yet he couldn't believe it. This isn't real, these are night fears, he thought. The troops stood in a line, close to he saw their faces were nervous. He might be inspecting them.

'Mr President!' one of the soldiers said peremptorily.

Chryssa was bewildered, since early morning there had been noises, voices, walking feet, as if the security forces were moving house. Determined boots stepped to her cell, the door was unlocked and pushed open, and she saw in silhouette the shapes of Major Klathas and Captain Kalokyris: the two of them paused there like hawks before swooping.

'Good morning, Mrs Tzavella,' the Major said cheerfully. Chryssa felt a sudden falling fear, they had her name, they had her now. But the Major was holding out his arm, as if he wanted to shake hands with her.

'Nice to have met you, Mrs Tzavella,' he said vigorously, and turned to his companion. 'Mrs Tzavella is an impressive woman, eh Captain, a woman of character?'

The Captain nodded jerkily, and smiled without humour; then they stepped apart, leaving the doorway clear.

'I can go?'

The Major slightly bowed.

'You've no more use for me, then?' she enquired, in trembling irony: still she couldn't believe it.

'Ach, Mrs Tzavella, those days are gone! There's no more for us to do, they'll put us out to pasture. That'll be a lame end to all our service for the nation, eh Captain?'

By now they were walking down the passage. 'What are you saying?'

'Well, Mrs Tzavella, you will not be sorry to hear that the tyrant has been overthrown –'

'What do you mean?'

'Patience, patience, my dear Mrs Tzavella. The President, the autocrat, has been arrested. A new government is being formed. Prisoners are being released.'

Chryssa stopped where she stood. 'Oh!' For a moment she felt weak as water, then every part of her wanted to soar. And yet, and yet, how could this happen? Wisps of doubt, unease, swirled round her.

'The army acted,' the Major said proudly. 'Even the army had had enough. He had become a tyrant. And that business at the Architecture School, that was too bad – as you said. All those students killed. The army is not there to kill Greeks, Mrs Tzavella.'

'All the prisoners will be released?'

'Ah, you think of your husband. He will be out. Not today, perhaps, I don't know. Obviously it will take time for those in the islands. But don't worry, Mrs Tzavella.'

Still, somewhere, Chryssa worried: but a weeping, laughing exhilaration danced in her, it begged to be released, to sweep her away.

'So you see, Mrs Tzavella,' the beaming pop-eyed Major said, as they stepped into the short alley that was Bubulina Street, 'the army does good sometimes. The Greek army is not all bad, eh?'

She found herself nodding, thinking the soldiers were brutes, but they were Greeks also: the massacre was too much, even for the army. Gazing round her in the clear November sunlight, seeing the Major with his red jolly face, his bulbing cheeks, his rolling pop eyes, she found herself thinking, Even him, he's human, he's a human being. Around her certain other officers were amiably seeing their dazed victims off the premises. She realized only the older and more important victims received this treatment: she perhaps received it because she knew foreign journalists. But still the parting had a weird sunny unreal atmosphere, as if they were guests taking leave of some friendly hotel.

One prisoner took it differently, she heard him exclaiming to a friend in anger and contempt, 'You arsehole, Demo, do you believe the new lot are any different? You'll soon see.'

His friend shrugged and sighed, 'Stelio, Stelio, the country has had enough. Even the army.' He looked compassionately at his friend, who looked back in focused contempt and repeated, 'You gullible arsehole,' as he limped down the alley. His narrow yellow face was ugly with scorn and pessimism, Chryssa shuddered when she saw it – the face of mistrust, it couldn't be right at such a time. Was she morose, a pessimist? She was bewildered. You must trust human nature: deep down there are forces you can't violate for ever, there is a limit to atrocity.

357

She walked down the street. The grey buildings of the city were dingy and flaking, yet the pale bright sunlight gave them a faint smile, and a flower seller smiled, and the person who was buying smiled at the blooms. Another street was blocked by students dancing and singing at the fall of the Junta. She walked home in a dream, on a delirious wave: she couldn't yet believe the nightmare was over, Vangelis was coming home, everything bad had turned to good.

She felt a slight sinking when she arrived at her flat and found it empty: she had caught herself believing he might somehow, crazily, be back already. She trembled with impatience and hope, Come come come, Vangeli, she murmured, as if her urging could bring him sooner.

She tried ringing the prison authorities, the justice department, the security agencies, to get information. All the lines were engaged: but of course they would be, today, she could only wait.

She rang friends, Clio and Simos came round: she gave them coffee and whisky, put on music, they celebrated the fall of the dictator. For that much was certain, the President had gone.

'Who *are* the new ones?' Chryssa asked.

'Ach, nothing's known,' they both said. 'It's an interim government, they're all unknowns.'

Clio said brightly, 'The new President is a general. They say he's a fair man, an honourable man, the sort of "good soldier" who had got just up to here with the Junta.'

Simos crumpled and puckered in scepticism. 'I don't know that I see it like that.' He said no more, he didn't want to sink their mood; but Chryssa pressed him.

'Well, Chryssa, this new President, he may be a "good soldier", I don't know. It doesn't matter, he's obviously just a figurehead. But this idea, that there's a *good* part of the army that's fed up at last, so it throws out the Junta, well. . . . When you start asking who the people are who *could* overthrow the President, who actually could do it. . . . When you think what their security has been, when you think who actually controls the troops. . . .'

Simos paused, Chryssa's face was angry. Though she thought she was divided still, not certain she could trust good news, she found she resented all Simos said. She heard herself ask him in a hard voice, biting, 'So what are you saying, Simo? That nothing's changed? That things are as bad as they were?'

He didn't answer; and she didn't insist further. She had been through much, she was not willing, so soon, to have new fears confirmed.

'I couldn't bear it,' she said firmly to Clio. She poured them more drinks, and put a record on loud; but their mood was spoilt.

The next day she tried again to contact the authorities: but again all the lines were engaged. She visited the offices, but they were besieged, and when she managed to get to a counter, it was only clear that no one was sure of anything. The civil service was in chaos, no one knew who was going or staying or what the new orders were; yes, some prisoners here were being released, but no one knew what was happening elsewhere. The officials she spoke to were frantic with uncertainty, there was nothing she could do but wait.

She got all the newspapers she could, and combed them. At the end of the day, on the phone, she compared notes with Clio. The Brigadier of Military Intelligence had loomed large at the swearing in of the new President – that was a bad sign. It was said that the new government had the support of young hardline officers, and this could not be good. Worst of all, in the official reasons given for the change of power, the massacre at the Architecture School was not mentioned once: on the contrary, the main reason given was that the country was being led to an 'electoral adventure'.

'It's not good news, is it?'

'It sounds very bad, Chryssa.'

'Clio, don't say that, I hoped you'd say, I don't know –' Chryssa could not stop herself crying, as they spoke on the phone. It seemed that when she was alone, all her doubts could not stop her hope growing, hope grew of necessity: then the doubts of other people felled it again. She felt she could not live if their doubts, her doubts, proved true.

'But Chryssa, they are still releasing prisoners. I think they will release Vangeli. The new people will have nothing against him. That's all you should think of.'

Chryssa nodded, and presently rang off. She hoped, but she feared. She went out on the balcony, and the quiet evening city reassured her, it looked like a free city, other families chatted on their balconies. It was only when she looked down, at a building across the road, that she realized there was a man standing in the lobby who did not move at all. Perhaps he was waiting for someone. Evidently she had caught his eye, for he was looking back at her: and he continued looking, till she realized for sure – he was waiting for no one, he was watching her.

As that came home, her legs turned to water, she staggered back indoors, collapsed across the sofa, her heart pounded in her to break her up: it must not it must not be that still the nightmare was going on.

She switched out the light, and all lights, and waited in the dark. Eventually, her nerves tearing, she stepped back on the balcony, and looked down. The man was still there, in the lighted lobby, he didn't try to hide; and still he was watching her flat.

She returned indoors: she couldn't walk any more, she crawled on the carpet softly moaning. Darkness bloomed over the city.

The next day she heard the releases had been slowed down; also, there were new arrests.

The new President, an elderly broadbacked officer with a short wiry crest of white hair, entered the reception with a steady walk but an anxious eye: evidently there was someone else he expected to see there, and could not find. The new Prime Minister, a lean diffident balding man, approached respectfully, stooping slightly in his uncertainty whether he should shake hands or bow. Their talk made jerky stops and starts, as the Prime Minister explained in a thin voice, a little too loud, a scheme for the redistribution of land.

A sharp-edged, assured voice was heard outside. There was a catch in the conversation of everyone except the President, who, slightly deaf, came to a halt a few moments later. Eyes turned to the doorway, as the Brigadier strode in: his eyes were hard, shining, excited; he came in with a swing of his arms, with a gait between a march and a swagger, his success was too fresh and too complete for him to hide the zest it gave him.

Officials and ministers hastened to greet him; he acknowledged them slightly as he crossed the room to the President, who turned to greet him as though their roles were reversed.

'Good evening, Brigadier, I am delighted to see you.'

His respects paid, the Brigadier moved slowly through the company, saying little himself, but pausing when others spoke to him, his bald Caesar's head slightly tilted in superior attention. When they finished he moved on, savouring grandeur. All his hopes had come true, more smoothly than could ever have been believed possible. So quickly, so easily, the old President, his old friend, fell. The new government had been received with rapture, with rejoicing in the streets, he could not have carried out a more popular action. And all the time his men watched at the ready, and all those who thought they could safely spout socialism, all those traitors who thought they were dancing on the National Government's grave, of all of them good note was taken. They had released some prisoners, small fry, the bigger fish they kept. Already the new arrests began, he had a thousand eyes, all over Greece his men were gathering in their greatest harvest. The power the last President had frittered away was working smooth and strong, he knew now truly events marched as he chose, he would be harsh at home and aggressive abroad, he would make Greece great.

The Foreign Minister approached, all compliance.

'Mr Minister, I shall call on you tomorrow if I may,' the Brigadier said. The Foreign Minister bowed, acknowledging the order: he would place his morning at the Brigadier's disposal.

The Brigadier dismissed him with a pleased nod: Greece's power had stagnated, tomorrow it would stir.

In the daytime, life in the barracks was normal, no different from before, but every night now he was back in the Architecture School, and he saw again the bodies mangled together, he thought they are all dead, then they started to get up, so they were cheating, they couldn't be dead, and the one in front of him coughed or choked, his throat was blocked, and then it cleared, and suddenly like paint poured from a bucket blood poured from his mouth and kept on pouring, blood, more blood than a body could contain.

He woke early, shivering, and for hours every morning felt sick and exhausted. In the daytime, it was only odd things he remembered like that great big communist, he'd wonder where the bullet hole was, this question would come into his mind when he was thinking of quite other things, and he would say over to himself, in the middle of conversation with his mates, 'What a big chap he was!' and they all stared, but presently things were back to normal, they laughed and joked, there were a lot of rough jokes round the camp these days.

But often too he would wonder about the way that tank ran over the students, he couldn't get it out of his head, but probably it wasn't part of their orders for that to happen, probably the man driving the tank didn't see too well through his little window, probably he saw the students jumping and thought they'd all gone, and then again once started he had to get through the gateway because if he just stopped, blocking the gate, how could the soldiers get in? And then again the students who were crushed were only dead after all, and how were they different from the ones who were shot?

These things nagged him more not less as time went on and they had nothing to do but sit around the barracks, and then one night he heard a shot in the next shed, and he went round there, and it was just like the Architecture School because here was another damaged head, the back of it blown out and blood and brains scattered back over the furniture, but this was no student, it was his mate Spanos, of all the people in the world Spanos had shot himself; this shook him more than the things he had seen at the Architecture School. He knew Spanos was troubled, he kept saying he couldn't sleep though he looked as though he had nightmares, yet after all he wasn't one of the ones who first went in shooting. He had said he only shot one student, yet now he had done this.

After Spanos' death he kept feeling the world hung off its hinges, and as to himself, he knew he wouldn't commit suicide, he wasn't that sort, but another soldier did, there were funny things happening, his memory had gone odd and the dreams didn't go away and wherever he looked there was an odd ragged glare in the corner of his eyes.

In the prison garden Vangelis, Christoforos and Stamatis sat piecing together the bits of news they got about the changes in Greece.

'Yes, but who *are* they?' Stamatis mused.

'Who do you think?' Vangelis said. 'It's just a change of guard in the barracks.'

'Well, that's all right,' said Christoforos. 'If there's a change of guard in the barracks, they should want a change of prisoners in the prison. They'll have their own enemies.'

'Let's hope they've had enough of us,' Stamatis sighed.

Vangelis shrugged, but then bethought himself, 'Yes, why shouldn't they want to be shot of us. What good does it do them to keep us here?'

'And then again,' said Christoforos, 'if they don't let us out, we may at least have new company. We may be playing *tavli* with ministers, Vangeli.'

Vangelis smiled.

Because boots make no sound on dug earth, they woke belatedly to the stout tight-uniformed prison guard striding towards them.

'What in the name of the Virgin are you doing? On your feet, all of you, don't you know this ground must be dug?'

Vangelis turned round to see him; and something in the sight of Vangelis' large, slightly scowling, defiant face seemed to irritate this guard, who for days had been trying to be friendly. He shoved Vangelis hard with his boot, so he fell over sideways; seeing him sprawl, he kicked him in the back.

Now he was shouting. 'Look at this earth. Do you call this digging? Dig it again, I want every inch dug.'

He strode off; he seemed pent up again in annoyance, in anger, as did the other warders. The prisoners knew by these signs that their hopes of change and release were vain after all, the new government in Greece had no presents for them, and life in the prison was back to normal.

'Never mind,' said Christoforos, 'one dictator's gone, and there's one more to go. We're half way there.'

He took his spade, and dug with force.

PART THREE

The Third Coup

1

At first the new dictatorship followed a policy of contradiction. Now they announced new releases, now new arrests and trials: now they promised reform, now they promised to discipline the nation. The changes kept Chryssa and everyone uncertain; and in the meantime the grip was tightened, so they all knew too late that they had been played with, and that the sacrifices were for nothing, and that they were worse placed now than they had been before.

Winter arrived. A needle wind from the north tore the palms, flicked grit in the eye, clattered old cans on cobbles and walls; under black cloud that dragged overhead nonstop like a lugged tarpaulin. Groups of shiverers watched a line of army lorries slowly pass; a soldier with his face screwed up into smarting sleet raced an armoured car through slithering streets. The blinded house fronts died from sight in the early dark: and all she saw spoke of sharp storms and cold torrents, dead hearts and winter despair, in the city of spies and hopelessness.

When she heard Alexis had been injured at the Architecture School, Chryssa visited Patra and Leonidas.

'How is he?' she asked them.

'How's Alexis? Huh! A good question!' Leonidas muttered; he slouched across the sofa, unaired, sluggish.

'Don't ask us that,' Patra said tightly.

'Why? What's happened?'

'He won't live here. He won't even see us.'

'Why not?'

'Because of Leonidas.'

Chryssa glanced at Leonidas, who sat forward: his face looked swollen, inflamed with emotion. But he wouldn't say a word about Alexis to Chryssa, and Patra looked aged and wizened, and didn't want to speak.

There were few topics they could meet on. The sisters spoke a little about their father: still his pension arrangements hung uncompleted, and in the meantime he had entered a new spiral of ambition. He spoke of buying a ferryboat: he had been on the phone to both of them, full of excitement and unclear conviction.

'A ferryboat!' Leonidas scoffed. 'Does the man want to be a shipowner now? Captain Nikos!' There was rant in his voice, as if their father's claim to be planning the impossible exasperated him to fury.

'Leonida!' both sisters shouted, 'he is our father!'

They left the ferryboat project. It seemed that the new government was the only topic Leonidas would allow to be spoken of, though at the same time he would say almost nothing about it. He would only repeat, with a dull irony, 'They are excellent men! Eh? Huh?' When Chryssa mentioned how she had been watched and followed, Leonidas inflated impatiently, and presently interrupted her, 'Chryssa, that's nothing! If they follow you from place to place, if they listen to your phone, if they read your letters, if they have cameras in the lavatory, I tell you that is nothing to what they do to us. Because we are the government before the last. We are dangerous. They watch us more than they watch anyone. You think you have troubles, Chryssa, but you have some friends. We have no friends. The nation hates us; the new lot hate us; the army hates us; our sons hate us.'

He laboured to regain his calm, then said to Chryssa in an urgent serious voice he had not used before when speaking to her, 'Well, well, you and I, Chryssa, we are very far apart. However, I will say one thing: I hope you are not up to any tricks – meetings, phone calls, leaflets, resistance groups – the sort of thing Vangelis did. Because they will catch you, and you should know that this government is not a joke. They are willing to do – very bad things. I worry a great deal, because of Alexis. Be careful.'

Chryssa didn't answer, and shortly afterwards she left; but this serious warning, coming from of all people Leonidas, stayed with her. She was no longer followed by spies – presumably they had more important prey – but still she would be seized by sudden alarms, and would stop and look round her in the street. Her fear woke curiosity in the nearby faces; and as they looked at her, she saw in them surveillance. Grey faces, motionless at winter windows, watched her.

368

She was back in the black world: it was as if, through her recent holiday of hopes, her own despair had all the time been waiting like a patient friend to rejoin her when she came in sight. She knew now Vangelis would not be released for years. The new dictatorship was more nakedly military than the old: it abandoned the pretence of popular support, and treated the country as an occupied zone. If there were resistance now, Chryssa didn't know, the rounding up and the scaring had been too thorough and too savage: and she herself was dangerous to talk to, having been arrested at the Architecture School. She must keep to herself, not lead the police to anyone.

As the days passed, she sank deeper in shadow. It took time for a tragedy like the Architecture School to come home, and it was only now she registered truly the deaths she had seen. In her dreams she returned to those days: again she stooped in the street beside the girl who had been talking and laughing and who lay there looking alive, but she was dead; or she was in the makeshift casualty ward where the bodies were laid out on desks in rows, and they moved and stirred, there were shrill cries muffled in distance, but when she reached them, they were dead. She saw bodies in the road, bodies on the floor, bodies on trolleys. Her memory retrieved other casualties from the past: cases that had come to Vangelis, the family of a girl who had died in prison, the tatters of the car, following the bomb explosion. Now newsreels and stories got mixed with her memories: photos of the dead in the Civil War, and in the World War, and in the Great War, and the stories of all the dead, and the speared children, in the wars with the Turk. All her life she had, without realizing it, been hugging the wall of the pit of death, moving downwards, and now she arrived at the trough at the bottom, and it was not black here but lit by a grey even numb light that showed bodies heaped on bodies beyond anyone's counting. When people laughed and chatted in cafés, it was all illusion, they were waiting to die. What was she doing now, but waiting to die? Vangelis in prison was waiting to die. The dead bodies at the Architecture School heralded this truth, that only dying was real, that everyone living belonged to death, and nothing else could matter, there was nothing else.

If she rose from this mood, she returned to it later. Her translation work, which had given her contact with a busy world, had thinned to a trickle, trade also seemed dead. She sought other work, but many now were out of work.

The wind wailed outside the closed windows, while she jotted or typed in the small pool of light from her lamp. Around her the darkness was cold, for the radiators in this elderly building had never been strong enough for mid-winter. There was in the flat an ancient elaborate wood-burning stove, which she and Vangelis had never dismantled, since they liked its decorations and also relied on it in the coldest days: she kept it at a low glimmer, for some extra heat, but still wore four cardigans. Somewhere far off the shrill sound of a siren rose and fell in waves.

Her doorbell buzzed: she knew who it was, but still, from habit, peered through the globular eye in the door. She saw a slender stalk of person, very tall, light-faced; she cranked back her locks and opened.

'Michael.'

He was out of breath, anxious, his longish hair blown awry, he looked as though he had run to Greece.

'Chryssa, are you well? – I heard such terrible things –'

'I'm all right,' she said briefly, and shut the door. He was inside, a too big figure, like a windblown tree come into her home. He took in her multiple cardigans.

'That's you wrapped up,' he said affectionately. 'You look like a Russian doll.'

They hadn't kissed yet, but now, abruptly, for all her cumbering cardigans, she launched up to kiss him hard on one cheek and hard on the other. The colour flared in his cheeks at the spots where she touched him.

He followed her into the living room. He wanted to embrace her, at the least to speak warmly, from all his concern and love and anxiety, but she had a tautness that kept him distant. He noticed there were no new plants.

She poured them each a glass of ouzo; they sat. He asked again about the Architecture School, and presently she told him; in a level voice, seldom meeting his eye, with intervals of pause where she was blank, numb, impenetrable to him.

He listened, stricken: what she told him was worse than any reports, even rumours, that he had heard.

When she finished, there was a silence; there was nothing he could say.

They became aware of a noise growing steadily outside: a clattering and rumbling like boulders tumbled and rolled. It approached them rapidly. No vehicle could make such a noise, but still the racket grew, echoing between the facing buildings till, even with windows shut, it was deafening.

Michael opened the glass doors onto the balcony, and understood. In the dimness, a large khaki block of iron, a tank, was driving fast below him. Behind it were other tanks, and ahead of it were tanks: from end to end the shadowy street was a single line of tanks, racing in colossal clatter on the damaged tarmac. Through a trapdoor in the top of each gun turret a soldier's head stuck into the air, in beret and earphones, watching the road ahead. The other traffic had slewed to either side of the road, the pavements were lined with people watching. It seemed that on every balcony of the block opposite a family had come out, men in shirtsleeves, women in aprons, children, old people in dressing gowns, all watching bleakly the passing convoy.

The last tank moved out of sight: already they had gone, they drove so fast. Their thunder receded behind the buildings. Michael returned to the flat, stunned; he had never seen an army in a city, meaning business.

'They do it often,' Chryssa said. 'They drive in convoy from one barracks to another, just to show us, to keep us in our place.'

'It's showing off as well, isn't it? Hideous! They're like, I don't know, cruel schoolmasters.'

'No, Michael, cruel parents – that's how they think. We're the bad children. It's nightmarish.'

'It is a nightmare.'

'No, I don't mean that, I mean life here is a *real* nightmare. Being watched, followed, wherever you go. Knowing there's something horrible round the corner in the road. Being alone in rooms with people who will do things to you that you daren't imagine. Those are the things that happen in nightmares, and those are the things that dictatorships do.'

'That's why you feel so helpless against them.'

'Feel helpless? You are helpless. What can you do against tanks and soldiers?'

He sat, tossing slowly like a man in a sack. 'Yes – but – how long can soldiers run a country?'

'I don't know, Michael. Things are very far gone, even the businessmen are sick of them now. But hatred doesn't get them out. And people talk of oil, they say there's oil in the Aegean, and if they get oil money. . . .'

Michael nodded; then, with energy, said, 'But doesn't the Architecture School give you hope as well as grief?'

She looked up, he had surprised her. 'Yes, Michael. That it happened. That so many people came together there. That does give hope.'

They went out to eat; afterwards, near her flat, she kissed him quickly and said, 'It's good to see you, Michael, I'm glad you've come.' She had an odd, tense, tight-skinned brightness.

'But you'd like to be left?'

'Do you mind?' she asked, perhaps with apology, perhaps with reproach.

'Of course not,' he said, as he had to.

The following day they met for lunch, and afterwards walked. With her unobtrusively, perhaps unconsciously, guiding him, they made their way eventually up the rock spike of Lykavittos. Once they cleared the housetops, the wind was raw and biting. The steep path zigzagged upwards between cactus plants with leaves as big as platters, jagged-edged, spined, tufted with thorns: a twisted forest which, uncannily, hardly moved in the hard wind.

They came out on a high terrace, and looked over the close-packed blocks, bleached white but grimy, dotted with black windows, receding through the grey air like a city cut out of chalk and covered in dust.

'Horrible city!' Chryssa muttered. 'Sometimes, Michael, I feel this is the end. I see only death all round. Do you know how many people died in the Architecture School? The newspapers here say half a dozen; the press abroad say twenty-five. The people I know say it was over four hundred. And there have been other deaths. Those who think they can imagine the worst just don't know what happens here. You don't know how dead I feel inside.'

She looked at him then: he flinched. Her face in the cold was pale, almost white; her Greek hair was dark, and her brown eyes, weeping in the wind, looked black. She was extraordinarily distinct, handsome, frightening.

'You're not dead, Chryssa, you're very far from it. You look,

I don't know, clearer, stronger, than you did before.'

She frowned into the wind. 'I don't understand that.'

'It's true.'

'I suppose the Architecture School has changed me. It's strange, when you see something as terrible as that, it brings home – what a *big* place the world is. Hundreds of lives can disappear – just like that, wiped out, gone, and there's no god, or anyone, who stops it, or steps in, or does anything about it. It's – beyond fear. It changes the way you worry about yourself. What can you do?'

'What do you do?'

'Sometimes I want to pray – not *to* anyone, just to the emptiness – it seems a way of meeting it.' She paused, her frightening white face still cutting the wind, while tears tracked down it. He wished her to say, 'Other times, I want to be in bed – I feel sex is all we've got.'

She turned to him; they had come to the point. She slightly raised her shoulders, lowered her head – his heart began to bang – he knew her words would break him.

'Michael, there's something I should say. I don't think we should go back to being as we were on the island. It's because of Vangelis, of course – he didn't take a pardon he could have taken, he chose to stay inside. How can I then . . .? And there's the Architecture School. You weren't there. Perhaps you couldn't be, anyway you weren't, and I felt you were very far off. And I was inside, with other Greeks. I felt I was with Vangelis, in being there with them.' Again she raised her hard eyes to him. 'We're in different countries, wherever we are. You've always got your ticket home.'

She spoke bitterly – almost, at the end, with malice. What could he say? – people in love make their own country. That was romantic, and her face was blunt, a door shut against him. But she said, 'Don't be angry, Michael. I don't have feelings for anyone at present.'

He blinked; did she mean they'd still be friends? But what sort of friends could ex-lovers be? Yet still the clockwork of courtesy turned: and they talked as friends, but with a catch in their talk, as they descended Lykavittos. In the steep drunken streets at the bottom they parted; it was not clear when they'd meet again.

There was something still which he hadn't told her: that this time he had no return ticket with him. He had fulfilled the resolution he had made on the island: he had given up his job, and had secured, from an agency, a half-pay commission to work in Athens. So here he'd stay; and sometimes see Chryssa. It was poetic justice. He would do the work which he had told others he was coming here to do; but he wanted to crack his head on the cold wall beside him.

In the following days he established himself in his flat. He was pleased with it: he overlooked the Athens flower market, a curious completely circular shed, with a circular path round it, and a zodiac circle of further sheds round the path. There was scant business these days, but he looked forward to spring and summer, when, his landlord told him, the whole ring would be a fire of colours.

Whenever he wasn't busy, fidgeting his furniture into the right angle to his typewriter, and clearing all surfaces in his austere shipshape style – but he had bought an ancient shadow puppet and attached it to the wall – he was restless at the window. He looked down on the concentric bare circles of the winter market, and thought about Chryssa. On his love, as on everything that happened to him, his restless thinking preyed. He knew what she said was true: he hadn't been here when he should have been, it had stamped him for good as what he was, the outsider, while she rejoined her country. He hadn't expected this: that what would come between them was not Vangelis, but Greece itself.

He remembered how moved he had been, when he first saw her feel she had lost connection with Greece: fear had splintered the nation into small guarded units, who trod warily round people like her. It was perhaps only at such a time that he and she could have come together: she, in isolation, half wanting to be rid of the country she was tied to, looking wistfully outside to Europe and the West as Greece always had done; and he, the outsider, looking in, moved, aghast, presuming he could help, and feeling at the same time that the world didn't care. So they came together, in the secret temporary love they needed. It had to be temporary: of itself, the dictatorship would generate new opponents, where Vangelis had gone they would follow, their numbers would grow, the nation would

374

stir, and start straining to heave off the dictators. And she must be with them, as she was in the Architecture School; where, as she told him, she felt all those gathered there were parts of one person, who for her was Vangelis. He was jealous of Vangelis; but how could he be jealous of a country?

He hung in uncertainty; he felt all he had was his love of Chryssa, if that were plucked out he'd drop in the street like an empty coat. Things that had not depended on her before did so now because he loved her.

In the meantime he must do what he'd come here to do. He began a full report on the Architecture School, following tips he'd been given by Chryssa, tracing witnesses and relatives. When not working on the report, he read slowly books in Greek, and – working like a careful surgeon – made repairs to his shadow puppet, who was somewhat the worse for decades of wear.

Whether the police were on his track he did not know: he did not seem to be followed, he couldn't find bugs. Probably, fortunately, they found him unimportant.

He was crossing the large road near his flat when a car, which he'd thought parked and empty, drove in his direction. He heard the frantic revving, thought, mad Athens drivers, glanced round – and saw the car growing bigger very fast, like a rock hurled at him. In that second he realized how wide the road was: and he was in the empty middle. He sprinted, the car slipped past. Arrived on the pavement, he watched it disappear over a hump in the road. His heart banged like a stone in a drum. It's some playboy, he thought, or youths – giving the foreigner a scare. In his head the car still hurtled at him; if he'd been dozy, or tripped, he'd be dead.

He bought the newspaper he had come for at the kiosk, and returned to his flat. The drink he took did nothing to steady him; he went out on his balcony for air. Was it possible, with all his reports, and his arriving now permanently to spy on them in Greece, that the Junta wanted to kill him? That's for the films, he thought. But then he thought, they've killed many people, why should they mind killing me? He realized that though in theory he knew the risks, in practice he took for granted the immunity of the foreigner. He would stay on now without that illusion; and without Chryssa. He had made his choice.

The cold air revived him. Presently he found he was used to what had happened, and less worried than he had thought: he must simply be precautious, always alert.

Returning indoors, his eye fell on the shadow puppet, lying on the table where he'd done his repairs: it was like the flattened body of someone run over in a cartoon. Smiling wryly, he picked it up carefully. He felt again between his fingers the strange stuff it was made of: it was stiff but semi-transparent, some sort of tanned and toughened skin that had been painted over so that, when it was held up to the light, the different parts of it glowed different deep colours, rich, burning, like a stained-glass window. He looked at places where the thread or wire held the pieces together: he was pleased with his work. It was a caricature person, a mountaineer or islander, with a big-nosed head and a belt stuck with weaponry. But what a curious object it was! He realized he was holding it in his arms as if it were a frail person, just alive; as if it were, personified, his Greece, his love of Greece, his love in Greece. . . . As tenderly as if he held a sleeping child he rested it on the table, and returned again to the balcony, and all his senses and thoughts and emotions, all of himself, stretched over the rooftops to Chryssa.

They met in the centre of Athens, on an afternoon that seemed the coldest of the year. Steadily the wind sharpened, till they felt it would blow all the heat from the world: you stepped round a corner into a blast that knocked you over. The sky blackened. It seemed as though winter were not a season, or a turning of the world, but a cone of cold force, or a god and his aura, that could descend on a region and chill it in minutes. They leaned steeper, into a gale that shrivelled eyes that streamed with freezing tears. And as the light failed, another visitor arrived that Michael had never thought to see in Greece: the air boiled with white flakes that stung the raw skin where they touched it. On dirty wings of flying sleet a staff car sped past them. They hurried back to Chryssa's flat, huddled to the blast.

They stood shivering, frozen, without even motion to warm them now.

'Michael, you've a way with stoves, let's have a proper fire.'

He busied himself folding papers and arranging sticks; and presently the fire took, and scorched their skins that knelt before it, and roared gale force in the teetering iron chimney that buttressed the wall.

He went to the balcony, and looked out: a few days before the convoy of tanks had sped past below them, like giant fish in a black river. Now he saw nothing but large white furry moths of snow descending steadily, evenly, down into the scurry of car lights at the bottom of the abyss of the street. The wind had died.

When he turned back to the flat, he saw Chryssa kneeling before the stove; firelight flickered in the leaves of her plants, so they seemed to stir. The domesticity of the whole occasion moved him, a couple warming by their fire. He went and sat, and watched her gazing firelit through the opened doors of the stove. Her face was slightly peaked, with the hypnotized expression that comes over fire watchers: she looked young, a girl; side on and sharp-lit, the vulnerable inquisitive curve of her profile moved him as it used to. He watched her in a grief of yearning. They talked occasionally, coolly and with friendship, but with a density of sadness round them: he felt the air would turn solid with sadness.

Later the snow stopped. They went out on the balcony: the air was still, and unexpectedly warm. Snow stood distinct on each sill and ledge.

He suggested he took her out to eat, and they went to a small restaurant nearby. The amber glow of its crowded, misted windows drew them. It was a pizzaria, but the Italian interest stopped at the menu: the walls were hung with lurid rugs depicting Holland, all windmills and tulips; and Chinese lanterns hovered in midair; while loud bouzouki music played from a tape. In the cheerful smoke-thick atmosphere they sat; ordered; and then couldn't talk. Opening remarks, beginnings of joke, petered to nothing. They had left the flat to escape the sadness, but the sadness accompanied them here. In whomever it began, it was quickly picked up by the other and deepened, till it was tangible as lead, a paralysing grief. It was clear to him then that love, and nature, didn't allow such meetings: they should separate completely, the 'good friends' friendship was not a possibility.

Abruptly, out of the obscure melancholy she had slipped

into, Chryssa glanced up and saw Michael gazing at her with a look of such racked yearning she was shaken in her frozenness as if she had been hit: she had never been looked at with such urgent wanting, not by Vangelis, not by anyone. Her eyes shivered quickly away; but she was thrown, confused, odd tremors and shocks disturbed her. She couldn't look at Michael; and the restaurant tables receded like packed desks, the smoky people were chattering ghosts, she saw bodies on the desks in the makeshift Casualty, she had fallen back to them, dead bodies, damaged bodies, damaged dead bodies.

They finished in silence. Chryssa seemed dazed, he escorted her out and they walked home through the snow. Every so often he glanced at her: her face was raised, but puckered as if she wanted to cry, or as if, quite silently, she were crying already. He had the impression that in some fine way, too small and quick to see, she was trembling from top to toe.

He put an arm round her, then both arms, for really she was shivering like a frozen person. He bent into a kiss, her cold mouth met his: they kissed hesitantly, then their mouths pressed, then their arms pressed and held.

Arrived at the flat, she stood quite mute, letting him undress her till they were both undressed. Softly he caressed her, all his constraints melting in his desire to kiss and touch her, to brush as with wings all of her that was cold and immobile, till a shiver ran through her that turned to a weaving coil of her body, and what had been frozen in her warmed and thawed and life flowed again to her arms and fingers that touched hither and thither on his back, while his hands felt again the lovely incurved small of her back that drew closer to him.

She wanted to feel this whole body, and be immersed in her loving of it, till she knew she was whole.

They lay still, warm under bedclothes in the cold flat, her head in a crook of his arm, their pains relinquished as time lost its hurry and became a slow river as wide as the world in which they, hardly moving, swam. She knew Michael would be staying in Athens, and she knew what she would do. There was nightmare round her on all sides; her hopes had accepted a long postponement; she would be with Michael, she saw nothing else.

Walking in the city the following day, they came to the gate of the ancient agora. Cypress trees, a temple, the restored arcade, stuck up through the uneven muffle of snow.

'No one comes here in winter.'

'But I like it,' he said. 'It brings the old world nearer, it must have looked just like this in winter.'

They walked through the ancient market place. The sky was black, the ground was white, the buildings nearby looked dark brown, earth-coloured. Darker black against the sky, a helicopter whirred overhead: hard to see clearly, loudly noisy, hovering then passing like a bad spirit.

He asked, 'You'll come to my flat?'

'Tonight you mean?'

'Tonight and often.'

She mused, then said, 'Yes, that's best.'

She looked round: flecks of snow were on her clothes, her hair, and momentarily sparkled then dissolved on her skin.

She laughed. 'This is my snow wedding.'

He smiled tenderly: the snow on them was like wedding white, the white ground her bridal train. A yellow trolley bus was to be their carriage, ferrying them between tanks and army transports and hooting cars to the solitary wedding breakfast, looking down on the flower market, imagining blooms.

The next day, she fetched a number of her things. It was better they were together at Michael's, her own home was made of different memories. In Vangelis' long absence his clothes, his books, his odds and ends, had come to seem like part of him: they should not be moved or disturbed, she had a piety for them. But Michael's foreign flat would be a small secret part, like a seed, of the world outside.

They moved just in time. Later in the day winter made new menaces, new gales shrilled, new whirlpools of snow volleyed over the acropolis. The city became an arctic planet, with ancient ruins, and modern blocks shuttered tight, side by side in blizzard: the streets were a turmoil of huddled, wrapped-up hurriers, crawling traffic, wind-spun flakes that burned like shot. They arrived back from shopping paralysed numb, their wet feet turned to club feet of frost. They laughed out loud as they chafed their skin and worked their tingling fingers supple, with sheer exhilaration at the extremity of the cold. It fired their skins red hot, their eyes sparkled with hot frost. They

379

drew the curtains, heated the flat to oven heat, and were warm, together, safe, shut off from the world.

In the morning, when he woke, she was already up: he padded to his small living room. She had brought with her some of her plants, and he watched her move among them, tending them carefully.

He said, 'You're like a mother bird, feeding its chicks.'

She looked up, smiled – and just then, momentarily, the winter sun broke through: it shone through the leaves, and through the silk of her kimono. All the flat was transfigured.

'I said to myself, if Chryssa brings her plants, that means she means to stay.'

She looked at him then, arms akimbo, narrow-eyed, friendly.

'Don't psyche me out, Michael.'

Finishing with her plants, she squatted down on the floor to read the paper. Exquisite in silk, she looked now like a beautiful water lily, with the broad leaves of newsprint round her. He loved the way she was willing to sit down all over his flat; it suggested that she felt at home. He enjoyed watching her when she was absorbed. Like a child playing at running from its mother, and then pelting back laughing to her, he would look away from her just for the delight of looking back again and seeing her there.

Later they went out. The sun had reappeared, the air was still, there was a white glare on the city buildings. Every facet and broken stone of the Parthenon, on its high crag, was brown and clear-cut as crystal. They walked in the Zappeion Park, passing slowly between the skeleton trees.

She clung close, rubbed her cheek on his sleeve.

'I'm so glad you came back, Michael.'

He held her tighter. She said, 'It's strange, we're back now as we were on the island. The island seems just a few days ago – but a few days ago, the island seemed to me *years* away.'

They walked. Under their feet the thin crust of snow did not give, but delicately snapped; it had thawed and frozen a dozen times, there were layers of ice between the layers of snow.

'It's funny how love can go and come. I thought love and sex were – *dead* for me, you don't know *how* dead. Now those things are alive again, and, I don't know, you're not the same person in one state and in the other.'

'Your ancestors called that different gods.'

'And that's right.'

They trod, the cold park tinkled. Later she said, 'You're very good with me, Michael, very patient, kind – and I'm difficult, I know, I'm an egoist, and up and down.'

'Yes, that's you, an egoist on a seesaw.'

'And when I'm down I hate everyone, and when I'm up I like myself.'

'I love the way you like yourself, it's not pompous at all, it seems to lift you from the ground.'

Her arm embraced him tight. Later he told her of the incident with the car, which possibly had tried to run him down.

'Probably it was a jay rider, giving me a scare.'

Her eyes half closed, her face puckered as if she hurt. 'Michael, you won't let them get you. It would kill me too.'

'I'm careful,' he said lightly, uneasy that she took the event so seriously. He realized he had been trying to forget it, now he couldn't.

He smiled to her. 'I won't let anything happen that could hurt you.'

The fragile sunlight was pale and clear; the cold park tinkled brightly and brittly as they trod to the gate.

Late at night they woke, and knew they were awake. In the pitch dark he was nothing but touches, she was a fragrant vibration of voice. Her whisper, very quiet, had a crackle: some danger, electric, was with them in the dark. She became more still, almost silently urging and suggesting. He pinioned her. She moaned. He was teeth tracing skin, pinching, biting. She found handholds in his flesh, her nails dug, her tight grip hurt. He grabbed her wrists together. She writhed slowly, not knowing where he'd hurt her next, in the delicious dark, the torment. He continued, each thing he did tore lesions in his mind.

Later in the dark she surfaced, still holding Michael. The love they'd made in torture seemed remote now, somewhere else. There were such different worlds of the night. Greece was nightmare in the daytime now, but the other nightworlds waited, the worlds of love in bed. Then she remembered her trip to Salonica, when she slept with her mother, and all the comfort of childhood returned. Even now, warm-drowsed in bed, she felt as if something of her mother were present, as if her mother's warm body had turned into the love she made. As she lay against Michael, listening to his quiet, so steady breathing, she felt, sinking, their lives flow like one, as if two streams could flow side by side, touching.

2

When the great discovery was made, it came only as the perfect completion of Kostas' pleasure: for everything had gone triumphantly well. He had risen to colonel; he was known and trusted by the Brigadier; the nation was in the hands of men like himself, young, patriotic, determined, fearless. The nation resisted, but the nation would learn. It was the same situation as faced any officer, when he fought to get control of a gang of village conscripts: he must first get their fear, then, through discipline, he'd command their respect.

'You're my general,' Kiki told him each morning, as she gave him little kisses through the car front window. Kostas smiled, and his eyes slowly closed; then he revved his engine, and left their new home in the pines of Kifissia. Using his horn sharply, he cleared a passage for himself through the crammed streets, and drove fast to the Pentagon, where soldiers and junior officers snapped to the salute, then ran for his instructions.

And now the great good news had come – 'the salvation of the nation' the President called it – the news that would change the economy from a pit of loss to a well of riches, that would change them from a weak nation to a great nation, that would still all complaints and make the people love them. Oil was found in the Aegean. For a long time there had been drilling and searching: now it was confirmed, the oil was there. They would depend on no one: they'd tell the world what to do. It was a new future for Greece.

There was one snag only: the oil was claimed by Turkey as well.

'What garbage, what rubbish, they've no claim at all! The Aegean is Greek!' Kostas would announce, echoing generals. 'There are Greek islands right to the Turkish coast. What we do is quite simple. We extend the boundary round every Greek island, so there's no free Aegean left at all. That's our answer to the Turks – the answer Metaxas gave to the Italians: no!'

This was the answer, the only answer: yet it could not be supposed the Turks would just say, '*Aman!* We're disappointed!' and walk away. No, there was only one action the Turks would respect: Greece must arm at once, prepare for war.

All the Pentagon came alive to the possibility. Life had been dreary, with so much deskwork, sitting around getting fatter and bigger-arsed and being no soldier at all. Now everyone was urgent and active and keen: the dingy yellow-walled sprawl of buildings stirred alert as one tense war creature, flexing muscles, stretching in readiness.

And not the Pentagon only, but all forces alerted. Messages crackled from shore to ship, from carrier to submarine, from jet to bomber to missile outpost. In every barracks and airfield were drills and alarms. Jets braked abruptly on carrier decks, young officers hurried to admirals, and gave their instructions and commenced inspections. Everyone had zest: for years they had done nothing but police work, now again they were an army, defending the fatherland.

How far these plans would go was still uncertain. Readiness for war was necessary, to warn Turkey off, and to secure a good agreement in negotiations: but probably the matter would be settled in that way, in negotiations. Again there was the question, would the Americans let them go to war? Kostas noticed that a number of officers who went ahead with energy preparing for conflict still could not believe they would really go to war. He himself knew they would. The Brigadier had made it clear he supported the Great Idea, he did not represent only Military Intelligence: he controlled the nation, he had ambitions for it, he would put Turkey down, and show the world the force Greece was.

Kostas was present not by accident when several officers met late one night in the war room. Many had gone home, the room was largely idle, half its large wall screens were switched off, only here and there a map or screen glowed dimly on the wall, where a watcher still sat over shadowy instruments. Some of the generals had their tunics off, they looked fretted and tired from the day's work; but they still rehearsed keenly the war plan – the dummy assaults and the real invasions from the islands, the thrust from the north – till one of the senior

generals there said gravely, 'Gentlemen, there is one problem
we still have not dealt with.' He brought his finger hard down
on the map. 'We must be able to attack from Cyprus.'

Kostas attended, for it was his job to receive intelligence
from Cyprus. Before he could comment, a lieutenant general
intervened, 'Poh!' he said, 'the Turk can destroy Cyprus. He
had only to reach out his hand.'

The General narrowed his eyes, put his head on one side.
'Well . . . in the long run, who knows where Cyprus will go?
But that's for the future. Here and now, we need it. Look
where it is, it's beautiful, it's a dagger at the heart of Turkey.
We must be able to invade from there.'

Kostas, anxious to have his authority known, said firmly,
'We can't do it, General. We couldn't get our tanks there.'

The General frowned at the new confidence of the new
colonel. 'And why not, will you tell me?'

'Because of the Archbishop, of course. He will never let us
in.'

Others there muttered the Archbishop's name: Archbishop
and President, he was a perpetual thorn to the National Government. But the General made short work of him, 'He must be
removed.'

'Right,' said the Lieutenant General. 'He's got to be kicked
out.'

'Oh no,' said the General. 'He must be removed. When a
man's as popular as that, he's got to be removed.'

'Do that, Lefteri, and you make a martyr of him.'

'*Let* him be a martyr, who cares about that? People forget, in
six months he won't even be a memory, and in the meantime –'

'We'll have Cyprus.'

'We'll have Cyprus. And we need it. So there's no question.'

The Lieutenant General still demurred, 'Well, Lefteri, yes,
but I mean – an archbishop! Who'll do that for us?'

'We'll do it, won't we? We've got men there. You liaise with
them, don't you, Colonel?' He picked out Kostas. 'I'd get on
with it, if I were you. The order'll come through soon enough.'

Kostas stiffened to meet his glance firmly; but he was still
shocked; he had not supposed his work involved 'removing'
an archbishop.

For Kostas, the following days were lit with a light that
shone from the future: his thoughts, his dreams, teemed with

385

landing craft beaching, bombers swarming, the new submarines Greece had bought from Germany sliding through the dark Aegean. Cyprus would be theirs. Still the Archbishop made him uneasy, there was a flicker of lightning round the thought of removing him. But he could not be spared, he was the figurehead of all their enemies. And he wanted Cyprus to go independent, in defiance of Greece, and NATO, and history. Kostas found himself working steadily angrier, when he thought of this cleric sitting safe on his faraway island, pretending to be their conscience, and being a hero to the Greek people when the Government should be the hero. He had a weird dream, where he stood on a globe or curved map of the world, and looking to the east he saw the black denouncing figure standing up tall like a great stake out of the tiny clump of his island, cursing them, condemning them.

The more he thought, the more outraged Kostas grew. For the army had always been loyal to the Church, its rallying cry was 'Greece of the Christian Greeks', it proclaimed the return to Hellenism. And the army now was the genius of Hellenism, the Church should bless it in its work. The Christ-loving armies of the Greeks fought under the blessing of the Church in the past, in the Revolution against the Turk Greek priests led the fighting. The Church itself, with its troops and ranks of black-uniformed priests, was like a second army: it *was* the spiritual army of Greece, the guardian of the spirit of Christian Hellenism. And this spiritual army was strict and militant, it should be the soul of the real army. If the Church and the army became opposed, it would be as if the army were fighting with its soul. Of course, there were atheists in the army who would not care; but Kostas was not one of them. The Archbishop must not bring them to this: he was a traitor to Hellenism.

Alone in his office, but still gingerly, furtively, Kostas took out of his desk a folder, and out of the folder a photograph, which he studied intently, in the manner of a man who kept secretly at work a picture of his girl friend. It showed an upright figure in black robes which fell gracefully downwards in a way that gave him height, height increased again by his tall dark cylindrical hat, which had its own mantle falling to his shoulders. The face framed by these robes was long, the more so because of the drooping nose that sank far down his

386

moustache, and because of the long dense beard; his eyes also were narrowed to slits, sloping downwards. These things together gave his face a look of great patient shrewdness: there was a glint in the eyes behind the folded slit lids.

Kostas's eyes flickered quickly round his office, to the door, to the window, then under his breath, nervously, with the thrill of the forbidden, he started to murmur to the photograph, 'So, Your Beatitude, and what will you do now? Because we're coming for you. Oh yes, your time will soon be up. You thought you were clever, eh? Your tricks have caught you now. You've no friends, Your Beatitude. The Turks know you're weak, and they're driving you back. And we're on the other side, lying in wait. Our men are on the island. EOKA hates you. And you thought you could keep us at bay by tricks. Are you afraid, Your Beatitude? I would pray if I were you. On your knees, Your Beatitude. Down and pray. But that won't save you.' Kostas studied the photo a few moments more, then sighed, and replaced it in his desk.

And soon the officers in the Pentagon heard: there was to be a special meeting on the subject of Cyprus. The Brigadier, the President and the Prime Minister would be there, and the heads of the services. Kostas would be summoned.

The day of the meeting came: officials arrived in dark-shaded cars, in a purr of outriders. Kostas was called, and entered a bright-lit room where field-marshals and admirals sat beside men in dark suits whom he did not know. But he recognized the lean, unconfident figure of the Prime Minister. The President wore full uniform; his raised face was immobile. But all of them were eclipsed by the assured figure of the Brigadier, his bald head gleaming, his sharp cuts of eye trained on the charts, still, tense, a centre of force.

Kostas gave his assessment, and afterwards the discussions continued for a further hour. Then the dignitaries left in their sleek dark projectiles.

It was only days later, and after other quieter meetings, that Kostas heard the decisions arrived at. The contingent of Greek forces, stationed on Cyprus to train the National Guard, would be steadily augmented, till in effect there was a Greek garrison on the island. Links with the leaders of EOKA would be strengthened, and plans coordinated. In due course there would be a revolution, the Archbishop would be a casualty, a new government would be appointed. This government would immediately offer certain territories and rights to the Cypriot Turks, to placate them, while it would quietly owe all allegiance to Athens, and be controlled from there. In a few days the situation would be calm, and immediately they would begin on the massive shipment of arms to the island, secret, disguised as aid, with tanks and missiles inside containers, till all Cyprus was a weapon aimed at Turkey.

'Yes, but when, when will it be?'

'Patience, Kosta,' his superior hummed, 'We must be well prepared, there must be no slips. It could take a year.'

Kostas sighed. 'It's a long wait,' he said.

'No, Kosta, it is not a long wait. It is the proper time. We are moving faster now.' The officer nodded to himself with a certain satisfaction, and then, more confidentially, said, 'You know, Kosta, what happened at the Architecture School was not good – shooting students, deposing a president. And yet, in the long run, it was for the best. We are out of our barracks now, and we won't go back.'

Kostas nodded intensely, thinking: it is true, we have found our leader, we have a destiny. Out of tact for his superior's own sense of greatness, he did not mention the Brigadier by name.

He saluted, departed. So there was to be further delay; and yet, for the first time in many months, Kostas felt serene. For there was a plan: as he marched down the corridor, all his hot thoughts went clear, transparent, and he knew he was seeing the shape of history. There were, in one sequence, *three* coups d'état, three great acts of will and fate. The first coup had brought the National Government to power. The second coup, after the Architecture School, had brought the true tough strength of the army to the fore: it had completed the national revolution in Greece. And the third coup, in Cyprus – that would be the great move, the move beyond their borders, the securing of control of all the Greeks. Then, oil rich, they would expand. On these three foundations would the Greater Greece be built.

Easter came. Kostas travelled to the barracks of his old regiment outside Athens: he wanted to share Easter with good

388

comrades, and he had a further incentive in that both the President of the Nation, and also the Brigadier himself, were going to be present.

It was late, and dark, when he arrived, the celebrations had begun. As he approached through the buildings and trees he heard singing, not just chanting, but full-throated singing. Under the powerful lamps, a huge troop of men were gathered round the regimental chapel, which itself was crammed with senior officers, all singing. Kostas began quietly, then, relaxing in the familiar company, he threw his head back, loosened his strong voice, and sang out tunefully.

He saw his friend Coulis: when the hymn finished, he joined him.

'Ach, Couli, what days these are!' He spoke hoarsely, with contained thrill. 'Now we are moving. Philipides is bringing his regiments up from the south.'

They discussed troop movements: from all over Greece arms and supplies were flowing north-east.

'Vouros has asked for more ammunition,' Coulis said.

'Vouros!' Kostas paused. 'Well, but Couli, what the hell does Vouros want more ammunition for? He's nowhere near the front. And he's got enough tanks, bombs and rockets for doomsday. That man! He just wants more ammunition the way a brigand wants more pistols to stick in his belt.'

'All right, Kosta. But war is war.'

A hush spread outwards from the chapel. Now they heard the voice of the aged priest, winding through his chants like a thin crooked wire; through the doorway they briefly glimpsed the robed figure, busy at the Table of Isaiah. Then the priest came to the door, so they all could see him. He was a gaunt wizened old root of a man, but stern and tough and grim for all his gold-embroidered robes. His thin voice was firm with authority, he addressed the soldiers' tough discipline from his own stern discipline in the Church. This was a priest who knew his duty.

Complete silence under the trees. It was midnight exactly. The old military priest looked severely round, then shouted vigorously.

'Christ is risen!'

'Christ is risen! Christ is risen!' the soldiers cried. Kostas shouted, 'Christ is risen!' All the soldiers shouted, they raised their guns and fired in the air, gunshot rattled into the sky.

The great men emerged from the chapel. The new President was glorious in his uniform, but even here he was still serious, not fully at ease, not part of the celebration. But the Brigadier was different: sharp-featured, bright-eyed, a little more plump than when Kostas last saw him, he chatted and smiled with the other officers, and made a discreet show of camaraderie. His bald head beaded with sweat moved through the gathering in a travelling eddy of admiring faces.

Kostas sighed: if elsewhere in the country was cringing complaint, here still, in the army, was passion and faith, the nation's heart. At the top of his voice he shouted, and others round took up the shout, 'God save the army! Long live the National Government!'

Across the sea in the east, in another and larger church, another celebration had drawn to its close. The entire cathedral was filled to bursting, outside also crowds pressed close, straining to hear and to peer inside.

On a dais in the centre, gloriously robed in jewels and gold, stood the man on whom all eyes were bent: his head was lifted as he chanted the long service, his voice was fine and musical. At last he sang,

'Christ is risen!'

Christ is risen: now the flame from his candle ignites other candles, and passes outwards in flickering lines through the church, till there is a sparkling firmament of candles, and all the voices with one voice chant 'Christ is risen!'

If there is concern for the future behind the solemn face of the Archbishop, as he stands upright as a prophet in the overweight sweltering armour of jewels, round which the crowds of the city press close – if any concern threads him, he betrays no sign as he stands on the dais like the summit of a hill, like the summit of the song that soars through the church.

> Christ is risen from the dead,
> defeating death with death,
> having given the gift of life
> to those in the grave.

3

Of all the new prisoners who came that spring, there was one especially that Vangelis remembered. He came hobbling into the yard on feet that wouldn't flex or bend: and this was a young man, who hobbled in like an old cripple. He could only be twenty, his young face was white and sharp, his black-rimmed eyes were holes into a bin of pain: in spite of the sun he huddled a thick coat round him. Vangelis and the others had also had their feet beaten, and would always limp from the damage done to the small bones of the foot, but still they were not so injured. Whether because he had resisted too much, or because his family were poor nobodies, or because his young good looks drew out something in his torturer that could not stop, he had been more badly beaten than anyone they had seen.

He limped a short distance, then sat on the ground with his back against a wall. Vangelis and Stamatis introduced themselves, but he hardly registered. He had the dazzled air of having lost somewhere a part of himself.

He was, he said later, a poet; and, brokenly, he told the prisoners that the poets were with them. Certain writers in Athens were protesting against the Junta, they would publish nothing while the Junta was in power.

'That'll make the President shit in his pants!'

The young man's pinched face, which was sharp from pain, and looked young and old at the same time, blanched in anger.

'We protest in many ways.'

Vangelis quickly said, 'You fought, didn't you, Thoma?'

Stamatis joined in, turning the talk, and Thomas' face regained its normal, its terribly haggard, aged look.

Later, pressed to it, he recited some of his works. Hunched to the wall, white-faced, in his frail voice he spoke the verses confidently. The poem was aflame with flowering images, a broken iron head descended in the sky, thorns blinded watching gods, the curses of endurance fell in burning dust on peacocks, shitflies and orang-utans. The poem was a tribute to the prisoners' sufferings, and they nodded and smiled, encouraging, but they made no contact with the beautiful humourless words.

'Bravo!' they said, without conviction.

Thomas' sunk keen eyes read their faces. Perhaps he realized that it was himself also he was describing, and found that his wild hymn of denunciation flew over the top of his own pain: for, confessing he had not himself joined the writers' strike, he quickly switched to a different poem, a political satire on the first dictatorship. The then president was recognizable as the dwarf mother-in-law declaiming, bouncing, haranguing the family from a precarious chair on the kitchen table in a shrill crazy speech of squawks, each squawk a terrible-wonderful senseless tangle of mixed political metaphor. And the long-suffering son-in-law imprisoned in a plaster cast so complete that he could only pee by looking in a wing mirror mounted on his fixed outstretched Heil Hitler arm, was Greece. His speeches were a deep-throbbing one-toned almost stifled music.

The audience laughed, cheered, said over lines and snatches, and bits of idiom and slang that reminded them of home. Thomas laughed too, while his starved eyes fed hungrily on their applause: visibly he strengthened, he seemed fuller in the huddled coat.

'Encore!' they shouted. 'Give us another!' But he was tired; he nodded agreeably, pleased, relaxed, almost asleep.

The following day Thomas limped to the prison library.

'You'll find nothing there,' Stamatis called.

'But perhaps I can write there.' He showed them an old bouzouki, that he had picked up in the corridor: it had lain around the prison for ages. He wanted to write ballads, like the ballads of the klephts, on the war against the dictatorship.

'The library's all right,' Vangelis told him, 'I work there, on and off.'

'Do you write?' Thomas asked him.

'No I talk, I'm a lawyer. But it's true, I have been scribbling something. There's one thing about prison, it allows you time. You'll write lots of poems here.'

In the friendly atmosphere of the prison Thomas began

slowly to open from the clench of pain he had been in when he came. He remained reserved, often he was abstracted, either in past suffering or in his imagination; and as the days passed the prisoners did not feel they came to know him better. But he liked to be in company, not speaking much but listening to what they said: their talk wasn't poetry, but it seemed that after his long isolation, he took sustenance simply from being where speech was.

They did not hear his new poems. One morning a squad of guards abruptly collected him and his papers. The other prisoners only heard later that he had been taken back to Athens. The authorities had decided that he knew more than he had told them.

He did not return, and it was a further month before the prisoners were told, by one of the guards, that Thomas had a brain haemorrhage while under interrogation. The authorities blamed it on the drugs which his liability to haemorrhage proved he had been taking. Between them the prisoners wrote down the poems they remembered. Of him they heard nothing more. In the blink of an eye he had come to them, and been withdrawn again, tortured further, and erased from life.

The cumbersome laden vessel of the prison slowly drove through the new doldrum year. Though Thomas had gone, others arrived, including many who had earlier been given amnesty. In a dark spirit Vangelis continued his book; at times, by demand, he gave seminars in law, though it amused him bitterly to be teaching prisoners the knowhow of the outside world, while they all sank together in the pit of the forgotten. He could be free in thought, but his world was shrinking to the prison itself. Sometimes in the dead of night he woke, and visited the storehouse where his hopes and ambitions were laid up. In the musty dark he made out their shapes through the dustcloths and the fur of dust: but if he pulled off the cloths, he found only a decay of rust, and replaced them tenderly with stone in his heart.

He looked at himself in the washroom mirror. His body was robust, from tilling the rock-hard prison soil. His cheeks had lost their waxy overweight look, much of his fat was turned to sinew, he could say to himself – there's a sturdy, strong-backed man. And his eyes were black and bright. But still, when he saw himself, he shook his head: was that man a lawyer, with spark and zest – an intellectual, a politician? Forget it, you can see what he is: a stocky, swarthy mountain peasant. Prison had made him resemble his ancestors, scratching their living among barren peaks: a dour breed, aggressive, with vigilant small dark eyes. That's what he was, why shouldn't he look it? – bleak men, a bleak life, barren. His city self was gone. He had his defiance still, he was unconquered; and perhaps his expression had been theirs also, closed faces, obstinate, defying harsh weather, the hostile sun: it was a look which he felt had sunk into his skull.

Spring arrived: showers pelted, gusts veered, small white clouds moved quickly through the sky, and even the few thorny shrubs in the prison yard developed buds, that globed and burst in fleshy stars. When the prisoners went outside on labour parties, they found the stony clinker of island hillside covered by flowers, tiny blooms speckled thick, and rich petals yawning. On still nights, the scents from the small garden of Christoforos hovered in a cloud, and made one corner of the prison sweet.

This growth and freshness came in strange mockery. Vangelis thought longingly of Chryssa. He could not see her because the new Junta had imposed additional obstructions in the way of visiting. And only very seldom, after weeks of delay, mail got through. Chryssa, and their home in Athens, were remote as the moon.

To shock his memory back to life, he recalled their fights in the early days: then she would be wild. He infuriated her once in his law chambers, and she hurled his files about the room, making huge havoc. When they lived outside Athens and used to drive everywhere, they'd quarrel in the car. Once, when he said something that offended her greatly, she attacked the car itself, she kicked in the glove compartment, kicked at the door, kicked under the dashboard where the cables were, she threatened to reduce the vehicle to a chassis and engine travelling the road. And in those days he was the masterful male, he picked her up in mid-quarrel once and hurled her on the bed, her shoe hit the ceiling like a rocket, at the shock they both laughed, and were making love as the flakes of plaster fell.

'That was a marriage!' He shook his head. How was she now? Quietly he wondered – Suppose she's seeing someone? The question, which had crept into his mind so calmly, sharpened to a piercing hurt. He said she shouldn't waste her life: but he clenched his eyes, he huddled forward, this thought could suck him hollow from inside. Anger, frustration, churned in him thicker than blood: hot, black, like lava rising: bodies kissing, bodies in bed: rising violence, he'd smash

He shivered, shook himself: what was he turning into? He'd had such pangs before, but never so biting, so brutal. And what were these thoughts? They were nothing but suspicions, mad fancies, while his mind festered. Yet it took him an hour to shake them off.

One day he picked up the old bouzouki Thomas had found, and took it into the prison yard. A string was undone: he wound it in again, and fiddled the pegs. He couldn't play it, he was no musician: but as he sat in the corner in the hot dust, the sterile stones behind him, he began to pluck and plink, he tried to make a sound that was not discordant.

As he tilted his ear to the notes, his eyes wandered the brown walls – till he found himself staring at one of the watch turrets. Was the guard up there signalling? He was definitely looking at him, and making odd movements with his hands. Then Vangelis realized: the guard was moving his fingers as though he were playing the bouzouki. He held an imaginary instrument at a certain angle, and plucked. Vangelis attempted to follow suit, and the guard nodded.

In the following afternoons, when that guard was in the watch turret, he would give Vangelis silent lessons in playing the bouzouki. He did so in short spells, when the officers were away: he did not want to be seen to fraternize. But one afternoon, when he was patrolling in the yard itself, he offered Vangelis a cigarette, and they discussed bouzouki music. He asked Vangelis why he was inside, and shrugged blankly when Vangelis explained; as for himself, he worked here because the money was better than elsewhere on the island. He was saving up so he could open a taverna.

Vangelis began to play tunes: the guard in his turret nodded the rhythm while down in the yard Vangelis plucked and strummed. He wore his makeshift plectra to splinters, and his nails raw, but he made music. In the sultry yard, louder than the buzz of flies and the sawing of the cicadas, the irregular tinny notes plinked from the bouzouki, and rippled where the hot air shimmered, danced in a corner where the dust-devil whirled, and like zigzagging butterflies climbed the walls note by note till they circled the watchtowers, and fluttered over the walls to freedom.

4

Summer advanced. The sun became a scorching eye, hot to destroy life. The steaming air almost ceased to move, and a white stifling haze settled over Athens like a curse. Occasionally, from excavations in the brown hills outside the city, the distant booming of dynamite echoed over the rooftops; occasionally too came a sharper, nearer bang as a bomb went off. Though everyone hid where possible in shadow, everyone was exposed, for everywhere were watching eyes – so many people the Government paid to watch other people – anxious eyes, guarded eyes, eyes in windows, eyes sharp in haggard faces: under the shrivelling scrutiny of the fireball in the sky the great city of gregariousness became more than ever the city of mistrust and fear. Every street stall and kiosk sold little blue amulets to ward off the evil eye; but there weren't enough, to Chryssa it seemed all Athens was the city of the evil eye. Police vigilance intensified. There was no safe place under this scalding sun; and no safe time, for the darkest, coolest hours of the night were the hours of greatest danger: then the arrests were made.

They did not take Chryssa, their interest was in other opponents and other groups now. She and Michael could only watch as one resistance organization after another was caught, and their members tortured till someone broke, and new information came, and yet new arrests were made. For if one business prospered in this tormented exhausted demoralized city, it was that underworld industry of questioning and pain; it prospered now and thrived in so many places, in cellars, warehouses, homes, wherever two or three policemen collected with a victim to hand. The security forces were hated as they never had been. As the hatred grew, so their reasons to be busy grew, so much so that their numbers grew, and in the turning of this slow dragging wheel of pain the city was grinding its people to powder.

Already, in early summer, security harvested. In a garden brilliant with cascading bougainvillaea a policeman stepped back slowly, paying out the wire to a listening device. On a hot summer's night a professor from the University was attempting from directions given him by a friend to make a bomb, when the explosives went off in his hands, and took with them a hand; in bright morning the police collected him newly bandaged from hospital and added their treatment. On a summer's midday Chryssa's friend Simos was visited on his balcony by men in shirtsleeves, and led away to offices where for many days he glimpsed no sun, no day.

In an Athens street, on her way to see Michael, Chryssa met her nephew Alexis. She had scarcely seen him since the Architecture School, she was struck by how changed he was from the schoolboy nephew she used to know. His young face looked mature, tough, battered; the shapeless young nose had become distinct and hard; his mouth had a permanent crinkle of irony and there were odd bulges and swellings round his jaw. He was taller too, she had to look up to him. But what struck her most was his bitter voice: it was new to her to hear this broken but still youthful voice, from which in the past she had heard jokes and demands for sweets, speaking in such harsh, hardbitten, withering tones.

'You're involved in resistance, aren't you, Alexi?'

His gaze sharpened quickly.

'You *must* be careful.' She felt herself very much – at this moment – the aunt.

'I'm careful,' he said, with a fidget of frustration. 'I know what these new ones are like. Do you know, they even follow me. Would you believe it? I go to school, and they follow me.'

'They're insane! They employ half the country to watch the other half.'

'How are things with you, aunt?'

'I've had bad news. Our friend Simos has been arrested. Have you heard of him? He's a lawyer like Vangelis, a great big man, a giant –'

'Yes, I know, Simos Dimakopoulos. He's been sent to Yaros.'

'Alexi!' Chryssa started, lost colour. 'How do you know that?'

Quietly, with the wry modesty of someone much older, he said, 'I know people.'

He told her what he knew, from relatives of prisoners, about Yaros. The old prison, on that salt rock of island, had been refurbished for the enemies of the new dictatorship. The regime there was harsher than in other prisons: there was a routine of the day, whereby the prisoners were put, one by one, in a large tub or drum, and spun round till they were sick; they were sent stumbling up a ladder to the roof of a two-storey building, and then tripped and kicked off it, so they fell spinning into a pit of sand. 'It's time for the tumble,' the guards would joke. The island seemed run on a system of sadism: the guards were bullied by the officers almost as brutally as they themselves bullied the prisoners, and by the same token, sometimes, they were fucked by the officers as they themselves sometimes fucked the prisoners. At the end, Alexis said, 'People die there.'

'Don't Alexi,' Chryssa's eyes screwing momentarily shut. And he stopped; he had gone further than he meant to.

'I'm sorry,' he said; while she watched him, mute, her eyes filling. Evidently he thought she was thinking only of the prisoners, but she was thinking of him. She remembered him as a child, pensive, big-eyed, meekly holding Leonidas' plump hand; and laughing, joking, silly with excitement, pestering his mother for one more chocolate; and sitting cross-legged, thoughtful, his eyes on Vangelis at a family picnic. And now she saw him in his last teens, scathing, sick with anger and frustration, bent to the fight as if all of Greece were the father he hated. Danger hung over him, and torture if they caught him, and possibly death. 'Alexi,' she murmured, 'won't you wait –'

'I can't wait. The things that happened at the School. . . . You don't know Rena, she was one of the students, I saw her up on the gate when the tank came in. . . .'

He stopped, his pale face quivered, suddenly his youth showed: he lowered his head. Then, as he raised his face, the tears, that had started to his eyes, dried. Chryssa saw there only a mature grief.

While they lingered, the throb of a distant engine grew louder, and from behind a massive apartment block a green helicopter flew forward, flying so fast so low it looked huge,

399

shocking, though what Chryssa immediately thought was how like a gigantic dragonfly it was, its bulbous head down, its green body tapering back to a point, its blur of blades like the haze of wings: unreal, surreal, too big, too low, it shot along the wall of buildings, in seconds it had vanished, its noise trailing after it like a long tail.

Alexis rolled his eyes briefly to heaven, heaved his shoulders in an ironic shrug. 'They're in a hurry, that's not good.' His face now was ageless, composed, sardonic.

He looked up, he must be on his way. 'Bless you, Alexi,' she said, and kissed him.

Watching him walk up the road – with a quick step, too free of fear – she suddenly felt, as she hadn't in years, close to her sister. Every day Patra must feel that anxiety – cuttingly when she saw Alexis, and numbly, constantly, on the days when she didn't see him.

In the dim yellow station the train was arriving: the varnished wooden carriages rattled to a stop. As she stepped on board, she thought: am I doing right, to leave all this? Then she wondered at the trick her mind had played, for she had felt, boarding the train that would take her to Michael, that she was leaving Greece, the nightmare country. In their few months together, his flat had come to be that for her – the refuge island, somewhere else.

She watched the window, a picture of black tunnel or night outside, with her face reflected back, pale as her own ghost riding beside her. What would Alexis say, if he knew what I'm doing? But he wouldn't say anything – but he'd be thinking about Vangelis. Yet I don't feel bad about Vangelis – perhaps I should, but there's a whole side of my life I've just – shut up, boarded up. But there was such death there – When will Vangelis come? And my feelings about Michael change all the time. The train rattled in the tunnel, she glimpsed wall slipping by: it's going very fast, will it crash, a wreck in pitch blackness under the ground? The eyes of her reflection looked back haunted. That's not how I feel! She smiled, and her ghost smiled: a happy ghost dimming as the light outside changed, they were slanting upwards.

Blink of dazzle, daylight in the train: always at this point her spirit soared, as the track and the train rose from the ground and continued rising: she saw housetops, smokestacks, hills between apartment blocks. It rattled but it flew, the train. It's all black in Athens, and I just feel happy travelling to Michael: and I don't know how we'll be today. A red-tiled roof flew past, deep-grooved, in rippling corrugation: and light leaves of plane tree, palm spikes. The train's got wings: it glided, hanging on the air as it slowed.

She left the metro, crossed an avenue, and presently was walking down a small road strewn with heads of flowers, bedraggled stems, a confetti of petals. Business was over in the flower market: buckets of water, with floating leaves, stood among old papers and straggled lengths of raffia; there was a sharp metallic clatter as empty buckets were stacked, or rolled against each other. Curious pleasant atmosphere of a market at the close of day: men and women, in the old clothes they used for work, stood round with shrewd but relaxed faces, shaking heads, going tst tst tst poh poh poh as they reviewed business. From childhood she liked markets.

'Good day,' she called, like a familiar customer.

'Good day,' they called brightly, cheered by her cheerfulness.

'Ah, you didn't sell those.' She'd spotted some survivors, bright cornflowers in a bucket.

'Those aren't for sale, madam. They are beyond price.'

'Cornflowers beyond price?'

'Well, all right. Twenty drachs.'

Chryssa hadn't bargained, she had simply stood by, liking the flowers. The flower seller cheerfully wrapped the blooms, and didn't trouble to count the coins.

'You are the flower, madam. Good evening.'

It seemed years since shopkeepers had flirted with her. She laughed, for it was true, she had chosen the blue flowers to go with her dress, so she could be part of the bouquet she gave Michael.

He, in his doorway, kissed her and liked the flowers; but afterwards looked slightly tense.

'Are you working?' she asked, disappointed.

'Hard,' he said. He led the way to his small kitchen, which seemed afloat with the ingredients of something – there were aubergines, mincemeat, cheese, spices, salad.

'What's this, Michael?'

'It will be – Imambaldi – the Imam swooned.'

Amused, she watched him quarrel with his Greek cookbook, which refused to state quantities, and told him simply to take a piece of this, add some of that, a pinch of spice, a little garlic, and cook until it's done. He concentrated gravely on his marshalled ingredients. Anyone less like a chef she had not seen: slender, bony, looking in his difficulties like a young Don Quixote, he seemed someone who didn't eat, let alone cook. She saw he was best left.

'I'll put on music.'

She sat in his living room, absorbing the light-hearted music till she felt she was afloat in it, dissolved in its notes. It was music from some German or Austrian court, as she listened she thought: it's like talk. The ripples and skirls of tune interlaced, met, interrupted, retorted to each other in laughter. It was the music of elegant court conversation. She sighed: if only we could go out tonight, see people. When she had lived alone, she was settled alone: now she was with Michael, she wanted other company too. I *am* gregarious, she reflected. But she didn't see friends when she was with Michael: and it was her choice, to keep her worlds apart.

In tune with her mood, a slow movement played: it touched the heart lightly, with a sweet unhurting reminder of pain. All the sadness in her seemed repeated in the delaying, limpid notes: the complicated causes of sadness withdrew, it was sadness itself, and sweetness; it was love in absence, a thinking of love. She looked at the shadow-puppet on the wall, noticing how carefully Michael had worked on it. Then she looked at Michael: in the doorframe he looked very tall, keen-limbed, pleasantly intent. Evidently his cooking was working better, he seemed to her now to be conducting the meal. She thought of the foreign life she lost when, years since, she hurried back to Greece: she was living it now.

Looking up from the table, Michael watched her listen. She sat quite still, as if every part of her attended to the notes. I don't listen like that, he thought: he mostly played music while he did other things, he was bad at sitting still. And he thought of Chryssa as in constant activity, following a rhythm from her family, her country, the torn lives: he marvelled at her stillness now, he felt he could see the notes pass through her. He watched, loving, and returned to his tossing of salad.

But the food, when they ate, got little mention: he was quickly businesslike, telling her his news. From his own enquiries, from other correspondents, he had details of troop movements. It didn't show in Athens, but in rumour, in report, there was throughout Greece a steady mobilization. Long convoys, tanks and artillery, drove steadily into the east. With every landing, new quantities of Greek soldiers, many in disguise and some in uniform, disembarked on the Greek islands next to Turkey.

'They're preparing for war.'

'They *can't* want war, Michael.'

'NATO can't – but who knows what these people want?'

'It must be a bluff, to make sure they keep the oil.'

'Suppose the Turks call their bluff? This "military government" has become so military, I don't see how they can avoid shooting someone.'

'No!' she said vehemently, and Michael stopped, in self-reproach: he had been speaking like a foreigner, not really imagining the cost of war.

But she asked him, 'What do you think will happen?'

'Who knows? It may be an oil war, maybe they'll move on Cyprus.'

'They *must* keep out of Cyprus.' Her voice throbbed, her brow knit tight: he was startled by her intensity. Their mealtime pleasure was quite shattered now.

'You're thinking about the Archbishop?'

'Yes, of course.'

Michael paddled his cutlery: they had a hidden disagreement about the Archbishop. He ventured, 'Isn't he a Machiavellian character?'

'Well, that's the English view. To us he is a hero of resistance.'

'All right. Still, he's not a hero to EOKA.'

She half closed her eyes at him. 'Don't try to be smart, Michael. EOKA wanted union with Greece, but union with Greece was never possible. The Turks would have jumped in straight away.'

He had stopped arguing, but she had not. 'I don't know about Machiavellianism, Michael, but if you want to lead a tiny country to independence, in the twentieth century, with the big powers breathing over you, then you have a difficult task – then, believe me, you need to be very clever, and very subtle, courage isn't enough. He has no army, the powers he had to deal with are a hundred times – a thousand times – the size of his forces. No, he needs to be very shrewd. Thank God he is.'

Michael nodded, but she hardly noticed what Michael did. 'And perhaps it's true, they'll try and get him, that's what all the soldiers are for. Because he is a free island, he's the bit of Greece that's free of them. Oh, I hope he beats them, I hope he throws them out, they *must* not catch him.'

Michael watched her, wary of her passion, also awed. The conflict had come very clear, the forces had separated, and gathered in armies. There was the Brigadier and his Junta, with their tanks and guns; and the Archbishop in the east who still defied them, who spoke out with a fierce denouncing voice. Chryssa looked to him, following each manoeuvre he made: and in this she was at one with the nation. She didn't need to feel physically engaged, as she did when she went to the Architecture School: passions were larger, more extreme, wherever she was she could feel herself part of an invisible multitude. He saw it in her raised bright face, cheekbones clear, eyes remote – as he saw it in other Greeks when the Archbishop was mentioned – all the souls in the nation drew together in one, an invisible communion that bent its urging and wishing to Cyprus.

He saw this communion: he was outside it. He couldn't be together with her, as she, at such times, was together with Greece. He felt a separation.

She told him about her meeting with Alexis: and it was clear to Michael, though she didn't say this, that that at this moment she felt closer to Alexis than she did to him. Of course – how else could it be? She had a sparkle of current, a certain bright tension, when she spoke to him.

Yet after their meal they went out on the balcony: and as they sat and talked, she returned from her place in the chorus. Her face, which had been intense, static, hardly individual, became mobile again with tender expression. She liked the Imambaldi, she liked his decision to cook with care, when previously he had been a mechanical eater. They were calmly together, watching the warm night wake the city. His eye cast

404

round for spies or watchers, for sometimes he was followed, though they had not again driven a car at him; but the streets were clear.

As they got up to go in, Chryssa stopped where she stood, closed her eyes, said to the night 'I pray he escapes them.' And Michael thought: the British are on Cyprus, perhaps at last they will play a part, trip the Junta. He prayed for that.

It was only when, in bed, he bent over to kiss her, that his earlier sense of separation returned: for as she raised her mouth to his she slightly turned her head, so she was rising both towards him and to avoid him, and at the same time she closed her eyes. Often she did this – perhaps she was unaware – and each time he saw in the dimness those large globes of closed lids, he knew, he knew – what by daylight he kept denying – that she didn't want to see him when they made love, she wanted to forget it was Michael she was loving. It was seldom that they spoke of Vangelis, but every time Michael saw those shut eyes he knew that Vangelis was there, between them, in her thoughts, in her heart, in the heart of her love.

They had loved, and he lay beside her cold. Whenever this happened, whenever Vangelis came between them in love, he felt annulled, cancelled, from being something in her life, he shrank in seconds to being nothing at all. He had blamed himself, taking Vangelis' place, and all the time the truth was otherwise, Vangelis was there, he could not be usurped. Michael moaned, coming again to this irremovable fact: then, he could not help it, he wanted her to forget Vangelis, he lay in the dark, cold but acid, he was jealous of Vangelis. He had loved Chryssa years, lived with her months, jealousy filled him, jealous resentment, jealous dislike, he wanted Vangelis out of the way. But always at this point he thought: how *can* I let myself be jealous of Vangelis? When he's suffered so much, when I've wronged him so much, how can I, on top of that, let jealousy attack him? He should hate me. Then in jealousy, guilt, self disgust, he felt himself shrinking to a shrivelled obscene creature of envy, venomous, something crawling that hissed and spat, the worm, the devil in man, the small coiled reptile of jealous self – something that should be stamped on, crunched out, but it couldn't be, it had a hard carapace, it was there at the base of him glaring with yellow eyes from where it hunched nursing poison.

405

Stealthily he slipped from the sheets, and slid on silent pads out of the room. Stealth came easy when he was in this state: and he couldn't be still, he couldn't lie down in the grip of these thoughts. He coiled, paced: he had said he had come as the friend, the helper, but he was the enemy, the outsider, the betrayer. He had lost touch completely with the state he had been in a few hours before, of pleased loving Chryssa, the two of them a couple. When things were good between them, he didn't think about the black side: he knew of it abstractly, he didn't face it. Then suddenly he tipped into the underworld of guilt, despair, and love of Chryssa out of sight.

He paced, worried, shivered, turned; put on the light, put it off, went out on the balcony and came in again. That habitual restlessness of his old normal state, which recently he had relaxed from, returned now magnified, a huge, a terrible restlessness, literally that, he was a person who could not, anywhere, rest. Was that what his unrest always was, guilt or a premonition of guilt? But that wasn't so, he was seeking something surely? But what was he seeking? He could see less than ever, he only knew he was receding, falling, backwards, downwards away from Chryssa.

He returned to the balcony, feeling cooler, settling towards a level despair. Each time he plunged in this cycle it was so: as he felt himself falling away from Chryssa, his jealous resentment of Vangelis declined, he accepted his guilt, he had wronged Vangelis but also he paid for it, he would never truly be with Chryssa. Visible, invisible, in prison, in death, Vangelis was beside her – it was right, it must be so, and he was far from both of them, in the darkness outside. They were Greece and he was the foreigner, soon to be the outcast.

He looked out from his balcony: the air had a freshness, it must be three, four in the morning, but even at this hour Athens was not quiet. From the main road near his flat came the noise of engines racing, squealing tyres, he saw white and red lights flashing; and far across the city he heard other traffic and a distant racket of music. Over towards the sea, hot light from the bouzoukis hovered on the darkness. Unsleeping city, there was nothing to soothe him here: at least its restlessness gave him a partner.

They lived in a swing of extremes, Chryssa also. She didn't so easily feel guilty for love, she had perhaps a sane southern sense that love affairs might happen within a loving marriage; she didn't swing as he did between free love cant and abject guilt, the hypocritic puritan after all. But he might say something very slight that however was complacent, that reminded her of his foreignness, of the oddity, disloyalty, of their affair: then he saw her brow knit, her face tauten, he knew with fear, with misgiving, that she had switched to hostility, he watched her self-questioning and fedupness grow, frustration with him and self-frustration building up to the split, the days apart in hostile isolation. At any place, in any conversation, that trapdoor could open, down they pitched.

He waited, smoked, pondered; as time passed and he grew colder, he also began to grow tired. He wondered, should he try to creep back into the bedroom? But how could he approach her, feeling as he did? He couldn't simply lie down again beside her, like an insomniac husband finally tiring. He put on more clothes and sat on the balcony, realizing, as he huddled tighter while the night grew cooler, that the distant lights and car lights were less acid and dazzling than they had been: slowly the blue-black overhead was giving way to a shadowy greyness. In the cold hour, the black barrier of buildings near him began to separate in shuttered blocks, grey and peeling.

He watched, fascinated: the sun was still invisible, but below he heard voices, a puttering engine. A small three-wheel truck turned into the street, and stopped. The market was stirring: a few voices called to each other, while the doors of separate booths were opened. A tailboard dropped with a sharp bang, the first blooms emerged, a dim glowing of yellow, pink, red, in the grey abyss.

So now, unhappy but used to his unhappiness, feeling tired and drained, he was occupied watching, like a slow hypnosis, the opening of the market. In the growing light lorries unloaded: from under their canvas what seemed a cornucopia, a river of flower heads, flowed. Large armfuls of rainbow blooms seemed to walk of themselves, bouquets with legs, to fill steadily the separate sheds, till the grey ring of tarmac round the central pavilion began to be hidden beneath clustered blue, yellow, bronze and flame-coloured flowers, a marvellous jigsaw of colours among chatting goodhumoured morning voices, while a glance in the east showed the dazzling jewel of young sun standing over the hills.

He must have nodded off and dozed for a time, for when he blinked his eyes again the circle of colours down below was complete and busy voices rose, energetic, shrill, arguing, bargaining, while trucks and three-wheelers and motorcycles and pedestrians came and went with clustered blooms and bunches and gross conglomerations of flowers: all in bright sunlight, while a dense cloud of scent, richly mingled, unbelievably sweet, rose in a steady stream with the busy hum of trade. He realized he was warm, he sat in hot sun, the city air was mild: and turning his head to look indoors, he saw Chryssa sitting in one of his armchairs, which she had brought into the doorframe so she sat in the sun: her legs curled under her, her face peaceful however their night had been. As he took her in, her yellow-brown eyes smiled to him. Evidently she had sat there a long time, watching him sleep. He felt oddly exposed, caught out: she knew something of him that he would never know. But perhaps he was a better person asleep, for she was gazing still with such tender affection. He felt oddly humbled, powerless, gazing back in surprise and gratitude.

For some time, in the daze of waking, disregarding the stiffness he inherited from his chair, he turned between the concentric circles of the sunlit flower market – looking down into its rainbows was like looking up into heaven – and Chryssa, sitting in the sun so calm and still and tender she seemed like a visiting goddess materialized on her altar while the scents of flowers streamed round her. Her smile was amused – amused at his surprise, and at being caught out in her surreptitious watch on him.

'My love,' she said with a cadence. He gazed: it was the first time she'd said it.

Lightly, in a swirl of silk, she uncoiled from the chair and stepped inside to bring coffee. Sipping, they sat in the sun, naming blooms. Moved by the flower trade now hectic below them, Michael reminisced about his fruit-farm childhood. How curious that his childhood surfaced now, for he was always speaking to Chryssa about other countries, but he had not once mentioned his English youth; now he wanted to. He described climbing in the fruit trees and falling out of them; and early mornings in the orchards, avenues of trees with a foliage of cobwebs, dewshot and shining, and his father moving among the trees, a tall figure in wellingtons, his large check shirt loose on lean shoulders, a lean chapped tanned face, who seemed to the young Michael preternaturally tall, reaching an arm into a tree as if he were reaching deliberately into the sky, gently touching the fruit and turning it slightly while with thoughtful eyes he studied it.

He realized, as he talked, he was not having to delve in his memories, the past had come forward with energy to join him. Ignorant of the apple trade, Chryssa was intrigued by his orchards, and by the cool barn of boxed apples, in towers of trays, he described to her.

'You and your barn,' she laughed.

'You and your warehouses.'

'Yes,' she said, 'that's true, we feel the same about them.'

'It's because they've both got lots of room, you can keep things safe in them.'

'They're like memory,' she said.

He looked up quickly. 'Yes. Let's be more than memories, love.'

She smiled. They talked on, pleasantly abstracted, as if their lives were clear streams collecting in a pool. At moments like this they had an ease together they never used to have: and with time this ease grew steadily more sure, whatever their crises, as the good times they did have added together. Michael wondered at the changes of the night: till the growing heat, and noise of traffic round the corner, woke them to thoughts of business, and the silver glint of patrolling fighters, tiny in the sky but hugely screaming, returned their minds to the movement of armies.

To Chryssa and Michael the troop movements are reports only; in the chat of Athens they are bluff and bravura, brandishing the sword; to Kostas, in his office deep in the Pentagon, they are markers on maps, or small lights on wide screens, that converge and cluster; but high in Macedonia, in the arm of Greece reaching far into the east, they have another aspect. For here the convoy passes through the village street, and it passes without end. Tanks reverberate down the tight passage taking fences and flower pots with them; they skid as they turn on the smooth stones of the square, gashing rock and powdering it to a white dust like sugar; and away uphill they rumble between other close houses, whose warped and sagging casements and balconies tremble and totter in the smoke and fume and thick haze of dust. On every balcony a white coating damps the scarlet geraniums. Undeterred by the smother the old men under the plane tree watch motionless, like rocks in mist. The café owner stands in his doorway cursing the army's haste, for thousands are passing, and none of them stop for a drink or a meal. The village priest, with his wispy straggles of beard, inches down the cobbles and stands with a trembling hand to his mouth as he keeps losing count of the vehicles that pass, none of which stop for his blessing. On the promontory of a high balcony, the star of the village, in a flaring crimson dress, her face made up pale, her lips made up crimson, blows smoke rings to pass the time, and uncrosses and recrosses her milk-white legs, as the soldiers pass and none of them stop for her. Vehemently the villagers talk and argue; from high paths and rooftops donkeys and chickens look down.

Night comes on and the only change is that the tanks and trucks put on their headlights, and hours into the night the village hardly sleeps, while harsh lights and spokes of shadow wheel across their ceilings. To either side of the village, the snake of moving lights stretches away into distance.

At the first cockcrow the boy is up, and begins herding the goats from their field beside the village to the higher slopes: and the dim streets are still, there is not a tank, not a truck, not a jeep, not a motorbike: the army has vanished as if it never came. The village cocks crow triumphantly over the enemy they have driven away.

As the boy climbs, light flows over the lower landscape, whitening the receding cover of mist from which the tops of the poplars project like spikes. But there seem to be more trees than before, or too many trees. As he climbs further and the sun rises higher and the mist disappears, a broad fall of light bathes the eastern plain, and he knows that what he saw in the distance, and thought a new forest, is not that: it is the army itself. He can hardly see the tanks, they are so far away; but he cannot mistake them, for there are so many of them, and trucks, and armoured cars, and guns, and rocket launchers, and fields of tents. As far as he can see to the end of the world the shelving plain is covered with brown armour, all still and at peace in the thinning haze, in the silver light of morning.

In the still shadowy hills at his back a thin trickle of sound now grows now fades, tiny in distance, till on the empty road he makes out a single light, a late headlamp in the morning, a solitary motorcyclist, khaki, a dispatch rider, buzzing tiny like an insect out of the west, roaring through the village, and speeding away with his messages into the east.

Cyprus

Such a sweltering furnace day it had been in the humid oven of Nicosia. Now the sun was low, there was a blessing of shade in the forecourt of the presidential palace, as the Secretary to the Ministry of the Interior left his car, and walked hurriedly into the deep arcade. In the shadows there, soldiers, heavily armed, stood guard; beyond them, a group of plain-clothes officers, chatting desultorily, glanced up swiftly, placed him, and nodded him through.

He was ushered into a bare white room. The droop-featured face of the Archbishop looked up from the large table where he studied papers: his half-closed eyes appraised the visitor.

'Please sit down, Mr Secretary,' he said, with formality, with courtesy, with a slight warmth of benignity, and returned to his papers. The Secretary watched the motionless black-robed figure: he seemed so still in thought that he made hot room cool.

With a deep breath, the Archbishop put the papers neatly aside. 'I have awaited your report.'

The Secretary started with nervous stumbles, 'Your Beatitude knows that this man we have arrested is of special importance, he is young but he is high in EOKA, we are sure there are many things he has to tell us, but as yet. . . . It is slow work, Your Beatitude. . . .'

The Archbishop stilled him with a raised hand, and in his habitual grave, somewhat thick voice, that paused a trace between each word, he enquired, 'Do we have, as a result of this arrest, the information we seek?'

'Not yet, Your Beatitude, but we expect much, we know he has contacts with the mainland, and contacts with the Greek officers in the National Guard. He has been the go-between with the accomplices of EOKA in Athens. Yes, we expect to know many things. . . .'

But he paused. The down-slanting eyes of the Archbishop

rested steadily on him: they were solemn, opaque, above such details as he was giving. He could not tell what the Archbishop wanted him to say.

Gravely, with emphasis, the Archbishop said, 'It is of the first importance that we get from him all his information.'

The Secretary slightly frowned. In his mind's eye he saw the young defiant face they were interrogating: the black trapped eyes gazing with desperate hunger like a man with a spinal injury. The man was passionate, fanatical, a patriot in his way: he would resist.

The eyes of the Archbishop rested firmly on the Secretary, in a steady reinforcement of what he had said.

The Archbishop stood up. 'Thank you, Mr Secretary.'

Dismissed, the Secretary withdrew, in an awkward, stooping movement that was half way between crossing himself and bowing.

The Archbishop slowly stretched his arms and worked his shoulders. Then he left his office and went into the large vestibule, where he conferred briefly, with a sharpened practical face, with the officer in command of his auxiliary guard. Presently a convoy of cars drew up at the veranda outside, and the Archbishop, and a troop of soldiers and plain-clothes men, stepped into these, and drove down through the trees to throbbing Nicosia.

As they drove through the winding streets he raised his hand in blessing to those who greeted him. The driver watched him nervously in the mirror; some evenings the Archbishop would chat, but today he said not a word.

They were nearing the new archiepiscopal palace. It was not large, but in the evening light and through the trees it shone as they approached. As he left his car and his guard, and walked inside, he relaxed truly: he had built it, it was his home. The walls were hung with paintings he had collected: they showed heroic scenes from the War of Liberation, with powerful figures in windswept tunics and skirts facing danger with storming eyes, defying the Infidel. As he took off his outer robes and his hat, he gazed at the rich colours of these paintings, and drank in their courage.

He ordered a briki of coffee from his servant and went out into the garden. For once, he had no reception, no appointment, no mountain of paperwork. The cool breath of evening brushed his bald head; absently he watched the breeze move through the garden, turning up the white backs of the olive leaves in slow waves. In the calm delicious quiet of the day his thoughts approached his fears, and touched them lightly as he fingered softly the cross on his chest.

Ahead, he saw only growing menace. The Turks of Cyprus pressed ever more insistently, more aggressively, as they saw his weakness, and his mistrust of Athens. And the mainland Greeks steadily undermined him, and smuggled their own men into his island, and were in league with the Cypriots of EOKA. If it came to war, either the Turkish army or the Greek army would swallow Cyprus, and that would be an end of him and of independence. Wherever he looked he saw hostile eyes moving closer: all he could do was delay, and give no sign to the Turks or to Athens that he was anything other than serene and sure.

As he faced the darkness his anxiety collected and sharpened, but he only sat more still, and slowly, without his kneeling or joining his hands, he sank into a quiet night inside him. He no longer, in his personal prayer, addressed God formally, 'O Lord, help thy servant', but he knew he was approaching his God. This island was special to God: older than the Church of Greece, older than the Patriarchate of Constantinople, old as the apostles themselves was the Church of Cyprus: here Paul struck blind the sorcerer Elymas. It was on the throne of Barnabus, the first bishop, that he himself sat. And in modern times it was he, of all the men in Cyprus, who was chosen to lead his people down a road of dangers. All the island's history rested on him now; all the enemies of Cyprus intrigued against him. Several times already they had tried to kill him: each time his life was spared, by a miracle of God. As he sank in deepening silence and stillness he moved closer to the God of Cyprus, till they were as one, he in the Lord, the Lord in him, his prayer no longer a plea but a willing: Let guidance come, let his enemies be smitten as Lucifer fell in lightning from Heaven, let a way open to him and his people as the sea opened for Moses.

He was again aware of the twilight garden: he stirred and sighed, he was weary and at peace, he had passed before the face of the Lord and rested still in the hush of that passage.

He had lost count of time; but presently he heard unsure,

respectful voices approaching through the trees: voices that hesitantly sought him in the garden. Led by his servant, a family had come to visit him: the father and sons stiff as machines in their smartest suits, the mother and daughters shy in rich dresses. They were distant relatives of his: the Archbishop greeted them, and they sat in a ring in the garden chairs. Mainly the father spoke, nervously fingering his worry beads, while the Archbishop listened, and nodded from time to time, and occasionally, gravely, with some sparkle in his eye, put in a word.

'How is Stavros faring?' the Archbishop asked.

'Extremely well, the Lord be praised!' Stavros was training to be a priest, he had one of the Archbishop's scholarships to Harvard.

'And our cousin Aristotle?'

'And he is doing well, Your Beatitude. As you know he went to England, and, the Lord be praised, he has made his fortune there.' The father sighed; he had not made so great a fortune, staying loyally at home.

The Archbishop's servant returned and served coffee. The family grew more at ease, the Archbishop seemed more like a kindly uncle, listening shrewdly, occasionally advising, a wise, subtle Cypriot; the click-clack of the father's worry beads slowed to an easy rhythm. They asked the Archbishop's advice on a family dispute.

The summer evening quickly grew dark, and the family took its leave. The Archbishop went indoors, and was preparing with his chaplain for the prayers of the evening when the Secretary was announced again. He hurried in without formality, his face had a glare of elation and shock.

'We have the information, Your Beatitude!'

He spoke excitedly, his words tripped: for the prisoner had been a wild spark, and yet all at once, as they worked harder on him, he gave in. He lay now in a heap as though he had no bones, his pride extinct. The Secretary confined himself to giving the Archbishop the information he wanted, with no word on how it was obtained.

Which information the Archbishop took in with no change of expression: he was a still pool in which huge things sank without trace. But when the Secretary left he breathed a deep sigh of thanksgiving, and his head sank in reverence. He knew

415

now all that he needed to know: and the guidance he prayed for was given with that knowledge.

He joined his chaplain and the waiting priests, and presently their voices rose in a long rippling climbing chant.

As they hurried down the corridor, Kostas found himself overtaking the robust and evidently flustered form of General Vouros, who, in a low murmur of anger, was complicatedly involved in getting his shirt adjusted to his trousers and his tie to his neck, his movements hindered by the jacket and cap he had also to carry. He scowled at Kostas, he saw no need for sudden assemblies in the middle of the weekend. When Kostas, ever courteous, held the door open for him, he rudely shoved past and walked into the room complaining vigorously, in a voice which continued the exact note of the quarrel with his girl friend Loula in which he had been interrupted. 'What the hell is all this?'

He saw, too late, that there were present not only brother officers, but the Brigadier himself, and also the Prime Minister. The Brigadier turned sharply, his face white with sudden fury: for a moment he could not speak: then, with control, he said, 'You came, General. I thank you.'

Vouros grunted; and sat; and still after sitting – it seemed the pattern of his meetings with the Brigadier – continued slowly flushing hotter.

The Brigadier stood up. Kostas had never seen him angry; and he had thought he never could admire, as he admired the Brigadier, a man consumed with anger. But the Brigadier today was a mountain of anger, an anger beyond any irritation with Vouros, an anger that put a wide stare in his eyes, and dilated his pupils, and left his face bloodless, and put a choked tremor in his voice; and yet still all was ordered, all was disciplined, all was directed force. Kostas was awed by his control.

'Gentlemen,' the Brigadier deliberately said, 'I shall tell you at once why I have called you here. Last evening the President received a demand from the Archbishop for the Greek officers on Cyprus to be withdrawn.'

He paused; an officer asked, 'Does he give a time limit for this "withdrawal"?'

'Yes, General, he does. He gives us one week.'

Now the exclamations came, in fury, shock, a rising wave of indignation. Beside the Brigadier the Prime Minister swallowed and worked his mouth.

The Brigadier continued, 'You should know two things further, gentlemen. The Archbishop's police have begun the systematic arrest of EOKA personnel. And he has created yet a further "auxiliary tactical reserve force". He is enrolling that force, and he is arming it, fast.'

Down the table, someone muttered, 'He knows, eh?'

Kostas asked, 'How much does he know?'

The Brigadier, his idol, dismissed the question. 'He knows enough, gentlemen. That is all that need concern us. There is now only one matter before us.'

A voice rose, angry but hesitant, 'You mean, bring our plan forward – bring it forward so many months – I don't know. . . .' Another said, as if to his neighbour but really to all of them, 'Uh! Act within days? We can't do it, it isn't possible.'

At the end of the table, near the Brigadier, sat the hollow-cheeked Major General who had described the war plan at the meeting on the yacht. Kostas looked to him urgently, thinking: He is one of our leaders, he will speak for action. And the Major General did now speak; but he was not resolute and decisive as Kostas had expected, on the contrary he sounded like a man caught deep in a dilemma. He said slowly, 'We must be certain of our strength, when we move' – and then he paused, and sat back: he was not yet ready to say more.

Kostas was surprised, dismayed. He thought, *Major* General – that's your mark. He saw the Brigadier also was disappointed, and further angered: his eyes now were shining. Kostas saw his opportunity.

'If I may speak, gentlemen,' he said distinctly. 'It is unthinkable that we withdraw from Cyprus – unthinkable that we withdraw any of our strength. It is vital that we hold Cyprus, if there are ever to be hostilities with Turkey. If we leave now, it is not only a victory for the Archbishop, it is a victory for the Turk. We must do all that is necessary to ensure that we stay.'

Vouros and the older officers looked askance at the whipper-snapper: but Kostas knew he had become the voice of the

Brigadier, he knew the strength this gave him.

The Major General asked, in a clear dry voice, 'Could I enquire who we will put in the Archbishop's place?'

The Brigadier turned his stark eyes on him. 'Negotiations are in hand, we have no worry there.'

With great seriousness the Major General said, 'I ask because we have very much at stake in this operation. If we make a wrong move, the Turk will be in there before you can snap your finger.' From face to face, his glance patrolled the table. 'What army have we got on Cyprus to fight the Turk?'

With a part-constricted voice, at the last stretch of patience, the Brigadier said, 'The Turk will not fight, the Americans say so. We give Cyprus to NATO, they hold back the Turk.'

Another asked, 'Yes, but what about the British?'

'Don't worry about the British!' the Brigadier snapped. 'The Americans have got the British by the balls!'

More questions were asked, but the Brigadier's anger would tolerate no more. Shaking, leaning forward dagger-faced over the table, he told them, 'Gentlemen, we shall not be humiliated by this priest. We will act. We will act within the time he has given us. That will be our answer to him.'

He turned to the Prime Minister, who nervously murmured about the honour of Greece. Kostas spoke in support, and others fell in: for they saw the fury of the Brigadier. It was agreed, their attack would be advanced. Instructions would be sent immediately, and certain officers would be air-lifted to Cyprus: among them would be Kostas.

The meeting broke up in a scraping of chairs; though little was said, Kostas sensed some misgiving, some feeling that with the sudden new power the Brigadier enjoyed, his capacity for anger had grown too great, and his patience had been damaged. But they dare not challenge him. The cowards, Kostas thought; for his part, he felt only enthusiasm. At last they were moving forward, and moving outside Greece: the great expansion had begun, and it had come even sooner than he had dared to hope. Greek soldiers would march; and he himself was at the heart of the attack. Leaving the room, he passed the Major General, who at that moment muttered drily in the ear of General Vouros, 'The policeman is cross.' Glancing sideways briefly, Kostas saw that the face of Vouros had assumed again that impenetrable, guarded, shrewd expression it had worn on the yacht. Kostas shook his shoulders slightly, to shake off acquaintance with these hesitant men, and strode fast down the corridor as though it led with no turning or diversion to the presidential palace of Nicosia.

All day the scorched buildings of Nicosia heated, and into the evening the air still burned; only at night could one step into the street, or onto a balcony, for pleasure and coolness. It was black deep night, close almost to the dawn of the following day, before the doorways and balconies, and all the windows open for coolness, finally were deserted. Only then, in the thick dark, in the hanging clouds of jasmine, could a man flit up the alleys being sure he wasn't seen, carrying a large package which he deposited in a doorway as lightly, as delicately, as a mother abandoning a baby; and so he is away, round an angle of the street. But a strange door, this, to abandon a baby at, the barred double entry to a large business premises; and from the package comes no baby's cry but flash, detonation, shatter, the door disappeared, stones falling, wreckage, and little flames like mice rippling here, there, on the shattered wood, starting to burn; while from burst windows overhead a light hail of glass splinters still tinkles in the road. Shouts, shrieks, lights in further windows and blear faces poke in shock; calling voices approach in the dark while fire catches in the blasted shop. Then, from two streets off, another crash, a leap of fire, more voices, steps, a scream; and from far across the city a further blast, and somewhere a siren; till all the city is dotted with explosions and shouts, and wreckage smouldering in the first glint of day.

Or, in a cellar in the city, the door suddenly splits in separating planks, armed men jump through, and the sleeping men inside scramble pell-mell fumbling for weapons and tripping half-tangled in sheets, while the militia already have grabbed them, knocked them hard against the wall, and kicked them upstairs into the waiting truck.

Emerging from prayers in the early morning the Archbishop meets his auxiliary troop – he is a black column surrounded by soldiers – and learns which of his supporters in the city have had their premises bombed in the night; while his own forces have caught, in this hiding place or that, so many members of EOKA. From new interrogations he learns how strong his enemies are, how many serpents are within the walls. The dragon of his enemy is curled round him, now it stirs, he pricks it while it rises alert, and when it is upright it will kill him. He must hope he has acted fast enough, that he has caught them too unready to succeed; if not, still he has grasped the danger, they are less strong than they would be later.

He announces to the world the ultimatum he has given: that the Greek officers, who control his own army, must be recalled. He announces that he fears a coup, and the plot leads back to Athens. He must hinder them, catch them, make it hard for them to go on: it is a question of days. All the while the Greek officers of the National Guard seem quietly intent on their business: stolid worthy cumbersome men, their faces blank behind black glasses.

The next night is worse, with bombings as before, and killings; gunfights in the mountains; and there are new arrivals too.

Among them Kostas: a lithe black figure untethering and disentangling from the rippling panting collapsing silk cloud on which he has slid out of the sky, and standing erect, a black shape on the slope of stones, who starts descending towards Nicosia.

A rickety three-wheel truck drove through a rear entrance into the barracks of the National Guard in Nicosia, and Kostas clambered out of the back. He felt stiff and sick from his cramped journey: it came home to him that after his long period of deskwork, he had put on weight, and was out of combat condition. But he breathed in deep, and shook and shivered himself to tautness: then he bid farewell to the EOKA agent who had brought him, and asked to be taken to the commanding officer. He was led through corridors towards a distant noise of heavy voices raised: a door was opened, and he looked on a scene that made all his skin prickle in indignation.

For *this* was the conference of the senior Greek officers of Cyprus: he had expected to see, as at the Pentagon, smart uniformed officers being formal, tough, insistent round a table; but what he saw, through a blue choking atmosphere of smoke, was a disorder of men who stood around with their tunics unbuttoned, with a flushed look of – what? – impatience, querulousness, a look above all of annoyance. These men were not ready for fighting: even now one of them was saying 'I can't take those tanks on the road, they'd overheat in half a kilometre. I'd go faster in an ox cart.' He broke off, scoffing to himself, 'Diesel, huh, the Archbishop's diesel-engined tanks!' Another was saying, like a man who expected war always to present its compliments before it arrived, 'How can we? Who do they think we are?'

At these grating, shrugging voices, Kostas thrilled with contempt. So what if plans had been advanced, the good soldier is always ready. He knew on the instant he must take charge.

'Good morning, gentlemen,' he said, in a bayonet voice copied from the Brigadier.

There was a large, powerful-necked, strong-featured Colonel in the centre of the group, he evidently was in charge. He had not been facing the door; but now he turned his large head at his leisure until he saw Kostas. Behind him, the others stared at the newcomer out of their anger, like villagers catching sight in the distance of someone on a donkey they didn't know.

'You from Athens?' the Colonel asked, heavily offhand.

'I'm from the Pentagon.' Kostas inspected the ragged line of them with a level cold eye.

'Congratulations,' the Colonel said quietly. 'So the Pentagon thinks we can bring our attack forward – forward by months – in two days?'

'The Pentagon thinks that we must. It is necessary. What are the obstacles?'

In a contained hot voice that delivered its phrases like a builder placing stone on stone, the Colonel said, 'The obstacles? Maybe you don't see the obstacles, over there in Athens. Well, I'll tell you one. Who's going to be president, when the Archbishop goes? None of the ones we want has said yes. They hint, but that's all.'

Kostas replied fierily: he knew he must quash this one at once. 'Poh! They won't say yes while he's alive! What would you expect? But afterwards – of course they'll take the job. Will they let Cyprus have *no* president?'

' "Afterwards" – that's easily said. And tell me, I beg of you, who is going to shoot His Beatitude?'

'Are we soldiers or what are we?' Kostas cried, his voice

421

rising sharp and high. 'It's easy enough to kill a man, in the name of God!'

The Colonel was unimpressed. 'It's easy enough to say it's easy. Look, my brave Athenian, you walk through our barracks – go out in the streets, if you like, and search Nicosia – and find me the man who will do it.'

Kostas drew himself tall, till he stood like a spear, upright, pale, before their massed doubts. He knew he had come to a turning point in his career: in a harder and sharper voice he said, 'The orders from the Pentagon are absolutely clear. We are to attack. Those are our orders.'

They stared back, hostile, he saw they were wondering whether to retort. He knew he was growing pale before them; but also deadly; and he felt inspired.

'We attack,' he said clearly. He felt a cold tearing in his mind, and he thrilled with electric strength, as he heard himself, without a quaver, confirm the sentence on the Archbishop.

The Colonel looked at him with a reddened face, with hot bloodshot glistening eyes. Eventually he said quietly, 'So be it.'

There was a change in the atmosphere of the room. 'The Archbishop has forced our hand,' an officer said. 'He has given us no choice.' The Colonel was heavily silent. The man who had complained about the tanks said, 'My men will do their duty.'

There was still great tension, but a readiness also: Kostas listened to them with strong excitement, he knew the difference he had made.

He had some inspections to make: for even with the smuggled extras, the arms of the National Guard were far from good. And it was known, too, that the Archbishop had smuggled in for his own men arms better than those he gave the National Guard. There was hard work ahead; but there could be no turning back.

Two days later, Kostas inspected with zest the sunlit yard, where the soldiers were busy round the lined-up tanks. There was a continual rattle as moving parts were checked. A soldier held out skeins of machine gun ammunition like an island woman holding hanks of wool. Everywhere in the clear morning was excited disciplined movement.

Kostas went over to the Lieutenant Colonel who had lamented before the state of the tanks.

'They're vintage models, all right!' Kostas nodded towards the antiquated diesel-engined rattletrap vehicles.

'The Archbishop bought them off the Russians,' the Lieutenant Colonel remarked; his mood was different today, he was impatient to start. 'Well, we've got enough of them,' – he gave the cumbersome tracks a kick – 'they'll serve the purpose.'

A sergeant approached, saluted, and shouted at them, 'Everything is ready, Mr Lieutenant Colonel!' Throughout the yard the soldiers had come to a pause, they all stood now motionless beside their tanks.

And so they waited; the signal to leave had not yet come. The Lieutenant Colonel and Kostas muttered familiarly to each other, as the people in charge, showing they were at ease. Yet the Lieutenant Colonel was not at ease, Kostas saw, nervous worry danced in his eye. Then Kostas realized that something of this nervousness ran through all the troop, they were too quiet, too still, even for men paused before battle.

'This waiting is bad for the men,' Kostas said.

'Uh!' the Lieutenant Colonel grunted; his fingers fidgeted, he couldn't hold easy the gun that he couldn't put down.

They waited still; the sun climbed; by the minute the morning air heated. The soldiers talked in fits and starts; swivelled guns; a walkie-talkie crackled intermittently.

A soldier hurried over from the barracks, shouting highvoiced, 'He has arrived at the palace.'

Briskly the Lieutenant Colonel gave the signal, the sergeants bawled it on; he and Kostas, and all their troops, climbed into their tanks. Clouds of black smoke rose, as the ancient engines fired and revved. The tanks advanced, soldiers shouted, gates opened; cramped in their tight hot ovens of armour, the troop set out.

Craning to small grills in the thick iron, they saw cars and people skid out of their way as they drove fast through the city; jarring, jolting, they swivelled at a corner, and juddered down a new, busy road. In the distance, through the small frame of vibrating iron, they saw a grand gateway, and beyond

423

it trees, tall black cypresses. Kostas looked slantwise at the Lieutenant Colonel, who looked tense ahead, pale, sweating, he looked like a man in a wash of fear. His eye swivelled, and caught Kostas looking at him; and his face sharpened, he resumed command. At that moment they drove through the gateway, and started climbing a winding road, between trees: they were in the grounds of the presidential palace.

'Must be the excitement,' Kostas murmured, watching his colleague; but still, as if he had caught a picture from the Lieutenant Colonel's eye, his own mind filled with pictures of the Archbishop: images that were hallucination clear, though they must come from old newsreels, newspaper photos, the picture he kept in his office, for he had never seen the man himself. But he realized, he is not grand: he saw the man's belly, pushing his long robes forward; and he is young, for all his grizzled beard; and he is not tall, it is only the high black hat that makes him tall. But still the Archbishop was bigger in his mind's eye than the cypress trees that passed them on the road, each of which jarred his mind as if in some way it were a standing shadow of the Archbishop himself. He was glad they were inside tanks. The last trees parted and they saw ahead the tall arched façade of the palace, its domed roof, its arcaded wings stretched out like helpless arms. It stood there white and frozen, no sign of life.

'Aim . . . fire . . .' the Lieutenant Colonel shouted to his tank, and into the walkie-talkie, and as Kostas watched, the top of the palace exploded in smoke, in a scatter of falling plaster, and as the smoke cleared the rough brickwork of the palace wall showed.

Over the engine noise Kostas shouted, 'Hey, we should surround the palace before we attack!'

'Don't worry, we'll flatten him,' the Lieutenant Colonel shouted back, in a rasping furious voice. Gold fire, a huge smoke, bloomed on the palace's face, and as that cleared they saw that the windows and window columns were all blown in.

The tanks fanned out, moving to either side of the palace. Now, looking through a side window, Kostas saw troops, their supporting commandos, dodging up through the trees. The tank shuddered again as it fired. He watched the shell burst: when the smoke cleared, the palace was for some moments a scarred but white still beautiful sunlit building: then abruptly

424

shots cracked from it, missiles fired from it, tracer bullets streamed from it, it seemed suddenly alive all over, weapons pouring from every window. As Kostas watched, there was a burst of smoke round the lead tank, red flame burned through the choking black, the tank disappeared in a burning cloud.

'The bastards! They've got bazookas,' the Lieutenant Colonel exclaimed. His tank fired again, and the other tanks continued their advance in a stream of fire from the palace. The two columns of tanks met at the rear of the building, swung inwards, and all now at will fired at the palace, while the commandos crept up between the tanks, and in sudden spurts ran from one piece of cover to the next. A soldier dashing across the courtyard suddenly flung up his arms dancing and collapsed. A grenade was lobbed in through a balcony arch: as it exploded, a man swinging his arms and a length of balustrade were flung outwards. Further along the balcony a young soldier came running from the shadows into sunlight, he was shouting to people behind him, then turned forward, his face lit: like a sinking ship he slowly slanted behind the balcony out of sight.

Fires had begun, smoke poured from several windows; the commandos were close to the palace walls, crouched in groups, they flung grenades: as soon as they burst, some ran and dived through windows, while others sprayed the façade with shot. There were bursts of firing, dazzle of shots through smoke, figures running low behind the parapet.

Those who had given the covering fire themselves now advanced into the palace, till all the troops had disappeared inside it, and there was only the muffled noise of shooting within the building, growing more distant.

The shooting stopped. The breeze removed the smoke that hung round the palace. There were pits and craters and great blackening sweeps of soot across the walls, from which the facing had fallen away; rough holes bigger than windows cut across the windows, balconies stopped, arches hung, unsupported, in midair. It was a ruin.

Kostas and the Lieutenant Colonel left their tank and walked cautiously into the building. Smoke hung under the ceilings, the floors were heaped with plaster and rubble, the young auxiliaries of the Archbishop's troop lay awkwardly, some dead, some moaning, among the stones; some of them stood in a shambling group being rounded up by the National Guard.

'Where's the Archbishop?' the Lieutenant Colonel shouted. The soldiers looked blank.

'Find him!' he shouted in passion.

The search began, posses of soldiers worked from room to room, the Lieutenant Colonel strode sharply back and forth through the building, snapping orders: every nook, every alcove, every cupboard must be searched, no place must be left.

At length the soldiers reported: they had searched every corner, they had not found the Archbishop's body.

'Has he got away?' Kostas gasped, voicing the horror-thought that had been with him all through the attack.

The Lieutenant Colonel stood breathing heavily, looking angrily round at his men: they would pay for their incompetence.

'We should have surrounded the palace first,' Kostas said.

'Don't tell me my business,' the Lieutenant Colonel said, and Kostas saw in his yellow eyes that all the man's fury was levelled at him.

As they left, the guardsmen fired the building. Glancing back at the gateway, Kostas saw the column of smoke from the burning palace rising high over the tree tops: for a moment, in the corner of his eye, it looked like a dark figure standing over them.

The offices of the British camp at Akrotiri were a shouting match of telephonists, 'We have no further information.' 'We are awaiting information from the Cypriot authorities.' 'We are not advised that British personnel have any cause for alarm at the present time.'

Leaving the briefing room, the Colonel made his way through the humid shouting office. As he came outside, a captain who had followed him finally caught up.

'Colonel, excuse me, sir.' He waited till the Colonel had stopped and attended: then he saluted, and took a formality. His face was flushed, his eyes were bright.

'Colonel, we have the forces. There is no question, we could put a stop to this.'

He stood in the Colonel's path now, his bright eyes staring emphasis of what he had said. Listening to him, the fair haired

Colonel compressed his lips and nodded; but at the end he said simply, 'London doesn't want us to intervene.' He didn't debate; he collected briskly the Captain's salute, and strode off to attend to his exigent duties.

With a sigh the Captain went back into the crowded hectic room, where voices shouted down speakers, 'We have no advice at present.' 'Ring later in the day.' 'I am sorry, but we cannot help you.'

Over the whistling car radio the brass band music stopped, and they heard the announcement, 'The Archbishop is dead. Long live the National Guard!'

The two soldiers nodded to the fifty-year-old man who sat between them in the cramped back seat of the car: a bald-headed, black-browed, thick-bearded man, with a drooping nose, who wore only a white shirt and a pair of dark trousers, but who still sat between them with a stateliness. Then, 'Down, Your Beatitude!' they shouted, and briskly the Archbishop crouched low. The timber workers, at their roadside camp, stared inquisitively at the strange car, battered, white with dust, that continued bucking and jolting up the steep track going nowhere.

Cautiously the Archbishop sat up, and looked about him anxiously. But they were high on the mountain now, even the pine trees thinned. Nicosia was a wheel of haze far below them.

They crested a rise, and losing sight of the lower lands drove onto a high empty plateau on the roof of the world: only lichen and a few grasses straggled across the crumpled rock; over the noise of the car engine they heard the tinkle of goat bells.

'We should see it by now,' the driver shouted back.

'This is the road,' the Archbishop said, then was interrupted by the soldier beside him. 'Stop, stop, switch off the engine.'

In the sudden silence, in the settling dust, their drumming ears strained, and just caught the distant gnat buzz of an airplane engine.

'We need cover,' the driver grumbled.

'Can you get to those trees?' The soldier pointed to a pair of wizened, leaning pines, some distance over the rock.

'You'll have to get out.' So the two soldiers and the bald, bearded man walked over the stones, while the car progressed gingerly, tilting this way and that, till it came in the lee of the sparse branches.

Watching anxiously, the four men crouched motionless beside the car, which fortunately was as grey with dust as the stones. The noise of the plane rose and fell, still they could not see it: then they glimpsed, far off in the sky, the tiny shining cylinder, that seemed to make an unbelievably slow insect progress between the peaks. The whine of its engine came to them thinly through the tinkle of the goat bells. Then it disappeared behind crags, and its sound thinned. They waited, easing their positions: then abruptly the sound swelled, and the plane crested the near horizon as if driving on their road. It passed rapidly, throbbing, over their heads; and then for a long time slowly grew smaller, slowly its thin cry failed and died.

The Archbishop sighed: and they made their way warily back to the road, and continued their drive. At a crossroads of faint stone tracks they argued.

'There it is, Your Beatitude.' One of the soldiers pointed to a stony shoulder of mountain where they made out a small clump of trees, and in it a bleak stone building like a large farm.

They drove carefully up the rough track, and eventually arrived in the tiny courtyard, just finding space to park between the piled stacks of new cut wood. A handful of monks and soldiers gathered round the car. As the Archbishop in his dusty clothes got out, the Abbot of the small monastery, a young, jet-bearded man, stooped and kissed his hand.

A tarpaulin was thrown over the car, and the monks conducted the new arrivals indoors, where they sat down to a meal of soup and bread.

'We have radioed the British,' one of the soldiers said bitterly. 'They will not take action, they're going to sit in their camps.'

The Archbishop looked at him with his heavy, drooping eyes, and presently said, in his slow voice which paused between each word, 'We shall not ask the British to intervene.'

The soldier blinked, and stared at the Archbishop who, deep in thought, continued his meal.

As soon as they had finished, the Archbishop rose, said a brief prayer, and detailed instructions to be sent by radio. Then he and his companions returned to the courtyard, the tarpaulin was jerked off the car, and they got in briskly. They were joined by one of the monks, who would guide them over the mountains.

They drove down the track, and presently took a new road which was hardly any road at all, but just a gully of boulders like a dried-up river course. The car slid and jerked and bounced from stone to stone, the driver worried and complained, but the wire-bearded, hard-faced monk who had joined them raised a hand and said gruffly, 'Be still, my child, this is the road.'

At the monastery gate, the monks and soldiers watched the car jolt down the stones, till it was cut off from them by a flank of crag; then the monks said a final prayer, and returned to their work.

In the crowded headquarters of the National Guard, Kostas paused in mid sentence and his ears pricked. The Brigadier himself was on the radio, speaking from Athens. All the officers leaned close, with troubled faces; and Kostas listened keenly, but with faltering admiration. He thought of the Brigadier's Roman head; but he heard, not the voice of a Caesar, but the hot spitting voice of a man out of temper.

'Why isn't he dead?' The Brigadier's voice blurred as he shouted. 'You had the troops, you had the tanks. How did he get away?'

The powerful neck of the Colonel inflamed: tense with chagrin, he began, 'It isn't so easy . . .' But the Brigadier shouted over him, 'I want the man dead. Comb every inch of the island, every hole. I want him dead by this evening.'

The Colonel didn't answer.

'Have you got a new president?' the Brigadier shouted.

'We thought it wise to delay, till we had definite information of the Archbishop's death.'

'Delay? Do you think we're playing tavli? I want the President sworn in!'

Curtly the Colonel stated his obedience, and walked away from the radio with a face of fire. But he was barely to the door when he was called back, a new voice came on the radio.

'Colonel,' the radio officer called, 'it's the playboy.'

'O my God!' the Colonel cried; he snatched the microphone,

429

shouted 'no!' and banged it down on the bench. To all of them he exclaimed, 'The EOKA playboy – he thinks he'll be president. He's mad!'

At the open door, he snapped, 'Mr Liaison Officer, come with me.'

Puzzled, Kostas followed, as they strode to a staff car. 'Where . . .?'

The Colonel grimaced, 'Where are we going? We're going to look for a president.'

The staff car hurled them through the narrow swerving streets. They stopped at a large, old-fashioned house, where a servant led them into an elegant room of old Balkan furniture and framed proclamations of the Sultan.

An elderly man in a white suit came in: he stared hard at them, still with anger.

The Colonel did not waste time. 'Sir, you will know the tragic situation of this island today. Faced with this grave emergency, we come to you now to submit our power to you. We beg that you will give us guidance – not on our behalf, but for the good of Cyprus.'

'What are you trying to say?'

'We ask, sir, if you will accept the office of President of Cyprus. We pledge to you all our support.'

The elderly eyes burned at them from the pale, lined face. 'It is impossible. The President of Cyprus lives.'

The Colonel drew breath sharply. 'It is not certain that he is alive. In any event, he is out of office, he has fled Nicosia, he is no one now. Therefore we come to you . . .'

Drawing himself taller, trembling with passion, the man said, 'It is impossible.'

They saw there was no point in staying, and withdrew. The Colonel snapped orders to his driver, and sat grim-faced as they again sped through the streets, and drew up at another house. Here they were led into a dim apartment, where a stout man half raised himself from a sofa on which he reclined, looking more like a Turkish pasha of the old days than like a Greek statesman.

He heard their urgent words; and said at the end, in a trailing, syrupy voice of insinuation, 'Gentlemen, I thank you, but of course . . . I am not sure if I am up to date . . . I heard that the Archbishop. . . .'

He paused; and the Colonel said nothing in the silence.

The reclining man studied them from under lowered waxy lids; then with surprising vigour, he said, 'Your proposal is unacceptable. I condemn the action you have taken. I disown your overture to me. You will leave my house immediately.'

The Colonel stared a moment, in such compressed anger Kostas wondered if he would have a heart attack; then briskly he stood up, and left without a word. Kostas followed, feeling that, somewhere, everything tumbled, nothing was happening as it should.

Again the hectic racing streets: they drew up at another house. The man they asked for was not there, he was not on the island, he would be away for several days.

Tears stood in the Colonel's eyes as he returned this time to the staff car. He sat down heavily beside Kostas but could not say a word to him, and for the better part of a minute he only sat, staring blindly ahead, as though in front of his eyes was no crowded street, but a stone wall.

But he gave the order, and sat back wearily; and they drove, not so fast, to an office building, and without ceremony walked through it to a room where men in battle dress crowded round a desk littered with guns, where a smooth-haired baby-faced businessman, the 'playboy' as the officers called him, rose smiling to greet them and said – his voice nervous and husky for all his elation – 'Good afternoon, gentlemen.'

In a clipped voice the Colonel said, 'We have the honour to beg you will accept the office of President of Cyprus.' It sounded like an order, rudely given.

His EOKA aides about him, the businessman made a speech, 'Gentlemen, you honour me deeply. I will labour to be worthy of the great trust you have placed in me.' He savoured the moment, he was on a cloud. His cheering aides hugged and kissed him. The Colonel turned to go, with a smart in his eyes, with an opaque face of duty.

All Kostas' skin burned, as ambitions came true in a world gone wrong.

At a kiosk in Constitution Square, Chryssa saw a newspaper with a large photo of the Archbishop, and the simple words, in huge letters, that he was dead. Her heart stopped. As soon

431

as she saw that headline, she knew the whole story: buying the paper and hectically scanning it did no more than confirm her guess. She tried to read it more slowly and carefully, but that was impossible, the words danced and dissolved before her eyes.

Clutching the paper, she hurried home, and as soon as she got indoors squatted on the floor. After several starts, she read the report properly, and read it with a terrible impatience, a terrible eagerness to know the worst. Far off on his island, the Archbishop had been a beacon of defiance: now they had killed him, as they had tried to before, and made a new dictatorship there as well. She knew the Junta had done this, there was nothing they wouldn't do, and the world connived in it. They only advanced, they only grew stronger: it came home to her again how greatly, how hugely, she hated the Junta. She had never before given herself up to hatred, but now, as she crouched on the floor, she consigned her soul to it. For the Junta she wanted death, but not quickly, not easily, they must have done to them what they had done to others, and they must be kept conscious knowing as one pain grew that worse would follow and only death was at the end of it.

She came to slowly. A long fire had burned through her till she was ember, dead clinker. It was dusk outside, the day had gone. She leaned back in an armchair, she felt only – exhausted. From time to time she trembled or shuddered, and wiped her hand across her brow as if some shadow or web stuck there.

Michael arrived. 'Chryssa, where were you? I thought you were coming to mine.'

She looked at him hot-eyed. 'Have you seen this?'

Between them, in the middle of the floor, the black figure of the Archbishop, and the tall black letters.

'I've seen,' he said, compressed-faced. But what use was his anger? She looked at him as he stood there helpless.

Eventually she said, 'They could have saved him.'

He knew she meant the British.

'They could have, couldn't they, Michael? What are they doing there?'

'They're sitting in their camps –'

'– having a whist drive.'

He muttered ineffectual anger, then clamped shut in chagrin.

They closed the blinds, switched on the light, took something from the fridge and ate indifferently.

Later, he switched on the radio: the channels boomed and died till he got the BBC. There was a news programme, he tried to tune it clearer but it hummed and buzzed, the voice came and went. They heard the word 'Cyprus', then 'dead' or 'not dead', it wasn't clear. All their hearing focused on the set. Then, with heavier crackling still, a different voice came on, a thick voice speaking Greek which they had heard before on the radio. It said only, 'I am Makarios. I am alive. The Junta will perish.'

The announcer resumed: the source of the broadcast wasn't clear, it might be a recording. . . . But Chryssa didn't listen. 'He has escaped them,' she said, her eyes slowly reflecting the sublime comedy of events.

Late in the day, after long detours in the mountains, jolted, battered, dented, a clatter of overheated iron in the centre of a white cloud, the car carrying the Archbishop had run down into the small ancient port of Paphos. Word of his arrival drove faster through the town than he did, when the shaking car stopped in the town square it was surrounded by soldiers and militiamen, by townspeople carrying arms, by bearded black-robed priests with skeins of ammunition round their shoulders like stoles. As the exhausted, bruised, unrobed, dust-covered Archbishop climbed out of the car they cheered and shouted his name and waved their guns and sang prayers, and shouting pressed close almost to crush him as he slowly moved through them.

At the small radio station he made his broadcast: and all that evening and night the road from Nicosia, and other roads into Paphos, dazzled with headlights as cars, motorbikes, trucks, lorries, crammed with men, queued to enter the town; the streets were crowded with men brandishing shotguns, rifles, guns captured from the Turks, guns captured from the Germans, guns captured from the British, guns bought from Czechoslovakia and Russia. The town was loud with men's voices, excited, intent; occasionally the Archbishop was seen, wearing again black robes, a tall hat, a cross, carrying again his silver-headed staff, grave, intent, consulting busily with his lieutenants.

The men lay down to rest where they could, but all night Paphos rumbled and glared with more heavy traffic in the narrow streets, bringing new reinforcements and new ammunition.

By morning, all arrivals had stopped, and the dawn light grew over still fields, empty roads, silence in the hills. Only, late in the morning, they heard a distant low vibration, like something vast being lugged across rough ground; and later a muffled booming, like thunder, like a mountain storm though the sky was clear, like dynamite echoing from a distant quarry.

At midday, silence fell; the armed men, in battledress or shirtsleeves, the priests with their machine guns, moved their weight restlessly, talked uneasily, it seemed the time before the battle would stretch out endless. Out to sea stood a Greek battleship with its guns trained on the town, but no movement came from it.

There was a rattle of shots up in the hills; then streams of machine gun fire rippling nonstop, shell bursts, smoke rising. For a long time they listened to the close noise of this invisible battle in the hills. Then, in new dust clouds, cars came driving fast down the road from the mountains, in growing clouds they drove straight into Paphos, and armed men got out of them and pulled out the wounded. The defenders of Paphos would not wait long.

The vibration grew louder. Tiny on the heights, far out of range, an armoured car appeared, then more, and then, slowly, all: an armoured heavy-engined convoy slanting down the hillside in a smoke of dust. On the lower ground, half hidden behind trees and houses, it became a brown cloud steadily growing as it rumbled nearer.

Two tiny puffs of smoke flowered on the distant warship: and an old large building in the centre of the town exploded in fire, bricks shooting like shells. At the same moment, up the road, there were flashes of gunshot, rising smoke, new shells flying in, buildings throughout the town exploding. Through the smoke, from between the distant tanks, soldiers started running nearer, diving, dodging for cover.

'Eh, Niko, is it you?'

The young trade unionist looked round, just as a priest of his own age came loping across the road, stooped low, and

434

plunged behind the same stone wall that he was using. He studied the pale, black-bearded face, slowly the name swung to him.

'Stefano!' They greeted each other with a clasp between a hand shake and a hug. They had not met in years.

The priest checked the contents of a large basket he was carrying, then asked, 'Have you seen Gregory?'

The other had not, but he had seen Yiannis and Michaelis. Alternately now they produced names, till it was apparent that nearly everyone from their village had come to Paphos for the present showdown: the Archbishop himself came from a village nearby.

'Have a fig, my son,' the priest said munificently, tipping his basket: Nikos saw that it was full of grenades.

'Thank you kindly, father.' Nikos reached in, and took as many as he could fit into his jacket pockets.

They peered between the stones of the wall; at intervals they would see one of the distant national guardsmen dodge to a new piece of cover. They were taking their time. The long waiting made Nikos ache with impatience to get a clear shot at them: he wanted to attack, not wait to be attacked. He could wait no longer: he gave the priest a bang on the shoulder, went sprinting up the road, and dived behind a further wall, which he had had his eye on. There, carefully, he removed a stone, and sticking his rifle barrel through the hole he aimed at a gate, where he knew a guardsman hid, and at the first movement, fired. Looking round, he saw that the priest also had run forward, and crouched in a doorway. Others also had advanced, he saw the barrel of a machine gun sticking through the plastic blinds of a window.

Through his loophole, he saw that the guardsmen had reached the other end of the street he was in. A soldier emerged from an alley: Nikos got a good sighting, fired, the gun kicked, the soldier dropped.

He shot again, again, another man fell. Bullets zipped past him, and ricocheted off the stones; behind him shells burst and rubble flew. Another squad of guardsmen appeared in the road. He shot at them, then, near, he heard a hoarse, in-breathed cry, and looking round he saw Stefanos, the priest, tumbling out of his doorway, he looked all blood, soft ropes of his guts hung forward, his unused grenades rolled out like

435

tumbled apples in the street. For a moment Nikos died at this sight: then he came to, cold, focused, and now nonstop he aimed and shot, aimed and shot. The enemy bullets chipped the stones near him, a bullet shaved his head, it had come through his loophole, it had taken off part of his ear: briefly he touched the incomplete ear and warm liquid running on his cheek. His insides drew together in a hard knot: he fired, fired, fired, till there was a great bursting and shatter near him, his wall seemed to swell in a wave then the stones of it flew, he buried his head as some of them came down on him. It felt as though a house had fallen on his leg.

He was tangled up with the wall: he wouldn't be able to get clear of it, but he felt no pain, and he was facing the right way, and he still had some cover from the mound of stones round him. He saw the guardsmen coming very close, crouching in the street, they were distinct people: he couldn't tell how many: but he shot at them and shot, while their shots flew round him. He couldn't tell any more whether he was hitting them.

He continued shooting, but at a certain point something in his head became detached from what he was doing. It was as if, in this short time, he had shot as many people as he could want to shoot, it would be great work to shoot any more, and also he felt that with each shot he was tearing some stretched white membrane inside himself. He registered also that the enemy were extremely close, only metres away, while the men on his side, who had come forward to attack as he had, had retreated; and he, mixed up as he was with this heap of stones, was not well placed to retreat. He found it odd that he still didn't hurt: and he had the curious idea that the white stones of the fallen wall were all bits of his broken bones. Nearby lay the priest, his front shot to bits, and another dead man who was wearing a sheepskin jacket, like guerillas in old photos. He thought, how can a sheepskin coat protect you from bullets? But then he thought, yes, it is an armour, an animal skin is armour.

He thought, I should be shooting, but he had stopped; and he saw the national guardsmen passing in front of him: Don't you realize I can shoot you point-blank, I can shoot you dead. But even if they glanced at him, they ignored him; he grabbed for his gun, but it wouldn't come, and also he felt tired. At the same time he felt the start of pain, he had a premonition that all the pain, which he had so far been too shocked to feel, would, in a few seconds, strike him. Fortunately he was sleepy, he would be asleep before the pain hit.

Steadily the national guardsmen advanced through the town. A priest up on the rooftops looked round from his machine gun: a black round shape, with long wings or blades spinning on top of it, came clattering towards him over the roof tops. It was the death angel: it was so big and loud he ducked low, though it wouldn't have hit him: and then, nearby, it simply stopped, hovering in the air, over the courtyard. Its racket was deafening, dust whipped in a whirlwind under it. An arm in the machine flung out a rope ladder. Looking down, he saw the Archbishop had come into the courtyard: assisted by others, he caught hold of the ladder, and, awkward in his black robes, climbed slowly up it, swinging round, dangling, till khaki arms reached out and pulled him in. The moment the Archbishop was inside, the helicopter heeled over and swung away back up into the air, as if it were on the end of a piece of string that were suddenly pulled. It slanted into the sky, while the men below hurried indoors to their continuing work.

The priest returned to his: but with shock, for looking back to his long view of roofs and domes and parapets, which had all been deserted before, he saw men – men climbing, running, jumping, from roof to roof coming his way, men in battledress: they came up quickly while he still stared at them.

Seeing him, they stopped: and there was a moment, an eyeblink, in which he stared surprised at the young soldiers, while they stared amazed at the aged priest, paused half turned from his rattling machine gun. His pink skin was pure as a baby's: his clear eyes flashed: his flying hair and fleecy beard were white and lovely as new washed wool. In his mind, old battle chants swelled, but he thought: why should he be shooting the Christ-loving armies, he ought to be blessing them as they marched to kill heathens. But they moved forward: he swung the gun round and started it rattling, their guns flashed, and the great war hymn that soared in his head soared out of hearing.

★

In the Pentagon, glasses clashed: with the announcement
'Paphos has fallen!' a cheer went up from the assembled
soldiers. So the Archbishop had got away, picked up by the
British; never mind, he was nothing now. The new President
of Cyprus had been sworn in, resistance was crushed, the
island was theirs. The uncertainty and expectation of months,
the strain and anxiety of recent days, all were eased. The
officers had to rejoice, they were ready almost to dance. They
pressed close in congratulation round a tall, knife-nosed, bald-
headed officer, whose skin had a pallor and shine, whose eyes
had the hot gleam of someone exalted, moved, by excess of joy:
the Brigadier. He did now, unusually, show his excitement.

'Gentlemen,' he said, glancing sharply round at all of them,
'we have a loyal brother government on Cyprus!'

Powerful voices applauded, and he in the centre smiled
tightly, savouring deeply the burning pleasure of his second
triumph.

A discontent quickly came into his pleasure. For the officers
were intoxicated, they couldn't stop making boisterous jokes:
about the mainland Turks, waking up goggle-eyed to find
they'd lost Cyprus; about the British who so conveniently had
looked the other way. Their humour grated on the Brigadier:
such a victory was not a matter for jokes. He himself felt only
a great relief; for it all could have gone so easily wrong, they
had been forced by the Archbishop to act in such hurry. Beside
him, he heard someone say: 'Thank God we got away with it!'

He turned: it was big-faced General Vouros, puckered and
blushing with shrewdness under pressure. The Brigadier's eyes
fastened hard on him: though Vouros had voiced his own
thought exactly, he found it infuriated him to hear it aloud.
So very quietly, coldly, he said to Vouros, 'It was not a matter
of luck, Mr General.'

'No?' said Vouros, too far gone to be polite. 'Well, I held
my breath!'

The Brigadier stared, then turned about and stepped sharply
away. He had to; he felt such rage at Vouros. Jokes, slyness,
cheers, whooping – were these men officers? This second
triumph was not like the first: then he just exalted, excited like
the men, but this time he found himself unexpectedly on edge,

438

displeased, irritable; as if he had wanted even more, as if he wanted now more than could be granted.

He strode abruptly from the room, and out onto the balcony to smoke in peace. He needed time apart: he heard their bellowing clatter of voices, Vouros among them. He jerked his head impatiently: they were not serious men – the 'officer corps', they were well-heeled, most of them, from city homes. At times like these he felt the difference: they didn't know, as he did, that living was deadly earnest work. For no reason he could think of, he remembered the old iron waterpipe in his parents' home, joining into the concrete wall. If his parents could see him, now Greece was his! Slowly he absorbed his victory, with a deep solemnity, almost sad. Cyprus had returned to Greece. He thought, I have made the country whole. The first great phase of the army's work, that began when they took power seven years since, was completed at last, and completed by him: all the Greek lands were under army command.

He stood quite still and grave, his eyes and blade nose down, looking more like a man on the night before battle than like a warrior returned in triumph. But he could not stop: he had extended his power outside the Fatherland, the great age of Greece was beginning now.

Kostas looked out over Nicosia. The teeming city was calm and still, and beautiful in the morning: there were no shots, no shouting, only the stir of early traffic. Eventually he succeeded in ringing Kiki: he made light of the fighting, it had been a clean operation, a bad problem was solved, he was well. As he hadn't in weeks, he spoke to her lovingly, joked relaxedly, blew kisses down the telephone wire.

At the barracks, all was congenial work: he oversaw parties that left to take out pockets of resistance in the mountains; he visited the wounded and promised honours from Athens; he ordered protective custody for certain bishops and politicians of the Archbishop's party. He spoke at length with Athens, arranging the integration of the Greek and Cypriot army, and of Greek and Cypriot intelligence. In all these tasks he was clipped and efficient, fresh, taut, clear.

The day went well, he was tired and satisfied at the end of

it. The Archbishop had absconded – out of sight, out of mind. And if the world still called him President, and ignored his successor, well, that would soon change as the Archbishop stayed by himself in the wilderness. And if the new president were not the world's greatest statesman, still, he was a hero of the island, and he had pledged before everything his loyalty to Athens. The third coup, in the great series of three, had come to pass.

Kostas slept a sweet, dreamless sleep, and the following morning, again a recharged dynamo, he registered more with annoyance than with alarm the growth of a new shadow. For there was, that morning, concern in the barracks. He thought: they're an anxious lot on this island, real worriers!

'What's the problem?' he enquired, with an edge of sarcasm, of that red-necked colonel who had been proved wrong before.

Levelly the Colonel told him: there were reports coming in of troop movements in Turkey. Men and armour were travelling to a port in southern Turkey close to Cyprus.

'They're gathering there!' The Colonel stabbed with his finger the scrappy wall map which was all the Cyprus war room had.

'Poh! It's a bluff!'

The Colonel turned to him, as before, his bloodshot eyes of menace.

'They won't invade,' Kostas insisted. 'We have intelligence in Athens. Why should they invade?'

The Lieutenant Colonel put in, 'They say we've achieved *enosis*. They say Cyprus is now part of Greece, and that is unacceptable to them.'

'That's nonsense,' Kostas exclaimed hotly, rehearsing with enthusiasm the statement he might presently have to make in public. 'The tyrant was overthrown by the Cypriot National Guard. The government of Cyprus is an independent government. Nothing has changed in its relations with Greece. As you know, the first thing the new president did was to announce fresh negotiations with the Turks. Turkey has no case!'

The Colonel smiled tightly and didn't exert himself to reply; a subaltern approached and made new marks on the map.

'Our submarines could blow them from the water!' Kostas said later in the morning. He blamed the British: if they had not saved the Archbishop, if they had let him be shot, then it would not have been so hard to find a new president. Someone better would have served whom the Turks would trust. Of course the EOKA playboy was a red rag to Turkey.

More officers had come. The earlier reports were confirmed: large convoys of tanks and personnel carriers were steadily, at their own pace, converging on a port in southern Turkey, where also destroyers and landing craft were gathering. 'It's a bluff,' Kostas murmured to himself, after he had stopped saying this to the Cypriot officers: and even if there were an invasion, if the war between Greece and Turkey started now, still it was the confrontation he had been wanting. It seemed that all the ambitions he had lived for were coming true, and coming true sooner than he could have conceived, and coming true with himself in the vanguard. Yet still the build up was slow. The Turks did not hurry, and for many hours nothing would happen, and on Cyprus they could only wait: in spite of himself, Kostas found that this gradual huge accumulation of armour, only a few miles across the sea, left him cold about the heart.

He began to say angrily to those nearby, 'Well, and what will the British do? They're guarantors of Cyprus. They've got soldiers here. Are they just saying to the Turks, "Go in".'

But no one knew what the British were saying. Later they heard there were talks in London: the Turkish premier had flown to attend: the fate of Cyprus would be decided there.

'*Now* I see.' Kostas nodded to the signs on the map of the Turkish build up. 'This is all laid on to impress the British. The Turks won't show their faces here.'

In the eyrie of his London hotel the black-robed Archbishop moved to the window and looked out on tree tops – strange city, as thick with foliage as if it had been built in a wood, grey beneath its damp low sky, sky leaden, ponderous with piled cloud – what a weight of water hung overhead. He shivered: how strange that events on the other side of the world, on his own scorched island, with its bare rocks, it orange groves, its cauldron cities where men shouted constantly and gathered arms while across the sea a colossal army crawled – that events so far off should be decided, controlled, in this sunken city on the cold banks of its winding serpent river.

To these talks he could not go; he could only watch from far, perhaps advise, eavesdrop from a distance, while the Turkish premier and the British Foreign Secretary discussed the fate of his island, under the shadow of the hand of America. He feared the result. Could they keep the Turks out? The British and Americans must be tough as granite, clever as the snake, to use fear of the Turks to get the Junta out of Cyprus, and yet still to hold the Turks back. He feared, he feared: the Greeks wouldn't go, and the Turks would invade. If the British and Americans let that happen, it would be a great crime, a great wickedness, blind folly too, for Cyprus it would be – catastrophe, the end.

Hovering at the window, he collected himself to pray: and yet that was difficult, he was far from his world. Soon he would be further, he must fly to New York. Cyprus, and the God of Cyprus, were tiny in distance, and he was isolated, hanging in air.

Down the long panelled room of elderly furniture the light slanted in beams of lit dust: it caught the red half of a hot fixed face, and a dazzling corner of paper on the reflecting lake of polished table. Instinctively keeping out of the sun, the Turkish Premier, energetic and angular, sat sharply forward, following with hungry concentration the foreign language being spoken.

The British Foreign Secretary was a large rounded shape at the end of the table, a fleshy face with learned glasses on, and a goodhumoured smiling expression that hung to his features though what he said, in his thick, slow, lugubrious voice had no joy in it. To the Turkish premier he seemed like nothing so much as some English country doctor seen in films, the family practitioner, whose curved genial avuncular face says for him 'cheer up, old chap, it could be worse' while slowly, flatly, he gives the bad news: a tired voice too, as if it had had to inform too many patients of too many serious illnesses.

The Premier's long-nosed head pointed forward, he frowned as he made out the jagged meaning of the heavy words. For, at last, the British were insisting: Turkey might threaten, but there must be no Turkish invasion of Cyprus. Britain, NATO, would not permit it, America would not permit it. All military aid and all aid would be cut. Turkey had been requested and urged, and now she was instructed, not to invade: and she was reminded how absolutely she depended on the West, so bankrupt, so indebted, so unprovided as she was. Helpless, dependent Turkey had no choice.

The Foreign Secretary sat back at last, that cheering but not relevant smile still hanging goodhumouredly on his face; and they all sat back, waiting to hear how Turkey would reply.

The Premier let the pause extend. He knew they thought he had no choice, he was forced to the wall; and this was true, though not in the way they thought. Somewhere in the room – but he shouldn't look round – an old clock ticked slowly.

Then he spoke, in a voice that pierced the thick air; the translator caught his crispness and his own voice cut. And what his clear incisions said was that it must be understood immediately that Turkey reserved all her rights to intervene in Cyprus if she judged fit; she would not be dissuaded by pressure or coercion; and on the contrary she wished to make it clear that if there were any form of interference with Turkish policy, Turky would withdraw from NATO, she would herself take over all NATO facilities on her territory, and she would begin discussions with the Soviet Union with a view to closer cooperation in the future.

Then he leaned back; and beside him the translator, his shadow, sat back defiant, and faced the British with folded arms.

But the British said little further; there needed clearly to be other consultations. The meeting broke up, the British looking at each other as they stood from the table, and looking askance at the Premier. He saw they were daunted, even awed, by such intransigence. He could not but glow with the lustre of that strength, even though he knew he seemed to have strength only because he had no choice. For he could feel, what they couldn't see, the hard poke of gun barrels in his back: behind him the Turkish generals stood, and they would go where they wanted to go.

As they moved from the room, the British Foreign Secretary came over, and sidled up to him like some large vessel hoving to.

'Strong words, I respect that,' he said, but then, quietly and confidentially, seriously, as getting the facts clear man to man, 'It's not on, you know. You know that.'

443

'What is not on?'

'You know what I mean. Turkey will never make an alliance with Russia. It's no good trying to scare us with that. It wouldn't happen in a million years.'

He studied the Premier, watching his words sink in to do their work at a depth. But the Premier for his part only smiled quietly, acknowledging: it was the smile of a man who records your opinion, a trace amused that you should say that. Behind his glasses the Foreign Secretary's eyes grew uneasy, and he withdrew.

The Turkish Premier returned to his embassy in the glow of his fearless intransigence: he had been firm as a rock, he could do no other, for the generals behind him had their gun sights set.

Evening in London, and the wind grown cold; birds home, while shadows cluster at eaves and overhangs, and thicken by thin columns in reiterate arcades. Behind black glass in a gnawed façade, two voices, one brisk and one lugubrious.

'You heard? The Americans have decided.'

'Well?'

'They're letting the Turks into Cyprus.'

'Oh!' and a long silence of exclamation; with at last the low reply, 'They can't believe Turkey would get together with Russia.'

From the other a shrugging silence; any watcher outside would see two pale faces swim slowly to the window.

'We could stop them if we wanted.'

The one turns sharply to the other, 'A foreign adventure? Are you joking?'

The faces turn out again; to where, before them, darkness thickens round a group of statues huddled in the crouched corner of a pediment: figures showing white in the hard soot round them, like pictures of bleached fear in the blast.

Finally loaded, the Turkish fleet puts out to sea; and for long hours, and days, the wide arc of armour steams towards Cyprus across the calm Mediterranean. It moves so gradually, this ironclad armada, that on the island they say 'It's not a serious attack, it's a threat, a bluff, they are holding back.' But yet it comes so steadily on that after two days of the slow invisible nearing, the other thought dawns, 'Is it a double bluff, a terrible cheat? Do they *want* us to think it's all a threat, so we make no preparations, and they get close, while actually they intend to attack? Having come all this way, will they simply turn round and go home?' Then true fear stirs. Slowly, in shimmer, the ships rise over the horizon till they make an iron wall, so that too late it is inescapably clear, of course they won't turn round, it was no bluff, they are here.

As the separate warships move closer inshore, out of distance behind them new engine sound grows, till a wing of ponderous transport planes, seeming to hang still in the sky, grows slowly larger in deep-throated droning, an airborne armada overhauling slowly the armada on the sea. Now the advancing planes are themselves overtaken, as in sudden screaming, flashing, in rattling of shots, fighters swoop unstoppably out of the sky.

In the Pentagon in Athens, a war of cross-voices, 'But they've landed, they're attacking in depth.'

'They can't have landed, the Americans told us –'

'Are you blind? They're all round Cyrenia. They've got tanks in the hills. Their paratroops have landed here, here –'

But he in turn is stopped, as down the corridor footsteps rap at their ears; steps they all know. Voices fall. The Brigadier has come, he stands rigid in the doorway, his face pale and shining, scanning them quickly with wide open eyes. In the shadows behind him dangles his Prime Minister.

Nervously a general asks, 'Brigadier, how has this happened?'

'What does this mean, sir?'

For a few moments still the Brigadier eyes them. He is breathing through his mouth, the only sound in the room is the slight slow rasp of inhalation, as slowly his deep chest rises and falls – till he says in a brittle crackle of voice, 'Do you ask what this means, gentlemen? It means war!'

Half the war room breaks into a weak cheer; others worry, an adjutant frets. 'But, Mr Brigadier, are we ready?'

The Brigadier ignores him, he turns to his Prime Minister, 'Have you got it?'

Standing tall uncertainly, swallowing hard, the Prime Minister hands him the crumpled paper he has been nervously fingering.

The Brigadier holds it at arms length and runs his eye down the hasty, blotched typing, voicing the words; officers nearby lean in and attend, it is the declaration of war against Turkey.

He writes on it, and briskly hands it back. 'Get their signatures.' The Prime Minister, dismissed, walks from the war room, leaning forward in his attempt at military dispatch: a hard task ahead of him, finding in an hour the scattered Cabinet and getting them to sign.

The Brigadier, in the meantime, is all over the room; his words direct armies, submarines, jets. Already he has ordered the mobilization of reservists and militia forces, and of all Greeks who have done military service. In hours the whole of Greece will be an army.

And then? Then the Turks will know his wrath. At his command there will be – such ferocity of attack; from the bombers overhead, such release of burden. And the Turks are strong – such a battle it will be, such slaughter, but back into the east he will drive the Turk.

The mobilization call finds Leonidas and Patra languishing in their villa beside the sea. Since he lost office no famous guests, and very few visitors, come to see them; and those who come find it no summer villa, but the house of dejection. Mostly Leonidas and Patra sit – either on the terrace looking out on earth where, in high summer, their thin-rooted grass parches brown – or on the beach among his unused vessels and toys; the rubber folds of his dinghy perish where it is creased, his neglected floats and beachballs deflate and pucker. Leonidas maintains only one of his old activities: he hunts. He sleeps badly, wakes early, and at the first crack of dawn he is up, and dressed, booted and armed in a twinkling. He stalks partridge through the waist-high vines, inhaling keen air, while the sun is still a white dazzle at the base of the eastern sky. Scuttle, flap and flutter, the bird flies, he aims, bang go the barrels, and he bags the fat panting limp-necked birds.

446

From field to field he stalks and shoots, and comes home hours later in a muck sweat, his satchels and his shirtfront and his pockets and arms full of the bodies of birds, and all are piled in the kitchen, day after day. And down on the beach he is busy with his harpoon, stalking fish and squid in the shallows. He hunts and kills, killing is all that assuages his hurt, and even so he cannot kill enough. The fridge overflows with corpses of the creatures of sea and air; the pantry stinks of them; Patra complains scathingly. They come to blows: but the catch won't be wasted, he will eat them all, he plucks in frenzy, feathers the villa, stirs full vats of stewed birds. Then he sits down to vast solitary meals and eats like a man who is eaten by fury.

The crisis on Cyprus brings him crouching to the radio. He urges on the National Guard, yes get the Archbishop, kick out the British, give the Turks one in the eye! When Turkey invades, his head explodes. Greece is mobilizing, he must waste no time, after all his frustration his day has come. He ransacks the house for any old bits of his military equipment; they are lost for ever, but at least he has his hunting guns. He bundles his weaponry into the car.

'Patra, I'm going!'

'Going where, Leonida?'

'I'm off to the barracks.'

'To the barracks? Whose barracks? What will you do there?'

'In the name of God, woman, don't you know there's a war?'

'Leonida, you're old, they don't want you.'

'Old? Old? With my experience . . .' He slams the car door, but pauses and is out again; they kiss tenderly before he sets out for the front.

'I'm away,' he says, and is: roar of car engine, crash of gears, lurch bounce and spring-smash of wallowing steel, he careers on regardless over the ridges and ruts of baked mud in the country track, he drives as if he were driving a tank.

At the metalled road he streaks away, and horn-blasts a path through other traffic. But the road to the barracks is blocked by a long double queue of cars: here he must wait. He grinds within, acid eats his stomach, to be delayed like this; yet also his soul soars and exalts, to see so many patriots streaming in. What an army this will be to defeat the Turk. He looks at the queue: Mercedes, small Fiats, three-wheel trucks, motor

447

scooters, from all walks of life men have come to swell the army.

He abandons his car and strides down the line, forcing his way through the crowd at the gates: and inside the barracks, what a scene of activity! Men in old uniforms, new uniforms, in different halves of uniform or no uniform; with rifles, pistols, old sten guns from the war or the Civil War, and ancient Balkan weaponry crusted with bronze. Tanks and jeeps are scattered through the crowd, flustered officers hurry, and all looks confusion and chaos but is really tense activity, the preparation of a country to go to war.

He joins a loose platoon of new arrivals: they look like experienced men, one fifty-year-old man even wears the uniform of a general – evidently he is one of those officers retired by the National Government. Well, they must all fight together; impressed after all by even relics of rank, Leonidas slides towards the General. But, what, have these men no discipline? For the Sergeant who evidently belongs to them is standing by, while a senior officer, a colonel, is shouting commands to them: and the men shout back! Leonidas listens incredulous.

'Get in your ranks, you men!' the Colonel shouts again; he is stout, hoarse-voiced, out of breath. And the men reply, 'Don't tell us what to do. We came here to fight, not to take orders from you.'

'You'll obey my orders or you'll be shot.'

One of the men who shouted looks away and spits; over his shoulder he says, 'Leave us alone, we've had enough, these years, of being bullied by the army. We'll say who we'll fight under. I will take orders from General Prevelakis.' He points to the General, who stands taut-faced, not shouting, among them.

'General Prevelakis is no longer an officer!'

'We'll take orders from General Prevelakis and no one else,' another man shouts.

'You'll take orders from me!' The Colonel pulls his pistol from its holster, but even so they shout back, 'Ach, run away, we've had enough orders from your lot. Military Government, National Government, Greece for Christian Greeks, clear off, we've had enough, we'll fight with General Prevelakis.'

Beside himself, the Colonel raises his pistol, but as it comes up he is surrounded, he is lost to sight in the scuffle, someone kicks his gun clear, there are violent voices shouting. Looking round, Leonidas sees there are similar quarrels elsewhere on the paradeground. It is too much, he will take over, he strides forward bawling, 'That's enough, get back in line! What discipline is this? How will we fight the Turks like this?'

They turn, amazed. 'Who the hell are you?' But someone knows him, a voice says, 'That's Leonidas Argiriou – remember, he was in the National Government!' As he sees their faces, Leonidas' voice fails, his insides melt, he knows pure fear. At a stinging pain in his face he reels, and as he goes down a knee comes hard into his groin: he is drowning in enemy.

They abandon him in disgust; as he gets up coughing, spitting, he realizes the steady voice he can hear is the voice of General Prevelakis calling for order. He hears running feet: staggering upright, he sees that the Colonel has returned with reinforcement, a line of alarmed boy soldiers stand with raised guns pointed at the crowd of men.

'Get in line!' the Colonel shouts; but still they shout back, 'Get away, you lot, you've fucked us for years. So shoot us then! Another Architecture School! Fine! Bravo! Shoot us, and go off by yourselves to fight the Turk.'

The Colonel's face twists like rubber, but he gives no order, while the line of soldiers breaks as the men approach them. All is confusion, the soldiers mixed up in a scramble with the men. Presently Leonidas sees the Colonel hurrying away; and he himself moves clear.

He wanders across a paradeground of disorder; a small knot of men harangue an officer, who flings his arms, arguing, protesting; new soldiers, armed, arrive in jeeps, but are unsure what to do; elsewhere the soldiers themselves are at odds, shouting accusations; all the paradeground is an argument, as still, through the gate, the new arrivals pour rapidly in and join the confusion.

Discipline! Morale! We must fight the Turk! Leonidas murmurs; but some other instinct takes control, and in a daze he finds himself hurrying not into the fray, but out of the gate, and back down the line of cars, and into his own car, where he sits collapsed, sighing and almost sobbing. What cruel irony: the army had intervened in government to save the country; and the result of that was that the army and the country had come to be at war; so that now, when real war comes, there is no army.

Men streamed towards the barracks, while he sat still. Then he started his engine, in a spin of wheels he reversed clear of the queue, turned, and drove full pelt, his face streaming hot tears, back down the road he had come.

In the Pentagon new alarm flows in, not from Turkey now or Cyprus, but from Greece: the mobilization a success in numbers, but a disaster in discipline; the larger the barracks the greater the trouble; in some instances, mutiny. Yet no one dares tell the Brigadier that the army he has called up is an army against himself; for he is all the time on the radio now, giving commands to the forces on Cyprus. There are fresh fears: the Turks are gaining ground, the tanks of the Archbishop are breaking down. There is a new terrible report, that the jets sent to Cyprus have been turned back by the Americans.

Now the Prime Minister is on the phone, broken-voiced, stammering, he hasn't got all the signatures yet, some members of the Cabinet he cannot find.

The Brigadier doesn't wait; he gets a direct radio link to the commander of the Northern Army.

'Do you hear me, General?'

'I hear you.'

'General, war is declared. I order you to attack. You will cross the Evros, and advance into Turkey.'

The General's voice snaps acknowledgement, and cuts off in crackle.

The Brigadier turns, 'Gentlemen, you heard. We are now at war with Turkey. We attack across the Evros.'

A General sits at his desk alone; dark glasses held motionless between thick fingers; dry eyes aimed ahead.

Before him a clock, and thin hands by invisible gradations sliding forward; perhaps he registers the clock, he doesn't move.

A glance sideways; through the window, in bright sunlight, are long lined gun barrels aimed into the sky; artillery receding

450

as far as he can see; a small glimpse only of sunlit armour, perfectly still; but the knowledge in his mind too that if the window were placed in any other part of the wall, or if there were no walls at all to his temporary HQ and he sat at his desk exposed in space, still he would see the same thing all round him: artillery and tanks, row on row into distance, rising in a wave where the land undulates, sinking from sight and reappearing far away, in a long line parallel to the border with Turkey.

It all waits one word. As calmly as might be, he could utter that word. In moments, officers would take it, would repeat and pass it on; as it travelled it would grow and divide, certain instructions would travel to the tanks, others to the guns, and others again to the airfields and rocket sites. From the artillery beside him, the bombardment would commence: each gun would mushroom, softly sink on its spongy springs, and already be loading and firing again; deafening noise continuing unceasing, and beyond the river obliteration, while the forward tanks advance over the border, and behind them more tanks prepare to move.

All this would follow if he said that word: it waits to happen.

He attends to the clock; the thin hand has turned a quarter since he spoke to the Brigadier. Already it is late; but it was already late, when the Brigadier called him. It was late, many hours ago. Across the river the Turk was ready then, the Turkish artillery were trained back at them, the Turkish tanks were ready to move. That enormous, that inconceivably huge army, had had the time to get itself ready, every gun, every man was waiting to fight. There too a general sat, waiting with a word; as his own guns fired, retaliation would be instantaneous.

Also, how ready was his army? The final alignment had been done in a hurry: they had been rushed, they had been told there would be no war yet. And how good actually were his arms? Such discoveries, in the recent mobilization: whole crates of ammunition empty, or filled with stones; army guns sold to the Arabs; tanks whose engines didn't work. Strange thing, that when the army had asserted strength, governing the country, it grew weak as an army. And so hated, never had the army been so hated, and the army should be loved by the nation.

But still, they were the army, they would fight to the death:

451

that was all the fight would lead to here – Armageddon. Was this a battle that could be won? Could he gain an inch of ground, for all the thousands who would die?

Sight returned to his heavy eyes, he again took in the clock; the thin hand had turned through half the dial.

The General sitting at his desk; and outside, the fresh sun bright on polished gunmetal, and on the equipment of the soldiers, standing ready in all directions away into the distance.

He picked up his receiver and asked for a radio link to the President: the President, his old friend, who had steadily lost power as the Brigadier gathered all reins in his hands; the President, who recently had been ignored in the Pentagon, and would today be attended to, and obeyed.

In the Pentagon war room, 'We have confirmation, Mr Brigadier, the Northern Army is not attacking. It has not moved.'

The Brigadier's eyes flared, 'Get me the General!'

'We cannot. The Northern Army is not replying.'

'Tell them it's me.'

'We have. They say the General is not available, the senior officers are engaged.'

In the Brigadier, a shock of chill. A moment, a second before, all the nation's war machine was in his hand: now the army he has commanded to attack does not move, and in that instant he has – no power. Already the precipice has opened where he stands: he is falling fast. And not only he falls, for he is the National Government, the Government is him: he has made it so, it is falling as he falls. All his great vision is lost, destroyed. Ahead for him there is defeat, humiliation, and the loss of Cyprus – for that, as well as tyranny, he will be blamed. For the loss of Cyprus he will be killed.

He stands motionless while the blade divides his body; there is nothing he can do, no reprisal he can order, the Northern Army has the tanks; drawing himself tall he says, 'Notify me as soon as the General is available. Where are our aircraft?'

He turns quickly to another chart, and in his edged brittle unmodulated voice demands up-to-date information on the movements of the Turk.

*

In northern Cyprus a tank crests a ridge of thorns, towering over the Greek soldiers in the gully like a whale rising from the sea. For a moment it hangs above them, showing all its underside of armour plate and track, then it swings bouncing down, and charges slithering on them. They scatter and flee as best they can, while, further along, the next tank tops the rise.

Reverberant, with threshing blades, the helicopter rises over the ridge and comes slanting slicing down the gully flashing fire, rattling its bullets.

The Greek survivors have scrambled to the opposite shoulder of hill, where glancing back they see the Turkish infantry crest the ridge, and stand in a straggled line along it.

Retreat: dodge: leap: run through the trees and rocks, back and again back; there are too many tanks and too many helicopters and too many guns; from stone to stone, tree to tree, territory to territory, back before the advancing Turks. They return at night, infiltrating the territory the Turks have taken, creeping up on any small Turkish patrol.

The Turks also are busy under cover of night; and so, if Greek, make no noise as you pass this village church. In the moonlight it is clean and new-painted; yet its windows are smashed and its door hangs askew, and in the field round the church is a scene of drunken labour, men stumbling, laughing, jeering, heaving large stones out of their way, as if drunk with the endlessness of treasure they've found; though this is terrible treasure, a long sack with flailing limbs goes flying over the wall, while the men can't stop whooping and shouting.

Slow footfalls in the dark to the nodding Turkish sentry, and suddenly an arm throttling his throat, and the knife plunged into him, deep as the Turkish thrust into Cyprus.

By daylight, mutilated bodies and desecrated graves; and renewal of fighting, as the planes scream overhead, a hotel filled with people sinks to rubble in a rising cloud of dust. And no pause, still the Turkish army advances, and in the Greeks only desperate fighting despair as they cannot stop the Turks.

The Turkish plane shrieked low; Kostas and the Cypriot officer dived for a shell hole, but the large-built Greek Colonel, who was also with them, ignored the plane and the petty, dust-puffing bullets, and walked at his own pace down into the shallow pit; there he sat.

'I don't believe it, it isn't possible,' Kostas said to him impatiently, resuming their argument.

Though the Colonel had walked calmly, his face was inflamed; he only said, 'It is true.'

Choking with bitter contempt, the Cypriot officer said to Kostas, 'You fool. Do you believe your "National Government" is going to help us? You know what you have done? You have given Cyprus to the Turk!'

So agitated that he stood up, ignoring the Turkish fighter that circled the hills, Kostas shouted, waving his arms without control, 'Greece will declare war! Greece will invade Turkey! She will spare no one!'

The Colonel studied him; quieter than before, he said, 'Greece will not fight Turkey. She will not send reinforcements.'

Nearby a shell burst, there was a brown explosion, moments later a light rain of grains of earth, chips of stone, fell pattering in their pit. Far over the hills they heard a change of pitch in the fighter's engine, as it returned in their direction.

Over the crest of the pit other soldiers sprinted and plunged to join them; they were Cypriots, one wounded in the shoulder. The Colonel got to his feet. To the Cypriots he said, 'We have betrayed you.' He climbed with difficulty the sliding side of the pit, and holding his gun ready walked towards the advancing Turkish tanks. They heard the shriek of the plane returning, for a second they saw its wings spread broad as it rose over the Colonel, who ignored it; its guns sparkled; they ducked, and when they looked again, the Colonel lay flat.

With clamped mouth, with burning eyes, the Cypriot officer looked round at his comrades; with no words they rose together from the pit and ran forward, sprinting for cover, diving and then shooting.

Kostas huddled down alone at the bottom of the pit, and held himself as if he were cold; he took out his revolver and nervously turned it round in his fingers. He sat there trembling, while his mood poisoned. When two Greek officers, retreating from the battle, passed nearby, he joined them; later, quietly, the three of them returned to Greece.

*

In a room on the other side of the world, with a view of lean buildings fencing the sky, the envoy approached a vertical figure in black.

'The Government in Athens has fallen, Your Beatitude.'

He spoke with some excitement, but the Archbishop gave no response; he only gazed back steadily with his droop-lidded eyes. But presently, slightly, he nodded, and said in his thick, reprimanding voice, 'They would not have fallen without great sacrifice. The sacrifice was Cyprus.'

The envoy withdrew; the Archbishop returned to his long view of skyscrapers.

Autumn 1974

The streets crowded, shouted, sang; unknown people hugged each other and joined in chains of dancers in squares, on the roofs of buses, on lorry trailers; they pulled down placards, stripped posters, heaved aside triumphal arches made of cardboard.

After the rumours, breaks of light, news on the radio she hardly dared trust, Chryssa rose hurting towards belief: it was difficult, there had been false alarms, could this be a new manoeuvre? She and Michael listened close, on the rack of apprehension. Yet each announcement made it clearer that the army had given up power, prisoners were released, a coalition government was being formed, to negotiate a ceasefire with the Turks and to prepare elections. The new government was made up of ex-prisoners and exiles. It was unreal, finding that only good news came, and more good news: steadily, inevitably, a climbing happiness rose in Chryssa, expanded, lifted, like a smile from the centre widening till it filled her. The joy of release released pent grief, happiness melted to strengthening sobs that tore deeper till she felt they'd tear her lungs out. Slowly she calmed to a steady free crying, where each sob was the bursting of some particular worry or fear that had eaten her, a part of her pain coming to the surface.

'Vangelis will be coming home,' she murmured, while Michael could only watch, sharing her joy with half his heart. An iron door was sliding between them: they could be inches apart, and it would be between them; they could be touching, and it was between them. He thought: now I'm dead to her, she goes back to her real life.

They made phone calls, and discovered that Vangelis should arrive next day by boat.

Michael accompanied her to the metro. On the way he let himself glance only briefly at her strong, fresh, clear-featured face. At the station she turned to him: but her voice was choked, and at first he couldn't catch her words. Then he understood: 'I must be with Vangelis now.' He had to agree: but how long the 'now' was, whether it meant 'from now on', or 'for these days' with a bitter decision later, he could not tell. This was what he must know: but her face as he looked grew only more troubled, and he could not bear to see her lose in this way all that had been clear at the moment of good news. Instead of asking the question he hung on, he heard himself say, the words hurting as though they were plucked from his flesh, 'You must forget about us for these days, Chryssa. Put it out of your mind, otherwise Vangelis won't have a good homecoming.'

She nodded, her eyes welled with tears.

They kissed, parted, Michael walked away fast.

Arrived in her flat, she cleaned and arranged, sorted embroideries, unable to be still. The good news overwhelmed her again, as if she had only just learned it: Vangelis was coming, and no police force could stop him now. The face of Michael swam again to her eyes, but she must not address it, she was swept away in the unbelievable. She had felt distant from Vangelis, but the shock news of his coming brought all her memories back. She saw him as clearly as if he had left hours before: she heard his voice, he called to her from the next room, he was coming nearer.

'Vangeli,' she murmured, 'My love,' and took out his clothes and held them close, as if any moment he would reappear within them, and within her arms.

She thought she would never sleep, but in happy hope her eyes closed and he joined her in her dreams. Only once she woke, frightened, there was something not right, something terribly awry; but that was not clear, her thoughts all spun. In the morning she could think of nothing but this day. She couldn't visualize Vangelis, she felt his arrival as some diffuse enormous light, or heart of love, travelling over the sea to her: her thoughts were suspended, she was nothing but a waiting.

She made her way to the quay: his ship had not come, there was no sign of it. Only then a new fear brushed her heart: mirages of anxiety, a mounded stretcher, a dead eye. Let it not be! But even as these fears came to sight, they dissolved,

457

she knew he was well, he was whole, he was coming.

All radiance of expectancy, her eyes fed on the horizon.

The prisoners were dazed, their thoughts fingered what they heard uncertainly, only slowly their dry throats opened to shout. The warders were effaced and foolish, at a loss, the prison was like a vessel that had lost its captain.

On the boat Vangelis stood with the others in the bow, which neither dipped nor rolled but drove on steadily over the uniform sea. The water was glassy, looking down they saw jelly-fish, white or dark red, hovering like tiny clouds in the green. For hours the voyage continued, the water stayed calm, the day only brightened: in new waves of realization he would repeat to himself, I'm free. Later they saw flying fish, racing the boat. It seemed an enchanted voyage, a passage to Elysium.

Christoforos said quizzically, 'Holiday's over then, Stamati. You'll have to do some overtime, if you want to catch up on your pension.'

'There'll be enough work for me,' Stamatis said quietly.

Vangelis eyed them, 'You two are all right. I'll have to tout for cases.'

Christoforos leered at him, 'I wouldn't say that. There'll be a lot of top rank officers looking for good defence lawyers.'

Vangelis raised his eyes till the whites showed.

Stamatis said, 'They'll put you on a tribunal, Vangeli. You'll be able to say what happens to them.'

Smiling, Vangelis jerked his head, 'tst'.

They chatted light-headed, gazing into the dazzle. A brown edge on the horizon slowly approached till they ran past a stony undulating coastline. As tiny houses began to appear, the mist ahead of them thickened to a purple-brown haze they could not see through: they knew then they were approaching Athens. Faintly the city appeared, white and dusty, its buildings looking like chips of chalk. As he started to recognize landmarks he felt oddly cheated that it looked no different from his memory of it: it was as if he had been away only a day, and his long exile was devalued.

They were heading now into a still sea that steadily grew more crowded with ships, with freighters and long tankers lying at anchor: it was a city of ships outside the city, becalmed on the doldrum sea that had here a dusty iridescent skin, it lay flat and heavy as oilcloth.

They threaded their way through the busy roads, and came round in a wide arc to the overbuilt coastline. He knew Chryssa would be there on the jam-packed quay, and suddenly he found himself curiously shy. He had been allowed to see her so little, he had been out of the company of women. He felt nervous as a boy approaching a girl for a first dance, while with love and shyness his mind empties.

As the ship docked, he searched the faces and found her: she had not changed. Had she seen him? Her eyes scanned, searching, but he hurried below, to disembark.

Police and port officials struggled to hold back the crowd that surged to the descending gangplank: reporters pressed ahead of relatives, holding up cameras and microphones, shouting technicalities. Chryssa struggled in the crush, walled in by shoulders. At last men emerged, sudden into sunlight, gazing round dazzled blind by the crowds and the flash bulbs.

She cast for Vangelis and at first didn't see him. He wasn't one of those who came striding straight into the arms of delegations. He came at his own pace, and in this first glimpse he looked his old self, dark-skinned, very solid – but quiet. He stepped ashore warily, testing his steps: while his black eyes darted at the crowd and away, not like a man come home but like a man landed in a foreign country. Still he hadn't seen her, he had difficulty facing the so many faces. Then his eyes found her, and her heart leapt crazy as she saw the relief, the pleasure, in those black eyes which didn't leave her for a second as he slipped through the crowd and stood over her. Senses she did not know she had, like invisible tendrils or feelers, stretched out gingerly and, like the touch of a blind man, felt their way over this hard-faced moist-eyed man till she found in him everywhere Vangelis. And his face softened, his cheeks puckered. In a leap she closed the small gap between them: in collision they hugged each other hard, shuddering, and kissed.

Flashbulbs burst at them, they realized they were at this moment newsreel stars: an eager man, mouthing, held out at them a grey bulb that trailed wire to his pocket. Vangelis glanced round, his old keen reconnoitre, and saw some of his

459

colleagues voluble with journalists, denouncing the Junta: it was a political opportunity. His face turned sardonic.

'Let's get out of here.'

They pressed hard through the crowd till they were clear of it, and got into the taxi Chryssa had kept waiting hours. As it headed into the city they sat back looking at each other, holding each other, taking each other in.

Chryssa unlocked the door, and he gazed at their home. With a long sigh he sat, and still looked round, renewing his acquaintance with the pictures and lampshades; the shelves and books; the knobbed and clubbed, gouged and graven blackwood table; the stately chairs carved to match. He could hug these things; the whole home had come back by a miracle. He held Chryssa's hand, shook his head, gazed at her in numb thanksgiving.

Shortly afterwards Vangelis' solicitor-associate Cosmas Matziris came round, with his wife Niovi, clattering unbidden into the flat laden with presents, drinks, flowers, and already celebrating.

'Vangeli! How are you?' Cosmas cried, hugging him vigorously then holding him at arms length and gazing at him shining-eyed.

'I'm well,' Vangelis nodded quietly. As they sat in the living room, Cosmas and Niovi alternately plied Vangelis with questions, and called to Chryssa as she hurried round with snacks. They asked about the people Vangelis knew in prison, and about the plans they all had now they were released; it was said that new political parties would be formed.

Vangelis hardly answered: he seemed abashed by their vigour, and reluctant to remember. He put his sentences together with care.

The others exchanged understanding looks, but were a shade disappointed also; and Cosmas, who had at first simply gazed on Vangelis admiring, presently began more confidently to opine. He became emphatic, the centre of talk. Vangelis sat back, listening to the noise of their voices rather than their words; Cosmas, who wore the same bow tie Vangelis remembered of old, had started now to dye his grey hair, and the black locks on top of his leathery face were not a good idea; the cheerful nervous laughter of his piquant fox-faced wife tinkle-crashed like breaking glasses. Vangelis seemed to watch

460

them from miles away, as if he saw them through the wrong end of a telescope. Remembering him in old arguments – sparkle-eyed, biding his time, retorting with zest – Chryssa was moved to see him sit on the sideline, the observer, while Cosmas boomed.

But the visitors gathered that Vangelis was tired, and presently they left: he met them most warmly as they embraced to say farewell.

When they'd gone, he said, 'I don't want other people. I want only you.'

They were then quietly together at home. In the brown lamplight, their things stood round them – the black suite, the unlit lamps – in the warm thick shadow of their old familiarity.

'You were right, Vangeli, not to sign that pardon.'

'I don't know. It meant another year gone from our life.'

'No, my love, you were brave and you were right. I was wrong, I was so stupid, even to bring it.'

Gently he headed his 'no' towards her, a 'tst' like a kiss.

Little by little he began to speak of the prison. He recalled the lighter, better things: his horticulture with Christoforos, Stamatis' unofficial pharmacy, his own seminars with the criminals. He paused, describing the bouzouki.

'My love . . .' She sat curled on the floor, her cheek on his leg. Very gently, as if amazed, he caressed her hair.

They went to bed, but did not love then. He lay in her arms still and quiet as a child needing to be held: he first, then she, subsided in sleep. In the early hours of the morning she woke confusedly: he was making love to her, though she realized that he too was only now waking, murmuring tenderly. Smokily his awareness woke, and joined his body's want of her. They didn't completely wake: in the warm pitch darkness he held her in a long loving, and sweetly they sank back into darkness.

In the morning they remembered dimly the sleeping love in which they returned to each other.

Vangelis stood on their balcony looking out over Athens; the traffic racket blared below, and the shout of a man working his way up the street selling watermelons rose high and then fell. Beyond the apartment blocks he saw the sea, dark blue, scintillating, busy with freighters. If he craned over the rail,

461

he could see the Parthenon. Everything that he had prayed to see was restored to him: yet he did not feel the emotion he expected. He had believed that if he ever returned, he would fling himself weeping on these dear objects: but instead of that he felt removed, as if the city were here right enough, but he had not got here yet, he was still on the way. Yet he felt at peace, as if he flew in white space: there was no hurry.

He breathed in, looked about him: he must get back to earth. There was an illusion in the peace he felt, an agitation he couldn't place, panic: then he had the sensation of a massive enclosure shrinking round him, it pressed his flesh on all sides. In the open air, he stifled.

'I'll go in,' he said breathlessly, and immediately moved indoors. Chryssa got up from her chair and followed.

He sat in one of the black wooden carvers, his arms on the chair arms, his head hard back. The room was dim from the thin day-curtains. He breathed in sighs, looked at her embarrassed, said, 'I'm sorry, I don't know –' How could he explain that the light outside, the endless space, everything free to fall off the world, had suddenly appalled him: then the prison returned, its stones closed round him.

She held his arm tight, her low voice, deeply assuring, said, 'Vangeli – you will be free.'

He breathed slowly, calmer, his vision cleared. Presently he said, 'There was one thought I often had, sitting in prison.'

'Vangeli?'

'I thought we should have children. It was I who stopped us, really. It was the worst thing I did.'

'My love.' She gave a tight, trembling smile, he saw he had startled her very much. And then, as if it were her turn to leave the room suddenly, she quickly got up and went into the kitchen. He heard her sob or cough: after a little while he joined her, together they cleared things. She had her head down, her eyes were red, she avoided looking his way.

The round face with drill-hole nostrils hovered closer, the mechanism on chains was pulled towards his stomach, they set it turning, scooping, it would pierce his navel and continue through him, and this was the deepest cell, no one would come.

'Vangeli – Vangeli –'

'Chryssa? What? Sorry.'

'My love. It's over.'

'Over? No, Chryssa, you don't know, there's been a new coup. It couldn't last.'

'You were dreaming, Vangeli. You're still dreaming. Come close to me, love. Lie close. You're home.'

'Chryssa.'

Slowly he sank in the warm dark of her embrace: but she now was woken, in a few seconds more she was wide-alert, turning. I must wake Vangeli, tell him – but how could she wake him, after that dream? How could she hurt him so? And tell him what? And somewhere in Athens Michael was waiting, not knowing what she'd say. Her love flowed to Vangeli; clung to Michael. Can a love be cut off, like a limb, abolished?

There is no exit from the labyrinth of night thoughts. Restrictedly she turned in the bed till first light; and, as Vangelis stirred, sank in belated sleep.

Simos also was home, they went to visit. Clio opened the door, a wan brittle face that lit with pleasure to see them.

'Vangeli! Chryssa! Come in, come in, how wonderful!' She led them in, almost weeping with excitement at their coming.

'Come and see Simo, it's so good you've come.'

They went into a room where, on a large sofa, the heavy-built form of Simos lay, in pyjamas. His head was rested up on a cushion, and they moved round till he could see them. His giant face had a rough growth of stubble, his eyes looked dully ahead, one of them more open than the other. They could not tell whether he saw them; except that there was a tremor, a movement, in his face somewhere.

'Simo, hello,' Chryssa said, kissing him.

'Simo, how goes it? It's good to see you home too,' Vangelis said. They both spoke with animation, and there was again the slight tremor and puckering in the large face. They talked on, hoping that somewhere he understood, while sorrow swept over them in waves. Clio turned back to them with swollen eyes, 'Sit down, sit down.'

They sat, in chairs that made a loose circle including the sofa where Simos lay. Clio perched neat on the chair edge, just

463

as she used to when they all went to the bouzouki, her hand raised like an elegant bird leg, holding a cigarette: the small, perfect, beautiful faced woman from Chania. She told them how Simos was brought home in an ambulance, with no warning to her of how he was: for the present, the Government provided a nurse. She said again, 'I'm so glad you came. I don't know if people will come.'

'People will come,' Vangelis said.

She nodded brightly, hardly hearing.

'The children help me.' Her face trembled. 'Can you imagine how it is for them?'

Suddenly, Simos started to shout. His mouth was open, his eyes stared, though his body lay still he was banging his head up and down on the pillow, up and down the large head bounced while from his mouth came a terrible cry that had no words, that was only sound, that in its intakes of breath and new cries was like the braying a donkey makes: heart-breaking noise, it could be animal or person, it went on and on, ripping them.

Clio approached him and passed her hand over his face; they were not sure how she treated him, but the cries paused. Then they began again, his head bobbed, his eye rolled, seeing them; she turned to them with a white harrowed face, cried, 'Please go, you must go at once, please.'

They left quickly, but out in the street they still heard the cries. The face of each of them was screwed up tight. They walked away like blind people, they could not stop hearing the continuous braying cry that tore their brains and hearts to shreds.

'Vangeli,' Chryssa said, holding her returned husband hard, while her eyes were wrinkled tightly shut. 'Vangeli, we're so lucky.'

He nodded firmly, holding her tight.

In the evening, Chryssa watched him at work: it was like one of their old evenings, before the Junta, restored by a miracle. In the pool of lamplight, his broad and slightly forbidding face was bent frowning over his papers, still in concentration. What a rock of a man he is, she thought. Already the shadow of his Balkan moustache had returned, like a ghost moustache materializing slowly. 'My love,' she murmured, musing as she watched him. Time passed: he hardly looked up, he worked solidly on into the night like a man who lived alone. And later it seemed to her there was something unreal, false, in the way everything looked just as it had been, when everything had changed. Vangelis had changed.

Chryssa had left Vangelis at the law courts, and was returning to the metro station in Omonia Square. She was watching the fountains in the square plume upwards like tall feathers when, as she approached the escalator, she saw Michael being lifted towards her out of the ground. Motionless as a statue he rose like a person ascending from the dead. Still she had not phoned him, she had been all the time with Vangelis. She had put off the crisis: now it met her. She stopped, the people behind cannoned off her confused. He saw her – his pale face broke in surprise, light – just as his feet touched the grill, and forcibly he came to life and stepped towards her.

For a moment they could only stare, like two people who had stumbled towards each other, unknowing, down a dark passage: now someone put the light on, the bright faces stared at each other astonished.

He got breath first. 'Chryssa, how wonderful to see you! How are you?'

Her eyes shied from him. She heard her voice answer in the distance; she felt thin and rattling, a bead curtain in the wind.

'How is Vangelis?'

'He's well, Michael.'

'I'm very glad.'

The unreal small talk continued jerkily. She still wavered; the wind tugged at them; beyond him she saw the fountains of Omonia Square weaving and breaking and steaming aslant in long banners of spray.

'Can we talk?' His blue eyes were haggard, he believed he'd lost her.

'We must talk, mustn't we?' But she wasn't ready, she needed time.

'Shall we go to the taverna?'

'We shouldn't be seen.'

They decided to go to Michael's flat.

465

'What's going on? What are you doing?' Her first thought was that the flat had been ransacked, the secret police had been. His work things, his pads, folders, lay against his books, that were piled in insecure towers on the floor. Nothing was where she was used to seeing it. The Karagiozis shadow-puppet lay like a crumpled person on the books.

'I've been sorting my things. I've sent some home.'

'Are you leaving?'

'Leaving here?' At that word his blue eyes shone; she was startled, for he had been a cool one. But he spoke clearly, 'I've got no plans, I have to find some. My commission here was to do with the dictators. Now they've gone, that's gone.'

'What will you do?'

'I'll find something, of course. It depends –'

'Depends on what?'

'On you,' he said, almost silently. She looked down. He cleared a chair for her. 'Sit down.' She didn't.

'How have you been, Michael?'

'Not good. Like half a man, really, hopping round on one leg, hanging onto things with one hand.' He smiled.

'I should have rung, I don't know how –' She paused; but he said affectionately, 'I can imagine how it's been.'

She looked at him directly, her low voice was distinct. 'Michael, I haven't rung you, and I haven't told Vangelis. Because – what to say? If everything were over with us, I'd know – if I could leave Vangelis for you, I'd know – But – I don't know what I should do. I don't know what I want. I thought that with time things would be better, clearer, but they aren't. I *can't* leave Vangelis, we've been very close these days. But also I *can't* just cut off from you and go back home and be the good wife. Perhaps I should do it, but I can't –'

He said – his voice more than usually hoarse, thick as if he wanted to cough, 'Come away with me, Chryssa.'

She blinked: at this slender-featured, energetic, terribly hungry man.

'Perhaps what I say is bad, selfish, what you shouldn't do, I don't know. But we haven't finished. Come with me – for a time – so you see what you'll do. Leave Athens –'

'I can't leave Athens, it isn't possible.'

She waited, silent: this is the moment, I must say nothing more.

466

Eventually he said, 'I should go?'

In the dim light his pallor was luminous, his tall boniness filled the room. His eyes leaned to her, yearning: how strange blue eyes are, sky-coloured, not earth-coloured like Greek eyes. She was under attack, the room's darkness swooped at her. It seemed yesterday that she'd been in this room, chatting on the balcony where she found him asleep. The changes were too quick. Michael was growing paler and bigger so his head would bang the ceiling: she was separating, coming apart like a jigsaw puzzle held up by the ears. She remembered the chapel on the island, where she glimpsed the other side of her life, the different life she'd live abroad. She must shut the door. She hurt as if his hands reached into her breast and gripped her heart and tugged to pull it out of her.

'Goodbye is what I can't say –' He choked, his eyes swam, abruptly he seized her hand and, stooping, pressed it to his lips and kissed it hard. She was helpless, it was all she could do to stay standing. He was a ball of brown hair before her, and a mouth on her hand. She touched his head to raise it, but raising it, held it.

The night sky was wild and tangled, she walked home through streets where paper peeled off peeling plaster, where walls crumbled to powder, where the shellshocked fronts of the buildings had hardly been renovated since World War II; down an alley where old newspapers cartwheeled in the funnelling wind. Through a chasm between buildings she caught a clear view upwards of the spotlit temple, pitched up on its crag: it looked yellow, flat, the torn sky came reeling over it so the temple seemed riding forward on a black wave to swamp the city. Afterwards she broke into a small isolated square of brilliant lights, crowded tables, arms in shirtsleeves pouring wine, glasses clinking; noise of laughter, shouting, harangue, celebration. But she followed the old papers, down a darkening alley with a cold sheen of street lamp at the end; where it turned, and opening unexpectedly brought her to the dead end of a small quay. Across a wide spread of sea hobbled boats rocked and tipped uneasily, in pitch-black choppy water that threshed the pebbles.

She walked on through the streets. People ate and laughed

and danced, as though everything were good again. But the country had been torn, Greek against Greek, and her life had been torn, and she'd been torn from what she had; now the enemy had gone, and Vangelis was back, but she was still tearing.

'Tell me, Chryssa,' Vangelis said. So seriously she had said to him, 'There's something – that happened while you were in prison – that I must tell you, Vangeli.' But there she stuck, her eyes fell, she sat gazing fixedly, frozen. He waited; he knew from her difficulty that what she would say would hurt him. Though she could not speak, he knew he must not relax the pressure on her of his waiting.

Gently he said, 'Chryssa, say.' Lips parted, she looked at him. He hurt from end to end with apprehension: he thought, this will be worst of all. Then he thought with chill – still not knowing – there is something here I have been avoiding.

'Chryssa.'

With difficulty, she told him of Michael: her own pain made the news hurt more. No jealousy burst; he wanted to cry. Tenderly he rested a hand on her, seeing her trouble he only loved her, and said, 'My love.'

She looked at him still with pain-eyes; and then he murmured, hoarse, 'It's over now?'

'It's over, Vangeli, it's you I love,' she said with emphasis, but, even as she spoke, voice broke to sobs, she dissolved in loud tears, and her words seemed to fall about Vangelis, the remnants of a sentence that broke to pieces at the moment it tried to fly from her lips. An arm resting numb on her, he gazed over her sobbing crouch with eyes in which sight died.

'What will you do? Will you go with him?'

'I don't know, Vangeli.'

'We'll talk tomorrow.'

But tomorrow brought no answer, only a new, quite different demand.

It was Patra who called, her voice shrill, 'It's come, Chryssa, he says we must all go and see it.'

468

'What's come, Patra?'

'The ferryboat. You remember dad said he'd bought a ferryboat? He's almost mad with it, we have to go.'

'I can't come now, Patra, it's a very bad time.'

'It's only a day. Chryssa, he's desperate, this is his success, we have to see it.'

'But Patra, he *can't* have bought a ferryboat. It isn't possible, there's some terrible mistake here.'

'You'll have to come and see.'

Chryssa sighed. Bewildered she took the plane, knowing she was in too great confusion to give concern to her family; it was only when she arrived at Salonica airport and saw her parents and sister drawn up in a line at the barrier, waving and calling, 'Chry-ssa!', that she thought how beautiful, what a miracle it would be, if she could step for a day into her family past, be herself younger, before the problems. Even Alexis was there, a taciturn man apart from the others: but he had, what she had thought she would not see again, a young smile for her. They all kissed, hugged, and walked to the large car of Leonidas.

'I'm so glad Alexis came,' Chryssa said quietly to Patra.

Patra shook her head gravely. 'He had his reasons for coming with us.' Then she smiled, 'But you're one of them. He said he'd come with us to the ferryboat, since you were coming.'

They began the drive across Macedonia, to the island where their father traded. Leonidas wouldn't look at Chryssa, much less at Alexis, he sat at the wheel tight lipped and aloof, like a man sitting on a great indignation. She saw he was determined not to feel abashed about Vangelis. He scowled at the road, drove savagely, and occasionally vented his feelings not on her but on her father, muttering with suppressed fury 'ferryboat!' Her father was too consumed with his own excitement and anxiety to notice Leonidas, or even his daughters; he sat forward, gazing at the road ahead with feverish eyes, while the knots of muscle round his jaw throbbed like small animals. He knew none of them believed in his ferryboat: the sceptics, they would see! Their mother sat beside him in a still grieving worry, murmuring from time to time to her own rhythm, regardless of them, 'Ach, my little God! Ach, aman!' They could not tell whether she believed in the ferryboat or did not believe in it.

469

'Is it this turning, Alexi?' Leonidas asked brusquely, and Chryssa saw that he was attempting to build a bridge with his son, asking his advice as an equal.

'No, father, it's the next one,' Alexis said, also brusque, businesslike. Otherwise he ignored his father, but to Chryssa he talked. He asked about Vangelis, he also told her his reason for coming to Salonica: it was not for the ferryboat, but because next day he would go with his friend Petros to the obsequies for Rena, who had been killed at the Architecture School. She came from Salonica.

'You saw her, aunt.'

'I don't think so.'

'But you were there!' Mature-faced, he looked for a moment close to tears: he could not believe that Chryssa had not seen her. And Chryssa realized that Rena was one of those students she had seen against the tank lights, up on the gate.

'I saw her.'

Leonidas, in front, sat with his head quite rigid, listening to them, not intervening.

'What is the time?' Chryssa's father asked, for the umpteenth time.

Eventually they arrived at the old city of Kavala, and took one of the worn, standard ferries to the island. There, the sisters found they had new travelling to do, for their father insisted that his ferryboat was to be delivered to a port on the other side of the island. Snarling in incredulity, and amazement that he was here at all, and indignation with the daughters for indulging the old man, Leonidas revved the huge car, and flung out of the island port in a fury of dust.

Finally they arrived at the other port: they ran past the few houses there, and pulled up on the quay.

'Well, father,' said Leonidas, leaning round from the front seat in a wide triumph he couldn't contain, 'and where is this ferryboat?'

Their father gazed out to sea, all the lines of his face working, his dry throat swallowing thirstily.

Leonidas lit a cigarette and sat where he was in the car, but with the door open, resting from the unnecessary drive.

Their parents got out of the car uncertainly: their father hurried to the waterfront, where he craned round, at a loss.

His daughters hurried after, exchanging looks of pity.

Patra said sharply, 'Father, who did you give the money to?'

'Money?' he murmured, with lost eyes.

'The money for the ferryboat, father. Who did you give it to?'

'The money? I gave it to the agent, to Mr Tsourkas.'

'Is Mr Tsourkas here?' They knew he wouldn't be.

But their father, after looking round with haunted eyes, said in a shattered quaver of voice, 'There he is.'

The sisters stared: for their father pointed to a man who stood on the edge of the quay with his back to them, a man so enormous they had never seen the like of him – broad bags of trousers taut over two gross planets of buttocks, a loose mountain of back just contained by a vast singlet stretched to bursting, round shoulders merging neckless to head.

The sisters quailed. Patra summoned Leonidas, who swallowed but steeled himself, and strode up to the quayside shouting aggressively, 'Where's Mr Tsourkas? I want to see Mr Tsourkas.'

The great man turned, and they saw, in the centre of the sack-like head, a long-nosed aquiline subtle face; with answering aggression he shouted back, 'And am I so hard to see then, Mr Sharp Eyes?'

Not to lose momentum, Leonidas shouted at once, 'I understand my father-in-law has placed money with you to purchase a ferryboat.'

Mr Tsourkas nodded provisionally and turned to see this father-in-law; catching sight of their father, he waved a salute, 'Good day to you, Mr Niko.'

'Good day, Mr Tsourka,' their father answered, his eyes of worry feeding on the huge figure.

'Right,' said Leonidas, getting into his hectoring stride. 'And will you tell us please – where is this ferryboat?'

With a slight flap of his arm – not to move too much in the great heat – Mr Tsourkas said nonchalantly, 'There it is.' The family turned: in seeking the ferryboat, they had made the mistake of looking out to sea. Now they looked along the coast, and saw, just rounding the headland, something sitting on the water that looked like a square black box.

'There's the new ferry,' Tsourkas said again; and even as he spoke, the word passed back, and in a crowd the villagers hurried past them to the quay. 'It's coming!' As they arrived, and lined the waterfront, a long hooting sounded from the distant boat.

With mixed feelings, the sisters, their mother and Alexis pleased, and Leonidas appalled, the family gawped. Chryssa heard a fisherman nearby say to his wife, '*There's* our ferryboat!'

She turned to him, 'This is *your* ferryboat?'

His eyes, his spaced teeth, glittered in his baked face, 'This is our ferryboat.'

At last Chryssa understood. 'You mean, everyone here has invested?'

'*Almost* everyone,' he nodded, and with a toss of his head he indicated a handful of villagers who stood at the back of the quay, scowling, muttering, lantern-jawed with dismay. These evidently were the sceptics.

The sisters understood: their father visited this island often in his business trips. When he heard of the ferryboat scheme, he had bought shares in it, and it was natural to him to have assumed from this that he was sole owner. He gazed now in a happy daze, as the square front of the ferryboat slowly grew larger. Its loudspeakers were turned on full blast and its music came to them over the waters. Beside their father their mother stood, looking out to sea with a rapt face while, in silence, the tears coursed down her face.

As it approached the quay, the boat slewed round, and all its long side and towered bridge were a dazzle of sticky-shiny white and blue: it was lined with coloured flags and pennants, and with festoons of light bulbs that would make it shine at night. In long bursts its hooter sounded. As it approached the quay, the iron jaw in its blunt bows opened: a sailor, spick and span in white, balanced casually on the iron edge.

The engines churned backwards, frothing the sea; it slowed; the bows just grazed the quayside: and at that moment all the village flowed on board. Chryssa's parents straggled in, in the rear.

A new ferryboat – Chryssa had never conceived of such a thing, ferryboats were always aged, grimy, dismal, foul. But all of this vessel was new and bright: the iron car deck was fresh green all over, shining in the sun, so the village seemed to troop in over sward. Everywhere in the passenger decks were small vases of plastic flowers blooming brilliant colours.

472

Throughout the boat the music was turned on deafening. Groups of villagers wandered in a daze; and through them strode Mr Tsourkas, who during the arrival had somehow put on an enormous shirt, dazzling white to match the new paintwork, and who billowed through the lounges like a sail boat within the iron boat, his eyes shining, shaking hands, clapping men on the back while they clapped him, exclaiming over and over '*This* is a ferryboat!'

Chryssa saw her parents come into the lounge; she had been separated from them in the crush. They were looking round the ship wonderstruck, but they were confused by the crowd, and the noise, and the events of the day, and the dazzle and newness of the boat. It touched Chryssa's heart to see her father, in his moment of triumph, when for once he had something to exalt in, wandering through this huge investment, dwarfed by it, looking shocked and lost in it. She flowed with love for him as she had not in years, and for her mother as she wandered in the ship bewildered, pleased, tired, not strong.

Later, more collected, they went on deck. As they stood in the bright sunlight their father gave a large wave of his arm that took in all the ferry and the village as well, as he cried, 'Ach, my love, my daughters, *now* this island will realize its value!'

They gazed over the brilliant boat; on the quay, they saw Mr Tsourkas fit himself into a tiny three-wheel truck, and putter off through the village, evidently to some further stage of celebration; looking up, they saw standing over them on the ship's bridge, Leonidas. He had been discomfited utterly by the arrival of the ferry; but Chryssa saw that, true to form, he had adjusted quickly, and introduced himself to the captain, and was now discussing, in a knowing way, the economics of a successful ferryboat line.

They returned to Salonica. Tired from the family day, Chryssa slept well: it had been a curious holiday. But in the morning she woke at dawn.

She slipped out of her parent's flat, caught an early taxi, and walked on a flank of Salonica mountain. She had been to school near here; from the close-packed yellow buildings that sloped to the sea rose the familiar racket of Salonica traffic, the bipping and beeping of horns, the buzz of scooters, the tinny flutter of three-wheeled vans, and the heavy-throated full-throttled chug as buses dragged themselves into motion.

It had been a windy and rainy night, there was still a strong wind blowing inshore, the air was very clear: the sky seemed huge, with different weathers in different parts of it. Out to sea was a storm, the rolled clouds were black over the shadowed water and between them swept dark wisps and skeins of descending rain; on the far side of the gulf was a pale but bright sunlit shore, with flat meadows of reclaimed land; to her right, from the factories trailing round the arm of the bay, a brown dusk of smoke rose to a smother of artificial cloud; while to the other side, and very far distant across the sea, she made out Mount Olympus, with white chariots and thrones of billowing cloud mounded and piled round it. Everywhere she looked she saw wind and water and shadow and sun teeming together over the world and changing, too much too varied too big to grasp. Cloud shapes tore and mended and changed, were thick in company then alone in space, and joined in new groups tearing clear, in endless ferment of destroying and making: a dividing nation, streaming history, her own life mending and tearing and love cleaving.

She saw, tiny and distinct, a plane slant up from Salonica airport, such as shortly must take her home. It came quite clear: this is the moment I act, I decide, no more delays. More and more her memory and all her thoughts fastened on one event, on the visit she had made to the prison island, when Vangelis had made his choice, his renunciation.

Alexis and Petros arrived together at Rena's home. In her parents' car, which was driven by her elder brother Panos whom Alexis hadn't seen before, they drove uphill to the large walled enclosure.

They walked past stalls selling huge sprays of crimson, saffron and cobalt flowers, all flapping sharply in the strong wind, and in through a large plain gateway of concrete. Then they hesitated, for they faced an endless recession of identical graves, undulating away over the broad back of the hill.

But Rena's mother knew the way. She led them through the winding low-kerbed aisles till they came to an area of new graves, where the small crosses sparkled clean and the small tabernacles at the foot of the graves held fresh, unfaded photographs. They passed other mourners, then, on one cross, they read Rena's name. Her mother stooped down, and took out the photograph and kissed it, then she passed it to her husband, then to Panos, and then to Petros, who passed it to Alexis. Rena looked at him out of the photo, black-eyed, her frizzy hair pinned back very tight behind her head: she looked older, more plump, more serious than he thought of her as being. Nervously, with a sudden piercing hurt of love as well as grief, he kissed the photo lightly, quickly – his one kiss on Rena's cheek – and, his lips burning, his eyes blinding, he returned the photo to her mother.

She replaced the photo, and threw out the old flowers and put in new. Panos relit the small lamp in the tabernacle. Then they stood remembering Rena. Her mother wept steadily, silently. Her father stood with his hands held slightly forward, like a man waiting to catch a voice on the wind. Panos stood with a pale angry scowling face: Alexis noticed now he was exactly like Rena, the same strong features, and the same frizzed hair, cut close. Every so often all the lines in his face would clench. Alexis looked at the grave, the tiny stone area, but couldn't connect it with Rena: there wasn't room for her, he couldn't feel any part of her was here.

Coming to themselves, they looked round for the cemetery priest, and finally made out the small black figure, attending a group of mourners far away down the hill. They waited, watching him, while he wound his way between the graves from group to group. The hard wind gusted and flapped continuously, and at times lifted the dry soil of the cemetery in brown clouds.

The priest took an age. Eventually Panos began to stamp and complain, he swore at the priest; Rena's mother felt faint.

Abruptly Panos could wait no longer: he snatched up the bottle of wine they had brought. 'We'll do the service ourselves,' he said, and began sprinkling and splashing wine on the grave. In a choked voice he tried to find words of remembrance, but he couldn't find right words, and he was aware of his parents watching him appalled: with a shout he hurled the bottle on the ground smashing it and stamped away, tears flinging from his eyes. Petros went and tried to speak to him.

At last the priest came: an aged man with white hair stretched back and tied in a tiny knot at the back of his head; with a peeling nose, and dusty glasses, and a gold-embroidered stole over his dusty black robes; holding in one hand a tatty black umbrella that he used as a sunshade, and in the other a prayer-book, and a polythene bag bulging with the bits of funeral bread the mourners gave him.

He blinked at them, complained mumblingly about over-work, and then stationed himself beside the grave and launched immediately into the obsequies, reading rapidly, slurring or swallowing parts of the service, and glancing up to read Rena's name off the gravestone, every time he needed a name. They all said the responses, except for Panos, who stood with his back to them, his arms folded, scowling.

Rena's father tipped the priest, and he hurried away to the next group of mourners.

They stood for some moments more by the grave. Rena's parents, and Petros, were moved by the prayers, but Alexis, the outsider, found he could not be, the priest's mumble of resurrection said nothing to him. In the photo, which he glimpsed in the little tabernacle, Rena seemed now further away: a raised, strong, dignified head, her hair pulled tight in an old-fashioned style, the face of an older Greece which had all the time been waiting behind the modern Rena. She joined her ancestors, and the other serious women and men com-memorated in sunbleached photos in the cemetery.

He looked round searching: the wind banged in his ears, his eyes watered in its gritty stream. Looking through the sunlit windblown cemetery, it seemed to him that all the world was marked by the absence of Rena, and that in some strange way her absence preserved her. He remembered her smoking and chatting beside him in the morning dusk in his best moment ever of company, when he lied to her, or possibly did not lie, that his career would follow that of his uncle Vangelis. Inside him she waited, watching, urging.

They took their leave and walked back through the windy graveyard to the car. As they drove down again towards the city, it occurred to Alexis that not only in him, and in Petros, and in all those who had been at the Architecture School, but also in many or all of the soldiers on the other side of the road, while still and in the future crowds ran

476

and reformed and tanks and soldiers wheeled in attack, Rena stands clinging to the iron gates inescapably defying them with her shouts of brotherhood.

While Chryssa was in the north, Michael visited Vangelis. At the door of the flat they shook hands briefly. It was years since Michael had seen him: in his lawyer's suit he was stocky, tough, a strong-backed man; he scarcely looked older, his hair was still jet; the skin of his face looked hardened, bleak. His eyes glistened, a trace wide: perhaps they glared.

'Come in, Michael.'

'I wanted to see you before I left.'

'You're leaving?'

'Soon, I think.' His words lingered: neither knew whether he'd leave alone.

They went into the flat, Vangelis motioned Michael to sit. With formality he said, 'I'm glad you came. I wanted to thank you – for your reports, your work. Chryssa has shown me the things you wrote, I know you did others too. You were very good. Thank you.'

'I don't think it made a difference.'

'That's not true. Everything that was said made some difference.'

'I meant, it didn't get you out.'

'I chose to stay in.' Vangelis' black eyes sparked momentarily with humour.

Michael looked round the flat, which seemed just as it had been when he first visited them: except that on many surfaces stood plants that Chryssa had bought.

'What will you do, Vangeli?'

'I'm resuming my practice.'

'Your name will be high, everyone knows of you.'

Vangelis laughed, but drily. 'So they say. But a name in politics is not the same thing as a name in the law courts.'

'But you had that already.'

'I had it, but that was years ago. It's – demanding, starting again from scratch.'

Michael nodded: he had not thought of this, the hard work involved in returning to the world.

'You'll be in politics?'

'Politics?' He smiled sardonic. 'Politics are politics, Michael.' He explained: there was contest already in the socialist party, between those who had been in prison, and the new men who rebuilt the party in exile. The prisoners might be martyrs and heroes, but the new politicians had done the rebuilding, they would not give up control, or office, to men who were famous, but out of touch.

'I don't believe this.'

'You'd be wiser to believe it. And of course, it was to be expected. But I'll tell you, Michael, it woke me up. Because when I came back, I was still in – a funny limbo, not properly back. And this brought me down to earth. Really you have to fight every inch, you cannot rest. And I didn't want rest, I've been festering years, I've got' – he touched his stomach – 'a great impatience here, a lot of black blood, no, they won't stop me. The only thing that would stop me would be – Chryssa's going . . .' His voice, sharp, cracked: he had spoken, at the end, more to himself than to Michael, but now he said, 'It's odd – because when I came back, I was – like a bachelor, in a way I'd got used to being alone, I thought sometimes I'm a dried-up block. Then when she told me about you – the future – it all fell down, our life, my plans. And you know I hadn't realized that *all* my life was tied to her.' He looked round the flat. 'It's so strange being here, Michael. Everything is hers, it's odd to be here, and she not here. Well, she must say. What will you do, when you go back?'

'I don't know, Vangeli. In my own way I've put everything into – Greece. I don't know what my "afterwards" is.'

There was a silence, then Vangelis looked up, his eyes focused sharp on the present. 'You know what I've said?'

Michael blinked.

'I've said she should go with you. Not just cut off everything in the middle, you can't do that.'

Michael gazed at him, blushing, in conflagration, a face of fire he should hide. He saw the goodness in Vangelis, and the change prison had made: a depth, a peace in grief, he saw how the words hurt.

Vangelis stayed taut. 'I should be clear. I am hoping it won't work, you and her – in time she will come back to

478

Greece. It's a dangerous hope, when couples part – they part. I'm only saying, don't think I'm your well-wisher, the magnanimous man. I'm not.'

Michael nodded; it seemed to him at this moment that Vangelis' black eyes twinkled in hate.

'She knows what you hope will happen.'

'Of course she knows.'

Michael shook his head. 'Can one *live* as an experiment?'

Vangelis didn't answer. Michael realized, there was no more to say.

He stood up. 'It was only now that I could come – while we don't know what she'll decide.'

'I'm grateful that you came.'

Michael was not sure how to bid farewell: he advanced, put out his hand – would they shake hands, like good sports in a film?

Vangelis said, 'In any event, this is the end of an acquaintance.' He took Michael by the shoulders, brushed his bristled cheek against Michael's on the right side, on the left. Michael went.

Returned to Athens, Chryssa went to the airport with Michael. They checked in the bags, and were swept in the milling crowd to the passport barrier. There they paused. A voice crackled from the loudspeakers, announcing a flight, departure gate so and so. Chryssa couldn't catch the words. Michael stood over her, his hands holding her hands: his lips slightly quivered, his eyes were blue-grey and shining. Everything must stop here. But the tide of passengers pressed on them, the voice in the air crackled again. She knew as he moved forward to kiss her that now she had lost him, this would be his last kiss, and he would go for ever. He kissed her, then slipped from her and began to move, the queue was swallowing him.

'Michael, I can't bear this.' She grabbed his hands again and held them hard. They kissed again; a full long embrace, they had not kissed so. Then he left, and as he moved from her she saw him today, and him in their previous times – in Omonia Square, in the snow, on the island, in the seaside restaurant – and the young Michael of the English lodging and motorbike, and her ambition of a life in the West, and the West itself, all together receding from her. Her uncompleted love for him welled stronger than ever. She hurt as though she were torn from head to toe; she was faint; she felt herself divide in two, as though, as in a film, she had a ghost self that could step out of her, and this other self or part or half of her was breaking free tearing all her fibres, and passing with Michael through the barrier, now standing beside him, blank-faced, blinded, looking back as he looked back, his hungry eyes making a last lasting snatch for her as he left. As he passed down the escalator he took this other self with him. Later she saw the plane fire steep at the clouds, wheel seawards as it climbed, and diminish in sky.

In the flat Vangelis waited, still on the rack, not daring to believe. The buzzer sounded, and he pressed the button that released the door down below. He held his breath, froze, all of himself a listening. Far down, muffled, he heard the lift door bang, then the whir of its mechanism. Let it not stop yet, he murmured: it had passed the first floor, now the second. He could not believe it travelled so slowly. He stood in the passage, at the door of the shaft, his hope and love rising as the lift carrying Chryssa rose up through the floors towards him.